Praise for Adam Baker's novels

'A compelling end-of-the-world story.'
Sunday Canberra Times on *Outpost*

'It had me on the edge of my seat from page one.'
Stephen Leather on *Outpost*

'A lock and load adventure of the highest calibre.
A tense, absorbing journey and a high speed collision
of military action and apocalyptic horror. *Blackhawk Down*
meets *Day of the Dead*.'
Adam Nevill on *Juggernaut*

'If you like zombies and survival horror then this is the
book for you. If you like to see just what man is capable
of doing when his back is against the wall then this book is
definitely the one for you.'
Starburst on *Juggernaut*

'An incredible, heart-pumping story, full of brutal action.'
Bookaholics on *Terminus*

'Baker's great at evoking the claustrophobic atmosphere
of the subway tunnels, the characters' sense of foreboding
and peril, of being trapped beneath the radioactive
wasteland that the city has become.'
Civilian Reader on *Terminus*

'Baker excels at taking a small group of individuals and
putting them in pressure-cooker situations where the enemy
isn't just the hordes of alien zombies but the darkness in the
hearts of the still living . . . Told in terse, James Ellroy-esque
prose, *Impact* is punchy and propulsive entertainment.'
Financial Times on *Impact*

'A tale that is worth staying with right until the very end.
It really does go out with a bang . . .'

Before writing his novel *Outpost*, Adam Baker worked as a gravedigger and a film projectionist. *Impact* is his fourth horror novel.

www.facebook.com/adambakerauthor
http://darkoutpost.blogspot.com/
Find Adam on Twitter: @AdamBakerAuthor

By Adam Baker

Outpost
Juggernaut
Terminus
Impact

IMPACT

ADAM BAKER

HODDER

First published in Great Britain in 2014 by
Hodder & Stoughton
An Hachette UK company

First published in paperback in 2015

1

A CIP catalogue record for this title is available
from the British Library

Paperback ISBN 978 1 444 75590 9

Printed and bound by Clays Ltd, St Ives plc

Hodder & Stoughton policy is to use papers that are natural, renewable and
recyclable products and made from wood grown in sustainable forests. The
logging and manufacturing processes are expected to conform to the
environmental regulations of the country of origin.

Hodder & Stoughton Ltd
338 Euston Road
London NW1 3BH

www.hodder.co.uk

For Ceri

IMPACT

IMPACT

CAUTION

TO DISARM:

INSTALL SAFETY PIN

**REMOVE CLEVIS PIN FROM HATCH INITIATOR
AND ACTUATOR FIRING MECHANISM**

EXPLOSIVE BOLTS

I

The limo approached Vegas from the east, high speed down the interstate, kicking up a dust plume. V8 turbo roar. A marine stood in the sun roof like he was manning a gun turret. Face masked by sand goggles. Shemagh wrapped round his mouth and nose bandit style. He held an AR-15.

Frost and her companions in the passenger compartment. Zebra upholstery. Blue floor lights. Jolt and sway. Clink of bottles in the mini-bar.

One of the grunts in the driver compartment turned and leaned over the partition. Full flak and K-pot.

'We call these trips Thunder Runs.'

'Yeah?'

'First journey was tough. Hotwired a Peterbilt and bull-dozed our way down the nine-five, shunting vehicles aside. Hung out the side door providing cover fire. Tore up my shoulder like tenderised steak. Stuffed tissue in my ears. Had to rotate weapons in case my barrel started to melt. Long fucking day.'

Frost nodded. She looked out the smoked glass window. Bleak desert.

'But now we got a route. A clear path in and out the city. Pedal to the metal. Don't stop for anything or anyone.'

She nodded.

'Mind you, it's never pretty. Infected folk hear us and walk into the road. Don't have the smarts to jump aside. Women, children. God awful mess. Sometimes it gets so bad we have to run the wipers.

'That's why we take turns to drive. Doesn't seem fair to put it all on one guy. Sight of them hitting the fender. Sound of them going under the wheels. Preys on your mind.'

She turned her attention back out the window hoping, if she broke eye contact, the guy would shut up.

'You don't have to look. Guess that's what I'm saying. When we reach the city. Might be best just to close your eyes.'

McCarran International Airport, Las Vegas.

Sentries manned the wire.

A two-man sniper team stationed in a squat watchtower. Faces striped with zinc cream like war paint. A crate of ammo and a piss-bottle. A portable sound system pumped Motörhead. Forty degree heat. Crazy boredom.

Rotted revenants, shambling skeletal things that had once been human, scrabbled at chain-link, anxious to reach aircrews they glimpsed walking between hangars and geodesic living quarters.

Scope reticules centred on a forehead. Focus/refocus. Distance-to-target calibrations.

'Check out the fat guy,' said Osborne.

'Which one?'

'Construction dude. Tool belt. Keeps looking up at the razor wire, trying to remember how to climb.'

'Hope he doesn't remember how to cut. If these bastards figure how to use clippers, we're all fucked.'

Osborne set his rifle aside. He drained dregs of Cuervo Gold and hurled the bottle towards the fence. Smash of breaking glass.

He picked up his Barratt once more and rested the bipod on the planked wall of the sanger. Eye to the scope.

2

The infected man climbed chain-link. Shirt streaked with blood and pus, face knotted with metallic tumours.

'Look at him. This guy's fucking Nijinsky.'

The rotted construction worker reached razor wire. Barbs tore his flesh.

'Give me some red tip. I want to light this fucker up.'

Standard full-metal jacket rounds swapped for a clip of incendiary cartridges.

Crank the charging handle. Cross-hairs centred on the bridge of the guy's nose. Black eyeballs. Pitiless like a shark.

The guy hissed as if he could hear the sentries seventy-five yards distant.

Lower the cross-hairs. Centre on his open mouth.

Gunshot.

Skullburst. Head blown apart. Blood-spray and magnesium fire. The guy's hard hat span and landed in the grass.

'Give me a drink.'

'All we got left is Bud.'

Tab-crack. Head thrown back.

'Fucking piss. We need to hit the supermarkets again. Liberate some fucking cigars and shit.'

Can-crunch. Belch.

A fresh survey of the crowd pushing at the fence.

Cross-hairs centred on a young girl, couldn't be more than seven. Ragged party dress. Metallic scalp tumours pushing through blonde hair.

'We should hose these fuckers in aviation fuel and toss a match. Save some ammo.'

'How many rounds we got left?'

'Couple of days. After that we better get the hell out of Dodge.'

Trenchman climbed the ladder. The shooters hurriedly threw a jacket over their beers and killed the music.

'How's it going, boys?'

'Pretty good, sir,' said Osborne.

Trenchman could smell booze-breath. He ignored it.

'The Hummer should be with us in five, ten minutes. Cover fire, all right?'

They listened. A silent city.

Distant engine.

'Any word when we might get out of this place, sir? Munition running low, and more of these fuckers every day, pardon my French.'

'Twenty-four hours and we're done with this shithole. Pack our gear and hit the road.'

'Can I ask where we might be headed?'

'Yet to be determined. But anywhere is better than here, right?'

'Fuckin' A, sir.'

'So stay sharp. You got our backs until then.'

'Gonna get bumpy,' shouted the grunt.

Elevated freeway. Blurred glimpse of incinerated storefronts and wrecked automobiles. Crooked phone poles. Burning billboard for a magic show at the MGM Grand.

A swerve down the off ramp like they were heading for The Strip, then sharp left and jump the kerb into the grounds of Bali Hai Golf Club. Manicured fairways turned to meadow. They tore across the grass, spraying turf. They skid-swerved sand bunkers and an ornamental lake, flattened a couple of marker flags, whipped a dead irrigation hose. The driver ran wipers to clear mud.

'Stay in the vehicle until we get through the gate. Gonna be plenty of shooting. Just sit tight until it's over.'

They jolted across Vegas Boulevard and slammed through a tear in the airport's old perimeter fence.

They headed for the inner compound. Razor wire, flood-lights and watchtowers. Troops corralled like POWs.

The shooting began. Distant crackle of cover fire. Infected mown down so the compound gate could be pulled wide.

A belt-fed .50 cal opened up close by. Concussions like hammer blows. Frost covered her ears.

The limo skidded to a halt. Frost almost thrown from her seat. She gripped the stripper pole for support.

'Remember,' said the driver. 'Just sit tight.'

Sporadic gunfire. Troops eradicating a bunch of infected that managed to infiltrate the compound when the gate pulled back.

A gum-smacking marine knocked on the side window. All clear.

Frost opened the door and climbed out. She shielded her eyes. Emerged from a bubble of smoked glass into brilliant sunlight. Heat radiated from baked asphalt.

'Watch your step,' said the grunt.

Bodies sprawled on the ground. Men, women, children, felled by precise headshots.

She kicked through scattered shell casings. Skull fragments crunched underfoot.

She looked around.

The airport terminal buildings had been abandoned to the infected. She could see deformed figures in the B Gate lounge and control tower. Atlantic arrivals. T-shirt slogans in French and German. Big-ass Nikons slung round their necks. She watched them butt themselves bloody against plate glass as they tried to reach troops milling down below. Some of the blood smeared on the windows was black and crusted. Must have been throwing themselves against the glass day and night for weeks.

Rather than defend the entire airport complex, the garrison had fenced two runways and a couple of hangars, made a temporary home in a bunch of tents and Conex containers.

Beyond that was the Vegas skyline. Burned-out casinos.

The onyx pyramid of the Luxor, punctured and smouldering like it took artillery fire.

Frost was joined by Pinback, Guthrie and Early. All of them in Air Force flight suits, backpacks slung over their shoulders.

They watched a couple of grunts park a baggage train loaded with cargo pallets to reinforce the gate.

'Anyone want to hit the town, play the slots?' asked Guthrie.

Captain Pinback contemplated the devastated city.

'Look upon my works, ye mighty, and despair!' He swigged Diet Coke and crunched the can. 'Or some such.'

The grunt stood beside Frost. He tapped a smoke from a soft pack of Marlboros and sparked a match.

'Welcome to Vegas.'

WARNING

Military Installation

It is unlawful to enter this installation without

written permission from the installation commander.

Sec 21, Internal Security Act 1950; 50 U.S.C. 797

While on this property all personnel are subject to search.

USE OF DEADLY FORCE

AUTHORISED

2

A Chinook flew low over the ruins of Vegas.

Hancock was strapped in a payload wall seat. The ramp was open. Fierce rotor roar. Typhoon wind. The tethered tail gunner trained his .50 cal on car-clogged streets below.

Hancock released his harness, stood and gripped cargo webbing. He looked out the porthole.

They cruised five-hundred feet above The Strip.

Wrecked casinos. Judging by school buses and ambulances clustered at each entrance, the casinos had, at some stage of the pandemic, become makeshift hospitals. Vegas residents, tourists unable to get home, all of them headed for refuge centres hoping for evacuation somewhere safe. Bedded down between the slots, the Blackjack tables, waiting for FEMA to truck in food parcels and bottled water. Must have been hell. Battery light. No air con. Dysentery, overflowing toilets, rival family groups battling over floor space and hoarded food. Then infection took hold. Screams in the dark. Panic. Stampede. Cavernous, blacked-out game floors turned to a slaughterhouse.

'Check this,' shouted one of the cargo marshalls. He beckoned Hancock to a starboard porthole.

He pointed at Trump International.

'What?'

'Look.'

A smashed window, midway up the building. Roped bed sheets, hanging down the facade of the hotel.

'Tells a story, don't it?'

Hancock gamed the scenario in his head. What would he have done? How could he have survived the situation?

The hotel overrun by infected residents. Bodies choking the stairwells, the corridors. Blood up the walls. Screaming, eye-gouge mayhem on every floor. And somewhere, up on thirty, some poor bastard barricaded in their room. Tough choice. Stay put in their fortified room and starve, or arm themselves with a table leg, open the door and attempt to fight their way level by level to the atrium.

Brainwave: they unlocked the door of their suite long enough to snatch a laundry cart. Spent a few hours lashing sheets together, testing knots. Then they put a chair through the window and repelled a couple of hundred feet down the exterior of the building to the parking lot.

'Tenacious motherfucker. Hope they made it.'

Touchdown. Rotor-wash kicked up a dust storm.

Wheels settled and blades wound to a standstill.

Trenchman at the foot of the cargo ramp.

Yellow warning beacon. A vehicle slowly emerged from the dark interior of the chopper. A wide wheelbase platform big as an SUV chassis loaded with something cylindrical under tarp. No driver. Electric motor. The heavy platform slowly rolled down the loading ramp. Hancock walked by its side, operating the control handset.

'Is that the package?' asked Trenchman.

Hancock nodded.

'Take me to the vault.'

They walked across a chevroned slipway towards a building signed: FIRE RESCUE. The heavy wheeled platform hummed beside them, advanced at two miles an hour, balloon tyres crunching grit.

Hancock looked around.

The runway perimeter fence, razor wire draped with shredded shirt fabric and torn flesh.

Terminal buildings, derelict and overrun.

He squinted at the watchtowers. The troops looked strung out. Mismatched fatigues. Scraggy beards.

'Where's your flag?' he asked.

'You're shitting me, right?'

'Military installation, Colonel. Ought to raise a flag.'

'I'll get right on it.'

'Have to say, discipline seems to be an issue round here.'

'I got forty guys, give or take, from a bunch of different units. Some are Reserve. Shit, some are navy. All of them have seen horrors. All of them have lost family. I got to protect them from infected bastards massing at the wire, and I got to protect them from themselves.' He gestured to graves dug in the dirt by the runway. Rifle/helmet markers. 'We average a suicide every couple of days. Know what happened last week? Two perimeter guys didn't report for duty. Found them in their tent, heads bust open with a golf club. God knows what went down. Brains everywhere. Maybe an argument went bad and somebody flipped. Point is: one of my guys is a double murderer and there's nothing I can do about it. That's the kind of bullshit going on round here. Place is a goddam madhouse. Yeah, I let the boys party. Try to keep them alive, try to keep them sane. Want to write me up? Complain to my commanding officer? Good luck with that, Captain.' He pointed to the eagle tab, the rank insignia stitched to his MARPAT field jacket. 'In the meantime, I'm CO of this joint and I'll run it anyway I damn please.'

Trenchman lifted a shutter and led Hancock into the empty fire house.

'This is where they kept rescue vehicles. You want a weapon vault? This is the best we can do.'

Hancock looked around the empty chamber.

'How many exits?'

'There's a side door. Chained shut. Fire escape at the back. We chained that, too.'

'I have a couple of equipment trunks aboard the chopper. I need them brought here.'

'Okay.'

'I'll need light. Any food and bedding you can muster.'

'All right.'

'And I need two guards outside the door at all times. No one comes in here but me, understood? Make this clear from the outset: anyone sets foot in this room without my permission, I'll shoot them in the fucking head.'

'Hey. I'm installation commander. I'll provide all the assistance you need. But anything happens to my boys, you're going to be answerable.'

'You got orders. I got mine. Anyone fucks with the weapon, anyone fucks with the mission, I will put a bullet in their skull. Tell your men. Make it clear.'

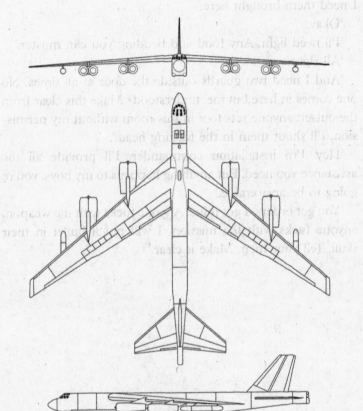

3

Trenchman showed the aircrew to their quarters. A freight
container.

TRANSPACIFIC LOGISTICS.

Three bunks and a couple of chairs. Flak jackets, magazines,
cross held to the wall by chewing gum.

'Where are the previous occupants?' asked Frost. She
checked out an oil drum washstand. Basin. Mirror. Old
toothbrush.

'Dead.'

'How?'

'Does it matter?'

'There aren't enough bunks,' said Guthrie.

'You won't be staying long. This is just a place to drop
your bags and freshen up. We got MREs, if you're hungry.'

'Like a fucking oven in here.'

'We got plenty of bottled water.'

'Anything refrigerated?'

Trenchman gestured around him.

'This entire camp is for your benefit. Remember that. None
of us chose to be here. We annexed the airport, secured this
section of runway so you folks could complete your mission.
You ought to be flying from Nellis, but it's out of action.
Don't know why. Biggest Air Force base in the region. But
some major shit went down, place is overrun, so instead we
got to hold this shitty runway so you folks have the distance
to take off.'

He checked his watch.

'Sundown. We aim to get you in the air before morning. Soon as you return, we pack our shit and haul ass out of here. Let those infected fucks take the compound. Welcome to it.'

'Where will you go?'

Trenchman shrugged.

'The war is over. We lost. Earth belongs to the virus. Personally, I aim to find somewhere remote and hold out as long as I can. You folks do as you please.'

Sundown.

They crossed a slipway to hangar seven.

Trenchman fired up a diesel generator wired to an external junction box.

'We keep the hangar doors closed,' he explained. 'Try to stay out of sight much as possible. Don't want to agitate prowlers out there beyond the wire.'

He opened a side door and let them inside.

Cavernous dark. Pungent stink of aviation fuel.

'Hold on,' said Trenchman. His voice echoed.

He threw a wall-mounted knife switch. Arc lights bolted to high roof girders flared to life.

A gargantuan plane filled the hangar. A slate grey B-52. Hulking airframe, wide wingspan, almost as big as a 747.

'*Liberty Bell*. Flown down from Alaska. Spent her twilight years flying stand-off patrols, edge of Russian airspace.'

'What happened to the original crew?'

'They went over the wire a couple of weeks back. Happens now and again. Couple of guys get together, figure they stand a better chance on their own. Desertion, I guess. Not that anyone gives a shit. If a bunch of them walk out the front gate, what am I going to do? Shoot them in the back?'

Captain Pinback gestured to the plane:

'What kind of condition is she in?'

'We got a Crew Chief. Used to maintain AWACS. Says she's not in great shape, but it's not like you're taking her on a long-haul flight. All she has to do is stay airborne long enough to deliver the package.'

Pinback walked across the hangar. Echoing bootfalls. He approached the nose of the plane, looked up at the flight deck windows. He patted the hull.

'How long to get her ready?' asked Trenchman.

Pinback shrugged.

'Couple of hours for a walk-around. Check her out, kick the tyres. Hour to finish fuelling. Hour or two to load and secure the missile. I'd say wheels up some time around two a.m.'

Pre-flight inspection. Frost and Pinback watched the Chief and his team conduct a nose-to-tail survey.

The names of absent airmen stencilled beneath the cockpit windows:

EMERSON

BLAIR

WALTON

KHODCHENKOVA

TRAINOR

It made Frost feel sorry for the abandoned plane, as if the half-billion dollar war machine had been orphaned.

A three-cable hitch to a power car supplied 205v AC/24v DC.

A fuel truck parked by the wing, hose hitched to a roof valve set in the fuselage spine, just back from the flight deck. Salute and wave for grunts pumping JP8 into the tanks.

The main gear bogies: four balloon tyres on white aluminium hubs, chocked, supporting thick hydraulic actuators.

The Chief knelt and checked tyre pressure.

He moved on and worked through his checklist:

Hydraulic reservoirs.

Accumulator pressure.

Moisture drains.

Pitot survey.

Shuttle valves.

Wing surfaces.

Engine intake/duct plugs removed.

All panels and doors closed and secure.

Frost glanced up into a gear well. She reached up and ran a finger across the hatch. Fingertip black with dust and grime.

'She's dying of neglect, sir. Hasn't been serviced in a long while.'

'Airworthy?'

'Barely. A junker. There are wrecks lined up in Arizona boneyards in better condition than this.'

Pinback shrugged.

'Single sortie. There and back. That's all she has to do.'

They walked beneath the port wing. Huge engine nacelles, each containing two Pratt & Whitney turbofans. Wide intakes. Fanned turbine blades.

Frost traced a rivet seam with her finger.

'Corrosion.'

'Not as much as I anticipated.'

'Yeah, but what can't we see?'

They walked the length of the plane.

The bomb bay doors.

The vast vulpine tail.

'What do you reckon, old girl?' said Pinback, addressing the aircraft. 'Want to put on your war paint one last time?'

Briefing.

The hangar office. Frost set metal chairs in a semicircle,

encounter group-style. Hancock dragged them to face front, reasserting traditional hierarchy.

Geodetic data, National Recon topographical maps and satellite images pinned to a noticeboard.

Trenchman polished thick-framed Air Force reg glasses.

'Simple enough mission. Proceed to the drop point. Launch the package. Fly home. Approximately four-hour flight time.

'Why us?' asked Pinback. 'Plenty of delivery systems. Pop a Tomahawk from offshore.'

'Tactical strike,' said Hancock. He sat apart from the aircrew, arms folded, aviator shades. 'Plenty of ships equipped to throw an H bomb big enough to leave a mile-deep crater. But we don't want to fry southern California. Just want to take out the target, clean and precise.'

'But why *Liberty Bell*? She was a beautiful bird, back in the day. But right now she's fit for a wrecker's yard.'

'Little choice. Original plan was to use a Minuteman RV to deliver the mail. 44th Missile Wing out in Dakota. They tried to fire up a mothballed silo, but the place got overrun before they could launch. You know the score. The world is falling apart. We have to adapt. Use what we can find.'

'B-2s?'

'Otherwise engaged.'

'Subs?'

'Lost communication. They must be out there, somewhere, under autonomous control.'

Pinback leaned forwards and peered at sat photos. A desert mountain range. Sedimentary rock. Rippling contours. Peaks, mesas, ravines.

'What's the target?'

'Classified. The missile will make the final leg of the journey on its own. You won't even see the aim point. All you have to do is confirm detonation, then return to base.'

'What kind of bang are we talking about?'

'Ten kilotons. Like I say: weapon release fifteen minutes from target. Just take position and watch the show.'

Trenchman turned to Frost.

'You're the radar nav, right?'

'Yeah.'

He handed Frost a plastic disk on a lanyard.

'Old school authorisation protocol. Dual key, all the way.'

Frost turned the disk in her hand.

'The arm code?'

Trenchman nodded.

'Captain Hancock holds the other one. Two minutes from the drop point, you will contact me for final authorisation to proceed. Once you've got the Go, your EWO will arm the weapon. Load both codes. Then you're hot to trot.'

Hancock looked around at sombre faces.

'Hey. First folks to drop an atomic weapon on US soil in anger. We're about to make history.'

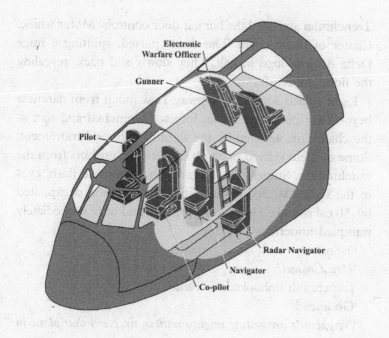

Electronic Warfare Officer

Gunner

Pilot

Radar Navigator

Navigator

Co-pilot

4

Trenchman activated the hangar door controls. Motor whine. Clatter of drum-chain. The doors parted, splitting a huge Delta Airlines logo in half. They slowly slid back, revealing the floodlit aircraft.

Light spilled across the slipway. Low moan from darkness beyond the perimeter fence. Infected wrenched and tore at the chain-link, agitated by the sight of light and movement. Some of them started to climb the fence. Gunshots from the watchtowers. Snipers momentarily lit by muzzle flash, eyes to the scope. Rotted bodies fell from the wire, decapitated by .50 cal rounds. They hit the ground, and were immediately trampled underfoot.

Osborne:

'Hey, Colonel.'

Trenchman unhooked his radio.

'Go ahead.'

'Neighbours are getting mighty restless, sir. Need that plane in the air, soon as practicable.'

'Roger that.'

Hancock rolled the weapon platform into the hangar on silent wheels. Two sentries paced behind the electric truck.

Pinback watched as he parked the truck behind the wing, flush with the plane's fuselage.

'Give me a hand.'

Pinback helped Hancock unrope the tarp and pull it clear.

First sight of the weapon. AGM-129 ACM. Twenty feet long. One and a half tons. Porcelain white. Forward-sweeping fins.

Hancock released canvas retaining straps.

'Better stand back.'

He adjusted the handset. The carriage wheels swivelled ninety degrees. The weapon truck slowly slid beneath the plane, easing to a halt beneath the open bomb bay doors.

Hancock ducked beneath the doors and looked up into the payload compartment. Frost stood on a narrow walkway looking down on him.

'Ten kilotons.'

'Yeah,' he said. 'Hiroshima, give or take.'

'You've done your sums, right? We won't get blasted out the sky?'

'We'll be fifteen minutes clear. Close enough for a grandstand view. Thermonuclear detonation, up close and personal. Not many folk get the privilege.'

He activated brakes. Steel feet extended and anchored the weapon platform to the hangar floor.

He pressed RAISE. Hydraulic rams began to lift the massive weapon into the belly of the plane.

The flight deck.

Pinback ducked beneath overhead control panels and lowered himself into the pilot seat. He secured the five-point harness.

Interior inspection. He checked avionic presets.

'Battery start.'

The external AC cart was disconnected and rolled clear. Thumbs up from the crew chief.

'*All yours.*'

Aircraft on internal power.

Trim check. Another thumbs up from the chief. He disconnected his external headset and stepped clear.

Pinback:

'All right. Engine start.'

Ground crew wearing heavy ear defenders fired up the start-cart. Air injected at 30 psi kicked engine pod two into life. Engines three and four boosted the other turbofans to motion.

'Starting one, starting two . . .'

Throttles to Idle. Check rpms.

A shudder ran through the plane. Escalating jet roar.

Start-cart rolled clear.

Chocks removed.

Clearance to taxi.

The lower cabin.

Frost secured the floor hatch and replaced the deck cover.

She strapped herself into the radar nav chair. She secured her helmet, jacked her oxygen feed and radio. She loaded cryptographic presets, slotted a data transfer cartridge and uploaded flight data.

It would be a quiet journey. Noble, the Electronic Warfare Officer, would have little to do. There would be no air contacts, no acquisition lock from enemy radar. They would fly through empty skies. Drum his fingers until the final moments when he would confirm authorisation to deploy, call the countdown, then hit WPN REL. The missile would drop from the payload bay. Boosters would fire and the ALCM would begin its journey, skimming the dunes at Mach zero-point-five. *Liberty Bell* would circle at safe distance and wait for the blast.

Ten kilotons. A mix of dread and exhilaration.

Guthrie leant close, conspiratorial:

'What do think?' he asked, gesturing up the ladderwell to the flight deck.

'Hancock? A true believer. A zealot and an asshole.'

Frost took gum from her mouth and glued her lucky coin to the console. She secured her oxygen mask and adjusted her harness.

Flaps lowered. Brakes released.

'Let's roll her out the barn.'

Pinback eased the throttles forwards.

The massive B-52 slowly rolled from the hangar out onto the floodlit chevrons of the slipway.

They followed lead-on lights to the runway. Slow taxi to the head of 19R.

The plane jinked starboard, aligned itself on the threshold, facing the nine-thousand foot strip.

Pinback secured his oxygen hose and mask. He jacked the interphone cable.

'Trench. You copy?'

'Ten-four.'

'Hit the lights.'

Runway lamps, centre line and edge. Brilliant white. A wide boulevard stretching to vanishing point.

First time Pinback had seen the perimeter fence from an elevated perspective. Hundreds of infected butting the wire.

'Jesus Christ. They can't hold them back much longer.'

'Not our problem,' said Hancock. He checked output dials. 'EPR good.'

'Ejector seat arm.'

'Ejector seat arm. You have the plane.'

'Time to hit the road.'

Pinback gripped the throttle levers and eased them forwards. Airspeed indicator crept from zero.

Increasing thrust. Pressed back in their seats by acceleration. Engine rumble rising to an earthquake jet-roar.

Hancock:

'. . . Twenty knots. Thirty . . .'

23

Pinback glanced down at the central alert panel. Winking red light.

'*Intermittent fuel warning on three.*'

The warning light shut off.

'*Cleared,*' said Hancock.

'*I'm calling abort. We need to put her back in the hangar and check it out.*'

'*Negative. You will fly the plane.*'

'*I'm ranking AC.*'

'*And I have tactical command. The warning has cleared. You will get this bird in the air and complete the mission.*'

Heading for the end lights and stopway. Moment of decision. Pinback increased thrust.

'*. . . sixty, sixty five . . .*'

Airspeed clocked seventy.

He eased back the control column.

Nose up.

Wheels left asphalt.

They took to the sky.

5

Frost woke face down in sand.

Her field of vision: a gloved hand viewed through the amber tint of her visor. A Nomex gauntlet. Seams, strap cuffs, and her, alive, looking at it.

She rolled onto her shoulder.

Dunes rippled heat.

She fumbled the sweat-slicked silicone of her oxygen mask and released the latch. She pulled off her helmet and threw it aside. It rolled. The airhose snaked in the dust.

Fierce sun. Blue sky. She shielded her eyes from the glare.

'Hey.'

Silence.

'Yo. Anyone?'

Nothing.

She patted herself down, ran fingers through her hair and checked her scalp for blood.

Typical injuries a person could expect to sustain during the 12g-force of ejection: bust ankles, concussion, compressed spine.

She tried to sit forwards. Shock of pain.

'Motherfuck.'

Her right leg. A sudden wave of dizziness and nausea.

She lay back, panting for breath. She was tempted to unlace her boot, slit her pant leg, probe her ankle and shin for broken bone. But if she unstrapped the injury, pain and swelling might render her immobile.

'Hey. Anyone?'

Sudden wrench. Hauled backwards six feet. She scrabbled at the parachute harness and flipped the canopy release. Nylon billowed and pulled tangled chute cord beyond the lip of a high dune.

She shrugged off the harness.

A morphine auto-injector pen in the sleeve pocket of her flight suit. She popped the cap, stabbed the needle into her thigh and delivered a 15mg shot.

Warm bliss diffused through her veins.

Her survival vest: nylon pouches slung on a mesh yoke.

She took out a PRQ-7 CSEL radio and pulled it from a protective plastic sleeve. She extended the antenna and maxed the volume.

'This is Lieutenant Frost, US-B52 *Liberty Bell*, anyone copy, over?'

No response.

'Mayday, Mayday, Mayday. This is Lieutenant Frost, United States Air Force, navigator tail MT66 broadcasting on SAR, anyone copy?'

She was transmitting on the standard military Search and Rescue frequency. The mid-watch radioman back at the Vegas compound should be on air demanding comsec validation: her day-word and a digit from her authentication number.

Nothing.

She cupped a hand over the screen to shield it from glare.

GPS hung at ACQUIRING SIGNAL. All base stations returned NO COMMS.

She shut off the radio to conserve power.

She unwrapped a stubby marine flare. She flipped the striker and tossed the pyro.

She lay back and watched red smoke curl into a cloudless sky.

★

27

Crawling up a steep gradient on hands and knees. Her lame leg gouged a trench.

She crested a dune. She shielded her eyes.

A rippling sandscape stretched to the horizon. Primal nothing, like something out of dreams. It was as if she had turned inwards and was traversing her own deep cortical terrain, a race memory bequeathed by early hominids. The hunt: tracking prey across sun-baked, sub-Saharan wilderness, spear in hand.

She checked her sleeve pocket. Two more morphine shots.

Somewhere among the dunes lay the slate-grey wreckage of *Liberty Bell*. A UHF beacon bedded in the debris transmitting a homing tocsin on 121 and 243 MHz.

Somewhere, in the Vegas garrison, a radioman would pick up the distress signal. Trenchman would call Flight Quarters. Alert 60. He would assemble a TRAP squad and order immediate scramble. The team would strap their vests, buckle helmets, distribute live ammo. The Chinook would be marshalled out of the hangar. Strap in, spin up, head west tracking their beacon. Touch down at the crash site, rotors kicking up a storm. The squad would descend the loading ramp. They would cut the twisted fuselage with oxy-acetylene gear, slice open the belly of the aircraft, suit up and take Geiger readings before entering the payload bay to retrieve the warhead. Finally they would fry sensitive electronics with thermite grenades, and begin a radial search for survivors. Scan the dunes for the six personnel that ejected from the craft.

She checked her watch. Chipped bezel, smashed face, hands jammed at the moment of egress: four-ten.

She unbuckled the watch and threw it away.

Sun high overhead. Merciless heat.

She peeled off her gloves and tucked them in a pocket. She unclipped her survival vest, unzipped her flight suit and tied the sleeves round her waist. An olive-drab T-shirt blotched with sweat.

Her face was glazed with perspiration. Half-remembered advice from survival school, Thompson Falls, Montana. Her instructor, Major Coplin: *'Don't towel sweat. It has a function. Let perspiration cool your skin by slow evaporation.'*

She should have retained the parachute. Used it to make a headdress. Hung it for shade.

She spoke, just to break the awful silence:

'Get it together, bitch. Don't let morphine mess your thoughts.'

The chute lay a hundred yards distant, pasted to the side of a dune.

Best move before analgesia wore off.

She slung the survival vest round her shoulders and began to crawl.

A journey out of nightmares. Fingers raked mineral dust. Massive muscular effort to advance a single inch.

Steep gradients. Sliding sand. Every time she stopped for breath she began to lose ground.

She paused at the top of each dune and sat a while, raised her head greedy for any kind of breeze.

An ass-skid descent. She spread her arms to slow her slide. An uncontrolled tumble might rip open her fractured leg. Jagged bone could tear through skin. Turn a painful injury into a life-threatening crisis. She would quickly bleed out, fresh arterial blood soaking into sand as she struggled to push flaps of wet muscle back into her calf and choke the wound with a boot-lace tourniquet.

She crawled the steep gradient on her belly and dug deep with her hands like she was swimming through dust.

She hauled herself to the crest.

The chute was gone.

She looked around. The breeze had dragged the parachute a quarter mile distant, far out of reach.

'Christ.'

She lay in the sand awhile, head in the dust, robbed of strength by an enervating wave of defeat.

Fierce, unwavering sun.

She galvanised heavy limbs, took off her T-shirt, draped it over her head and shoulders. The sweat-sodden cotton burned dry in seconds, leaving salt rime at the seams. The sun seared her bare back.

She unzipped a vest pocket. Three small water sachets bound by a rubber band. Vinyl envelopes of vacuum-sealed liquid squirmed between her fingers. She ran her tongue over parched lips. She gripped a tear-tab, fought the urge to rip open a packet, throw back her head and suck it dry. Three hundred and seventy-five millimetres in total. Best conserve liquid as long as possible. She rezipped the pocket.

She shielded her eyes and scanned the horizon. Distant mountains veiled by heat haze. Venusian peaks. Cliffs, buttes and mesas, insubstantial as cloud. Might be the Panamint Range. The plane was on target approach when the engines crapped out. Seven minutes from the drop, crew psyching themselves to launch the ALCM. Which put her somewhere in Death Valley and a long way from help.

No smoke plume. No sign of wreckage.

She cupped her hands. Loud as she could:

'Pinback? Guthrie?'

She held her breath, listened hard.

'Hello? Can anyone hear me?'

Silence.

She thought back to her final moments aboard the B-52. The plane tearing itself apart. Thick smoke. Shudder and jolt. Flickering cabin lights. Shrill stall warnings, Master Caution and ENGINE FIRE panel alerts. Frantic chatter over the interphone as Pinback and Hancock fought to save the plane:

Two's down. Shutting crossfeeds.

'We need to put her on the deck.'

'No time. Give me more thrust.'

'That's all she's got.'

'Nose up. Nose up.'

'Power warning on Four. Wild RPMs. We're losing her.'

'Restart.'

'Nothing. No response.'

'Full shut down and restart.'

'Negative. She's not spooling.'

'Hit the ignition override.'

'She's stone dead. Time to call it.'

'One more go. Come on, girl. Give me some lift.'

'Losing airspeed. Can't keep the nose. I'm getting hydraulic failure. Oil pressure is dropping through the floor. I got red lights all over.'

Momentary pause. Pinback running options, trying to figure some way to save the plane.

'All right. That's it. She's going down. Out of here, guys. Eject, eject, eject.'

The crew punched out one by one as the plane slowed to a fatal stall. Tripped their ejector seats before the crushing g-force of a nosedive froze them in their chairs. They adopted the posture: elbows tight, back straight, then wrenched the trigger handle between their legs. Hatches blew, rockets fired. Pilots through the roof, navigators through the floor. They must have landed miles apart.

Channel select from Guard to Alpha.

'This is Frost anyone copy, over?'

NO SIG.

'Pinback? Early? Anyone out there, over?'

NO SIG.

'Come on, guys. Sound off.'

No response.

She set the handset to Acquisition, held it up and watched numerals flicker as it scanned wavebands.

31

Nothing. No military traffic, no civilian.

Sudden signal spike. A weak analogue broadcast. She held the handset at arm's length, swung it three-sixty and tried to get a lock.

FM interference replaced by Hendrix. Churning guitar reverb floated across the dunes. 'The Star Spangled Banner'. Woodstock. Face-paint peace signs. *Get Out of Nam*. The ghost of old wars.

A voice cut in. Click of a pre-recorded message interrupting the transmission:

'You're listening to Classic Rock, Barstow. We have suspended our normal programming at this time as part of the National Emergency Broadcast System. Please stay tuned for important updates and announcements by Federal Authorities regarding current quarantine regulations and refuge centres in your area. Remember, it is your responsibility to stay informed.'

Another snatch of improv feedback.

Click. *'You're listening to Classic Rock, Barstow. We have suspended our normal programming at this time as part of the National Emergency Broadcast System . . .'*

She checked battery levels and switched the handset to transponder mode. The screen flashed BEACON to let her know a homing signal was broadcasting on SARSAT 406.025 MHz.

The sun was getting high overhead. Several hours must have elapsed since *Liberty Bell* went down. The Vegas garrison would have been manning their comms gear, waiting for the B-52 to confirm target strike. Instead, the plane was out of contact and long overdue. Trenchman should have scrambled a TRAP team a while back. Fired up the Chinook and sent it west. She should be back at the compound by now, lying in a bunk, leg in fresh plaster, sipping Coke through a straw.

Pang of pure grief for all the times she took air con and ice cubes for granted.

Insidious thought:

The boys back at Vegas have a single chopper. They need it. They won't send it into deep desert to search for a downed plane.

She told herself to shape up.

Hold it together. They won't abandon you. They won't leave seven guys to die of thirst in the desert. And they sure as hell won't forget the warhead.

She inspected her weapon. A 9mm Beretta with a twelve-round clip slung beneath her left armpit in a passive retention holster. She blew dust from the pistol. Function check: she shucked the slide. She dug a plastic bag from her survival vest, wrapped the gun and returned it to her shoulder holster.

This is not adversity. This is not your Great Test. You've got a bust leg and you need a drink. Improvise. Adapt. Overcome.

A fierce struggle to stand upright. She balanced on her good leg and looked around at surrounding dunes.

An impact crater fifty yards to her left.

She crawled on hands and knees.

She slid into the bowl-depression and dug. She excavated a heavy nylon pack. The ejector seat survival kit. The pack had been strapped beneath her chair and released by barometric trigger as she plummeted to earth.

She brushed sand from rip-stop fabric and pulled zippers.

Emergency gear packed for patrol over the pack ice and sub-zero waters of the Bering Sea.

A life raft and a plastic oar.

An Arctic immersion suit.

Woollen mittens.

A woollen hat.

'Fucking sweet.'

She rubbed her eyes. Merciless glare. Forearms already cooked red. Couple more hours in the sun would inflict first degree burns. Weeping blisters. Peeling skin.

The guys back in Vegas had looted plenty of supplies from

abandoned supermarkets. Cans, water, cigarettes, pharmacy shelves swept clean. She wished they had had the foresight to snatch some high factor sun cream.

She took out the life raft. Rip cord. Gas-roar. Tight-packed polyurethane plumped and unkinked as buoyancy chambers filled with CO_2.

A black one-person raft with a low tent canopy.

Frost dragged the raft to the crest of a dune, oriented it to catch the near-imperceptible breeze, then climbed inside, glad to be out of direct sunlight.

She drowsed in the shade, choosing to conserve sweat until the noonday heat began to abate.

She closed her eyes and breathed slow, worked to induce sleep. No sound but the oceanic diastole/systole surge of pulsing blood vessels in her ear canal.

She felt the raft buoyed by swells. She heard waves lap the side of the boat.

She slept, and dreamed she was adrift on a vast, moonlit sea.

USAF Crewman Survival Vest

(Contents vary depending on theatre of operation.)

Ultimate Survival Technologies 'Air Ace' Survival Vest

Fenix E35 Flashlight (CR123A x2)

Marine MK124 Signal Flares x2

Gryojet Flare Pen with 7 Flares

Petzl Pixa headlamp

Boeing CSEL Radio

MS-2000 Xenon strobe with IR filter

Hydrex 4.227 Fluid Ounce water sachets x3

GI Lensatic Compass

Signal mirror

Camouflage face paint

Wool hat and gloves

Multitool

Sponge

Tourniquet strap

First Aid Kit –fishing kit, surgical closure, adhesive
bandage, gauze bandage, towelettes, wire saw, razor, insect
net, soap, matches, water purification tablets, energy bar.

Survival Evasion and Recovery Manual

M9 Beretta (9mm parabellum, 15 round clip.)

6

Adrift on a storm-lashed ocean. The blackest night. Driving rain. The raft rode thunderous, titanic swells. She gripped the side of the boat, tried to stabilise the roll, braced for the inevitable capsize.

She jolted awake and shook off heart-pounding delirium. She wiped sweat from her eyes, licked parched lips.

She pulled back the raft canopy.

Mute desert. Cruel, unrelenting light.

She tried the radio. Hendrix and the Emergency Broadcast announcement.

She pictured the deserted streets of Barstow.

Crow-pecked bodies and burned out cars. A dead neon pole sign: *Classic Rock FM*. An edge-of-town office with a sixty-foot mast.

The abandoned studio running on back-up power. Scattered papers and toppled chairs.

An unmanned production desk: preset sliders and twitching output needles.

An empty sound booth.

'. . .*We have suspended our normal programming at this time as part of the National Emergency Broadcast System. Please stay tuned for important updates . . .*'

The looped transmission would run until power failed, console lights flickered dark, and Jimi was abruptly silenced.

Selector to BEACON. She set the radio aside.

She flexed her leg. Intense jolt, like a high-voltage shock.

'Jesus fuck.'

She lay back, waiting for the agony to subside. Pulsing pain, like someone driving a nail into her flesh.

A second morphine shot. Stab. Press.

She closed her eyes and rode a warm rush of well-being. Slow, shivering exhalation.

She tossed the hypo in the sand.

She tore the corner of a water sachet and sucked it dry. She had left her survival vest outside the tented raft. The sachets had cooked in the sun. Hot like fresh brewed coffee.

She ripped open the empty pack and licked residual drops of moisture from the plastic.

The sun had moved from its zenith. Shadows lengthened and coagulated in the depressions between dunes.

She wanted to hear the heavy beat of chopper blades. She wanted to look up and see the belly of a descending Chinook fill the sky.

She reached down and unlaced. A swollen foot prised from her boot. Gym sock peeled away, fraction at a time, teeth clenched against the pain.

She gently rolled the right leg of her flight suit. Her foot and calf were swollen, skin livid and stretched tight. She caressed her shin, traced her tibia with the tip of an index finger, gently probed for some kind of subcutaneous ridge that might indicate splintered bone. Nothing. Maybe her leg had suffered a hairline fracture rather than an emphatic break. Or maybe her leg was intact. Maybe she had suffered some kind of catastrophic sprain that would subside in a couple of days.

She gripped her ankle and checked for a tibial pulse. She flexed her toes. Still got circulation. Still got feeling.

She eased the sock back over her foot. She slid her foot into the boot, barked with pain as she pulled laces taut.

A plastic oar. She broke it over her good knee, and tossed the paddle.

She snapped the shaft in two.

Nylon cord ran around the lip of the raft. A handhold to help a downed airman pull himself into the boat.

She sliced the cord with her knife.

An improvised splint: oar sections either side of her injured shin, lashed in place with nylon cord. Snorts of discomfort turned to a thin, growling scream by the time she tied the final knot.

She punched the vinyl floor of the boat, lay and tried to get her breathing under control.

Fuck self-pity. Injured leg. Fleeting. Inconsequential.

She closed her eyes and stroked the Ranger emblem stamped on the leather sheath of her knife.

Injured leg. An inconvenience, nothing more.

She limped across dunes. She paused for a compass bearing. Flipped the lid of the lensatic, watched the liquid-damped needle swing and settle. Maintaining steady progress north. She snapped the case shut.

Backward glance. A trail of footprints. The raft was a distant dot.

Maybe if she covered a few miles she could raise someone on the CSEL. If she couldn't bounce a signal off a satellite, if the MILSTAR network were down, NCASEC and TACAMO off air, she would have to coax an unboosted analogue transmission across the mountains to habitation. Tough job. Distant crags were marbled with uranium ore radiating magnetic anomalies that could potentially jam a radio signal.

She kept walking. Each jolting step made her leg burn like she was hung over a fire rotating on a spit, but if she stopped to rest, she might not be able to get moving again.

Nagging doubt: hard to know where the parachute brought her down. Maybe she was walking deeper into the wilderness, walking further from help.

Her father had been a Ranger. If he were here, keeping pace as she trudged through the desert, he would say: *over-deliberation fucks you up. A samurai will reflect for seven breaths then commit to a decision. So roll the dice and God bless you.*

A monotonous landscape.

She glanced at a map before the flight. Geodetic data tacked to a noticeboard in the briefing room. A USGS chart: California/Nevada border. Blank terrain. Terra incognita. Mile upon mile of jack shit.

She couldn't recall topographic detail, but she remembered names. Memorials to early settlers that headed west in covered wagons and found hell on earth.

Furnace Creek.

Dante's View.

The Funeral Mountains.

A glint in the periphery of her vision. She stopped, turned and shielded her eyes.

Something metallic at the tip of a high dune. Probably a fragment of fuselage. Couldn't be much else.

Hard to estimate distance. Rough guess: quarter of a mile. She couldn't discern shape. Too much glare.

Quarter of a mile. A lot of energy, a lot of sweat, to reach a hunk of scrap metal. Her leg hurt so much she wanted to fall to the ground and puke. But a scrap of wreckage might provide a little shade, a spot to rest until nightfall.

She limped towards the distant object. Each step was teeth-jarring torment. She absented herself from her body, put herself on a wooded hillside, enjoyed the cool hush of the forest floor and let the pain and exertion happen somewhere else.

The top of a dune cratered like a volcano. An ejector seat sitting upright, bedded in sand.

Someone strapped to the chair. An arm hung limp. The sand-dusted sleeve of a flight suit. A gloved hand.

'Hey.'

No response.

Frost climbed the dune on hands and knees. She caught her breath, rested in the shade. Then she gripped the back of the chair and pulled herself upright.

A dust-matted body strapped in the seat.

She brushed sand from the name strip: GUTHRIE.

Legs askew, head slumped on his chest. His face was veiled by a helmet visor and oxygen mask.

Frost checked the seat restraints. Jammed.

The guy had been killed by some kind of release failure.

The moment Guthrie, the route navigator, reached between his legs and wrenched the yellow egress handle a roof hatch would have blown. He would have been propelled up and out the plane, hitting 12g in half a second. A mortar cartridge behind the headrest would have immediately fired and deployed a drogue to stabilise the seat as it fell. Guthrie would have remained strapped in the chair, breathing bottled oxygen during freefall. At twelve thousand feet a barometric trigger should have unlatched the chair harness and released his main chute. The seat should have fallen away, letting Guthrie float to earth unencumbered.

Instead he remained shackled to his chair, achieving a terminal velocity of over two hundred miles an hour before he slammed into the ground.

Dead on impact.

Frost crossed herself. She wasn't religious, but she half-remembered Guthrie pocketing a rosary as they suited up.

It should have been possible to hit a manual release to ditch the seat. He should have pulled a shoulder-mounted rip to deploy the chute. Maybe air-pressure and g-force pinned him to the heavy steel frame as it fell to earth at sickening speed.

Or maybe his oxygen supply failed and he lost conscious-ness. Succumbed to hypoxia. Desperately slapped and clawed at harness buckles as his vision narrowed and his mind began to fog.

Or maybe he chose to die. A dark supposition: Guthrie watched mesmerised as the ground rushed to meet him and became gripped by the same strange throw-yourself-on-the-track death wish that tugs at subway commuters as their train emerges from a tunnel and pulls into the station. The world in ruins, everyone he knew and loved dead or worse. Maybe he couldn't find the will to grip the parachute cord and save himself.

'*Via con Dios*, brother.'

Pat down. She unzipped sleeve and thigh pockets.

A Spyderco lock-knife. She tossed it. She would stick with her old K-Bar survival blade.

Morphine shots. She stuffed them in her pocket.

She searched his vest. She took water, batteries, matches and flares. Felt like grave-robbing, but the guy would under-stand. He would want her to live.

She tried his radio in case her own were defective.

'This is Lieutenant Frost, US-B-52 *Liberty Bell*, any one copy, over?'

No response.

'Mayday, Mayday. This is an emergency. Airmen in need of rescue. Does anyone copy this transmission, over? Any one at all?'

NO COMMS.

She dropped the radio in the sand.

She ejected the mag from Guthrie's Beretta and stashed the clip in her survival vest.

His head jerked and trembled.

'Jesus. Guthrie?'

She leant close, examined his chest for the rise and fall of respiration.

41

He slowly raised an arm. His gloved hand gently pawed her shoulder.

She knelt in front of him. She squeezed his hand.

'Hold on, dude.'

She unlatched his oxygen mask. Shattered teeth. He drooled blood.

She gently lifted his head, and raised the smoked visor.

'Oh Christ.'

She jumped backwards, stumbled and fell on her ass.

Guthrie's upper face was a mess of suppurating flesh. Metallic spines anchored in bone, protruded through rotted skin like a cluster of fine needles.

'So they got you too.'

He wretched and convulsed. He reached for her, clawed the air, constrained by his seat harness.

Jet black eyeballs. Guthrie, his mind and memories, replaced by a cruel insect intelligence.

He raged with frustrated bloodlust.

Frost struggled to her feet. She watched him thrash in his seat. She contemplated his onyx eyes, his livid, bruise-mottled skin.

A choking, inhuman howl. He spritzed blood and teeth.

She unholstered her pistol and shook it from its protective bag. She racked the slide and took aim, anxious to silence the guttural vocalisations, the imbecilic aks, das and blorts of a friend succumbed to dementia.

'Sorry, Guss. Best I can do.'

Point blank through the right eye. Whiplash. He slumped broken doll, wept blood from an empty socket.

Sudden silence.

She blew the chamber cool then reholstered.

She sat in the sand beside the dead man.

She contemplated the view.

The desert. Harsh purity, endless dunes and the widest

42

sky. The kind of place a person might come to confront an indifferent God. Like Buzz Aldrin said, standing in the Sea of Tranquillity, looking out at an airless wasteland: *magnificent desolation*.

Good place to die. Better than a hospital bed.

A water sachet. She sucked it dry and crumpled the plastic envelope.

A morphine syrette. She bit the cap and injected her thigh.

She limped east, leaving Guthrie dead on his throne, marooned in vast solitude.

TEAR

EMERGENCY

DRINKING

WATER

EAU POTABLE - DRINKWASSER

APPROVALS:

US-Coast Guard No. 160.026/55/0

9028 BV/MCA   9028 BV

Canadian Approbation de Garde-côte-T.C.210-005-003

HYDREX~INC~

HURON, SD 38721 U.S.A.

SATCHET CONTENTS: 4.227 FL OZ   (1/8 U.S. QT) – (125 ML)

MFG DATE

Lot No

7

Sunrise.

Hancock lay sprawled in the sand. He got dragged a quarter mile through dunes before he regained consciousness and released the chute harness.

He knelt in the sand at the crest of a steep rise, concussed by the explosive force of egress.

He reached up with a gloved hand, fumbled a latch and unhooked his oxygen mask.

Cough.

Spit.

Phlegm wet the dust. A string of saliva tinted pink with blood.

He released the chin-strap and eased the helmet clear. It rolled down the side of the dune kicking up dust in its wake.

Head shake. Blurred vision.

He held up a gloved hand and tried to focus. He moved the hand back and forth.

Blind in his right eye.

He pulled off gloves and gently touched his face. He flexed his jaw. Unbroken. Fingers crept up his right cheek delicately exploring skin swollen tight.

Flaccid eyelids. A vacant socket. Pulped flesh. His right eyeball was gone.

He fell forwards, crouched on hands and knees a long while, trying not to puke.

Enough. Get your act together.
He sang:

> 'Oh, I'm a good ol' rebel,
> Now that's just what I am,
> And for this yankee nation,
> I do not give a damn.
> I'm glad I fought again'er,
> I only wished we won.
> I ain't asked any pardon for anything I've done.'

He sang because, despite his injury, despite the pain, he was still, defiantly, James Hancock.

Maimed. He'd lost part of his body. Grieve for it later.

He straightened up, returned to a kneel. He shrugged off his life preserver and survival vest.

His bicep pocket. Three morphine auto-injectors which could render him numb in an instant.

He examined the hypodermics. A moment away from opiate bliss:

Bite the cap.

Stab.

Press.

Warm wash of analgesia.

Throw the depleted hypo aside.

Instead he returned the unopened syrette to his sleeve pocket.

No point fleeing pain like a bitch. Got to keep an unclouded mind.

A signal mirror the size of a playing card tucked in a zip-pouch of his vest. He held up the tab of polished metal like it was a powder compact and examined his face.

He'd taken a massive blow to the head. The right side of his face was bloody and swollen. Ripped forehead, ripped cheek. Barely recognised himself. He gently lifted his right

46

eyelid. Wet muscle. Severed optic nerve. Giddy realisation: he was peering deep inside his own head.

Careful scalp examination. A classic aviator's flat-top buzz-cut matted with blood. He ran fingers through his hair. Split skin. Possible skull fracture.

He unzipped his flight suit. The force of ejection had ripped the hook-and-loop patches from his sleeve and chest. The stars and stripes, Second Bomb Wing insignia, and Pork Eating Infidel emblem were gone. His name strip had survived: HANCOCK, J.

He tied sleeves round his waist.

The CSEL. He held it up to his good eye, squinted as he tried to discern function buttons.

'Mayday, Mayday. Pilot down, anyone copy, over?'

Dead channel hiss.

'Mayday, Mayday. Anyone copy on SAR? Air Force personnel in need of assistance, come in.'

Nothing.

The CSEL should have been unaffected by atmospherics. It should have been unaffected by nearby mountains. But if the USSTRATCOM net were down, if the military had become so degraded Tactical Air communication hubs had been abandoned and satellites were floating dead in orbit, if all AWACs were grounded, then he was truly on his own.

He sat a while and looked around.

Fierce sun.

Endless dunes.

No trace of *Liberty Bell* or its crew. No chutes, no wreckage.

Oppressive solitude. No roads. No pylons. No sign humanity ever walked the earth.

Cupped hands:

'Hey. Anyone?'

The desert sucked all power from his voice, made him sound weak and small.

'Anyone hear me?'

His helmet lay at the foot of the dune. He slid down the gradient and picked it up. The composite crown had been split by a massive impact. The padded interior was crusted with blood. Something gelatinous smeared across the cracked visor. He touched and sniffed, then gagged as he realised the tips of his fingers were wet with the remains of his eyeball.

Head-spinning nausea. He threw the helmet aside and sat head in hands.

One eye. He would never fly again. Desk job or discharge. Next time he filled out a form he would reach DISABILITIES, and instead of ticking NONE, he would have to specify PARTIALLY SIGHTED.

Fuck it. The world was falling apart. He'd watched it on TV. Safely garrisoned behind concertina wire and HESCO baskets at Andrews AFB. Big plasma in the canteen. Every news outlet live-streaming Armageddon. Crowds of infected charging Humvee roadblocks with demented aggression, barely slowing as .50 cal rounds blew holes in their flesh. Channel surfing montage: tent cities, corpse-pyres, cities under martial law.

One by one stations went off air, cellphone signals died, and grieving base personnel were left to picture dead family members bulldozed into a grave-trench, bedsheet-shrouded bodies doused with quicklime or gasoline.

There would be no desk jobs, no carefully worded résumés. A post-pandemic interview would involve a guy trying to plead his way into a barricaded community: *'Are you one more useless mouth to feed, or do you have a skill?'* Hancock had basic EMT training and could field-strip/reassemble/function-check an AR-15 in forty seconds. In this new, brutal world, that made him bad-ass ronin. The new American stone age. Cave clans warring over canned food. Folks would offer everything they had – booze, women – to live under his protection.

Crush this reverie. Face the here-and-now.

Better bandage the wound. Ensure his eye socket was kept free of dust.

A rudimentary first-aid kit in a pocket of his vest. He tore open the pouch. Gauze dressing folded into a pad and pressed to the vacant socket. He held the dressing in place with a cross of micropore tape.

Better shield his head from the unrelenting, blowtorch intensity of the sun.

The chute lay spread over a nearby dune. He strode towards it.

Headrush. The world tilted sideways and smacked him in the face. He got to his feet, stood and picked his way slow and careful, swayed like he was crossing the deck of a storm-tossed ship.

He threw himself down near the chute, pulled the cord hand over hand and brought the fabric within reach. Flipped open his pocket knife and slashed the material, cut a bandana square and tied it round his head. He adjusted the drape of the headdress so it covered his bandaged eye.

He coughed. Bruised lungs. Might have cracked some ribs.

More blood in his mouth. He tongued his gums. A missing tooth.

Supposition: the roof hatch misfired. Should have blown clear soon as he triggered the ejection sequence, but maybe the rim charges didn't detonate. His seat must have punched it clear as it propelled up and out. Lucky he didn't lose his legs. Lucky his head wasn't wrenched clean off.

Death Valley.

Tough choice. Head east and cross the Armagosa Range and back into Nevada. Or head west and enter the Panamints, hope to find blacktop road, an easy route into southern California. Either journey would require superhuman endurance.

49

Best shot at survival would be to locate the wreckage of the plane and wait for SAR extraction.

He unholstered his Beretta, blew dust from the weapon, checked the magazine and chamber.

He slung the survival vest over his shoulder and began to walk.

'I hates the yankee nation and eveything they do.

I hates the declaration of independence, too.

I hates the glorious union, 'tis dripping with our blood.

I hates the striped banner, and fit it all I could.'

High dunes. Treacherous, sliding sand. He followed contours as best he could.

His balance was shot. Lurching like a drunk. Each time he looked down the ground flipped up and smacked him in the face like he'd stood on a garden rake. He resolved to stare straight ahead. Distant dunes gave a fixed reference point. Best treat them like an artificial horizon gimbal monitored during a night mission. Imagine he was watching the tilt of a line marker by the eerie green glow of an EVS terrain scope, alert for any pitch deviation. Pretend he was strapped inside his skull, steering his body like a plane.

He felt dizzy and traumatised. The adrenalin rush, the near-miss euphoria he felt when he woke and discovered he had survived the crash, had ebbed and been replaced by all-pervading fatigue that robbed his limbs of strength.

He stopped and caught his breath.

He could barely see. He blinked perspiration from his remaining eye.

Sweat burned his split scalp and empty, swollen socket as if someone had poured vinegar on the wound.

Utter exhaustion. His hand kept straying towards his bicep pocket as if it were seeking out morphine of its own volition.

Time to rest.

He made for the highest dune, the best vantage point to sit and survey his surroundings.

A parched wind blowing from the east. He closed his eyes and turned his face to catch the breeze.

Awful, last-man-on-Earth silence.

That which does not kill me makes me stronger.

One of the tough-guy mottos pinned to the wall of the gymnasium annexed by Hancock and his clique of steroidal muscle freaks each morning. Planet Fit, Temple Hills, just off Andrews AFB. They bellowed encouragement and motivational abuse, buckled powerlifter belts, added plate after plate. Vein-popping exertion. Chalked their hands, struggled to bench their own bodyweight, pumped to collapse. They swigged protein shakes, admired their ripped musculature in wall mirrors, daydreamed of acing special forces induction.

Pain is just weakness leaving your body.

Time to put that Spartan ideology in motion.

Remember the warrior creed:

'I will always place the mission first. I will never quit. I will never accept defeat. I will never leave a fallen comrade.'

You are still in the field, still combat effective. You've been tasked. You have a mission to accomplish.

He reached the top of the dune, stumbled to regain balance. He drew his pistol and fumbled the gun. A clumsy Weaver stance, squinting down the sight with his remaining eye, taking aim at vast nothing.

'Picked the wrong guy to fuck with,' he shouted, addressing desolate terrain. 'I'm ready. Been ready my whole goddamned life.' He spread his arms wide. 'Give it your best damn shot. Come on. I'll break you. I'll take anything you got.'

He dropped his arms and laughed at himself.

Losing it. Totally losing it.

He stowed his pistol, clumsily slotted the weapon into the

passive retention holster. Then his legs gave out. He rolled onto his back and lay there a long while, hand pressed to his pounding head.

Merciless fucking sun.

He yearned for nightfall.

He got to his feet and forced himself to walk.

Lost track of time. His Suunto watch was smashed. The cracked LCD display projected weird, scrambled digits like it was alien tech.

The sun was still high. Felt like it had been noon for ever.

A chunk of wreckage.

Sheet metal protruded from the sand.

He gripped the panel and dragged it free.

An ejection hatch. One of the portals blown clear when the egress sequence triggered. Riveted steel streaked black by the detonation of explosive bolts.

He thought it over.

Implication: he was walking along the debris trail. Detritus scattered during the plane's terminal descent. His current bearing would bring him to the crash site. A chance to inspect the fuselage. Because the debrief would begin the moment he boarded the Chinook. Trenchman would demand an immediate sitrep. Hand him bottled water, then clamp earphones to his head so they could communicate above the rotor-roar. *What's the status of the aircraft? What's the condition of the bomb?*

Seventy yards north-west: an ejector seat. The seat had fallen out of the sky, rolled down an incline and come to rest at the foot of a dune.

He slid down the slope.

A chute had been balled and stashed beneath the chair frame. Another airman survived the crash.

He cupped his hands:

'Hey. Sound off.'

Pause.

'Anyone?'

A white scrap of garbage at his feet. He tugged it from the sand.

A torn water sachet.

Someone impulsive. Someone without the smarts to conserve water.

He crumpled the plastic in his fist and tossed it aside.

'Lieutenant Early? You out there?'

Lieutenant Early. Youngest of the crew.

Hancock stumbled to the crest of a dune and sank to his knees. He shielded his eye from the sun's glare and scanned the horizon for any sign of the crewman.

Hoarse bellow:

'Hey. Early?'

A discarded flight helmet. He picked it up, turned it in his hands. Undamaged.

Blurred footprints heading out into the wilderness, away from the plane, away from any kind of help.

He thought it over. Head for the wreckage, or pursue Early into deep desert?

Poor kid must be terrified. Alone in the wilderness. Struggling across the dunes, mile after mile, head full of panic and fear. He wouldn't last long.

Hancock unholstered his pistol and fired a signal shot.

One final shout:

'Kid, you out there?'

No sound but a rising, mournful wind. Sand blew from the crests of dunes like smoke. The desert transformed to a smouldering, infernal hellscape.

I will never leave a fallen comrade.

But:

I will always place the mission first. I will never quit.

53

Best find the plane.

He threw the helmet aside and headed north.

A column of smoke on the horizon. Hard to judge distance.

Black fumes. A fuel fire. Must be the remains of *Liberty Bell*.

Each crewman carried a radio which could switch to transponder mode and act as a homing beacon. Geostationary SAR satellites would pick up the signal. Just set it beeping and wait for rescue. But if comms were down, they would need to make themselves visible from the air. Surest chance of deliverance would be to reach aircraft debris.

Downside: the bomb might be damaged. Radiotoxic spill. The core assembly might be split open, projecting lethal gamma radiation. He might reach the wreckage and find himself walking among scattered fragments of fissile material. Sub-critical chunks of plutonium, plutonium oxide, uranium tamper. A calculated risk. If he stayed within the vicinity of the fuselage he would catch a dose, but any incoming SAR team would surely find him.

It was his best shot.

He kept walking, because it was better to act than sit on his ass.

'Three hundred thousand Yankees

Is stiff in southern dust.

We got three hundred thousand

Before they conquered us.

They died of Southern fever

And southern steel and shot,

I wish there were three million

Instead of what we got.'

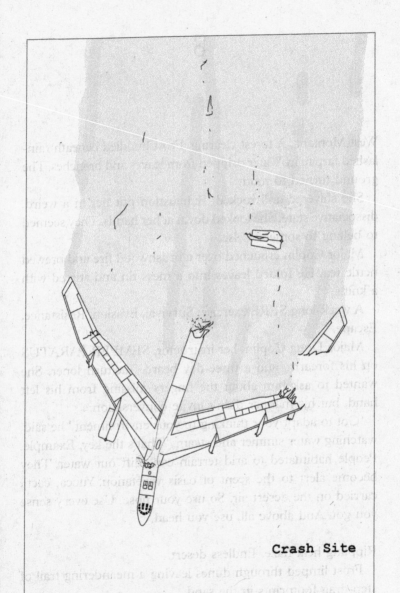

Crash Site

8

West Montana. A forest clearing. Frost huddled beneath rain-lashed tarpaulin. Water dripped from leaves and branches. The ground turned to mud.

She shivered and rocked. Exhaustion put her in a weird, dissociative state. She looked down at her hands. They seemed to belong to someone else.

Major Coplin crouched over a brushwood fire and brewed nettle tea. He folded leaves into a mess tin and stirred with a knife.

A week-long SERE exercise: Survival, Evasion, Resistance, Escape.

Major Doug Coplin, her instructor. SEMPER PARATUS on his forearm, and a three-day beard. Taciturn loner. She wanted to ask him about the fingers missing from his left hand, but his manner didn't invite conversation.

'Got to adapt your thinking to your environment,' he said, watching water simmer and steam. 'That's the key. Example. People habituated to arid terrain can sniff out water. They become alert to the scent of oasis vegetation. Yucca, cacti, carried on the desert air. So use your nose. Use every sense you got. And above all, use you head.'

Rippling heat haze. Endless desert.

Frost limped through dunes leaving a meandering trail of step-drag footprints in the sand.

She stopped and sniffed the air. An unplaceable scent carried on the breeze.

Brief, olfactory misattribution. Flowers. The heart-tugging hope of a verdant, tree-fringed oasis.

The aroma soured and grew strong. Burning plastic. Spilt aviation fuel. Ruin and incineration.

A column of black smoke unfurled behind a distant rise.

A steep gradient. The last of her strength. Crawling on hands and knees, weak with thirst and exhaustion.

She reached the summit, lay face down and regained her breath.

She slowly lifted her head, face dusted with sand.

The plane:

Liberty Bell. The massive, shark-grey B-52H lying crooked on the sand.

Heat rippled from the long, windowless fuselage, the sweeping, vulpine wingspan.

A deep gouge behind the plane. An impact trench wide as a six-lane highway.

An uncontrolled descent would have resulted in a nose-dive. Nothing left of the plane but an unrecognisable ball of super-compacted metal at the bottom of a deep impact crater. But the fuselage was largely intact.

Pinback's roof ejector port was still in place. Maybe his seat failed. Had to bail through the lower cabin floor. Or maybe he stayed at his station. Fought for control as the plane fell out of the sky, two remaining turbofans locked at maximum thrust. Jammed the throttle quadrant, wrenched the control column, pulled the plane out of a stall and brought it level enough to achieve a rough crash-landing. Nose slam, then a long, shuddering belly-skid. Three-hundred-ton airframe scything a succession of dunes before coming to rest.

Frost struggled to her feet and surveyed the wrecked war machine below her.

The tail had torn off.

Three of the four propulsion pods had been ripped from the wings. One of the detached engines lay half-buried to the east of the crash site. Flames licked between turbine blades. Acrid smoke.

The wing tanks had burst. JP8 aviation fuel leaked from split panels, leeched into the sand, stained it black.

Cupped hands:

'Hello?'

No sound but the steady pop and crackle of the burning engine.

'Anyone?'

Her shout turned to a cough. Parched throat. She fumbled a water sachet from her vest, tore and drank. She squeezed the plastic envelope dry and threw it aside.

She slid down the dune in an avalanche of dust and limped towards the plane.

She hobbled across the sand towards the gargantuan, sand-matted hulk.

She threw herself down in the shadow of the nose, lay beneath sortie decals and caught her breath.

Merciful shade. The intense, skin-searing pain of direct sunlight suddenly, blissfully, withdrawn.

She lay a while, fighting sleep. Lame, exhausted, dehydrated. All she wanted to do was rest.

Coplin turned a couple of rabbits on a twig-spit. Cooking flesh sweated grease. Flame-licked fat popped and boiled.

'Gonna be a cold night. Tempting to throw on a couple more logs. But like the man said, white folks build a big fire and sit away from it. Indians build a small fire and sit close. Conserves effort. Conserves wood.'

He probed the meat with the tip of his knife.

Frost drowsed in her poncho, lulled by the steady drum of rain on tarpaulin. She chewed a twig to dull hunger pangs.

'Ain't nodding out on me, are you?'

She shook herself alert and rubbed her eyes.

'Adrenalin is a drug like any other. Person builds a tolerance. You got to keep your shit together, girl. Wire-tight, until the mission is done.'

She got to her feet.

Headrush. An uncontrollable shiver. One-twenty in the shade, and she had the chills. Onset of heatstroke messing with her ability to regulate internal temperature. She made it to the plane just in time. Another couple of hours spent stumbling across open desert would have meant delirium and death.

Lengthening dune-shadows. Heading into afternoon.

She looked up. The flight deck fifteen feet above her head. A couple of the polycarbonate windows smashed from their frame, leaving skull-socket vacancy.

'Hey. Hello?'

Pause.

'Anyone up there?'

Deathly silence broken by a gunshot.

She threw herself against the plane, turned, and snatched the pistol from her shoulder rig.

Trembling hands. She scanned the dunescape, tried to locate hostiles.

Pop and spark from the burning engine. Components within the turbine stack combusting like firecrackers. Each retort puffed flame through titanium blades.

She reholstered the Beretta.

She began to walk the length of the plane, nose to stern.

No way to get inside the aircraft. Under normal circumstances the crew would enter the plane via a ladder-hatch in the underbelly, forward of the landing gear. But the crash had put the hatch out of reach.

She ducked beneath the massive port wing. Fetid cave-dark. Hand clamped over her mouth and nose. Aviation fuel dripped from fractured wing plates. Metal already streaked with oxidisation. Overwhelming stench of JP8.

Out into daylight. She straightened up. A backwards glance. The mid-wing spoiler panels were raised. Air-brakes deployed to create maximum drag. Someone had tried to slow the plane at the moment of impact.

She reached the rear of the aircraft. Ripped and ragged metal where the tail had been torn away.

Twisted spars. Trailing cable. Fluttering foil insulation. Central crawlway crushed flat.

A crash trench behind the plane. An avenue of raked sand flecked with wreckage.

The foreground: an undercarriage quad bogie ripped from a wheel well. Four huge balloon tyres on aluminium hubs. The stumps of piston actuators. Frayed hydraulic line. 'Anyone?'

Oppressive silence.

Maybe she was the sole survivor. Maybe the rest of the crew died on impact, or expired as they wandered, lost, through the desert.

Sudden, gut-punch anxiety. A child's pre-verbal fear of abandonment. What if the rescue team had already come and gone? Picked up survivors and returned to base, leaving her marooned in the desert.

Frost, LaNitra. Written up MIA presumed KIA.

Shrill note of panic in her voice:

'Can anyone hear me?'

Dear God, don't let me die here alone.

. . . *above all, use you head.*

She thought it through.

No footprints.

60

The dunes surrounding the plane were pristine. The rotor-wash of a heavy rescue chopper would have churned a shitload of sand, left a visible LZ.

And the body of the plane was pretty much intact. If a TRAP team had touched down at the crash site, they would have cut open the central fuselage to retrieve the warhead.

Liberty Bell had sat neglected, silent and still, since the moment she hit the ground and came skidding to a halt.

Relief quickly soured to strength-sapping fatigue. She was tempted to shoot-up and sleep in the shade.

Better conserve morphine. Hold out until nightfall.

She stepped out of shadow. Sun hit with skin-blistering force. She flinched from harsh light like she had taken a slap to the face.

She walked the starboard side of the plane and headed back towards the nose.

She leant on the hull for support but snatched her hand away. Metal hot as a grill plate.

The starboard wing. Three thousand square feet of aluminium alloy shimmered heat. Ruptured tanks dripped fuel.

The aircraft's remaining engine pod bedded in sand.

She ducked beneath the wing.

Dust saturated with JP8. A stinking, petroleum quagmire. Her boots bogged down, sucked like she was pulling them from deep mud.

She reached the nose.

She craned to see if someone were in the pilot seat. Dark, sand-occluded polycarbon.

A vertical rip in the aluminium skin of the plane. Popped rivets and buckled panels. She examined the fissure. A shoulder-width tear in the fuselage that would, with effort, allow access to the crew compartment.

She gripped torn metal and pulled herself inside.

*

The split-level crew compartment.

Lower cabin: navigator, radar navigator.

Upper cabin: electronic warfare officer, tail gunner, co-pilot, pilot.

Frost let her eyes adjust to the dark interior of the plane.

Low ceiling, tight walls. The place stank of smoke and cooked metal.

Multi-function displays seared by shorting electronics. Exposed circuits. Smashed scopes. Roped cable hung from a conduit.

The few sections of wall that were free of instrumentation were quilted with soot-streaked insulation pads.

No crew seats in the lower cabin. Both Frost and Guthrie had blown floor hatches and ejected from the plane.

Frost gripped the lip of her radar navigation console. An internal fire had caused the central sweep-screen to sag and melt bowl-shaped.

A silver coin tacked to the radar panel with gum. Kanji courage symbol on the obverse, ALWAYS ON THE BATTLEFIELD stamped on the back.

Membership token of an off-campus dojo she joined during her years at UA, Tuscaloosa. An austere fight-space above a laundromat. Crash mats. Punch bag.

A poster pinned to the wall. Jim Kelly throwing a high kick. And next to it, fourteenth century bushido text hung in a clip-frame:

It is related that a famous warrior known as the master archer used to have a sign on his wall with the four words he applied to everyday life: 'Always on the battlefield.' I note this for the edification of novice warriors.

She peeled the coin from the switch panel, rolled it finger to finger, and put it in her pocket.

The interior of the fuselage was furnace hot. Frost dropped her survival vest, carefully pulled off her boots, and squirmed out of her flight suit.

She took the authenticator lanyard from around her neck and dropped it into her boot.

Grey, PX-issue underwear.

She tipped a wall-mounted drop-seat. Vinyl padding hot against her thighs. She sat as still as she could, tried to slow her metabolism, allow a little yogic calm to lower her body temp.

She looked around.

Floor detritus. A packet of moist towelettes. Hand-wipes that used to hang in a wall pocket next to the plane's fold-down urinal.

Desert dust wiped from her arms, shoulders and face.

She wrapped one of the towelettes round her little finger as an improvised Q-tip and cleaned sand from her ears.

A locker to her right. A folded flag. A couple of two-quart canteens.

'Sweet mother Mary.'

She hurriedly unscrewed a cap and drank deep, panting between gulps.

That's enough. No point guzzling everything you've got. Might trigger some kind of cerebral oedema.

She set the canteen aside.

A wall-mounted trauma bag, big as a parachute pack, to her left. The WALK: Warrior Aid and Litter Kit.

She flicked the release clasp. The bag hit the floor.

She slid from the seat, sat beside the kit and unzipped side pockets. Wads of sterile dressings. Airway tubes. Surgical tape. Trauma shears.

She snipped the paracord lashed round her leg. Cord unravelled. The improvised splint fell away.

She let her leg rest a while.

Lying on slip-tread floor plate. Sun shafted through the fissure in the cabin wall. She watched light inch across the deck.

The fuselage creaked. Metal flexed and contorted as the wreck baked in merciless day-heat.

She cleaned her fingernails with the tip of her knife.

Maybe she should get some sleep. She set the knife aside and closed her eyes.

Thud.

Movement in the upper cabin.

She sat up.

'Yo?'

Her voice hoarse and loud in the confined space.

Craning to look up the ladderway into the cabin above her.

'Pinback? Hancock? That you?'

She tried to stand. Fierce pain. She winced and fell to the floor.

She dug into the trauma pack, found an immobiliser and clamped the stainless steel brace round her injured leg. Nylon tethers hung slack.

She put a webbing strap between her teeth and bit down. Fuck it. Morphine.

Jab. Discard.

She took deep breaths and mouthed a silent three-count. Brutal double-wrench. She pulled the splint-straps tight.

She crouched on the deck lost in white pain. It flooded her senses. Overwhelmed her vision like oncoming headbeams. A buzz-saw shriek in her ears.

She waited for the opiate to hit.

Knife-thrust agony diminished to a dull burn.

She grabbed the canteen and took a swig. She poured a splash of water over the back of her head.

She gripped the ladder and pulled herself upright. Knees and palms branded with the chevron tread of the deck plate.

She looked up through the hatchway into the flight deck above.

'Anyone there?'

Pause.

'It's me, Frost. Anyone up there?'

No reply.

She pulled herself up the ladder, executed an arduous hop-climb to spare her injured leg.

The upper cabin.

She rolled onto deck plate, gripped the EWO situational display for support and got to her feet.

The blast screens had been lowered. Each curtain fringed by a halo of daylight.

Banks of dead instrumentation.

Scintillating motes of dust.

She looked up. Open sky. Sunlight shafting through vacancies left by two jettisoned roof hatches.

The back-facing Electronic Warfare chair remained in position. The seat rockets must have failed. Lieutenant Noble, the EWO, would have followed a well-drilled back-up procedure. He would have unhitched, slid down the ladder, dropped out a vacant floor hatch and been snatched away by the airstream.

The co-pilot seat had fired. Hancock propelled clear before impact.

The pilot seat was still in place.

She could see the arm and shoulder of a flight suit.

'Pinback? Can you hear me?'

She released her grip of the Warfare console and limped towards the pilot seat.

Captain Pinback. Crazy bastard rode the plane during its terminal descent. Fought 'til the end. Stayed aboard the smoke-filled, depressurised flight deck. Didn't want to abandon the aircraft, the weapon.

'Captain?'

A gloved hand twitched and clenched.

She circled the seat, kept her distance, held the bracket rails of the now-absent co-pilot chair for support.

'Cap?'

She reached for her shoulder holster, realised she'd left the pistol below.

Pinback sat slumped in front of inert, fire-streaked avionics, his face veiled by his visor and oxygen mask.

Frost tentatively reached forwards.

Pinback took a shuddering breath.

She jumped back.

A gasping, heaving convulsion.

'Cap? Hey. Daniel. Can you hear me?'

Tentative approach. She reached out a hand and slowly lifted his visor.

He raised his head, groggy like he was waking from deep sleep. Blue, unclouded eyes. Free from infection.

He stared at her face, struggled to focus.

'Christ. Can you hear me? Can you talk? How bad are you hurt?'

Right arm folded across his belly. He lifted it aside. He was sitting crooked in his seat, lower body twisted like he'd been cut in half and jammed back together at a weird angle. Shattered spine.

'Jesus. Hold on, Captain. Just hold on.'

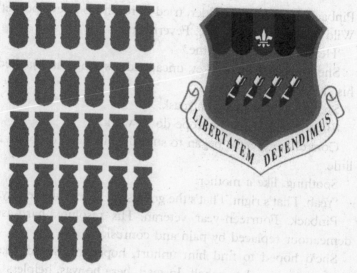

9

Pinback pawed his shoulder, tried to reach his sleeve pocket. Wild eyes. Contorted face. Feverish pain.

'Hey,' said Frost. 'Let me.'

She unzipped the pocket, uncapped a syringe and jabbed his shoulder.

She released his oxygen mask.

'Breathe slow. Let the dope do its work.'

Convulsive breaths began to subside. His head drooped a little.

Soothing, like a mother:

'Yeah. That's right. That's the good shit. Ride it all the way.'

Pinback. Fourteen-year veteran. His resolute, hard-ass demeanour replaced by pain and confusion.

She'd hoped to find him unhurt, hoped he would take charge, think on her behalf. Instead, here he was, helpless.

She lifted the blast screens to get more light.

She stood over the pilot seat, unbuckled his chin-strap and lifted his helmet clear.

She ran fingers through his hair.

'Take it easy. Just got to sit tight until Trenchman decides to show up.'

His lips moved.

She leaned close.

'Get me out of here,' he whispered.

'Help will come soon.'

'Get me out of this fucking chair.'

'Not such a great idea. You've suffered a significant thoracic injury.'

'I don't want to die strapped to this fucking thing.'

'You're not dying anywhere, sir.'

Pinback impatiently swiped his hand as if her bullshit, you'll-be-fine platitudes were buzzing his head like mosquitoes.

'Help me up, Lieutenant.'

'You've hurt your back, sir. Probably broken. Don't want to make a bad injury worse.'

'I'm fucked beyond repair. Moving me around won't make a damned difference.'

'Best wait for the EMTs.'

'Do as you are told, airman. Get me out of this chair.'

'Afraid I cannot comply with that order.'

'Come on. Don't leave me scrunched like waste paper. I'm done, anyway you cut it. Lay me out, let me have a little dignity.'

She thought it over.

'I'll get the WALK.'

She fetched the trauma kit. Brought it up from the cabin below slung over her shoulder.

She threw it down.

Headrush. She lay a while and tried to recover her strength.

The back-frame of the WALK pack was a bunch of self-locking aluminium rods which snapped together to form a litter.

Frost assembled the stretcher and laid it on the flight-deck floor behind the pilot seat.

'No two ways. This is going to hurt.'

'Just do it,' said Pinback.

'Internal injuries, sir. It's a concern.'

Tabloid horror stories from the New York subway. Commuter slips and falls as a train pulls into the station. Gets pinned between the subway car and the platform. Twisted at the waist like a corkscrew. So there he is, the besuited commuter, trapped but feeling fine, trading wisecracks with first responders. He waits for the fire department to show, tilt the train with a Hurst tool and pull him clear. He wants to call his employer, let them know he has been delayed, promise to work late to make up the time. It's a glitch in his day, an anecdote to tell co-workers when he reaches the office. But MTA cops lay the hard truth: 'Dude, you're beyond help. Your spine is shattered, your insides are messed up. Moment we tilt this train, you'll bleed out and die. Anyone you want to call? Any message we can pass on?'

'Reluctant to move you around, Daniel. Might have repercussions.'

'Want me to beg? I'm all-the-way fucked. Help me die, Lieutenant. Least you can do.'

Frost leant over the injured man and unclipped his harness.

'Got to ask one last question, sir, before I pull you out the chair. Did you transmit a Mayday? As they plane went down, did you broadcast a distress?'

'We were squawking on all channels.'

'Did you get a response? Do they have our grids?'

'No. Couldn't raise a soul.'

'Christ.'

'Come on. Get me out of here. Make it quick.'

She put a hand between his shoulder blades and pushed him forwards. He barked in pain.

'Want me to stop?'

'No.' Panting through clenched teeth. 'Keep going. Get it done.'

She stood behind him and hooked her hands beneath his armpits. She slowly toppled sideways dragging him from his seat, across the centre console and onto the floor. They both screamed. His back. Her leg.

She caught her breath.

'Finish it,' he hissed.

She dragged him onto the litter. More screams.

70

She arranged tie-down straps, got ready to buckle him tight. He pushed her hands away.

'We ought to get you rigid, sir. Put you in a neck brace.'

'Forget it.'

She unclipped the drogue chute from his seat and put it behind his head as a pillow.

She crawled across the deck and sat with her back to the cabin wall.

Both of them pale, sweating, exhausted.

'What's the time?' asked Pinback.

Frost looked out the cockpit windows. Long shadows. The sun heading for the horizon. The sky tinged red.

'Late afternoon, heading into evening.'

'What day? How long have I been here?'

'The plane crashed this morning.'

'This morning?'

'You've been here fourteen hours, give or take.'

'Feels like a lifetime.'

'Yeah. Yeah, it does.'

'What happened to your leg?' croaked Pinback, gesturing to the splint clamped to her calf.

'Took a knock when I punched out.'

'Broken?'

'No idea. Hurts like a son of a bitch.'

'Cry me a fucking river. Give anything to feel my legs right now.'

'Yeah. Well. Looks like we'll both be eating hospital food a while.'

He nodded. Eyes struggling to focus, like he was fighting sleep.

He raised his hand and fumbled the zip-pull of his sleeve pocket. Frost leaned forward, gently pushed his hand aside and took out his two remaining morphine injectors.

'What's up? Need another shot?'

71

He shook his head.

'For you.'

'You're messed up, sir. You'll need them.'

'No,' he said. Sad smile. 'No, I won't.'

Frost unscrewed her canteen. She lifted his head, held capfuls of water to his lips and let him sip.

He lay back, nodding gratitude.

'What about the others?' he asked.

'Guthrie's dead. Infected. Must have been hiding it the whole time.'

'Infected. Jesus. When?'

'Vegas, at a guess. Someone in the camp wasn't quite what he seemed.'

'Anyone else make it?'

She shook her head.

'Far as I can tell, just you and me.'

She gently wiped his face with towelettes.

'So what happened up there?' she asked. 'Why did the engines fail?'

'Wild guess: tainted fuel. Simple as that. Sediment in the tanks.'

'Yeah?'

'You saw the situation back at Vegas. Place was falling apart. Barely enough guys to man the wire. Some poor, half-trained bastard filled the tanks with sour JP8. Fuel must have been sitting in that truck a long while.'

'And that was the flame-out?'

'Sure. Pod two choked and blew, peppered the wing with debris. Took out the firewall isolator valves. Ruptured the lines. We were fucked from that point on. Losing fuel, losing oil pressure. Pod one starts to burn, and suddenly we had electrical fires all over. Pods two and three die in a matter of minutes. Pointless to apportion blame. We caught a dose of bad luck. Leave it at that.'

'Yeah,' said Frost, thinking it over. 'I buy it.'

'Cascading system failures. It's like you said. This bird belongs in a museum. She shouldn't have been in the air.'

He winced.

'Sure you don't want a shot?'

He shook his head.

'You should have punched out,' said Frost.

'Thought I could bring her level. Thought I could bring her home.'

Frost gave him more water.

'So what was the objective? Why were we out here, in the middle of nowhere, prepped to bomb dirt?'

'Classified.'

'Come on, Cap.'

'Classified. Seriously. They gave me coordinates. A map with a cross. That's all. It was Hancock's deal. He was running the show. S2 intelligence. That's why they put him aboard the flight.'

'Where's the target data?'

Pinback gestured to a soft vinyl document wallet propped beside the co-pilot position.

'There are the particulars. Be my guest.'

Frost retrieved the wallet.

Cover stamp: RESTRICTED ACCESS. CO-PILOT ONLY.

Zipper.

She thumbed pages.

Latitude/longitude.

A grease-pencil flight path plotted on a map.

A sheaf of National Recon Office aerial photographs: dunes and a limestone escarpment.

'Doesn't make sense. A ten kiloton strike on absolutely nothing. Sand. Rocks.'

'Think of the effort that went into this operation. Trying to marshal the resources for a nuclear drop while the word

73

falls apart. Didn't happen on a whim. The continuity government, bunch of generals and politicians, wanted to hit this site real bad. Sealed in their bunker, shouting orders down the phone. Expended their remaining assets to see the mission carried out. Must have been a big deal.'

'Crazy.'

'Rich man's war and a poor man's fight. Same as it ever was. Above our pay grade, Frost. Don't sweat it.'

Pinback suddenly gripped the side-poles of the litter and screamed through clenched teeth. Frost punched another morphine shot into his neck. He slowly relaxed.

They sat a while and watched sunset turn the cabin interior gold.

Pinback started to shiver.

'Damn,' he murmured. 'Freezing in here.'

She checked him out. His face was white. His lips were blue. She put a hand on his forehead. Running hot.

'Guess it's the evening chill,' she lied. 'Night falls fast in the desert.'

He exhaled, like he was trying to see his breath steam in cold air.

'Got a blanket or something?'

'Think I saw a coat down below.'

'I'd be obliged.'

Frost gestured to her injured leg.

'Got me running all over the damn place, you sadistic fuck.'

He smiled.

She climbed down the ladder to the lower cabin. An NB3 parka wadded and lashed to the wall.

Easiest way to carry the heavy coat up the ladder was to wear it.

When she got back to the flight deck Pinback was dead.

She took off the coat and laid it over his body so she wouldn't have to look at his face.

74

1. PUSH LATCH TO OPEN DOOR
2. PULL 'D' HANDLE TO JETTISON HATCH

RESCUE

10

A backpack stashed in the EWO footwell.

Frost sat in the pilot seat, held the bag in her lap and unzipped the main compartment. Noble's stuff:

A handful of snack bars.

A video camera.

A copy of *The Little Prince*.

She examined the book. She flipped pages.

To Malcolm, Have a very happy birthday, All my love, Dad.

She'd met a bunch of military personnel in the past few months. Most ditched keepsakes. Eschewed reminders of all they had lost. Kids, partners, parents. Out of contact, almost certainly dead. Hard to think of them without succumbing to suicidal despair. Better to be surrounded by impersonal PX-issue clothes and accoutrements. Olive-drab, mil-spec gear that held no evocative power.

She turned the camera in her hands.

Noble had been ordered to film the blast.

How it should have played out:

The target run.

Frost, strapped in her seat at the radar navigation console. She and Guthrie plot course; make sure the aircraft reaches the precise drop point.

Hancock maintains heading.

Pinback rides the throttles, monitors airspeed.

Couple of minutes from target Pinback radios Vegas for permission to deploy. He gets the Go. Hancock and Frost formally concur. They hand their authentication codes to Noble. He keys the digit sequence into the weapons console and arms the device.

Cue for Frost to unzip her breast pocket, take out a stopwatch and call the sixty second count.

Twenty seconds to target: low rumble/thud as the bomb bay doors fold open and lock.

Pinback issues the final command: proceed with launch sequence.

Countdown from ten.

Noble reaches for the overhead Special Weapons panel, lifts switch covers and hits WPN REL.

Clamps retract and the ALCM drops from the payload compartment. Solid fuel boosters fire, fins unfold, and the missile begins its journey to the target site. Warhead: a Mod 4 CS-67 tactical nuke dialled for a ten kiloton yield.

The plane banks and enters a holding pattern. Standoff until detonation.

They drop blast screens and wait. Minutes pass.

Pinback:

'Brace, brace, brace.'

A shuddering shockwave buffets the aircraft. Noble unbuckles, crouches between the pilot seats with his camera, and lifts one of the blast screens. He and the pilots are bathed in the unholy light of a slow unfurling mushroom cloud.

The crew had sat in the plane while it was hangared at McCarran and drilled the procedure until it was instinctual. Everyone knew their part.

But then the centre console flashed ENGINE FIRE. An ominous moment that seemed to signal bifurcating reality. One timeline in which the plane completed its mission and returned to base. Another in which Frost found herself marooned among wreckage.

Frost set the camera on the avionics console and pressed REC.

'LaNitra Frost, Lieutenant, Second Bomb Wing. Radar nav aboard *Liberty Bell* MT66.

'We crashed in the desert a few hours ago. Lieutenant Guthrie and Captain Pinback are both KIA. Noble, Hancock and Early are missing. As far as I can ascertain, I am the sole survivor.

'Sun is about to set. Must be twenty-one-hundred, or thereabouts.'

She could see her own face in the camera's little playback screen. Sunburn. Cracked lips. Crazy, sand-dusted hair. Looked like the kind of raddled meth casualty you might see shaking a cup on a street corner. She reangled the screen so she didn't have to look at herself.

'I spoke with Captain Pinback prior to his death. It was his supposition that the explosion of engine two triggered a sequence of systems failures which, in turn, caused the plane to lose airspeed and stall. There will be no investigation, no forensic examination of debris, so I guess we'll never know for sure.

'Pinback sent a bunch of distress calls before the crash. There are multiple locator beacons broadcasting from this site. The plane, the missile, the ejector seats are all transmitting a homing signal. Hopefully the guys at Vegas will scramble their chopper and pick me up.'

She wiped her brow.

'It's hot. Too damned hot. Truth be told, it's been a long fucking day. Guess there's nothing I can do but sit tight and wait for rescue.'

She pressed OFF.

She turned in the pilot seat and looked over her shoulder.

Pinback lying dead on the flight-deck floor. An Arctic parka draped over his face. Frost could see the outline of his head.

The mystery of death. Hard to believe there was no longer a person under the coat. Speaking to the guy a moment ago. Injured but animated. Strong voice. An entire universe behind those eyes. Now her friend and Captain was a cooling slab of meat. Mind and memory dissipated the moment his heart stopped beating.

Better move the body. She didn't want to share the cabin with a putrefying corpse. It wouldn't be long before he started to stink.

She grabbed his feet and dragged him to the ladder way. She gripped his wrists and lowered him through the hatch. He hung for a moment, feet brushing the deck of the lower cabin, standing upright one last time. Then Frost released her grip and he fell dead-weight to the floor.

She slid down the ladder and stood next to the grotesquely sprawled corpse. Ought to feel bad about throwing the dead man around, think of it as brutal desecration, but that kind of sentiment died months back with the rest of the human race.

She dragged him outside, hauled him through the rip in the cabin wall, flight suit shredded on torn metal.

Pinback laid out on the sand. Lips parted, eyes closed, face already mortuary white.

She placed his hands across his chest, wrapped a parka round his legs. She fetched the flag from the locker, a cheap Walmart stars and stripes evidently used as a dust cover for the avionics. She tucked it round his upper body like she was saying goodnight. His head shrouded in stars.

Sunset. Pale azure. Delicious evening cool. Day heat already evaporating into a cloudless sky as the earth turned and put her on the dark side.

79

Frost climbed a high dune in front of the plane.

She sat awhile and massaged her leg, glad to be away from the stink of aviation fuel and burned cable insulation.

She powered up her CSEL and extended the antenna.

'Mayday, Mayday, this is Lieutenant LaNitra Frost, United States Air Force, requesting urgent assistance, over.'

Nothing.

'Can anyone hear me, over? Air Force personnel hailing all channels, please respond. Does anyone copy this transmission?'

Nothing.

'If anyone, anywhere, can hear my voice, please answer.'

The backlit screen: NO COMMS.

She shut off the radio.

A rippling ocean of silica. Pale dune crests, deep wells of shadow.

She could see tracks in the sand, the trail left as she crossed the desert and approached the plane. The footprints had begun to soften and blur. In a couple of days, all trace of her passage would be erased.

Skin-crawling unease. She pictured herself dead of thirst. A desiccated corpse consumed by the desert. Nothing left but bleached bone next to a corroded fuselage. A few tattered scraps of flight suit. A couple of wind-scoured dog tags. A sand-filled skull.

She had never felt so small, so utterly alone.

She pressed REC.

'Night is falling. Couldn't raise anyone on the CSEL. Hoped a change in atmospherics might extend the range, but I guess not. Half remembered something they taught us during Basic: high frequency analogue signals are less likely to be absorbed by the ionosphere at night. Doesn't seem to have made much difference, though. Haven't reached a soul.

'The plane itself has several communications systems, but none of them are operational. The power is out. Reckon that's my next job, once I've grabbed a little rest. See if there's life in the aft batteries. Coax a little juice to the flight deck, fire up the UHF and TACAN.

'Truth be told, I'm scared to try. What if I can't re-route the power? What if the batteries are dead?

'Worse still: what if I restore current to the deck systems, broadcast on every channel, and get no reply? Thing of it is, Guthrie was infected. Must have been sick before he got on the plane. Can't blame the guy for covering his illness. He was scared. If he'd sought help, told anyone at Vegas he was infected, they would have shot him in the head where he stood. But when did he get bit? The virus must have breached the wire. Someone brought it inside the airport compound. Maybe one of Trenchman's boys got tagged during a supply run. Brought it home and spread infection across the base. Bunch of guys convinced searchlights and perimeter guns were keeping them safe. But the virus was already inside the garrison, picking them off one by one. Maybe we got out just in time. Maybe they are all dead.

'That's what I have to face. There's a very real possibility that the last military installation in this time zone has been wiped out.

'So what if I'm marooned in this god-forsaken place? That's the question I've been trying to avoid. I'll send out regular distress calls. But what if help doesn't come?'

The plane itself has several communications systems, but none of them are operational. The power is out. Reckon that's my next job, once I've grabbed a little rest. See, if there's life in the air reservoir, there's a little air — to the flight deck, the up-tide OHF and TACAN.

'Truth be told, I'm scared to try. What if I can't re-route the power? What if the batteries are dead?

'Worse still, what if I restore current to the deck systems, broadcast on every channel, and nobody's there? Thing of it is, Culture was at sea — he goes —

'There's what I have to face. There's a very real possibility that the last military installation on this time zone has been wiped out...

'So what did I transposed in this god-forsaken place?' That's the question. I've been trying to re-route, I'll send out regular distress calls. But what if help never arrives?

I I

Frost lay in the sand and looked up at the stars. Constellations emerged from the darkening sky. Cassiopeia. Pegasus. Andromeda.

She enjoyed the evening cool. A sensual, skin-prickle chill.

She switched on her flashlight a while and let the beam shine upwards into the sky. No moths or mosquitoes dancing in the beam, batting the lamp. No insects of any kind. Implication: no water for miles.

A distant shout.

'Hey.'

Frost struggled to sit upright.

A silhouette at the top of a high dune. A guy in a flight suit.

He fell. He tumbled in a cascade of dust.

Frost scrambled to her feet and limped towards the prone figure.

Hancock. Head bandaged with blood-blackened chute fabric.

She knelt beside him.

He fumbled at a pocket of his survival vest. She gently pushed his hands away, extracted a water sachet and tore the corner tab. She lifted his head and held the pouch to his lips.

He sucked the pouch dry. Feverish thirst.

'Another?'

He nodded.

She tore the tab and watched him gulp a second pouch.

83

He lay back, panting.

'More water on the plane, right?' he asked.

'Some.'

'Anyone else make it?'

'Pinback and Guthrie are dead for sure. No sign of the others. Poor bastards must be out in the desert. I'll start a fire at first light. Put up more smoke. Maybe they'll see it.'

Hancock held up his CSEL.

'Couldn't raise anyone. Not a living soul.'

'The airwaves are stone dead.'

'Thought my radio might be damaged.'

Frost shook her head.

'There's no one to raise. It's as if the whole hemisphere has gone dark.'

'Still,' he said. 'Glad you made it, Frosty.'

He held out a hand. They shook.

Frost gestured to his injured head.

'Want me to patch you up, sir?'

'Been walking all day. I'm beyond tired. Let me rest a while.'

'Looks like you took a substantial knock.'

'Woke up minus an eye.'

'Lost some blood, by the looks.'

He nodded. He gestured to his scalp.

'Itches like I-don't-know-what. Hard to stop myself scratching the wound right open. Torment. How about you? You okay?'

'Messed up my leg.'

He checked out the splint.

'You can walk. You can put a little weight on it. So I guess it can't be bust.'

'Morphine dulls the pain. Not sure if that's good or bad. Might encourage me to exacerbate the injury.'

'You'll be okay.'

'Does your head hurt?'

'It's like my migraine has a migraine. Can't hardly see straight. A thousand drills boring into my skull.'

'There's a trauma kit aboard the plane. Plenty of dope. I'll fix you up. Get you high as a Georgia pine.'

He shook his head.

'Pinback is dead, is that right? Then I guess that makes me AC. Better keep a clear head. Responsibilities. There's a whole new day tomorrow and it ain't been touched yet. Plenty to do.'

'Maybe you ought to take a shot. Help you concentrate on the tasks at hand.'

'No.'

'With respect, being AC doesn't mean a whole lot right now. The mission is over, sir. Not much to be done. Just got to sit tight and wait for rescue.'

Hancock started to get to his feet. He looked resolute, like he was ready to take charge and issue orders. Then his strength gave out and he fell on his back.

'Seriously, sir. You're played out. Better rest a while.'

They lay and looked up at the brilliant starfield.

'No planes,' said Hancock. 'A dozen flight paths used to intersect over this desert. Few months ago we would have see contrails, running lights.'

'We ought to concentrate on our immediate situation.'

'A silent planet. Nothing moving on the highways. No ships at sea. Imagine the cities. New York. LA. The stillness. The silence.'

Long pause.

'What if we're the last people on Earth? If Vegas got wiped out, if the airwaves are dead, maybe there is no one else but us. End of the species. Could be us. Right here, right now.'

'You want to procreate, is that what you're saying?'

Hancock smiled.

'Appreciate the offer, but right now I barely have enough energy to blink.'

They lay in silence a while.

'Thought I was going to die out there, Frost. Die among the dunes. Thought my end had come.'

'Yeah. Me too.'

'Least we survived, right?'

She nodded.

'Yeah,' said Hancock. 'Least we survived.'

12

Frost got to her feet.

'We'll freeze if we stay out here. We better get inside.'

She held out a hand and helped Hancock to his feet.

They leant against each other as they walked to the plane.

The body.

Pinback shrouded in the stars and stripes.

Hancock stood a while, leaning against the hull of the B-52, and contemplated the dead man.

'Don't mean to speak ill of the departed. Understand he was your friend and all. But the dumb bastard should have punched out.'

She helped Hancock squirm through the fissure in the fuselage and enter the darkness of the lower cabin.

He lowered himself to the floor, sat with his back against the nav console.

Frost crouched and found her survival vest by touch. She unzipped pouches and found her little Fenix flashlight. Cabin lit by a weak pencil-beam.

'There's a big Maglite in that locker,' said Hancock.

Frost threw him a parka.

She zipped her flight suit and stepped into unlaced boots.

'Try to sleep,' advised Frost.

'If there is stuff to be done, we ought to set to work before the sun comes up and heat starts to build.'

'You're in no fit state. Get some rest.'

She pulled a tool pack from a floor locker. Duct tape. She twisted the reel onto her wrist like a bangle.

'I'm going up top. See if I can patch a few holes, trap a little heat.'

She climbed the ladder to the flight deck.

Two of the roof hatches were open to the starlit sky.

Sections of the cabin roof and walls were insulated by padded blankets clipped to the superstructure by poppers. She pulled a couple of blankets free.

She stood on a trunk stamped LIFE RAFT. She bite-ripped strips of tape and patched the vacant hatch frames with insulation.

She pulled down blast screens to curtain the missing windows.

She climbed down the ladder and set the flashlight on the nav console.

She pulled another blanket from the wall, held it against the split in the fuselage, measured it for size, prepared to seal the plane against a rising night wind.

'I feel bad,' said Hancock. 'Sitting here, watching you work.'

She shrugged.

'No point messing yourself up any further. Just add to my problems. Want to eat? We've got food.'

'I'm okay,' he said.

'Let me know if you get hungry. I'll fetch snack bars.'

She tore tape with her teeth.

'Reckon they'll show up? Trenchman and his gang?' she asked.

'Only hope we got is that nuke,' said Hancock. 'The Joint Chiefs, whoever the fuck it was ordered this mission, will regard you, me, the whole damned crew, as an expendable asset. No point crying about it. Came with the uniform, right? The moment we tied our boots. But promise you this: no way will they shrug off the loss of a tactical nuke, just leave it lying in the sand. They are desperate to erase something out there in the desert, and we got the only warhead at their disposal. If they're still alive, if they're still down a bunker somewhere issuing commands, they will make our rescue an absolute priority. Help will come. Just got to sit tight and not panic ourselves into anything stupid.'

A flicker in the sky outside. Pinprick, brilliant white, falling out of view.

She squirmed from the plane, limped to a nearby dune and scrambled to the top. Hancock stumbled in pursuit.

'What can you see?' he asked, looking up at her from the foot of the dune. He tried to stand, but fell on his knees. 'A searchlight? A chopper?'

She waved hush and squinted at the distant horizon.

A distant star shell slowly fell to earth.

'A flare. Somebody else survived.'

Hancock and Frost stood at the ridgeline. They looked out over moonlit desert.

She flagged a Maglite back and forth.

'Sure it was a starshell?'

'Yeah.'

'How far?'

'Couple of miles.'

She continued to flag the light.

An hour later:

'Hey.'

A voice calling from the desert darkness.

'Who's out there?' shouted Hancock, hand on the butt of his pistol.

'Noble, two-nine-five-five-six.'

Frost trained the Maglite.

A figure strode towards them across the sand. Noble. He wore a chute fabric headdress. He shielded his face with his hand.

'Get that light out my eyes.'

He climbed the dune to meet them.

'Good to see you, Frosty.' Back-slapping hug.

She looked him up and down. No sign of injury.

'You all right?'

'Yeah,' he said. 'I'm good.' He gestured to the splint lashed to her leg. 'How about you?'

She waved the question away.

'Glad you made it,' said Hancock. Brief handshake. 'Thought we'd lost you.'

Noble checked out the bloody bandage wrapped round his head.

'Looks like you both took a bruising.'

They stood a while and contemplated the wrecked war machine.

'Breaks my heart to see a bird like that in the dirt,' said Noble.

'Yeah.'

'Iraq. Afghanistan. Not a scratch.'

'Hunk of metal,' said Frost. 'No earthly use getting weepy. Want some water?'

He licked parched lips.

'I want all the water in the world.'

She led Noble down the side of the dune.

She stumbled. Noble put an arm round her shoulder and helped her walk back towards the plane.

The lower cabin. They sat cross-legged on floor plates.

Noble gulped from the canteen.

He wiped his mouth with the back of his hand.

'We could put up flares. Fire them at intervals. You never

know. If Early is out there, stumbling around the desert, it might lead him home.'

'Not much point,' said Hancock. 'Judging by the direction of footprints, Early headed away from the plane, away from help. Maybe he panicked. Maybe his compass was fucked. Either way, the guy is almost certainly dead.'

'We can't give up on the kid.'

Frost nodded.

'It won't hurt to send up a shell at the top of each hour.'

Noble spread a map on the deck. Frost trained her flashlight on the chart.

Miles of beige nothing. Shallow contour lines. Grid squares chequered with the legend: *dunes*.

'Hard to get a fix on our exact location. Couldn't get a clear lensatic reading. Couldn't raise a soul on the CSEL, either.'

'Plenty of metal deposits hereabouts,' said Frost. 'Iron salts. Manganese. Uranium. All kinds of shit. We're probably sitting in the middle of some weird electromagnetic anomaly. Won't clear radio interference until we reach the mountains and climb.'

'Given our direction of travel, given that we were about six or seven minutes from the drop point, I'd say we were here.'

He circled a central section of wilderness.

'That's a long fucking walk,' said Frost. 'A shitload of desert any direction you care to choose. On foot? Person couldn't last more than a couple of days in this kind of environment.'

'It would have to be our very last resort. But hey. There's always the chance Trenchman will show up at first light. Long shot. But he might have spent the day fixing a fault with their Chinook, trying to get it back in the air. Can't rule it out. This time tomorrow we could be feet-up in Vegas sipping a cold one.'

'Perhaps,' said Frost. 'But I'd feel a whole lot better if we got power to the flight deck and actually raised someone on the damned radio.'

DRAG PARACHUTE LATCH MECHANISM ACCESS PANEL

13

The upper cabin.

Frost sat in the pilot seat and cycled the AC selector.

Noble, from below:

'Anything?'

She tapped a volt gauge. The needle remained unresponsive.

'Total flatline.'

The lower cabin.

Noble helped Frost lift a fuse panel from the wall behind the EWO console. The primary distribution bus. He held the flashlight steady while she examined tangled cable.

Burnouts. They trimmed and spliced cable.

They replaced the fuse panel. All load switches set to green. She returned to the pilot seat and toggled for power.

Nothing.

'We should be getting twenty-eight volts DC from the auxiliaries. Enough to restore essential systems.'

'Line break?'

Frost shook her head.

'Cells must have shorted out, drained dry.'

'Dammit.'

'We've got one more shot,' said Frost. 'There is a backup power cell, a nickel-cadmium battery in the aft of the plane.'

'Yeah?'

'So I guess someone will have to take a walk and find the tail.'

★

Noble and Hancock looked out over the moonlit dunescape.

A wide debris trench, like preliminary construction for a highway. The trench was littered with wreckage. Structural spars, scraps of fuselage, a massive undercarriage bogie ripped from a wheel-well.

'Can't be too far,' said Hancock.

They set off.

Noble looked towards the horizon. Pinnacles and flat-top mesas, a jagged ribbon of black against a fabulous dusting of stars.

'Funny. You can make out the mountains clearer than day.'

Hancock stumbled a couple of times.

'You all right?' asked Noble.

'Concussion.'

'Maybe you should sit this one out.'

'It'll pass.'

'How much ground you reckon we've covered?' asked Noble.

'Quarter of a mile, give or take.'

'Can't be too far.'

'Better watch where you tread,' said Hancock, stepping over a torn wing panel. 'This shit wants to cut you wide open. Like walking through a field of razors.'

'Think we're the first humans to set foot on this patch of ground? Sure, plenty of people criss-crossed the desert. Pioneers. Prospectors. But this particular stretch of sand. Think we're the first?'

'Pretty good chance we'll be the last.'

They kept walking.

Their breath fogged the air.

'Freezing.'

'Enjoy it,' said Noble. 'Sunrise in a while. Another hot day.'

'Shame about Early.'

'Let's not write him off just yet. He's green, but he's not stupid.'

'You and Frost are pretty tight, yeah?' asked Hancock.

'The whole crew. Been flying a long while. Four, five years.'

The tail section sat in the middle of the debris trench a quarter of a mile from the main fuselage. A massive cruciform silhouette against the stars.

They trudged towards the wreckage until they were within the moon-shadow of the stabiliser fins.

Tail number: MT66.

The sand was carpeted with fluttering foil strips spilt by the underwing chaff dispensers.

The orange brake chute was spread on sand behind the empennage. Fabric wafted and rippled.

The rudder gently creaked and swung in the night breeze.

They kicked through foil.

Noble banged his fist on the fuselage. Hollow gong.

'Early? Yo. Nick. You in there?'

No reply.

Hancock looked around.

'No footprints, that I can see. Nobody here but us.'

They peered into the cave-dark of the fuselage interior. The flashlight beam played over twisted spars and ripped fuselage panels.

A tight crawlspace.

'Think there might be snakes? Scorpions?' asked Noble.

'Not this deep in the desert. Nothing can survive out here.'

They climbed inside.

The tail section of the plane had been designed to house four 20mm Vulcan cannons remote-operated by a gunner stationed on the flight deck. The quad weapon and feed chutes had long since been removed and the gun ports welded shut. The compartment was now home to a rack of electronic countermeasure gear. Ammo drums replaced by a radome and omnirange antennas. Access via a crawlway that ran the length of the plane from the crew cabin, through the bomb bay, to the rear.

Hancock shuffled along a short section of access tunnel on his hands and knees. Sheet metal slick with hydraulic fluid. Dancing flashlight beam.

Noble squeezed into the tight compartment. They crouched shoulder-to-shoulder, ignoring each other's body odour.

The flight recorder. Mission data housed in a steel cylinder: FINDER'S INSTRUCTIONS – US GOVERNMENT PROPERTY. IF FOUND PLEASE RETURN TO THE NEAREST US GOVERNMENT OFFICE.

The UHF beacon. A winking green light confirmed the beacon was active, operating on internal power, broadcasting a homing signal on SAR.

'How long will she transmit?' asked Hancock.

'Four weeks, give or take.'

The backup cell. Twice the size of an automobile battery. CAUTION – SHOCK HAZARD.

'Is that it?' asked Noble.

'Yeah.'

He disconnected the terminals.

'Watch yourself.'

They unscrewed hex bolts and jerked the unit from its rack.

Noble constructed a sledge from a section of deck plate. He cut a length of power cable and lashed it as tow rope.

Hancock watched him work.

'Feel like an idiot. Sitting here while you break sweat.'

'Best kick back awhile. Take it easy.'

'Head keeps spinning. Can't hardly see straight.'

'You need rest. No use pretending otherwise. Normal circumstances, a head wound that bad would have you laid up in ICU a long while. CAT scans, the works. Weeks before the nurses let you throw back the sheet and put your feet on the floor. Soon as we get back to the plane, you ought to shoot some morphine. Pop a couple of Motrins, at least. You need to recuperate.'

'Fuck that shit.'

'You got to be dispassionate. Set the macho bullshit aside. Your body is equipment in need of repair. Treat it as such.'

'Let you in on a secret,' said Hancock, contemplating the dunes. 'Truth is, I love it out here in the desert. I want to be awake every awful minute. Yeah, the situation is desperate. I want to get home same as you guys. But this is why I joined the military. Didn't want to stare at the world through an office window. Wanted a mission. Clarity of purpose. Something real. Something fundamental.'

'A true believer.'

'You're goddam right.'

Noble loaded the battery onto the deck plate.

'Hold on,' said Hancock. 'I got to fetch something from inside.'

He struggled to his feet, climbed into the tight crawlspace and retrieved a ballistic Peli case from behind the battery rack.

Noble helped drag the Peli case from the tail.

'What's in this thing?' asked Noble as he stacked it on the sled.

'Something that might save our collective ass.'

A star shell to the south. Frost. A flare to guide them home.

They gripped the tow rope and began to haul the battery across the sand.

The nose.

Noble reached up and brushed dust from the hull of the plane. He flipped latches and unhinged a panel beneath the cockpit window.

A seven-pin power receptacle: four pos/negs, two grounds and a redundancy.

Frost dumped the battery in the sand beneath the open power panel. She ran jump leads from the battery pack to the terminals, clamped them with heavy alligator clips. Crack and spark as she applied the second clip. She snatched her hand away.

'Better watch out,' said Noble. 'Whole fuselage is soaked in fuel.'

Frost sat in the pilot seat. Noble stood behind her.

He held a flashlight trained on the AC switch panel.

'Here goes.'

Frost cranked the selector from AUX to EXT.

Spark-shower from the overhead air refuel panel. They ducked and shielded their eyes.

Power up hum. Winking console indicators. Cabin lights fluttered and glowed steady.

Faces lit harsh white. Each shocked by the deterioration they saw in their companion's condition. Exhaustion and thirst. Stubble, sunburn, peeling skin.

They laughed. High-fives.

'About time we caught a break,' said Noble.

'Well, let's not waste precious volts,' said Frost. 'Pass me the headset.'

He handed her the pilot helmet. Brim stencil: PINBACK.

She hesitated for a moment, then pulled on the helmet, creeped to be sharing skullspace with a dead man.

She plugged the interphone jack into the side-console, switched on the command panel above her head and began to flip through pre-programmed frequencies.

She switched from INTER to VOX. Speaker hiss filled the cabin.

She keyed the radio.

99

'Mayday, Mayday, anyone copy, over? This is B-52 *Liberty Bell*, tail MT66 requesting aid, please respond.'

White noise.

'Mayday, Mayday, this is B-52 *Liberty Bell*. We have crashed in the desert north-east of the Panamint Range, we require urgent assistance, over.'

The unbroken susurration of empty wavebands.

She flicked toggles, turned dials.

'No good?' queried Noble.

'Quick II is giving me nothing on Guard. DAMA and AFSAT are returning No Comms. Line-of-sight is no fucking good with these mountains boxing us in. Best bet is the ARC one-ninety. Sooner or later, someone ought to respond. Don't want to believe we're the only folks broadcasting in the entire western hemisphere.'

Frost turned to Noble.

'No point waiting around. Might take a while to raise anyone. Best if we take half-hour shifts. This could be a long night.'

Frost, alone on the flight deck, feet propped on the avionics in front of her. She had removed the pilot's helmet. She toyed with the CSEL in her lap.

She'd managed to pick up fragments of BBC World Service. A news update which was, she suspected, days old, cycling from a console in an abandoned studio somewhere in central London.

British voice:

'. . . *extent of the pandemic . . . research centres across the world . . . no firm hope of a cure . . .*'

The transmission momentarily overwhelmed by a strange tocking sound, an electronic pulse that rose and fell as it washed across the wavebands.

'. . . *refuge centres overrun . . . advise extreme caution . . . place of safety . . . away from major cities . . .*'

Feedback whine. She tweaked Acquisition.

'. . . *asting from the United Sta . . . taken command of the continuity government . . . ecretary of State . . . sworn in at NORAD headquarters . . . continued state of emergency . . . executive posi . . . recall of overseas forces . . . concluded with a prayer . . . their trust in God . . .*'

She shut off the CSEL and threw it aside.

America's slow death evidently playing out like the final hours of Hitler's entourage sealed in their Reichstag bunker. Guys awarding themselves meaningless titles. Studying maps, debating strategy, issuing futile orders. Pathologically competitive alpha males jostling for status even as the power failed, the lights and air con died, and they were left in choking darkness. Bad fucking joke.

She reached above her head and powered the ARC-190. She held the oxygen mask to her mouth and keyed the mask-mike.

'Mayday, Mayday, this is the crew of B-52 *Liberty Bell* requesting urgent assistance. Can any military personnel copy this transmission?'

She scanned wavebands.

'Anyone out there, over? Anyone at all?'

A ghost-murmur behind interference. She sat still, held her breath.

Could be an auditory hallucination. Maybe she was creating syllables out of static, brain-shaping patterns from chaos.

She upped the volume.

'Say again, please. Say again your last.'

A voice. Male. Distant, desperate.

'. . . *For the love of God, can anyone hear me? Please, tell me I'm not alone . . .*'

'Hey. I'm listening.'

'. . . *Tired. Dog tired. Don't know how long I've been . . .*'

'. . . I'm right here, I'm right here, brother. Talk to me . . .'

'. . . can't be the last. Have to be others . . .'

The plane's UHF transmitter too weak to make contact. No way to boost the signal.

She sat back and listened to the phantom voice.

Frost and her distant companion. Two lost souls, pleading with the airwaves, voices shot with hopeless resignation, overwhelmed by the pathetic message-in-a-bottle futility of committing Maydays to the ether.

She stepped outside.

She leant against the fuselage and listened to the silence.

She glanced down. Pinback, shrouded in the stars and stripes, dusted in sand, slowly claimed by the desert.

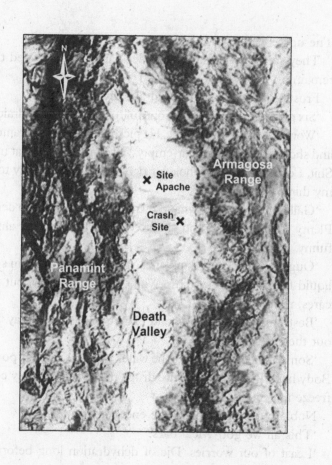

14

The upper cabin.

They sat cross-legged on the deck and contemplated their remaining water.

Frost spoke what they could already see:

'Six pouches. Two canteens: one full, one pretty much drained.'

'Won't last long,' said Noble. He picked up one of the canteens and shook it. It sloshed near-empty. 'Two or three days, at most. Shit, I could drink the whole lot right now. Would barely touch my thirst.'

'Gallon a day. That's what they recommend for deep desert. Plenty of water, rest, and shade. We're so fucked it's almost funny.'

'Ought to check out the plane. Might be able to drain some liquid from the sub-systems. Won't taste too pretty, but who cares, right?'

'Best limit perspiration,' said Hancock. 'Sleep by day. Stay out the sun.'

'Someone ought to carry the water pouches in their pocket. Body heat. If the temperature drops much further they could freeze and burst.'

Noble picked up one of the energy bars.

'This all we got? Meal bars?'

'Least of our worries. Die of dehydration long before we get hungry.'

The cabin lights flickered.

'How long will that power cell last?' asked Hancock.

'Longer than us,' said Frost.

'Any luck with the radio?'

'I would have mentioned it.'

'Nothing at all?'

'A weak signal. Some poor bastard calling for help. We can't reach him, he can't reach us. Pretty much the state of the world. So yeah, we'll keep transmitting an SOS. But it looks like we'll have to help ourselves.'

Noble pushed aside canteens to make space for the map. He moved the water pouches as carefully as he could. If one of the plastic envelopes snagged on a floor-bolt and tore, they would have to get down on their knees and lap moisture from the deck like a pack of dogs.

He shook open the chart and laid it on the floor.

He contemplated featureless terrain. Saltpans and washes.

'Every time I look at this damn map I hope to see something I missed,' said Noble. 'A water hole. A Park Ranger station. Something that might save our asses. It's like I'm working through Kübler-Ross. I've done denial and anger. Now I've moved onto bargaining. Been pleading with God, in my head. Each time I open the chart, hoping to find a symbol magically appeared. He hasn't obliged so far.'

He tapped the red grease-pencil circle at the centre of the map.

'Like I said. Pretty sure that's our grid. Might be a little further north-west, but it doesn't make a whole lot of difference. Several days from any roads, any habitation. A true country mile any direction we take. In this heat? We'd tap out pretty quick. We'd be crow bait within hours.'

'It can be done,' said Hancock. 'Weaker men have overcome tougher odds. Just got to set our minds. Sleep by day, walk by night. It's not like we have a whole lot to carry.'

'Last resort,' said Frost. 'But I guess we've already reached last resort territory.'

'There is another option,' said Noble. 'You've cracked your head, and Frost has messed up her leg. Neither of you are in much condition to undertake a long desert trek. But I could go. I'm in good shape. I could cover a lot of ground on my own. Move at my own pace. If I climbed the mountains and reached blacktop road, I could summon help.'

'How much water would you be looking to take on this expedition?' asked Hancock.

'I'd need to cover twenty miles each night. That's a punishing pace.'

'So how much water?'

'A bunch.'

'Yeah. That's what I thought. If it's all the same to you, we'll stick with a straight three-way split.'

The debris trench.

Scattered wreckage half submerged in sand.

Frost held a flashlight while Noble crouched and dug. He slowly excavated a massive tyre.

Frost helped him heave the wheel upright. Chest-high, white aluminium hub. Part of the aircraft's forward quad-bogie, ripped from its wheel-well during the crash.

Frayed rubber. The tyre abraded by countless runway touchdowns.

'Jeez,' said Frost. 'Virtually no tread. Damn thing is as smooth as an egg. When was the last time this plane got an overhaul?'

Noble shook his head.

'Pinback was right. Should have aborted take-off and put her back in the hangar.'

He rolled the wheel hand over hand back towards the plane. Frost walked beside him, trained the flashlight.

They ducked as they rolled the tyre beneath the wing.

'Keep going,' said Frost. 'Want to get well away from the fuel before we light her up.'

They rolled the tyre fifty yards in front of the nose.

'Here's good.'

Noble kicked the tyre. It toppled flat.

Frost limped back to the plane. She fetched a wad of pages from the flight manual.

A wing reservoir leaked fuel. She held the paper beneath the leak, let steady drips of JP8 soak into the pages, stain them translucent.

She returned to the tyre and scattered the sheaf of papers.

She took a Zippo from her pocket. Burnished brass. Ranger insignia.

'That belong to your father?' asked Noble.

'Yeah. Three tours.'

'And that old knife?'

'His too.'

'Did he make it?'

'Yeah, he got home.'

She crouched.

'Stand back.'

She held the Zippo at arm's length, flipped the lid and sparked a flame. Fuel vapour combusted with a thud. A mini-mushroom cloud blossomed into the night, lit the crash site flickering red.

Paper blackened and crisped. The tyre began to smoke and melt. Ethereal blue flames.

'Burn a long while,' said Frost. 'Won't smell too pretty, but it'll put out a shitload of smoke. Visible for miles during daylight. If Early is out there, he'll see it.'

Noble covered his mouth and nose.

'Man, that stinks.'

'Should be okay as long as we sit back from it. Tell Hancock to get over here if he wants to keep warm.'

★

Frost climbed a dune and put up another flare. The white starshell screamed skyward. She stared into distant darkness in case, miles away, Early put up a reciprocal shell to alert them he was alive.

The flare lit the crash site cold white, lit Hancock dragging a Peli trunk towards the fire.

Frost descended the dune to meet him.

He had a balled-up parka beneath his arm. He threw it to Frost.

'Thought you might be cold.'

Frost threw it back.

'Thanks. But I can't walk around snug while everyone else shivers.'

'There aren't enough coats for us all.'

'Then I guess we just sit and look at it.'

Hancock flipped latches and opened the trunk.

Frost craned to see inside. Comms gear. A folded tripod antenna.

'What the hell is this?'

'Uplink to STRATCOM. Back-channel authentication for the bomb.'

'Why the fuck didn't you mention it earlier?'

'The digital equipment in the aircraft, the CSELs, the onboard, rely on the same satellite network as this thing. If the plane couldn't get a lock on the command net, I doubt the spectrum analyser on this kit will pick up a signal. Truth be told, I'm booting it up because we've got hours to kill and nothing to do.'

He unfolded the dish antenna and planted it in the sand facing east. He ran cable to the uplink.

Boot sequence. Flickering loading bars. A brief function menu, then the screen hung at ACQUISITION.

They watched the screen a while. A clock glyph cycled as the terminal tried to raise a response from a low orbit milsat.

'There's got to be someone out there,' murmured Hancock as he studied the screen. 'The entire US military. Got to be someone left alive.'

Frost turned away. She sat on the sand and massaged her leg.

Rubber bubbled and popped like gum. A column of filthy smoke rose into the night sky.

'Can you navigate off the stars?' asked Hancock. 'Appreciate it's been a long time since Basic. If we had to walk out of here, could you orient yourself?'

Frost shrugged.

'I can find Polaris easy enough. Truth is, doesn't matter much which direction we go. Desert and mountains on all sides. Same quotient of suffering, all points of the compass.'

She looked at the surrounding dunes, a dark ridgeline against the stars. She thought about the bleak, pre-human wasteland surrounding the plane, the journey that might lie ahead. Dunes seared by merciless sun, scoured by freezing night wind.

She stared into flames and heard herself say:

'We're all going to die out here.'

e. *Presets.*

(1) Set **CHAN** to **1**.

(2) Set **MODE** to **SC**.

(3) Set **RF PWR** to **HI**.

(4) Set **VOL** to mid range.

(5) Set **DIM** full clockwise.

(6) Set **FCTN** to **LD**.

(7) Set **DATA RATE** to **OFF**.

f. *Single Channel Loading Frequencies.*

(1) Obtain **SOI**.

(2) Set **FCTN** to **LD**.

(3) Set **MODE** to **SC**.

(4) Set **CHAN** to **MAN, Cue,** or desired channel (**1** to **6**) where freq is to be stored.

(5) Press **FREQ** (display will show **"00000,"** or the frequency the RT is set to).

(6) Press **CLR** (display will show five lines).

(7) Enter the number of the new frequency.

(8) If you make a mistake with a number, press **CLR**.

(9) Press **STO** (display will blink).

(10) Set **FCTN** to **SQ ON** .

15

McCarran International Airport, Las Vegas.

The hangar office.

The radio operator sat at his console and scanned wavebands. Trenchman stood at his shoulder.

'*Liberty Bell*, do you copy over? MT66, we are listening on SAR two-four-one, please activate your transponders.'

Nothing but static.

'Sure it was them?' asked Trenchman.

The radioman sat back, removed his headphones and consulted his notes.

'It was weak. Real weak. Faded in and out. But I got "LaNitra Frost" and I got "Mayday".'

'You're sure? Couldn't be mistaken?'

'Yeah, I'm sure.'

'What about the plane? Is the nuke intact?'

'Like I said. A couple of words. Nothing coherent.'

Distant gunfire.

Osborne kicked open the office door, breathless and panicked.

'They breached the wire, sir. End of the runway.'

'Can they be repelled?'

Osborne shook his head.

'Way too many.'

'You're sure?'

'We've lost the base. We have to get going right now.'

'All right. Hit the floods. Give us as much light as you can.'

Trenchman turned to the radio operator. 'Pack your shit. We're out of here.'

A floodlit slipway.

Trenchman ran up the Chinook cargo ramp.

Troops loaded crates and weapons.

A soldier climbed aboard with an arm full of bedding. Trenchman grabbed it and threw it out the rear onto the runway.

'Food and ammo. Much as you can carry. Nothing else. Wheels up in two minutes. Don't get left behind.'

He ran through the cluttered cargo compartment. He opened the flight-deck door. Both pilots suited and strapped, ready to haul ass.

'We really ought to go, sir.'

They looked out the cockpit windows at the runway ahead. Receding edge lights.

Movement in the overrun.

Distant figures.

Infected had breached the wire. Troops falling back in cover/fire formation, expending clip after clip, efficient headshots left the asphalt littered with bodies. They could hear the distant crackle of gunfire. They could see flickering muzzle flame.

The pilot adjusted his grip on the joystick like he was itching to bolt: raise the ramp, spin up and take to the sky.

'Hold your nerve, airman. Orderly evacuation. If fear takes over, we're all fucked.'

Osborne climbed aboard the fuel truck and floored the accelerator. He drove up the runway. Full headbeams. He switched on cab beacons and hit the horn, a signal to troops to get the fuck out the way.

He swerved left, smashed edge lights and skidded to a halt.

He jumped from the cab. He unhooked the fuel hose, hauled it to the centre line and threw it down on the asphalt.

The side box. PUMP START. Green light, motor hum. The hose twitched and unkinked. Fuel spluttered from the lock-cuff and washed across the runway.

A spreading lake of kerosene.

The troops fell back.

Infected shambling towards them. Fifty at least. Lurching, misshapen things, flesh torn by metallic carcinomas. Foul stink-rot. An oncoming tide of putrefaction.

'Fire in the hole.'

Osborne struck a flare. Spit and fizz. He tossed it towards the spilt fuel.

Ignition. Blossoming flames. He backed away, shielded his face from sudden heat.

A fireball mushroomed in the night sky.

'Get to the chopper.'

They turned and ran.

Osborne glanced back. Movement behind the wall of fire. Infected revenants walked straight into the inferno. Most of them fell amidst the flame. Major muscle groups, biceps, triceps, quads and glutes, quickly cooked and contracted, pulling them down, curling them foetal. A couple of figures made it through the fire. They walked clear, columns of flame, clothes and flesh ablaze. They stumbled blind, fell to their knees and died kneeling upright. Carbonised skin lacquered black. Bodyfat burned blue.

Trenchman stood on the Chinook loading ramp and supervised the evacuation.

'Move your fucking asses.'

Troops grabbed what they could from tents and freight containers. Rifles. Ammo. Boxes of bean cans.

One of the soldiers ran to the chopper carrying a bag of

children's toys. He had a large, blood-stained teddy bear under his arm. He glanced at Trenchman as he ran up the loading ramp, caught the glance of disapproval.

'Fuck you, sir. I'm bringing it.'

Trenchman stepped from the helicopter and glanced up the runway. Osborne and his men sprinted towards him. The fuel fire was already starting to die back.

'That's it,' he bellowed. 'We're out of here. Everybody in the chopper. Get inside and strap in.' He pointed to the jumble of ration boxes and ammo crates. 'Throw a cargo net over that shit. Get it secure.' He grabbed a guy wearing sergeant stripes as he sprinted up the ramp. Name strip: DAWSON.

'Make one last sweep. Check the tents. Check the freight containers.'

The sergeant looked like he wanted to argue. He didn't want to turn away from the cargo compartment, the light and promise of safety. Trenchman put a hand on Dawson's chest and pushed him towards the tents.

'Go. Make sure no one is left behind.'

Trenchman ran to the Humvee limo. Flame light from the runway fire turned white bodywork pink.

He checked for keys.

He opened the passenger door, threw a couple of AR-15s and a case of ammo into the passenger compartment.

He ran to a jumbled stack of supplies. He grabbed bottled water and a jerry can full of fuel. He threw them inside the car.

He ran back to the Chinook.

He stood at the lip of the loading ramp. Quick survey of the cargo compartment. Twenty-six guys strapped into side-seats. Sweating, fearful, desperate to be gone.

Dawson ran past, anxious to get aboard the chopper. Trenchman grabbed his arm, held him back.

'Nobody left behind?'

'We're clear.'

'You're sure?'

'I'm fucking sure.'

Dawson tried to pull his arm free. Trenchman maintained his grip.

'You're in charge now, sergeant. Get the boys somewhere remote, somewhere safe.'

'What about you, sir?'

'I got business elsewhere.'

Trenchman stepped from the loading ramp onto asphalt. He took out his radio and buzzed the pilot:

'That's it. Get the fuck out of here.'

Escalating motor whine. The Chinook's massive twin blades began to revolve.

Osborne unlatched his cargo seat harness and ran down the ramp to Trenchman. He shouted over escalating rotor roar.

'What the hell are you doing?'

'I'm going after *Liberty Bell*.'

'The crew? They're dead.'

'What if they're not?'

'Then it's a crying shame. But you don't owe them a damned thing, Phil.'

Trenchman pointed to the flag on his sleeve. Engine scream so loud Osborne had to read his lips:

'Got to do what I can.'

Osborne stayed by Trenchman's side. Warning klaxon. They watched the loading ramp rise and seal shut. Last glimpse of the ribbed interior of the hold, troops strapped in opposing rows.

They crouched and covered their ears as engine noise

reached a crescendo. Typhoon rotor-wash tore at their clothes, enveloped them in dust.

The Chinook ascended into the night sky.

Engine noise quickly diminished. Running strobes headed north.

Osborne lit a cigar and tossed the match. He watched infected shuffle through the dying flames of the fuel fire and head towards them, clothes ablaze.

'Guess it's time to go.'

They strode towards the limo.

Voices behind them:

'Hey. Wait the fuck up.'

Two soldiers running across the slipway, screaming, trying to flag down the long-gone chopper.

They skidded to a halt, bellowing at distant strobes.

'Get in the damned car,' shouted Trenchman. He ran, grabbed them both by the shoulder and propelled them towards the limo.

They tumbled into the rear passenger compartment.

Quick glance:

MORGAN.

AKINGBOLA.

Sweating, terrified kids.

'What happened to you guys?' asked Trenchman. 'How the hell did you miss the chopper?'

'Manning a tower. Didn't realise what was going down until it was too late.'

'Don't shit your pants. I'm not kidding. Combat stress. Clench, for God's sake. We could be in here a while.'

Osborne took the wheel.

The limo pulled away, swung a wide arc and headed down the runway towards the burning figures. Cadaverous creatures reached for the automobile, got flipped across the hood, slammed aside by the fender. A cop went under a wheel, got

balled up and jammed in the well. Bone-snapping disintegra-
tion, thick-tread tyre spraying fabric and flesh chunks like
slurry.

Osborne ran screen-wash and wipers.

They drove through the fuel fire. Brief flurry of smoke
and flame beyond the windows.

They accelerated down the runway, headed for the collapsed
section of perimeter fence.

Jolt across the kerbs of Vegas Boulevard. Trenchman and
the two grunts thrown around.

The vehicle lurched across the grounds of the Bali Hai
Golf Club. Headbeams lit ghost figures stumbling aimlessly
across the fairway.

They joined the two-one-five and headed out of town.

Trenchman relaxed on the bench seat. He turned to
Osborne.

'Either put out that damned cigar or raise the partition.'

Osborne cracked the side window for air. He opened the
glove box, scattered CDs on the passenger seat. He found
Cypress Hill and fed it into the dash.

Trenchman tapped a booted foot to 'Ain't Goin'Out Like
That'.

Osborne shouted over his shoulder:

'Looks like The Luxor is burning pretty good.'

Trenchman glanced out the window. The great bronzed
glass pyramid. Infernal glow from deep within the structure.
Flames licked from the broken apex. It looked like a volcano.

'Sin City,' he murmured. 'Abandon all hope.'

They headed down the interstate.

PREMIERE LIMO

SAVE $$$ ON YOUR VEGAS TOUR!

During Our 4 hour Trip Of The Strip You Will View:

- ✓ 'Welcome to Las Vegas' Sign.
- ✓ Fountains at the Bellagio.
- ✓ Mirage Volcano in the Tropical Gardens.
- ✓ Sirens of Treasure Island Theatrical Show.
- ✓ Fremont Experience Laser and Sound Show.

Complimentary glass of champagne.

No Matter How Big Your Group We Have a Deal For You.

Ask about our bachelorette parties.

- 3 Flat Screen LCD TVs
- DVD-CD Overhead Combo Player
- Hi-Fi Multi Speaker, Multi Subwoofer Surround System
- Contour Leather Coach Style Seating
- Rear Lounge/VIP Seating
- Fibre Optic Ceiling Lights
- Fibre Optic Bar and Accent Lighting
- Floor Lighting
- Digital Touch Pad Controls
- Tinted Windows
- Chrome Mag Wheels

CALL NOW TO RESERVE YOUR LIMO

16

Salt flats gave way to dunes. The limo lurched across sand. Heavy tyres cut deep chevron tracks.

Osborne, Morgan and Akingbola sat in the rear, rocking on a bench seat, sipping Diet Cokes.

Trenchman had the wheel.

'Doing okay so far,' he shouted over his shoulder, 'but if the terrain gets worse, might have to park and walk.'

Morgan leant over the driver partition.

'I don't mean to speak out of turn, but maybe this rescue mission isn't such a good idea. After all, we've got finite gas.'

'Crew of the *Liberty Bell* are out here, somewhere. They're counting on us. For our own peace of mind, we've got to do whatever we can.'

Noon. Tinted glass and air con shielded them from the worst of the sun. Osborne swigged pretzels from a bag and looked out at unbroken desolation.

'They must have bailed out the plane, right? Some kind of engine fault.'

'I guess.'

'Wouldn't want to find myself alone in this fucking place. Dead as the moon.'

Akingbola contemplated the shimmering heat-haze horizon.

'Hate to say it, but if we don't find these guys within twenty-four hours, well, this little rescue party will become a burial detail.'

*

The limo rolled to a halt, parked amidst an endless vista of sand.

They got out the car. Fierce heat. Fierce light.

Morgan climbed the ridgeline and looked around

Akingbola took a piss.

Trenchman and Osborne leant against the car. They contemplated the dunes a while.

Trenchman licked his academy ring and squirmed it from his heat-swollen finger. He threw it as far as he could. It arced out of sight.

He climbed onto the hood, then stepped up onto the roof.

He tuned his radio.

'This is Colonel Trenchman, US Army, calling the crew of *Liberty Bell*, anyone copy, over?'

No response.

'*Liberty Bell*, anyone out there, over? Anyone hear my voice?'

No response.

Suddenly tired, suddenly angry. Maybe Morgan was right. Perhaps he should have stayed aboard the Chinook, pushed the 'copter's range to reach somewhere defensible like Alcatraz instead of risking his neck prosecuting a futile rescue mission.

He rubbed his eyes.

'Come on, guys, talk to me. This is Trenchman, acknowledging your Mayday. I need your grids. If you can't manage verbal communication, switch to transponder.'

Dead channel static.

BROADCAST

EMERGENCY ACTION NOTIFICATION

MESSAGE NO. 2

These instructions must be posted at the Studio and Transmitter Control Point.

All NDEA Primary Broadcast Stations shall follow these procedures.

Upon receipt of an authenticated **EMERGENCY ACTION NOTIFICATION** all broadcast stations shall do the following:

1. Discontinue program and broadcast the following announcement:

   WE INTERRUPT THIS PROGRAM. THE OFFICE OF CIVIL DEFENSE HAS ISSUED THE FOLLOWING MESSAGE. THIS IS AN EMERGENCY, REPEAT, THIS IS AN EMERGENCY. IMPORTANT INSTRUCTIONS WILL FOLLOW IN 30 SECONDS.

2. Transmit an EMERGENCY ACTION NOTIFICATION ATTENTION SIGNAL.

   a) Cut the transmitter carrier for 5 seconds

      (sound carrier for TV stations).

   b) Return carrier to the air for 5 seconds.

   c) Cut the transmitter carrier for 5 seconds

      (sound carrier for TV stations).

   d) Return carrier to the air.

   e) Broadcast 1000 cps steady-state tone for 15 seconds.

3. Make the following announcement:

   THE OFFICE OF CIVIL DEFENSE HAS ISSUED THE FOLLOWING WARNING: THIS IS AN EMERGENCY, REPEAT, THIS IS AN EMERGENCY. THIS STATION HAS INTERRUPTED ITS REGULAR PROGRAM AT THE REQUEST OF THE UNITED STATES GOVERNMENT TO [Cont'd]

17

Frost, alone on the flight deck.

She set the camcorder on the pilot console and pressed REC.

'First night in the desert. It's cold. Damn cold.' She exhaled, watched her breath steam in chill air. 'My fingers are numb. But I got to relish every second because, few hours from now, the sun will rise and we'll burn in hellfire all over again.'

She rubbed her eyes.

'It all happened so fast, you know? World fell apart so damned quick. Entire cities wiped out in a matter of weeks. Shit, by the time we realised we had a fight on our hands, we were already beat.

'Must admit, I didn't pay much attention when the outbreak began. Safe on an airbase. Whole thing: Not My Problem.

'Spokane. Barely made the news. Some poor bastard found a half-melted lump of space junk out in the woods. Guy was some kind of survivalist. Headed into the forest with his bug-out bag to snare squirrels or some shit. Fucking ironic, right? Doomsday, end-of-the-world guy brings on Armageddon. Seems he came across a bunch of toppled trees and a smoking crater. Chunk of Soyuz buried in the soil. Remains of a fuel tank coated in some kind of carbonised residue. Dug it up thinking it might be worth a buck or two. Drove it to town strapped to the back of his pick-up. Posed with his boot planted on the thing like he was some big game hunter standing over his kill. Day later, he was quarantined in an ICU oxygen tent. FEMA locked down the hospital, taped the windows, the doors.

TV crews and their satellite vans ringed the perimeter. Footage of trucks pulling up outside, guys in biohazard suits getting scrubbed in decon showers. National Guard rolled out concertina wire, set up searchlights and gun posts. Nobody in or out.

'Know what? Looking back, they could have stopped it right there. Sacrificed the town. Dropped a nuke. Sterilised the region with a well-placed airburst. Would have killed the virus dead. But they dithered. And the moment passed.'

She sighed, looked down at her hands a while.

'Guess that's all it took. A few hesitations, a few bad judgement calls, cost the world.'

She hit OFF.

The lower cabin.

Noble pulled a quilted insulation blanket from the wall.

Ducting. A cluster of aluminium pipes.

He traced one of the pipes to an overhead vent.

'This one. Air con.'

Hancock handed him a wrench.

He rapped the pipe with the wrench. Hollow chime.

'Empty?'

'Hard to tell.'

Noble adjusted the wrench and began to unscrew a bolt joint.

'Ready with that canteen.'

He pulled the pipe from the wall. Metal squeal. Hancock held out the canteen and caught a brief piss-dribble of moisture.

'Guess that's all she's got.'

Noble shook the last drips from the pipe. He licked the bolt-joint dry, grimaced at the metallic taste.

'Window wash?' suggested Hancock.

'Thirty per cent ethanol.'

'Maybe we could distil it clean.'

'How?'

'No idea.'

'We could take a look at the wing, I guess. Took off with a thousand gallons of water, give or take. Engine boost. If we cut into the injector feeds we might be able to rescue a few cupfuls.'

'We'll need a siphon hose and some sort of container.'

Noble looked around.

'Anyone use the urinal while we were in flight?'

'Not that I saw.'

'Then let's see what we can scavenge.'

Frost went outside. She climbed a dune, sought a little solitude.

She surveyed the dark horizon, the lip of the world, the point where the starfield met the dunes.

She looked north-west. An irregularity on the horizon. Distant mountains. A snag-tooth ridgeline. The peaks had been obscured during the heat of day, but were now visible in outline as they eclipsed low constellations.

Somewhere out there was the target site. The god-forsaken stretch of wasteland they had been dispatched to sear with nuclear fire.

A distant thud. She turned round. The massive, broken airframe lit by moonlight. She watched Noble haul himself up onto the starboard wing. He held a plastic two-gallon piss bottle and a length of hose. He crouched, extended a hand and pulled Hancock up onto the wing beside him.

No doubt they were trying to siphon residual water from the plane's sub-systems.

Probably ought to help, but she didn't have the energy.

Noble walked the wing. Popped rivets. Split panels. He knelt, held his breath against the stink of JP8 and shone his flashlight into a fissure.

The interior of the wing. Fuel tanks. Spoiler servos and screw jack actuators.

The main manifold had broken in a dozen places. Every strut and spar greased with leaked aviation fuel.

'Here,' called Hancock.

The hydro-feeds.

Water injected into the turbojets on take-off, boosting each engine to seventeen thousand pounds static thrust.

Noble kicked at a buckled wing panel with his boot, hammered the aluminium sheet aside. He crouched and peered into the wing cavity.

'The waterline is cracked. Might be able to siphon some dregs. Pass me the hose.'

He fed tube into the mouth of a fractured aluminium pipe, sucked until he drew liquid.

He convulsed, choked and spat.

'Hot damn. Fuel. Tainted with fuel.' He gagged. 'Mouth full of freakin' carbon tetrachloride.' He bent and wretched. 'Man, that's nasty.'

'Better check the other wing. Maybe the fluid lines are intact.'

'You be taster. I got a tongue coated in gasoline.'

Frost stood and contemplated the stars. She found an austere consolation in the fact ten thousand years of human civilisation, the slow rise and abrupt fall, had been a fleeting moment of cosmic time, and the universe would continue regardless.

Movement in the periphery of her vision.

A figure, fifty yards away, silhouetted against the stars. It seemed to be watching her.

'Hey,' shouted Frost. She fumbled for her flashlight. 'Early? That you?'

She glanced over her shoulder. Hancock and Noble walking the starboard wing.

She turned back. The figure was gone.

Cupped hands:

'Early. Early, can you hear me?'

No reply.

'It's us, man. You made it.'

No reply.

She stumbled in pursuit, followed footprints down the side of a dune, anxious not to be drawn too far from the crash site in case she became disoriented in the darkness.

'Wait up, dude. You're not thinking straight.'

She struggled to climb a steep rise.

'We got water, we got meds. Come on. Let us help.'

She reached the top of the ridge. She swept the surrounding sands with the beam of her flashlight.

A trail of prints heading out into deep desert.

The lower cabin.

Noble pulled insulation from the back bulkhead.

A simple crank-handle hatch. A pressure door that allowed access to the crawlway that ran the length of the aircraft.

He pulled the door wide, crouched and shone his flashlight inside the tight passage. Sheet metal slick with hydraulic fluid. A rat-run that led through the ECM equipment bay, to the payload compartment.

'Step aside,' said Hancock.

'You don't looks so great.'

'Let me do my job.'

Hancock unzipped a tool pouch and took out a compact Geiger handset.

'Real bag of tricks you got there,' said Noble.

Hancock scanned the crawlspace interior. Flickering numerals. Steady background crackle.

'Guess the warhead survived the crash. Otherwise this thing would be singing to high heaven.'

'You're sure?'

'If we were sharing this plane with a bunch of spilt plutonium, we'd be puking blood already.'

Noble climbed inside the crawlway and lay on his back. He held out his hand. Hancock slapped a cross-head screwdriver into his palm. He began to unscrew the panel above his head.

Twelve screws. The panel dropped loose. Hancock helped manhandle it clear.

Noble shone his flashlight into a dense nest of cable and pipe work.

A large water tank bolted to the airframe above his head. Reservoir for the engine injection system.

'Can you see the tank?' asked Hancock.

'Yeah.'

'Can you reach it?'

'Yeah.'

'Is it intact?'

'Ripped open. But not all the way. Give me the hose.'

Noble reached up and fed siphon hose through the cracked skin of the tank. He squirmed out the crawlway.

'Give me the bottle.'

Noble sucked the pipe until he drew liquid. He caught a mouthful, then jammed the pipe into the neck of the two-gallon bottle. The bottle began to fill.

'Drinkable?' asked Hancock.

Noble swilled the water round his mouth with relish. He gave a thumbs up.

Sudden commotion. Frost threw herself through the rip in the cabin wall, tripped and hit the deck. She crouched beside her survival vest, hurriedly checked the pockets and extracted a flare.

'What's up?' asked Hancock. He clapped for attention. 'Hey. Lieutenant. What's going on?'

She didn't reply.

She gripped the flare and headed outside.

They followed.

Frost hurriedly limped to the peak of a high dune and fired a star shell.

The crash site lit brilliant white.

Noble waded up the gradient and joined her. They looked out over the desert.

'What can you see?' called Hancock from the foot of the dune. 'Is someone out there?'

Frost tracked footprints, pistol drawn and chambered. She followed the trail, flashlight trained on the ground ahead of her.

'You saw somebody?' asked Noble, keeping close in case her leg gave out and she fell. 'Who is it? Early?'

'Couldn't say for sure.'

'You didn't see a face?'

'No.'

'Flight suit?'

'I think so.'

'Then it's got to be Early. Couldn't be anyone else.'

The prints came to an abrupt halt halfway up a dune, as if whoever made the tracks winked out of existence mid-stride.

'What the hell?' murmured Noble. 'It's like the fucker grew wings and took off.'

Frost crouched and raked the sand.

The star shell above them fluttered and dimmed.

She peered into the surrounding darkness. Growing apprehension.

'I think we should get back to the plane.'

AFT CRADLE POSITION

18

The lower cabin.

'So what did it look like?' asked Hancock.

'A silhouette,' said Frost. 'Couldn't make out a face.'

'Did it speak?'

'No.'

'A man?'

'Yeah.'

'You're sure?'

'A guy. For real. Wearing a flight suit.'

'How could you tell?'

'The outline. Boots, pockets, straps.'

'Early?'

'Couldn't be anyone else. Not unless there's a second aircrew wandering around.'

'Guthrie was infected, right? Bitten back at base. What if Early turned as well? Maybe that's how he survived the desert. Maybe that's why he won't approach.'

Frost thought it over. She shook her head.

'You saw those prowlers back at Vegas. Hoards of the bastards butting the wire. Dumber than plankton. Dumber than rocks. I talked with the sentries. Said they thinned out the crowd with gasoline every couple of days. Sprayed them down and lit them up. Stinking fucks just stood there and burned. Shit, even the average roach has an instinct for self-preservation. These bastards haven't got a thought in their heads. You can shoot them point blank, run them

130

down with a truck. They won't do a damned thing to save themselves.

'I rode shotgun on a supply raid to Grand Forks a few weeks back. Six Hummer convoy. Cover fire while we liberated canned food from a Hugo's and brought it back to base. One of those sorry skeletal things spotted us from a furniture store across the street, slammed into plate glass time and again like a trapped wasp. Damn near beat his brains out.

'You know what I'm saying, yeah? These things don't have an ounce of cunning. They don't make strategic decisions. They don't hang back and pick their moment. They attack. They bite. That's all they do. If Early had turned, he'd be on us until he sank his teeth or got a bullet in his brain.'

'So why would he lurk out there in the dark?'

'He spent a long day in the sun. Maybe he's not thinking straight. Be a tragedy if he died in the dunes, yards from help.'

'Reckon he might be dangerous?'

'Danger to himself. Anyway, we each got a gun, right?'

'So does he.'

Hancock suddenly cocked his head and held up a hand for quiet.

'Hear that?'

'What?' asked Frost.

'A noise.'

'Care to be more specific?'

'A sort of scratching sound.'

They listened.

'Can't hear anything.' Frost gestured to the ladderway and the cabin above. 'The windows and hatches are taped up. One of them might have come lose, started flapping in the breeze.'

'No. It's down here, with us. It's real close by.'

They listened.

'Sure you can't hear it?' he asked.

'It's just the wind. Sure as shit isn't mice.'

'Scratching. Don't know how else to describe it. There it goes again. Hear? Plain as day.'

'The airframe is broke in a hundred places. She'll creak day and night.'

Hancock put his ear to the bulkhead like he was eavesdropping on an adjacent room.

'Could be the pipes,' said Frost. 'The fuel lines, coolant, hydraulics. All of them bust open and drained dry. They'll make weird music as the plane expands and contracts.'

Hancock shook his head. He signalled hush, listened a while, ear still pressed to the wall.

'Hard to explain. The noise. It's not structural. It's not mechanical. How come you can't hear it? Just sit quiet and listen. Really listen.'

They sat a while.

Frost shrugged.

'Sorry, Cap.'

'Scratching. Like claws. Like nails. Plain as day.'

'Don't take this wrong, but maybe we should have a look at your head.'

Hancock seemed ready to argue, then gave in to a wave of fatigue.

'Whatever.'

She sat beside him.

She hooked the trauma kit with her foot and dragged it close.

She gestured to his head.

'Does it hurt?'

'Cranium feels like I've been hit with a bag of nickels. Constant ache. Wearing me down.'

'How's your balance? Any improvement?'

'No. Each time I stand up the ground bucks around like I'm riding a bareback bronc.'

She carefully pulled at the chute fabric that bound his injured head. It was stiff with dried blood. It was gummed to his hair.

She carefully lifted the filthy rag clear and threw it aside.

'Oh, man.'

The side of his face was swollen and crusted black.

He pulled a Spyderco folding knife from his pocket. He flipped open the blade and examined his reflection.

'Puts paid to my modelling career.'

'Probably looks worse than it is. Lot of dried blood. Bet if we clean you up, it won't be so bad.'

She tore open a packet of towelettes and began to dab flakes of dried blood from the skin surrounding his vacant eye socket.

Awkward silence. Strange to be up close, face to face.

'So how much water does that tank contain?' she asked, by way of conversation.

'No idea. Twelve-hundred-gallon capacity, but it's ruptured. Not much left. Might give us a couple more days. Best to tape the cracks, see if we can limit evaporation.'

'Maybe we should share it right now.'

'Three-way split? What if you ran out before me? Got enough self-control to watch a guy sip a drink while you die of thirst? You and Noble might go back aways, but all that good feeling won't count for shit once we are down to the last drop.'

'We're not animals.'

'That's exactly what we are.'

Frost probed the split in Hancock's scalp.

She said:

'Apparently, when Eskimos share fish, the guy who does the cutting gets last pick. Helps keep portion size honest. Read that somewhere.'

She dabbed dead and hardening skin. She dabbed exposed skull.

'Lot of sand in this wound. We better rebandage your head when we're done, try to keep it free from dirt.'

'Okay.'

'Any pain?'

'No.'

'Can you feel anything at all?'

'A little.'

'You got a wide lesion. I can see bone. We ought to stitch it up. If we leave it untreated the skin could die back further. State of the world right now, we got no one to pull a tooth, let alone perform a graft.'

'So get sewing.'

She used surgical scissors to trim hair surrounding the scalp wound. She tore open an antiseptic wipe and disinfected the wound.

She found a suture pack. A curved needle and eighteen inches of monofilament.

'Let me give you a shot. For the pain.'

'No.'

'Come on. There's no one here to impress.'

'Fuck that shit. Mind you, if you've got a hip flask about your person, I wouldn't say no.'

Frost tore another antiseptic wipe and disinfected her hands.

She ripped open the suture pack and threaded the needle.

'Don't expect fine embroidery. Not much of a dressmaker.'

'Always wanted some bad-ass scars.'

'Reckon I ought to stitch your empty eye as well. Best way to keep the socket clean.'

'Do it.'

He adopted a meditative posture and prepared to tough out the pain.

She leant forward, ready to sew skin.

'Hold on,' said Hancock. He sat straight and pushed her hands away. 'There it is again. Hear it?'

Frost sighed.

'There's nothing.' She froze. She cocked her head. 'Hold on. Yeah. Yeah, I hear it.'

She set the needle and suture aside.

'A scratching sound.'

'Yeah,' said Hancock.

A persistent abrasion like dragging nails. She slowly turned her head left and right, tried to pinpoint the locus of the noise. She looked down at her feet.

'It's beneath us. It's under the plane.'

A red grating set in the cabin floor. It hid the egress hatch, the ventral door and fold-down ladder that would, under normal conditions, allow the crew to enter the plane.

Frost knelt, knitted her fingers through the grate and lifted it aside.

The hatch had been ripped away during the crash. They looked down on sand.

The scratching sound abruptly ceased.

'Could it be snakes?' murmured Hancock. 'Scorpions? Some kind of burrowing thing?'

She shook her head.

'Middle of the desert. No bugs, no brush, no nothing.'

'The sound. It was a living thing. Something moving with purpose, deliberation.'

'I think you might be right.'

Frost reached down like she intended to dig sand. She hesitated, fingertips an inch from the surface, then slowly withdrew her hand.

MILSAT GLOBELINK™ PORTABLE SATELLITE TERMINAL

Front Panel (fig1)

Laptop On/Off

Military Grade System Controller

GPS Receiver

Tx Monitor

Rx Monitor

Modem Status –

      Receive

      Transmit

      Status

      Network

Rear Panel (fig2)

On/Off

Power Supply

Control Out

In: 115/230 VAC-50/60 Hz 7/4A

Fuse T7A 250V

DC/SSPA Control

Tx IF 50Ω N Female or N(f)

Rx IF 50Ω N Female or N(f)

Tx Monitor IF 50Ω N Female or N(f)

USB

RS 232 Console

Control In

Baseband

19

Hancock tied a fresh length of chute bandage round his stitched scalp and eye socket. He clenched teeth as he knotted and pulled tight. He sweated with pain. His skin steamed in the night air.

He sat cross-legged with his eye closed, locked his face in a mask of calm. He rode out head-pounding discomfort, let it peak and dull.

'Thought the wound was numb,' said Frost.

'That was before you got to work with a needle and thread.'

He relaxed and opened his eye as pain began to abate.

Frost sat with her back to the bulkhead. She pointed to the grate covering the ventral hatch.

'Maybe we should stack a few boxes,' she said. 'Don't know what the hell is down there, but I'd feel better knowing it can't get in.'

'Let's not freak out,' said Hancock. 'We've got more than enough bullets to greet anything that might come knocking.'

Frost bit the cap from a morphine auto-injector and punched the needle into her thigh. She waited for the opiate to hit.

'Okay, Cap,' she gestured to her injured leg. 'Your turn to help me out.'

'What do you need?'

'Release the splint. Let my leg breathe a while. Check my foot isn't about to rot off.'

Hancock knelt beside her. He released splint straps. She winced.

Her calf bruised black.

'Looks all right,' said Hancock. 'Messed up, but not gangrenous.' He examined her foot, checked it for warmth. 'You've still got circulation. Guess your leg will be all right, given time. Want me to strap it up?'

She shook her head.

'Give me a minute or two. Got to psych myself. Bound to hurt like a motherfucker.'

Frost stepped outside and leant against the fuselage.

The moonlit crash site surrounded by a high ridge of dunes.

She bent and massaged her strapped leg. She studied shadows, did it sly, glanced around without moving her head. Half expected to see a solitary figure watching from the darkness.

She straightened up. She stopped her hand as it strayed towards her shoulder holster.

'Everything okay?' called Noble.

He lay on his back looking up at the stars.

Frost nodded, non-committal.

Sunstroke. Early driven out of his mind by thirst and unrelenting light. Only thing that could account for his behaviour. He no longer recognised fellow crewmen, saw them as threatening strangers. In which case he would soon die in a wretched delirium, like a rabid dog. Succumb slow and nasty. Stumble through the dunes ranting and raging. Too dangerous to approach, too far gone to accept help. Nothing they could do but let him prowl the wreckage-strewn perimeter, screaming at the sky, until he fell dead in the sand.

Lieutenant Nicholas Early.

A serious-minded kid, with a degree in aeronautical engineering. Had a young wife somewhere. A likeable guy. Sad to think of him lobotomised by the cruel sunlight.

Hancock crossed the sand towards the signal fire. He swayed. He stumbled. He kept his eyes fixed on the flames to help him walk straight.

He popped the restraining strap of his shoulder holster and kept a hand on his pistol butt. Couldn't aim worth a damn. One eye, no balance. But at close range it wouldn't matter. Lieutenant Early might have been driven mad by the sun, degenerated to a raging berserker so demented he couldn't feel pain or injury, but a couple of 9mm hollow points centre-of-mass would put him down for good.

Hancock dropped to his knees next to the satcom.

Battery at seventy-three per cent.

The screen still hung at Acquisition.

He cancelled and selected preset Alpha.

Comsec sign-in:

AUTHENTICATE

He keyed:

VERMILLION

He hit Enter.

THIRD AND SEVENTH DIGITS
OF PERSONNEL CODE

He keyed:

8 1

The screen cleared. Winking cursor.

He glanced around at dunes lit by weak flame light, checked for any sign Early was watching from the shadows.

Nothing but darkness.

He wondered what the deranged airman might be doing at that moment. Stumbling among the dunes. Or sitting in the moonlight, rocking back and forth, head full of phantasmagoric torment. Or lying dead in the sand.

Hancock turned back to the screen and typed. Same message he'd typed a dozen times:

USAF MT66 VEGAS
REQUEST URGENT ASSISTANCE
MISSION FAIL
DECLARE IKARUS
PACKAGE INTACT AND SECURE
BEACONS ACTIVE
PERSONNEL IN NEED OF MEDEVAC
2 KIA
1 MIA
3 IMMEDIATE EXTRACTION
PLEASE EXPEDITE
ACKNOWLEDGE AND ETA

He hit Send. Then he shut down the terminal, folded the antenna, and began to drag the case back towards the plane.

Hancock hefted the trunk onto his shoulder and heaved it up the ladderway, onto the flight deck.

He climbed the ladder and sat on the trunk a while to catch his breath.

He lifted a blast screen. A glance out the flight-deck windows. The signal fire.

Strange sight:

Two figures lit by weak flame light.

He hurriedly leaned across the pilot seat, tried to wipe dust from the windows with the sleeve of his flight suit for a clearer view.

The figures were gone.

'Noble?' he shouted. 'You still down there?'

Noble, from the lower cabin:

'Yeah.'

'Were you outside just now?'

'Been right here.'

Hancock wondered how much he could trust his own vision. One eye. No depth perception.

'Stay sharp down there, you hear? Don't nod out on me.'

He flipped latches and threw open the lid of the trunk.

The antenna packed in foam. He lifted it free. Tripod extended. Segmented aluminium petals fanned into a dish.

He stood on the trunk, reached up to the roof and tore back the insulation blanket masking the gunner's vacant ejection hatch. He pushed the antenna out onto the roof and adjusted alignment.

The terminal. Coaxial cable jacked into a side-socket.

Boot up. Scrolling BIOS. Flickering loading bars.

Comsec sign-in:

AUTHENTICATE

He keyed:

VERMILLION

He hit Enter.

He keyed:

7 3

He hit Enter.

The ticking clock glyph of signal acquisition.

Clatter of boots on ladder rungs.

Noble climbed up onto the flight deck. He stood beside Hancock and looked at the screen, the endless sweep of the clock.

'Nothing left, is there? Nothing coherent. The Joint Chiefs are probably down a bunker someplace. Maps. Time-zone clocks. Yelling into their war-phones, issuing orders to units that no longer exist.'

'We played our part,' said Hancock. 'Did our duty. Reason to be proud.'

Noble shook his head.

'We should have made for Canada while we had the chance. Hit the coast, found a boat, headed for Vancouver Island. You can bet a few other folks had the same idea. The last of humanity. That's where they will be.'

Frost, from down below:

'Guys, you better come outside.'

They went outside. They stood beneath the starlit sky. Breath fogged the night air.

Frost held up the sand-dusted flag.

She trained her flashlight on a depression in the sand.

'Captain Pinback is gone.'

FUEL SERVO PLATE LOCATED IN INTERPHONE CONTROL BOX LEFT FORWARD WHEEL WELL

20

Survival, Evasion and Escape exercise, Thompson Falls.

The forest at night.

Incessant rain.

Frost shared body heat with her instructor, Major Coplin, as they huddled beneath a brushwood lean-shelter.

She shivered. No allocation beyond the standard flight suit and survival gear she would have if she had punched out and parachuted into thick tree cover.

Coplin held out his hand and caught raindrops in his palm.

'You got lucky. Rain will throw off the dogs. Wash away your scent. Downside: plenty of mud. You'll leave tracks when you move out tomorrow. Take a lot of ingenuity not to leave a trail.'

She pictured restless German Shepherds pulling at a taut leash chain, waiting for handlers to unclip their collars and send them darting into undergrowth.

'Has anyone made the full eight days?'

'Five. That's the record. Cajun kid. Inbred, banjo-strumming runt. Worked in a chicken plant before he signed. Plucking, beheading. Should have seen him with a knife. He could gut a kill in seconds, make music with that thing. Lad could barely write his name but, damn, he was whip-smart. Know how he beat the dogs? He climbed a tree. Moved branch-to-branch while the hounds scoured the forest floor below him. Got two miles down the hill without setting foot on the ground.'

'Outstanding.'

'Managed two days in the Red Room before he gave up his key word. Most guys tap out after a couple of hours. Stubborn motherfucker. He broke hard.'

'So who are the capture team?'

'Ex-Delta. Real snake-eaters.'

'And you?'

Coplin smiled. He pulled up the sleeve of his camo coat to expose his forearm. A faded Hemingway quote:

There is no hunting like the hunting of man, and those who have hunted armed men long enough and liked it, never care for anything else thereafter.

'Tell the truth, you've done well to make it a third day,' he said. 'Most guys panic. They run through the woods, no plan, no direction. Don't think to climb in the stream to mask their scent. Get chased down by a German Shepherd soon as their lead time expires. Back in the truck by lunchtime.'

'Do the capture team use infrared?'

'They've got all kinds of shit. All you got are eyes. Still ought to move at night, though. Best way to see in shadow? Don't look directly at your target. Look to the side. Probably told you this before, but it's worth repeating. Centre of a person's sight is good for colour and focus during the day. At night, peripheral vision is sharpest for shape and movement. Remember that. Might save your ass.'

Frost put up a star shell. Desert lit cold white.

She stood at the top of a dune, survival blanket drawn over her head and shoulders like a shawl.

Hancock joined her. He checked his pistol. Loaded. Chambered.

'How many of those flares we got left?' he asked.

'Plenty.'

They looked out over the Arctic landscape. A three-sixty survey.

'There should be night-vision gear aboard *Liberty Bell*, right?' said Hancock. 'Standard kit. Monoculars, somewhere on the flight deck.'

Frost shook her head.

'You saw the plane, saw the state she was in. An antique. Pretty much out of commission. Probably flew Arc Light missions back in the day, bombed the crap out of some Hanoi railyards. She was mothballed. A reserve. Hadn't been in the air for months. Sitting in an Alaskan hangar collecting dust and webs. Final flight would have taken her to an Arizona boneyard to be chopped. Turned into washing machines or some shit.

'She's got no standard inventory. Most of the lockers are empty. Nothing but a bunch of Arctic survival gear.'

Frost contemplated the featureless landscape. Scalloped dunes. Flare light transformed the desert to a vista of rippling dream-forms.

'No tracks,' she said. 'Not a single footprint.'

'My first thought? Vultures. Wolves. Pinback got snatched while our backs were turned. Something big, with a taste for carrion.'

'He weighed over two hundred pounds in flight gear,' said Frost.

'Just running through the possibilities.'

'Said you saw two guys standing by the fire. Two. If one of them was Early, who the hell was the other guy?'

'Not sure what I saw,' said Hancock. 'I got one eye. Can't see too clear. Might have been nothing. Nothing at all.'

'Maybe there are preppers out here. Kind of remote location a survivalist might build a refuge for himself and his family. Cache weapons and cans during the good times.'

'But why take Pinback?'

'Running low on food.'

'Perhaps he was infected. Dead, but not dead.'

'Maybe. Maybe he got up and walked. By like I said: no tracks.'

The star shell fell to earth and died. Dark dunes and a starlit sky.

'Bullshit aside,' said Hancock. 'Someone's out there for sure, watching us, determined to fuck with our heads.'

The lower cabin.

Frost unclipped an insulation pad from the wall, exposing cable runs and pipe work.

She examined pipes. She wanted a section of tubing thick enough, strong enough, to support her weight.

The wrench. She unbolted a four-foot section of inch-thick hydraulic line. She unscrewed restraining brackets and lifted it clear. Residual hydraulic fluid dripped and pooled on the floor.

She measured the pipe against her body, wedged it beneath her armpit, tested it as a crutch.

A good fit.

She sat in the nav seat, unsheathed her knife and began to slit the insulation pad.

Noble joined her.

He shook sand from his hair, slapped dust from his clothes. He looked around the lower cabin, assessed its potential as a defensible redoubt.

He nodded approval.

'This is good. This is secure. One way in or out. We ought to barricade this opening, though. Block it with a couple of equipment cases.'

He picked up a canteen. He rubbed the cool canister across his face and neck, and set it down unopened.

He gestured to the upper cabin.

'Not much we can do to block the flight deck windows. The blast curtains could deter snipers, I guess. Deny a target.'

Noble stood at the ragged fissure in the fuselage wall and stared out into darkness.

'Why don't they attack? Couple of determined guys could take us out anytime they want. Wouldn't break a sweat.'

His hand strayed to his shoulder holster. He stroked the polymer grip.

'Must be toying with us. Psy-ops. Some kind of mindfuck.'

Frost padded the crutch with insulation fabric, and lashed it with cable cut from the sixty miles of wiring that snaked through the conduits and cavities of the plane.

'Got to keep a little perspective. Easy to go nuts in a place like this. The space. The silence. Easy to fill it with our fears.'

'Pinback is gone. That's real enough. And whatever took his body snatched it quick and clean. Didn't make a noise, didn't leave a trace. Sure as hell wasn't Early. Not without help.'

'I suppose.'

'What if we have to walk out of here? Think about it. We've got precious little water. You and Hancock are hobbled by major injuries. We'd struggle to cover ten miles a night. And if we had hostiles dogging our steps? Bastards intent on taking us out one by one? We wouldn't stand a chance. We'd be easy prey.'

Frost tested the crutch. She walked back and forth. She glanced at Noble. He looked exhausted, strung out.

'Take a moment. Get your head together. We're armed. We've got plenty of ammunition. We're badder than anything cat-stepping around those dunes, all right? Just got to watch our backs until daybreak. If anyone is out there, messing with our heads, they won't try anything after sunrise. Too much exposure.'

Hancock, called from outside:

'Guys. Better get out here.'

'My turn to bring bad news.'

Hancock held up his CSEL.

A voice, heard through crackling interference. Male, stern:

'. . . cabinet officers . . . terms of The 1947 Presidential Succession Act, I have assumed that grave respons . .'

'Is this the BBC?' asked Frost. 'Is this a live transmission?'

Hancock mimed hush.

'. . . unthinkable, only to be countenanced as an absolute last resort. But, I have to tell you now, at five o'clock, eastern standard time, I gave that terrible order. Our courageous armed forces, both at home and abroad, did their duty . .'

The voice swamped by static. Hancock held the radio above his head to regain signal.

'. . . San Antonio, Dallas and Detroit. And I ask anyone who can hear this broadcast, whether you are a citizen of the United States or not, to pray for their souls . .'

'What's the guy talking about?' asked Noble.

'Evergreen,' said Hancock. 'He's talking about Evergreen. I heard rumours. Didn't think they'd go through with it.'

'Evergreen?'

'OPLAN eight-oh-eight. The final roll of the dice. If they couldn't stop the virus, if major cities become hot-beds of infection, they could invoke a doomsday option.'

'Jesus,' said Frost, catching the obvious implication. 'You can't be serious.'

Hancock nodded confirmation.

'Nuclear strike. Incinerate every substantial metropolitan area.'

'. . . both Berlin and Munich . . . still no word from our French correspondents . . . lit the northern sky . . . no further communication from Paris . .'

'Dear God.'

'Enhanced radiation weapons. Tritium/deuterium nukes. Sandmans. Way more lethal that the tac we've got in our hold. The blast itself is pretty low yield, but they pulse intense gamma radiation at the moment of detonation. No hiding place. Cuts through concrete and steel. Any mammal within a ten-mile radius; human, whatever, will sicken and die in hours.

'The blast itself will spread cobalt-sixty and a bunch of other isotopes over the surrounding area. Lethal contamination. Long half-life. Even if we make it out of here, we will have to keep away from cities. They'll be dead zones. No cats, no dogs, no birds. Centuries before a person could walk the streets.'

'Jesus fucking Christ.'

'What else could they do? Only way to purge the virus. Destroy the world in order to save it.'

'God in heaven.'

Frost looked towards the starlit horizon.

'So what do we do? America is a wasteland. Even if we make it out of this desert, where on earth can we go?'

ACTIVATION		TERMINATION	
1	CHINAMAN	1	HERALD
2	BACKDOOR	2	COMANCHE
3	CATWALK	3	GRAPEVINE
4	FORTRESS	4	DEEPFREEZE
5	DOWNFALL	5	GUITAR
6	BRITISHER	6	BERLIN
7	HITCHHIKE	7	PROVERB
8	LAYMAN	8	RIDGEPOLE
9	PIGMENT	9	DELUXE
10	STOIC	10	SOFIA
11	CANYON	11	AZURE
12	FANFOLD	12	WINDLASS

21

Frost, Hancock and Noble climbed to the top of the ridgeline and watched the sky lighten with the first trace of dawn. They were cotton-mouthed with thirst, each determined not to be the first to break resolve and gulp their morning ration from the canteen.

'Twenty-four hours since the crash,' said Noble. Dry cough. 'Feels like a month.'

'We need a plan,' said Frost. 'An actual plan. We've spun our wheels twenty-four hours. Time to face reality. No one is coming for us. So we better decide, here and now, how we intend to get back to the world.'

They sat in the sand and looked out over the crash site. The eastern sky turned fine azure. One by one, stars faded into oncoming day. The sun would break the horizon within the hour. Nightmare light. It would quickly cook the desert like a blowtorch flame, turning the dunes to a heat-rippling hellscape by mid morning.

'I saw a flash last night,' said Noble. 'A pulse of light to the west. Flickering white, like summer lightning. Didn't pay it any mind.'

'Must have been Los Angeles going up.'

'And one to the east, a couple of minutes later.'

'Evergreen,' murmured Hancock.

'I suppose we're part of it,' said Noble, gesturing to the saurian hulk of the B-52. 'We got the last tac nuke in the arsenal. Last one they could lay their hands on, at any rate. Something out in the desert they wanted vaporised with all the rest. Not sure I want to be involved.'

Frost paced the crest of the dune. She kicked at sand. She tried to picture the atomic devastation that lay beyond the horizon.

New York in ruins. The broken skyline of Manhattan. Toppled skyscrapers, avenues clogged with rubble.

Los Angeles. Gridlocked freeways seared by a nuclear firestorm. Automobile bodywork scorched down to base metal, seats reduced to frame-springs, tyres melted to bubbling tar.

Atlanta. Scoured by uncontrolled block-fires, street grid razed, ten kiloton airburst repeating the destruction wrought by the Confederacy before they ceded the city to Sherman.

Had Europeans bombed their major conurbations? The Russians?

Maybe astronauts marooned on the International Space Station were looking down on Europe and the United States at that moment, watching the smoke of burning cities taint the stratosphere, filthy soot plumes carried on prevailing winds.

Nuclear Winter. How long before a radiotoxic haze encircled the earth, and darkened the world to a grey twilight which would last centuries?

Maybe snow would fall on the desert. Flakes grey with ash.

Maybe, as she and her companions trekked across the sand, day would be overtaken by premature dusk. The temperature would plummet. Shimmering heat would give way to a fierce blizzard. They would trudge onwards, leaning into a driving snowstorm, until they succumbed to hypothermia and dropped dead among the dunes, bodies feathered with ice.

'So,' said Noble, calling her back from her reverie. 'Canada or Mexico?'

Frost thought it over. She opened her mouth, intending to say Canada, but Hancock cut her off:

'We find the nearest functioning military unit and report for duty.'

'The war is over, sir,' said Frost. 'The virus won.' She lifted the dog tags from around her neck, disentangled them from the code lanyard, and toyed with the tin tabs. 'Rank. Insignia. Flag. Not sure they mean a great deal any more. Just souvenirs.' She tossed the dog tags onto the sand beside her. 'Feel like secession troops after the surrender. Ragged losers. Column of Johnny Rebs trudging home.'

'Best put a lid on that shit, airman.'

'We got beat. Time to be realistic. All that's left is survival.'

'You are an officer in the United States Air Force. Still bound by oath. Don't fucking forget it.'

Noble spoke up, aiming to divert the argument.

'This valley extends a long way south,' said Noble. 'Unbroken desert. Certain death. North, east or west: that's the only real choice we got.

'If we head west, we've got a long walk across dunes, then our troubles really begin. We'd hit the Panamint Range. Barren as the moon. Like crossing the Himalayas with nothing but the clothes on our back. And then we have to repeat the trick. Cross Saline Valley and the Inyo Mountains, and onwards into the Mojave. Miles of impossible terrain between us and Edwards. It's not an achievable journey. Certain death, unless we got lucky, real lucky. Stumbled across an RV or something.'

'And we'd be heading towards the ruins of LA,' said Frost. 'Walking into a lethal fallout plume.'

'Well, the journey east isn't much more enticing. Miles of desert, then we hit the Black Mountains. Not much on the other side. Could make for Vegas, I guess, but it's probably a smoking crater. Or we could head through the Amargosa

Desert which is also, let's not forget, the Tonopah Bombing Range. Dirt peppered with unexploded munitions. If we made it across the Amargosa, beat thirst, exhaustion, the prospect of getting our legs blown off, we might finally reach Nellis Air Force Base. But we took off from Vegas precisely because Nellis has been overrun.'

'Hangman's choice,' said Frost. 'Want to flip a coin?'

'West,' said Hancock. 'We head west. Hike till we find a highway. This is a National Park. There are blacktop access roads running through the hills. All we got to do is find a car, start it up and we're home free.'

'We got enough water to last about five days, more or less. Journey like that could take a couple of weeks. Our luck would have to make a one-eighty turn.'

'It can be done. Just depends how badly a person wants to live.'

'What about our unseen friends?' asked Noble, gesturing to surrounding dunes.

'We're well armed. Once we are out in the desert we'll have an unimpeded sight-line. Hard to see how anyone could mess with us.'

'Pretty hopeless plan,' said Frost. 'But I guess it's all we got.'

'We'll leave tonight. Wait till the sun sinks to the horizon and the day begins to cool. Yeah, we're not in great shape. But if we summon a little determination we should be able to set a decent pace, cover ten, fifteen miles a night. Rest during the day. Take a chute so we got a little shade.'

'We got some Gatorade, a few No-Doz,' said Noble. 'Bit of sugar and caffeine might boost us a couple more miles.'

'The will to live. That's the bottom line. If we set our minds, we can drive ourselves past the point of endurance, past the point at which regular folks would lay down and die. We'll make it.'

Hancock got to his feet and began to walk back to the plane.

Frost and Noble watched him stagger and sway, each calculating bleak odds of making it out the desert alive.

'All that believe-in-yourself bullshit,' said Noble. 'Tired of it already. We're constrained by reality. Can't cross those mountains on foot any more than we can flap our arms and fly.'

'Where the hell are my tags?' asked Frost.

She raked the sand beside her.

'My dog tags. They were here.'

'What do you care?'

'They're gone, that's all I'm saying.'

She stood and kicked at the dune.

'Swear to God, they were right here.'

Noble looked up. Sky tinged red. Mid morning, but it looked like sunset.

He walked towards the eastern ridgeline. He broke into a run. Growing sense of panic and urgency. He scrambled the gradient and stood at the crest.

'Get up here guys,' he shouted. 'Take a look at this.'

Frost and Hancock climbed the dune. The three aircrew stood side-by-side.

A red blur on the horizon. An oncoming wall of dust.

'Sandstorm. Heading this way.'

RESTRICTED

DOS-06

APACHE – GROUP OPERATION DOSSIER

JOINT FEMA/USAMRIID

SITE APACHE

OPERATIONAL PROTOCOLS

TOP SECRET/APACHE GROUP EYES ONLY

22

They watched, mesmerised, as the dust storm approached. A wall of sand, infernal red, half a mile high. It rolled like a wave hitting the shore, a wave that wouldn't break, wouldn't disperse, just kept coming, slowly blotting out the sky.

'Damn,' muttered Noble.

The wind rose to a steady moan. It tugged at the fabric of their flight suits. It ruffled their hair.

The signal fire guttered and died. Burning rubber smothered by driving sand. The column of black smoke rising from the smouldering tyre snatched by the wind.

'How long do you reckon we got?'

'Looks like it will hit in ten, twelve minutes,' said Frost. 'It's a long way off, but moving fast. Look at it. Big bastard. Don't want to get caught in the open. It'll flay the skin from your bones.'

'We got the plane, right? We'll be okay.'

'Better get as much stuff stowed as we can.'

They hurried back to the plane. Noble supported Hancock, held his arm to keep him upright. Frost limped behind.

'Best head inside, sir,' advised Noble.

Hancock leaned against the fuselage and looked up at the sky.

'Seriously, sir. Better head inside.'

Hancock looked like he wanted to protest, but couldn't argue with the sense of it. He was a liability. Slow. Disorientated.

If he were caught in the open when the sandstorm hit, Frost or Noble would have to risk their lives to save his ass. Better to head to the flight deck. Stay out of trouble.

He ducked inside the plane.

Frost turned to Noble:

'Go with him. See if you can reinforce the windows and hatches. Keep the storm out.'

Frost picked up equipment and supplies scattered on the sand.

Toothpaste.

A canteen.

Remains of the flight manual.

She gathered an armful of gear and stashed it in the crew cabin.

She glanced up at the darkening sky. Wind whipped her clothes and hair. She looked east. An oncoming tsunami of sand. She could feel it. A hot magnetic charge. She ran a hand through her hair and felt it crackle with static. Saltating particles pushing an intense electromagnetic field ahead of them.

The nose section.

Hancock sat in the pilot seat, tore fresh lengths of duct tape and re-enforced blast curtains covering the broken windows.

He stood and looked up at the cabin roof. Two vacant ejection hatches patched with insulation blankets.

He stood on a trunk, pulled the satcom antenna back inside and resealed the hatch frames with tape.

Noble climbed the ladder to the upper deck.

'How's it going?' he asked.

'Not sure how long these taped sections will hold,' said Hancock. 'Guess we'll have to keep up running repairs. Stick them down each time they tear lose.'

Hancock stepped from the trunk. He lost his balance, fell, hit the wall and slid to the floor.

Noble held out a hand and helped him to his feet.

'Feel like a freakin' invalid,' muttered Hancock. 'Sick of it. What kind of shape are we in? Did we get everything inside?'

'Yeah,' said Noble. 'We're locked down.'

'Temperature is dropping. Soon be cold as a meat locker.'

Patched windows began to flap and billow. The fuselage creaked.

Noble slid down the ladder to the lower cabin.

He and Frost stood at the fissure in the wall, shielded their eyes and looked out at a curtain of driving sand.

'Best close the plane.'

They slid equipment trunks across the floor, shunted them against the fractured wall and shut out the storm.

The flight deck.

Storm winds raged outside. The fuselage shuddered and flexed. Broken struts and spars deep within the war machine's superstructure ground like fractured bone.

Noble placed his hand against the cabin wall. Static crack. Blue spark.

A fine vibration ran through the hull. High velocity granules scouring the aluminium skin of the plane.

So dark he could barely see. He switched on the cabin lights.

He lifted one of the blast screens that curtained an unbroken window and looked out at swirling red twilight.

'Nasty out there,' said Noble.

'Silicosis,' said Frost. 'Get that shit in your lungs, well, I'm not a doctor. But you'd catch a real graveyard cough.'

One of the nuclear blast curtains tore open. The silvered nylon screen flapped and whipped. The cockpit was filled with swirling dust particles and hurricane wind.

Hancock threw himself into the pilot seat. He shielded his remaining eye from the gale. He pressed the curtain back in place, secured brass popper studs set in the window pillars.

'Get tape,' he shouted, fighting to keep the screen from ripping open once more.

Frost fetched duct tape.

Hancock tore strips and lashed the curtain with a triple layer.

He sat back. He rubbed sand from his ears and spat dust. 'Check the hatches. See if they are secure.'

Noble trained a flashlight and inspected the hatch seals. 'Good. So far.'

A sudden buffet slammed the fuselage. Groaning metal. The cabin gently listed starboard.

Noble stumbled, then regained his balance like he was walking the deck of a ship in high seas.

'Jesus,' said Noble. 'This thing isn't going to roll, is it?'

'She's bedded pretty tight.'

'What can you see from the window?'

'Not a damned thing.'

Frost sat cross-legged on the deck plate, back to the wall.

She switched on Hancock's survival radio. Thirty-seven per cent battery. She set it for Acquisition and watched numerals flicker.

'Why bother?' asked Hancock. 'We know the score. The world is in flames. We're on our own.'

'What if someone is trying to contact us? One in million. But what if they were? And we were off air?'

She sat, staring into the speaker grille, listening to whistling interference. The symphonic storm. Charged particles. Swirling, shimmering waves of electromagnetic interference.

Song of the desert. A living landscape. Vast. Unearthly. Implacably hostile to human life.

'This is B-52 *Liberty Bell*, crew in urgent need of assistance, anyone copy, over?'

She broadcast a Mayday every sixty seconds.

'This is the crew of *Liberty Bell*, tail MT66, hailing anyone who can hear my voice. Please respond, over.'

'Seriously. Forget it.'

'The storm might work in our favour. Atmospherics. You never know. It might extend our range.'

'Doubt it.'

Flickering strength-bars. Brief signal lock.

Frost maxed the volume. White noise merged with raging wind. She retuned. A woman's voice. Calm, digitised:

'. . . *four, seven, two, three, zero, four, three, nine, three* . . .'

'What the hell is that?' asked Noble.

'Sounds like a long-range numbers code. Odd to hear on this frequency. Usually broadcast on shortwave.'

'. . . *two, five, zero, zero, zero* . . .'

'What do you reckon it means?'

'Wild guess: blanket instructions for US service personnel overseas. Battleships patrolling the Strait of Hormuz. Arctic subs cruising beneath the ice. Imagine the message cedes command authority. Tells crewmen they are on their own. Better find safe harbour where they can. Head for the southern hemisphere. Australia. New Zealand. Some place like that. Good place to hold up.'

'God bless them,' said Noble.

'Tough break for the commanding officers.'

'Why's that?'

'Those vessels are a radiation hazard. A floating Chernobyl, a floating Fukushima. Reactor-powered engines, nuclear-tipped missiles in the firing tubes. Can't leave them moored, unmaintained. Death-traps. I guess they'll drop most of the crewmen in the antipodes, then a skeleton team will sail back north. Scuttle the boats in deep water.

Position themselves over an Atlantic trench, then fire a bunch of hull charges.'

Hancock turned in his seat and watched Frost continue to scan wavebands.

'You know, it's okay to enjoy it.'

'Enjoy what?' she asked.

'Doomsday. The enormity of the destruction. We got a front-row seat. Get to witness the dying days of humanity. No shame admitting there is an element of dark exhilaration.'

'Can't say I ever rubbernecked.'

'Come on. New York in ruins. The mushroom cloud. The falling towers. Admit it. Must have been quite a show.'

A new voice from the radio. Male, shouting in panic and fear.

Hancock and Noble sat forward.

'Is that English?' asked Noble. 'Can't make out a word.'

'Think it might be Russian. Some poor bastard in the Vegas suburbs, most like. An émigré, cowering in a cellar. Sick, irradiated, convinced he's back in Minsk.'

Frost pressed transmit.

'Mayday, Mayday, we are US Air Force personnel in urgent need of assistance, do you copy, over?'

The Russian continued to sob and plead.

'He can't hear you,' said Hancock.

'Mayday, Mayday, do you copy this transmission?'

'He can't hear a word you're saying.'

'Fuck.'

'Might be a ghost signal.'

'A what?'

Hancock stood and stretched.

'Ever seen a mirage?'

'Saw plenty of thermals yesterday, out in the desert. Shimmering lakes.'

'I saw a bunch back in the day. Rode on a few supply runs

between Baghdad and Sadr City. We saw some weird shit out in the desert.

'One time we pulled over to the side of the highway for a piss break. Needless risk, plenty of insurgents, but after a while you get careless. War becomes a game.

'Mid afternoon. Rippling heat. Hot. Hotter than this, but we had air con and water, so we didn't give a shit.

'So anyway, I was standing in the middle of nowhere, unzipped, looking out over the dunes. Then I saw a car. A white Land Cruiser, riding along, a couple of miles out in the sand. It pulled up. A guy got out. Fat guy. Blue uniform. Looked like a local cop. Acting real furtive. He took a pair of binoculars and checked around. Seemed to be looking straight at us. We waved, tried to get his attention. Trained our weapons, signalled "hands up". Fucker ignored us.

'He dropped the tailgate, dragged out a couple of heavy garbage bags and dumped them on the ground. Then he got back in the Jeep and drove off, quick as he could. Span the wheels, kicked up a ton of dust, then floored it.

'We drove out to the spot he dumped the bags. You know what? No bags. No tyre tracks. No trace of any kind.'

'Jeez.'

'The guy was real enough. He wasn't a ghost. Somewhere, out in that desert, he stopped his car and dumped a couple of bags. Might have been over a hundred miles away. But heat played tricks. Refracted his image, projected it miles from his actual position.'

'You think the sandstorm could echo a radio signal?' asked Noble. 'Bounce it around?'

'That Russian could be a thousand miles away. Shit, he might even be in Moscow. A big-ass static storm could turn physics on its head.'

Frost shut off the radio.

'So what do you reckon was in those garbage bags?'

164

'Glad I never found out.'

The target dossier protruded from Hancock's backpack. RESTRICTED ACCESS. CO-PILOT ONLY.

Frost unzipped the vinyl document wallet.

'Hey,' said Hancock. 'That's classified.'

'Hardly matters, does it, Cap? No secrets worth keeping any more.'

She thumbed pages.

The flight-path map. Red dashes across featureless terrain. Staging coordinates.

National Recon photos. Dunes and a limestone escarpment. Bleak as the Sea of Tranquillity. Each image stamped EYES ONLY.

'Hundred miles to the aim point, give or take. We were so damned close. What the hell were we supposed to bomb, Captain? Was it Chinese Whispers? Bunch of guys passing bad orders down the line without question?'

Hancock shook his head.

'The mission parameters were very clear. They knew what they were doing.'

A target image. Desert wilderness, and the centre of the picture, a black redaction.

Frost held up the picture.

'What's this? What's hidden? What are we not allowed to see?'

Hancock didn't reply.

'But you were briefed, right? They told you the nature of the target?'

Hancock crossed the flight deck and took the sheaf of notes from her hand. He stuffed the wad of documents into his backpack.

'Like I said. Classified.'

T-22 OFF ROAD SPEC

ADVANCED TREAD

CENTURION™ PUNCTURE RESISTANCE TECH

HEAVY DUTY RIM GUARD

LONG WEAR

ALL TERRAIN TRACTION

SIZE	LT395/70GH
LI/SS	121/118S
SIDEWALL	BSL
LOAD RANGE	D
PRODUCT CODE	856363278
MATERIAL NUMBER	1336
APPROVED RIM WIDTH (INS)	8.5-10.0
MEASURING RIM WIDTH (INS)	9.5
SECTION WIDTH (INS)	12.7
OVERALL DIAMETER (INS)	34.5
MAX LOAD @ INFLATION (LBS)	3,195 @ 50
TREAD DEPTH (IN 32NDS)	16
REVS/MILE	610
ORIGINAL EQUIP FITMENT	HUMMER H2

23

The limo swerved between dunes.

Osborne had the wheel. Trenchman sat beside him.

'I know you want to be a hero,' said Osborne. 'I know you want to ride to the rescue. But let's face it, we can't travel much further. We were okay back on the salt flats. Smooth driving. Here? We're going to bog down and stall any minute.'

'She's a big V8. Good tread, plenty of clearance. She can cope.'

'We don't even know where we are headed.'

'We know the plane's target and flight path. That gives us a pretty tight search field. Soon or later, we'll find wreckage.'

Trenchman pointed to a level stretch of sand up ahead.

'Stop there, would you?'

'Best if we kept rolling.'

'Stop for a moment. I got to check something out.'

They pulled up.

Osborne jumped from the Humvee. Cool air con replaced by desert heat.

He beckoned to Trenchman.

'Thought I could feel her pulling to the left. Looks like we've got a flat.'

Trenchman crouched and examined the flaccid tyre. Something white embedded in rubber. He worked the shard lose and held it in his palm.

'What is it?' asked Osborne.

'I believe it's a chunk of human bone.'

'Hope to God we have a spare wheel.'

'We do. It's in the trunk.'

Morgan climbed a dune and looked out over the sandscape. Akingbola joined him.

'Can you feel it?' asked Morgan. 'A rising wind.'

'Air getting colder by the minute. How often do you reckon it rains in a place like this?'

'Once a decade at a guess. You can bet it's a big fucking deluge.'

They looked around.

'You'd think there would be smoke. A fuelled-up B-52 nosedives into the desert. You'd think there would be a big-ass crater.'

'Check it out,' said Akingbola. He pointed east. 'Something on the horizon. See? A red blur.'

Morgan shielded his eyes and peered at the distant haze.

'Christ. Sandstorm. Heading this way.'

Trenchman climbed onto the limo roof. He cracked a cream soda, took a swig, and set the can down by his feet.

He powered up his radio, extended the antenna and did a three-sixty sweep.

'Anything?' asked Osborne, standing beneath him.

'Think I got some weak transponder hits. Hear that? The tone? Very weak. Can't get a lock.'

'Atmospherics?'

Trenchman gestured to distant crags.

'All kinds of metal in those hills. Copper. Nickel. Uranium. Playing merry hell with the signal. They could be sitting in the sand a hundred yards away, broadcasting Mayday after Mayday. We wouldn't know a damned thing about it.'

★

Osborne opened the trunk. He pulled back carpet and lifted the heavy wheel free. He rolled it to the front of the vehicle and propped it against the wing.

He returned to the trunk to fetch the jack.

'How's it going?' asked Akingbola.

'Five minute job. No big deal.'

'Looks like there's a sandstorm heading this way.'

'How close?'

'Miles out. Looks big.'

'We'll be all right. Just climb in the limo and sit it out. Might have to do a little digging once the storm has passed.'

Akingbola gestured to Trenchman standing on top of the limo. He spoke low so he couldn't be overheard:

'I guess you and the colonel are pretty tight.'

'Give or take.'

'He wants to save the aircrew. That's great. That's admirable. But we're putting our necks at serious risk out here. Totally reliant on the limo. If anything happens to the vehicle, we're fucked. We lost one wheel. What happens if we lose a second? Long fucking walk.'

'He saved your ass back at the airfield. Remember that.'

'Yeah, I get it. Believe me, I'm grateful. But it won't help a soul if we die out here on some kamikaze rescue mission. Talk to him. Make him see sense. We need to find a highway, start making long-term plans.'

Osborne grabbed the jack from the trunk. He threw it down beside the flat wheel. He ducked inside the passenger compartment and ripped the door from the snack cabinet.

He shoved the laminate door beneath the front axle, used it as a base to stop the jack sinking into sand.

He took off his field jacket, stretched his arms, then began to work the crank. The wheel slowly lifted out of the sand.

He crouched and prised the chrome hub. He threw it aside, skimmed it like a Frisbee.

He unscrewed retaining nuts with a four-way cross wrench and lifted the heavy radial clear.

He turned to Akingbola:

'Check the ignition is shut off, okay? Don't want to kill the battery.'

He examined the burst tyre. It was a run-flat, military spec, should have retained pressure even when punctured. But a chunk of femur had punched a hole big enough for his finger. Put the tyre beyond repair.

Faint cry behind him.

He turned around.

Morgan, gesticulating from the crest of a high dune.

He waved back.

'Yeah. I know. Sandstorm.'

'Help,' screamed Morgan. 'Jesus Christ, help.'

Osborne sprinted up the steep gradient.

Morgan was waist deep in sand and sinking fast.

Osborne gripped his arms and pulled. Trenchman and Akingbola joined him.

'Something's got me,' said Morgan. 'Something's got my legs.'

'Quicksand?'

'There's something in the sand. Something alive. It's gripped my leg.'

The three gripped Morgan's arms and pulled hard as they could. Hard to get a firm footing on sand. Morgan screamed and grimaced, shoulders at the point of dislocation.

'A snake?' asked Trenchman, desperately trying to make sense of the situation. 'Some kind of sand snake?'

Morgan was now wrenched neck deep.

'Oh Jesus, help me.'

Osborne and Akingbola gripped his wrists and pulled. Trenchman crouched behind Morgan and dug with both hands, feverishly scooped sand aside like a dog burying a bone.

Morgan's head hauled below the sand. He screamed and coughed dust. Osborne and Akingbola fell to their knees and dug to expose his mouth and nose, restore his airway.

'Mother of God.'

Trenchman stood back, drew his side arm and expended a full clip into the sand behind Morgan.

A final, whimpering scream, then Morgan was jerked below ground. Osborne gripped the stricken man's hand.

Final wrench.

Morgan was gone.

They stood back and contemplated the depression in the sand.

'What the fuck just happened?' said Akingbola.

The sand in front of Trenchman's feet shifted and bulged.

'Shit.'

He jumped backwards, slotted a fresh mag into his Beretta.

They began to edge back towards the limo. Osborne and Akingbola drew their pistols and trained them at the ground.

The ground in front of Osborne swirled and seethed. Something beneath the sand was moving towards them with a purpose.

'Run.'

They turned and sprinted back to the limousine. They vaulted onto the hood, scrabbled for purchase, then jumped onto the roof, boots skidding on slick metal.

They stood, looking down at the sand surrounding the vehicle.

'This is fucking insane,' murmured Osborne.

'Isn't happening,' murmured Akingbola. 'Can't be happening.'

Trenchman adjusted grip on his Beretta.

'Make them count.'

The ground beside the limo bulged and heaved. They opened fire, triple volley of gunshots merging to a continual roar, air filled with gun smoke and dust.

TARGET-FMJ

9mm LUGER HIGH PERF

CENTREFIRE CARTRIDGES

Cartuchos de Fuego Central

Cartouches Percussion Centrale

(9x19mm)   **115 GR.FMJ** (Bala Encamisada)

50 CARTRIDGES   STEEL CASE

NON-CORROSIVE BERDAN PRIMED   MADE IN USA

Keep out of the reach of children

Mantengase fuera del alcance de los ninos

Gardez loin des enfants

24

They sat in the limo and listened to the storm rage outside. Semi-dark. Nothing beyond the windows but swirling sand. Dust accumulated against the windshield, slowly blocking out the light.

The typhoon buffeted the vehicle. Whistle and moan. The car rocked on its suspension.

None of them spoke. Each locked in their own private horror.

Akingbola loaded an AR-15 and chambered a round.

Osborne picked up Morgan's helmet and turned it in his hands. He contemplated the interior webbing. Nylon stained with sweat. Trace evidence of Morgan's physicality, testament he had, moments earlier, been a living, breathing thing.

Akingbola lay the rifle across his lap and cracked a Coke.

'Take it easy with those,' said Trenchman. 'Best save a few for later.'

Osborne took a cigar from his breast pocket and bit the tip. He chewed the unlit Cohiba.

'We got to change that tyre.'

'Better wait for the storm to pass,' said Trenchman.

Osborne shook his head.

'The thing beneath the sand. God knows what it is. But it tracked us easy enough. Not sure how. Body heat, footsteps, whatever. But the storm might give us good cover. Lots of noise, lots of dust. A chance to haul ass before it realises we're gone.'

Trenchman thought it over.

'Yeah. Worth a shot.'

'But we got to do it from the car. That's the trick. We got to bolt that wheel in place without setting foot on the ground.'

Trenchman pulled back the sunroof and emerged into the storm. Shemagh wrapped round his head, eyes shielded from driving sand by wraparound shades.

He climbed out onto the roof, crouched and braced against the buffeting wind.

Osborne followed.

Akingbola stood upright in the vacant sunroof, rifle at port arms, ready to provide cover fire.

Trenchman lay on the hood. Osborne knelt behind and gripped his legs.

Trenchman hung over the left wing of the limo. He pushed the punctured wheel aside. It rolled a couple of yards then toppled flat. He waited to see if the vibration of the falling tyre would lure whatever nightmarish thing snatched Morgan beneath the ground.

No movement. Just shifting, wind-driven sand.

The spare tyre stood propped against the side of the vehicle. He rolled the heavy radial into position in front of the vacant wheel-well. He struggled to lift the wheel, line it with the hub bolts and slot it home.

'Lower,' he shouted. 'Get me lower.'

Osborne pushed him forwards. Trenchman's entire torso hung from the car, letting his arms reach the ground.

He raked the sand. He found the cross wrench. He probed the dust trying to locate the eight lug nuts. He unearthed them one by one, tried not to think what might be hiding beneath the sand, ready to seize his hands and drag him head first beneath the dunes.

He engaged the bolt thread and screwed the lugs finger-tight. He used the cross wrench to wind them secure. His ballistic glasses fell to the ground. He ignored them and continued to anchor the wheel.

'We're done,' he shouted.

He reached for his Oakleys. The sand bulged and puckered, and suddenly they were gone.

They dropped through the sunroof. Akingbola secured the window, shutting out the storm. Typhoon wind howl abruptly silenced.

'We cool?'

'It's still out there,' said Trenchman. 'Whatever the fuck it is. Circling like a shark.'

'So let's split.'

Trenchman climbed over the driver partition and took the wheel.

Ignition. Revs. He worked the shift, rocked the vehicle forward/reverse until he jerked the limo clear of the jack. Wheels hit the ground. Sudden traction.

The limo pulled out and swung a wide arc slewing sand.

'Where we headed?' asked Akingbola.

'Out of this fucking desert.'

Trenchman retraced their route as best he could. Visibility down to a couple of yards. Headbeams lit driving sand. The car lurched and rocked. Osborne clung to the passenger dash. Akingbola gripped the stripper pole.

Heavy thud.

'What was that,' said Akingbola.

'Think we left the trunk open.'

Second thud. They looked up.

'Something on the roof.'

Akingbola reached to pull back the roof window.

'No,' said Osborne. 'Let me.'

He crouched on the passenger seat. He drew his pistol and hit the side window control.

DOWN.

Motor whine. Typhoon wind and blustering sand.

He pulled the Beretta from his chest rig and squirmed out the window. He gripped the doorframe for support.

Something squatting on the roof. A malignant thing glimpsed through the swirling storm. It crouched like a spider, arm poised like it was about to punch through roof metal into the compartment below.

Quick front-sight aim. Instinctual. He pumped the trigger. Six shots, rapid fire. Bullets smacked flesh. Torn muscle. No blood. The creature took the impacts like they were nothing.

It lunged.

Osborne lost his grip on the doorframe and toppled backwards. He hit the sand and rolled.

Trenchman jerked the car to a halt and kicked open the passenger door. He leant out the vehicle, hand outstretched.

'Get in here. Get off the sand.'

Osborne snatched up his pistol. Scrambled to his feet and ran. He dove into the limo and slammed the door. He hit UP. Motor whine. The window raised halfway, then rotted fingers gripped the glass.

Skull face. Empty sockets. Yellow teeth.

'Hit it.'

Trenchman stamped the accelerator.

Osborne fired point blank, emptied the clip, shattered the window, blew chunks of skull, jaw and teeth.

The creature released its grip and fell away.

Driver compartment full of gun smoke.

The vehicle sped across the sand, lurched side to side, threw Osborne and Trenchman around.

Osborne reloaded his pistol.

'What the fuck was that thing?' muttered Osborne.

Trenchman opened his mouth like he was about to speak.

Then the limo hit a bank and rolled. He hit the brakes, but it was too late.

The vehicle on its side. He and Osborne thrown together.

The limo on its roof. Buckling metal, shattering glass.

Gun discharge.

A final roll. The car toppled upright. Suspension rocked to a standstill.

Abrupt silence.

Upholstery dusted with glass. Passenger compartment filled with dust and swirling sand.

Trenchman unsheathed a knife and stabbed the airbag. Shattered nose. He snorted blood. He used his shemagh to mop his mouth and chin.

He turned in his seat.

'Everyone okay?'

He looked over his shoulder. Akingbola lying on the carpet floor of the passenger compartment. Deep shock. Rifle in his hand, smoke from the barrel, a spent cartridge smouldering on the carpet by his side.

A ragged bullet hole in the upholstery of the driver's partition.

Osborne sat in the passenger seat, hands clamped over a hole in his belly, blood pooling in his lap.

40% Alc./Vol. (80 proof)

IMPORTED

25

Trenchman unwound the shemagh from Osborne's neck, balled it up and pressed it to the wound.

'Hold it tight. It'll slow the bleeding.'

He helped Osborne press bloody hands to the wadded fabric.

'There. That should help.'

It was something to do, something to say. The rifle round had ripped a massive hole in the man's gut. Torn him wide open. Shredded organs. Massive internal haemorrhage. He had a couple of minutes left to live.

'Hey,' said Osborne. 'Akingbola.'

'What?'

'It's all right,' said Osborne, gesturing to the blood-soaked wound in his belly. 'Shit happens. Don't beat yourselves up over it.'

He sat looking out of the shattered windshield. His face was white. Blood on his lips. Eyelids drooped in a terminal drowse.

Trenchman cranked the ignition, tried to get the engine to engage. Weak revs. He gunned the throttle, worked the gears forward/reverse. No traction.

Akingbola leant out the shattered side window, shielded his eyes from swirling sand. The wheels were bedded so deep they were barely visible.

'We're not going anywhere.'

Trenchman turned up the air con. He angled dash vents so Osborne got a cool blast on his face.

'Probably ought to save the battery,' said Akingbola.

'For what?'

Osborne watched sand accumulate on the buckled hood of the limo.

'Infected,' he murmured. 'Pretty far gone. Almost rotted down to bone. But smart. Never seen them act that way. Sly. Strong.'

'Yeah,' said Trenchman. 'Swimming around in the sand. I'd call bullshit, if I hadn't seen it with my own eyes. Something new.'

'You think the fuckers can learn? Evolve?'

'Maybe there are different types. Maybe we shook a nest of boss-level dudes.'

Osborne took a deep, shuddering breath and sagged in his seat. Then he straightened his back and widened his eyes, like he was trying to stay awake, fighting for a few seconds more life.

'Red jumpsuit. Notice that? Thing was wearing a red jump suit.'

'Must be pretty close to the target point. Agency black site. God knows what they were doing out here.'

'Might be more of the bastards. Head west. Get to the hills. Three or four miles of dunes, then you reach hard ground. Face the fuckers in the open.'

Trenchman nodded.

'Okay.'

Osborne reached out and stroked the dash vinyl. He looked at his right hand front and back, rubbing his fingers together like he was saying goodbye to his sense of touch.

'Guess you guys have a choice. Leave now and face the storm, or wait until later and face killer heat.'

Trenchman nodded.

'Personally, if I were in your position, I would wait until later. Wouldn't want to be blundering around in a cyclone.' He smacked dry lips. 'Got a drink? A real drink?'

Akingbola tossed Trenchman a plastic miniature cognac. Trenchman unscrewed the cap and held the little bottle to Osborne's lips. He sipped. Blood diffused through the bottle of amber liquid turning it near black.

Osborne reached for a vest pouch with a trembling hand and popped the flap. He gave Trenchman two clips of 9mm. He opened another pocket and took out a compass.

'Take every can of Coke, every pack of peanuts. Fill a bag. Don't leave anything behind.'

Trenchman nodded. He took the compass and mags, and stuffed them in a pocket.

Osborne leaned forwards, like he had something urgent to impart.

'And don't forget. They'll need you in the winter garden.'

'Winter garden?'

Osborne closed his eyes, leaned back and died.

Trenchman watched him a while, watched residual colour drain from the dead man's face.

He turned to Akingbola.

'Let's go.'

'What about the storm?'

'Fuck the storm. Let's get out of here.'

Nutrition

Serving Size 1 bar (65g) **Calories** 280 Fat calories 80

Amount Per Serving	%DV*	Amount Per Serving	%DV*
Total Fat 9g	14%	**Potassium** 190mg	5%
Saturated Fat 5g	25%	**Total Carbohydrates** 40g	13%
Trans Fat 0g		Dietary Fiber 1g	4%
Cholesterol <5mg	1%	Sugars 18g	
Sodium 150mg	6%	**Protein** 10g	20%

Vitamin C	35%	Vitamin E	60%	Niacin	20%	Vitamin B12	20%	Zinc	20%
Calcium	4%	Thiamin	20%	Vitamin B6	20%	Phosphorus	10%	Copper	15%
Iron	10%	Riboflavin	20%	Folate	50%	Magnesium	8%	Manganese	6%

* Percent Daily Values (DV) are based on 2,000 calorie diet. Not a significant source of Vitamin A.

26

The storm at its height.

The fuselage buffeted by a heavy crosswind. Slam and jolt, like in-flight turbulence.

Hancock sat in the pilot seat. He balanced a signal mirror on the flight console, angled it so he could see his reflection. He flicked open his lock knife and attempted to shave. He slowly dragged the blade across stubble.

The cabin shook.

He cut his upper lip.

Brief flash of anger. Fingers tight around the knife hilt in a white-knuckle death grip, like he wanted to stab.

He gently massaged his bandaged scalp, breathed slow and willed shit-happens acceptance.

He blotted a bead of blood on the cuff of his flight suit.

'You okay?' asked Noble.

Hancock ignored him. He looked out of one of the unbroken windows and watched swirling vortices of dust.

Noble got to his feet. He gripped a wall spar and braced against the roll.

Energy bars scattered on the gunner's console. He ripped a wrapper with his teeth, spat plastic, then ate.

He offered Hancock a bar.

'Hungry?'

'Better save those,' said Hancock. 'We'll need them for the trip.'

Noble gathered up the bars and stuffed them into a backpack.

'What time is it?' asked Hancock.

'Eleven, give or take.'

'Aim to set out around eighteen hundred. Sundown. Day turning to evening, desert starting to cool. We ought to get some sleep in the meantime, I guess.'

A sudden gust shook the plane. The flight deck shuddered. A blast curtain tore open. Hancock flinched from the stinging sand-blast. He reattached fasteners, lashed the screen back in place with fresh tape.

Frost leant across the pilot seat and looked out of one of the intact windows at the storm.

'How long before it lets up, do you think?'

Hancock shrugged.

'No idea. Got to blow itself out sooner or later.'

Frost looked down on Hancock's head. Swollen, angry flesh beneath the chute bandage.

Faint smell of rot.

'How long since that wound got cleaned out?'

'About twelve hours.'

'Maybe I should take a look. Dress it fresh.'

'I'm okay.'

'Looks pretty inflamed.'

'Unless you can pull a fully manned ICU out your ass, there's not much to be done.'

Frost sat next to the backpack. She took a map from a side pocket and shook it open.

'We reckon to cover between ten and fifteen miles a night, is that right?'

'Yeah. Although we have no real way of charting our progress, no way to measure the miles. Basically, we walk until we reach water or drop dead in the dirt.'

'I've been mulling it over,' said Frost. 'We've got to head

north. Not right away. But once we reach habitation and get ourselves fixed with a vehicle, we ought to head north soon as we can. Best chance to escape radiation. Bombs were just the start. Sooner or later every nuclear power station in the world will blow. Failsafe cooling systems can keep reactors stable for a while. After that: meltdown. There are a bunch of atomic power plants to our south in California. Diablo Canyon. San Onofre. Another big one at Palo Verde, Arizona. Best head in the opposite direction, put them far behind us. I vote we head for British Columbia.'

Hancock shifted in his seat. He folded his arms and closed his eyes.

'No need to over-think the situation,' he said. 'No need for elaborate plans. Got to take things day by day. Right now, all we can do is walk and hope to strike lucky. Best thing we can do is rest.'

Noble lay on the floor and dozed, soothed by gentle white noise from the CSEL positioned near his head.

He snapped awake.

He snatched up the radio and held it to his ear.

'Hear that?'

Frost jolted from sleep. She rubbed her eyes.

'What?'

Noble upped volume and held out the radio.

Steady hiss.

'All I can hear is static.'

'There's a voice,' insisted Noble.

Frost took the handset. She held it to her ear and listened hard.

'Nope. Can't hear a thing.'

'A voice. I heard "*Liberty Bell*". I heard "rescue".'

Frost listened a full minute. She shook her head.

'No. Nothing.'

Noble grabbed the radio from her hand. He pressed Transmit.

'This is US Air Force *Liberty Bell*, MT66, do you copy this message, over?'

White noise.

'There,' said Noble. 'Hear that? A response. Can't make out words. But they can hear us. They know we're alive.'

'Your mind is playing tricks. There's nothing.'

Noble impatiently turned his back and listened some more.

'I heard them. I heard them for sure. Voices. Got to be close by, right? So much interference. We couldn't pick them up otherwise.'

He slowly lowered the radio and looked towards the ceiling.

'Listen.'

'Can't hear a thing.'

Noble mimed hush. He cocked his head.

'Rotors. Yeah, rotors. They're here. They found us.'

'Ain't nothing but the wind.'

'We've got to get out there, put up a flare. This weather, they could fly right over our position and not see a damned thing.'

He slid down the ladder to the lower cabin.

'Nothing out there, dude,' shouted Frost from above. 'Sandstorm. Choppers can't fly in this shit.'

Noble ignored her. He began to haul aside the equipment trunks that blocked the fissure in the fuselage wall.

Hancock stood at the head of the ladderway and looked down into the lower cabin. Sand blew through the split seam in the wall, dusting the deck plate.

No chopper noise. Just the mournful moan of desert wind.

Frost stood in the wall fissure, shielding her eyes, looking out into the storm.

'Is he okay?' shouted Hancock.

Frost didn't reply.

Best leave Noble to his madness.

Hancock headed back to the pilot seat, holding the wall for support.

He stepped round the satcom case, attention immediately drawn to a winking green light.

He crouched beside the transceiver and lifted the lid. The screen blinked to life.

Comsec sign-in:

AUTHENTICATE

He keyed:

VERMILLION

He hit Enter.

FIRST AND NINTH DIGITS
OF PERSONNEL CODE

He keyed:

4 3

He hit Enter.

INCOMING EAM

He sat back and watched a loading bar slowly progress towards 100%.

Noble stumbled from the plane and was immediately brought to his knees by a gust of typhoon wind which hit him between the shoulder blades like a shove to the back.

He tied a bandana round his face, masked his mouth and nose bandit-style. He cupped hands over his eyes to shield them from driving sand particles.

Rotor noise. A deep, pulsating beat audible beneath the wind-howl.

He shouted into his radio:

'This is *Liberty Bell*. You are above our position. You are right overhead. Put down immediately.'

He switched his CSEL to transponder mode. He held it above his head, let it chirp a homing signal, an urgent electronic tocsin pulsing through the swirling electromagnetism of the storm.

Chopper noise getting stronger. A heavy, powerful machine. Sounded like a Chinook.

He braced for lacerating downwash, expecting to see the helicopter's belly-shadow descending from the dust churning above his head.

Hancock's CSEL on the floor next to the pilot seat.

The tiny speaker relayed Noble's voice as he tried to raise the phantom rescue party:

'*This is* Liberty Bell. *You are above our position. You are right overhead. Put down immediately.*'

Hancock ignored the CSEL.

He crouched beside his satcom unit and contemplated the decrypted communication.

CONFIRM STATUS ACTION-READY

He cleared the screen.

Winking cursor.

He typed:

REQUEST IDENT

He hit Enter the sat back, cross-legged, and waited for a response.

Deafening chopper noise.

Noble stood buffeted by wind, hand shielding his eyes, staring up into the broiling sky.

He waited for the belly of a Chinook to descend from of the storm, wheels settling on the desert floor.

Nothing.

Engine noise began to dwindle.

Noble threw the CSEL aside. He fumbled a marine pyro from his pocket. He held it above his head and fired. The star shell rocketed into the cyclone and glowed like a darting, storm-tossed sun.

'Hey. Hey, we're right here.'

He screamed into the typhoon, spat and coughed sand.

The spent shell dropped out of the storm and hit the ground in front of him, smouldering like a hot coal.

And then the flare was abruptly pulled beneath the sand leaving nothing but a wisp of smoke snatched away on the wind.

27

The storm abated.

Frost left the plane and took a look around.

The nose section of the fuselage was banked like a heavy snowdrift. Every upper surface, wings, fuselage, nose radome, loaded with dust.

A transformed landscape. Peaks and valleys, grown familiar over the past twenty-four hours, replaced with a new topography. A fresh maze of peaks and depressions.

A residual breeze stirred the dust, made the dunes smoulder like brimstone.

The tyre that served as a signal fire was completely submerged.

High sun burned through a residual red haze. Noonday heat cooked the plane.

Sand had accreted against the starboard engines. Dust choked the intakes, the turbine blades.

Noble emerged from the plane and sat near the nose, back to the fuselage, shifting position every couple of minutes to stay within a shrinking shadow. He looked tired, subdued.

Frost limped across the sand and joined him.

'You okay?'

'Thought I heard something on the radio. A voice, shouting our call sign. Thought we were about to get rescued.'

'Really?'

'And I heard a chopper. Deafening. Sounded like it was hovering over our position, ready to land.'

'All I heard was the wind.'

'It was right overhead. A Chinook. Real as anything.'

'Helicopter couldn't fly in that kind of brown-out. Choke their filters. Couldn't leave the ground.'

'Hancock said I wasn't thinking straight. Said it was all in my mind. Guess he was right. Know what? I thought I was holding it together pretty good. Congratulating myself for keeping a clear head. The madness. It sneaks up on you.'

Frost shrugged, traced patterns in the sand with her boot.

'Desert can fuck with a person's head. If we stay here long enough, we'll all go batshit. End up talking to thin air, sipping JP8 like fine wine, swimming in the dust like we're splashing in a pool. Won't take much to push us over the edge. Just a couple more days cooking in this heat.'

Hancock pulled down the remaining blast screens to block out the sun.

Fetid cave dark.

He sat on the flight-deck floor beside the satcom unit.

An incoming message:

CONFIRM YOUR STATUS ACTION-READY

He reflexively touched the crude bandage that patched his empty eye socket and bound his fractured skull.

He typed:

CONFIRM ACTION-READY

He pulled off the bandage and scratched his scalp. He leant forwards and examined his head wound, using the transceiver screen as a dark mirror.

Crude stitches. The swollen, puckered gash across his forehead. The empty eye socket.

Another incoming transmission. Buffering, then:

PRIORITY COMMAND
COMPLETE MISSION
PROCEED TO TARGET SITE AND INITIATE
PACKAGE
ACKNOWLEDGE

He sipped from his canteen.
He typed:

PLEASE IDENTIFY YOURSELF

He waited a long while. No response.

PLEASE VERIFY AUTHORITY
DESIGNATED COMSEC PROTOCOL
AS PER MISSION SPEC

No reply.
He typed:

WHO AM I TALKING TO

Incoming:

ABSOLUTE PRIORITY
CONVEY WARHEAD TO TARGET SITE
INITIATE PACKAGE
ACKNOWLEDGE
ACKNOWLEDGE
ACKNOWLEDGE
ACKNOWLEDGE
ACKNOWLEDGE

The screen continued to scroll Acknowledge until he hit Break.

He thought a long while, then typed:

MESSAGE RECEIVED
CONFIRM COMMAND
PROCEED TO DESIGNATED MARKER AND
TRIGGER DEVICE

Frost watched, mesmerised, as heat rippled from the upper surfaces of the starboard wing. Hallucinatory haze turned the wide expanse of metal to a shimmering, insubstantial thing so ghostly she felt, if she were to reach out to touch the steel and aluminium structure, her fingers would pass through it as if it were smoke.

The sandstorm had shielded the crash site from the morning sun. But now there was no respite. Searing, blistering light.

Better cover as much skin as possible. She zipped her flight suit, pulled on gloves and turned up her collar.

Hancock emerged from the plane. He dug beside the nose.

'What's he after?' asked Noble.

'No idea.'

They watched him work.

'Need any help?'

Hancock ignored them.

Frost sat in the pilot seat. She lifted a blast screen. The vast dunescape. Barren mountains veiled by heat haze.

From her position in the cockpit she could look down on Hancock as he worked outside. He was digging in the sand, excavating something buried by the storm.

The sled. Deck plate lashed with a cable tow rope. The chunk of grate he used to drag the battery from the tail section. He gripped the cable and hauled it clear of the sand.

Noble climbed the ladder to the flight deck. He stood beside Frost and looked out the window.

'Think he's lost it?'

'Hard to say.'

They watched Hancock pull a long length of injector pipe from the sand. He shook out the dust-matted flag and tied it to the pole.

He stabbed the pole into the ground. The flag hung limp. Inverted stars and stripes. A futile signal of distress.

The crawlway.

A tight, steel-sided tunnel, little wider than an air duct.

Hancock on his hands and knees. He held a flashlight between his teeth like a cigar. He pushed the backpack ahead of him. He dragged the satcom unit behind.

The bomb bay pressure door. A heavy hatch secured by crank handles.

He turned the handles. The door wouldn't open. The frame had distorted during the crash. He curled foetal, turned in the tight crawlspace and kicked at the door with booted feet. Metal shriek. The door swung open.

Stifling darkness.

He crawled inside and stood upright. A wall-mounted toggled switch. He flicked On. Immediate crack and spark-shower from cabling above his head. He flinched from the sparks and flicked Off. He traced cable with the beam of his flashlight until he found a frayed break in the line. He stripped and twisted copper wire.

He flicked the switch again.

Secondary lights burned steady. The compartment lit blood red.

He surveyed the vaulted weapons bay.

Dead power cable and data lines hung from roof conduits like jungle vine. He ducked beneath them.

His boots crunched sand. The payload doors had been ripped away, leaving a wide aperture in the floor open to the desert.

The centre of the bay was dominated by a rotary launcher: a drum-rack that could house at max five ALCMs and position them, one by one, above the open payload doors ready for deployment.

An eighteen-foot Tomahawk missile held by clamps. Solid-propellant power plant and intakes at the rear. TERCOM terrain mapping radome in the nose.

The warhead was housed in the payload section behind the nose. A Mod 4 CS-67 tactical nuke prepped for a ten kiloton yield.

He ran his hand over the surface of the weapon. White lacquer, like bathroom porcelain. The missile appeared undamaged.

He took a compact Geiger counter from his pocket. He took a reading, passed the sensor the length of the bomb. Steady background.

He unzipped his backpack and pulled out a flat Peli trunk the size of an attaché case. He flipped clasps and opened the trunk.

A laptop bedded in foam. Beside it: tools, cables, replacement fuses. Battlefield triage. Everything he would need to monitor and maintain the missile up to the moment it was jettisoned from the plane.

Titanium torque keys. He selected a key, lifted it from its foam trough and set to work.

The payload compartment of the ALCM was studded with twenty-four hex screws. A laborious task to release each screw. He had to crouch beneath the weapon with a flashlight. Had to pause every couple of minutes to shake fatigue from his fingers.

The final bolt. He set it turning, threw the wrench aside, and unscrewed by hand.

A faint click as the bolt cleared the thread. The cowling dropped loose. He carefully lifted the panel clear. It was heavy. Hardened steel alloy.

The core. An anti-radiation jacket held in a titanium frame. A featureless cylinder wired to a bundle of fusing and firing circuits. Uranium 235 hemispheres, plutonium 239 and a tritium/deuterium booster, all of it jacketed with hexagonal plates of high explosive to force a millisecond of super-compression.

Critical mass. Cascading fission. Stellar light. Nova heat.

Arming the warhead for manual detonation would take all the cold-sweat delicacy associated with defusing an IED. The slightest error would transform the weapon into a giant paperweight.

A nine-pin data port bedded in the surface of the confinement case.

He placed the laptop on the sand floor of the bomb bay. Flickering boot sequence. He ran cable and jacked into the warhead.

A winking cursor.

A black plastic tag hung round his neck on a lanyard. He lifted the lanyard over his head, snapped the tag in two and removed a small slip of paper.

He unfolded the paper and typed the ten digit authenticator code:

J8492N3399

The code input field was immediately replaced by a status screen. The arming sequence and fuse system. The heartbeat of the weapon.

FNL PAL ACTV

Permissive Action Links.

A five-stage authorisation protocol which would enable the bomb. Unless the weapon were activated in sequence a series of barometric, impact, and rate-of descent lock-outs would render the warhead inert to prevent accidental detonation. It could be consumed by fire or dropped thousands of feet with no chance of triggering thermonuclear reaction. It could only be detonated by specific human intent.

Four of the PAL cut-outs flashed green. Final authorisation flashed red.

The B-52 crashed on target approach, just before it reached the hold coordinates, the point at which Hancock would have checked in with USSTRATCOM and requested go/no-go authorisation. Once the order had been received, Frost would have armed the warhead and directed Noble to jettison the missile.

A deliberately fragmented protocol that would ensure a lone individual couldn't launch a nuke on a whim.

SCNDRY AUTH

- - - - - - - - - -

A single ten-digit code would complete the arming sequence and render the warhead live.

He booted the satcom, unfolded the antenna and set it on the sand floor of the bomb bay facing east.

REQUEST GO TO ARM WEAPON

He waited.

The reply:

CONFIRM EXEC AUTHORITY TO DEPLOY

He typed:

WHAT IS SECONDARY ARM CODE

Reply:

RADAR NAV
HOLDS FINAL AUTHENTICATION

He typed:

RADAR NAV NON-OPERATIONAL
UNABLE TO PROVIDE FINAL AUTHENTICATION
REQUEST OVERRIDE CODE
FOR SINGLE KEY LAUNCH

Reply:

RADAR NAV
HOLDS FINAL AUTHENTICATION

He sat back and massaged chin stubble.

Frost, the radar navigator, held the final code. It was printed on a small strip of laminated paper sealed in a plastic tag hung round her neck.

Without her ten-digit authenticator, he couldn't detonate the warhead.

NO LONE ZONE

TWO MAN CONCEPT

MANDATORY

28

Frost held a scrap of thermal print in her hand.

EMERGENCY ACTION MESSAGE
PRIORITY COMMAND
COMPLETE MISSION
PROCEED TO TARGET SITE AND INITIATE
PACKAGE
ACKNOWLEDGE

Message time-stamped one hour earlier.

She handed the note to Noble. He studied it.

She turned to Hancock.

'Did the sender identify themselves?'

'USSTRATCOM.'

'For sure? Did they actually authenticate as Roundhouse?'

'They had full knowledge of our mission and payload. Couldn't be anyone else.'

'To be clear: they did not use their designated comsec call sign, is that right? They didn't identify themselves as Roundhouse?'

'Disrupted chain of command. Can't expect rigid protocol.' He pointed to the paper in her hand. 'The order is clear.'

'I can't assent to the deployment of a nuke based on an anonymous message,' said Frost.

'We received clear confirmation of our orders back at Vegas, direct and unequivocal: launch the missile. We have to abide

201

by the doctrine of Commander's Intent. We have received no further communication from STRATCOM, nothing that countermands our original instructions. The mission still stands.'

'I respectfully disagree. Fluid circumstances. We have significant circumstantial reasons to believe the mission parameters have changed. We need to confer with STRATCOM, establish their current intent. Until they are back on air, I cannot assent to deploy. Anyway, why are we even having this discussion? Whole thing is academic. We lost the plane. We have no means of launching the missile.'

'We could carry it.'

'The sled? You want to drag the missile on the sled? It weighs over three thousand pounds. We'd need a dozen able-bodied men to make it budge an inch. A friggin' team of oxen.'

'The warhead could be removed. We could transport the core, the physics package, to the target.'

'I refuse to throw away my life.'

'You took an oath.'

'To a nation that no longer exists.'

Hancock fetched satcom gear from the bomb bay. He hefted it up the ladder to the flight deck.

He angled the antenna and booted the transceiver.

A blank screen. A winking cursor.

He turned to Frost and swept his arm in a be-my-guest gesture, inviting her to sit and type.

She lowered herself to the deck in front of the transceiver, laid her bad leg straight.

She keyed:

THIS IS MT66
USB52H *LIBERTY BELL*
STRATCOM HAIL
PLEASE ACKNOWLEDGE

She hit Send.

Immediate response:

TRANSMISSION FAIL

'Atmospherics,' said Hancock. 'The signal comes and goes.'

Frost leant back against the flight-deck wall.

'I don't mean to pry into your private life, sir. We're all hurting. We've all lost family. But you must have someone, somewhere, who needs you to live.'

He waved a dismissive hand.

'I could talk about duty and honour, but I doubt the words mean a whole lot to you. You're clearly the type who joined for the benefits.'

'Surely it's time to be pragmatic. Why die here, in this miserable corner of desert? What's the use? What good will it serve? No one will know. No one will care. If we get out of this damn place we might be able to find some folks who actually need our help.'

'I have tactical command, Lieutenant. This isn't some kind of town hall debate. I'm still AC. And I say we complete the mission.'

She pressed Resend.

> TRANSMISSION FAIL
> TRANSMISSION FAIL
> TRANSMISSION FAIL
> TRANSMISSION FAIL
> TRANSMISSION FAIL
> TRANSMISSION FAIL

Frost climbed into the crawlway. She sucked pipe hanging from the water tank, drew liquid and refilled her canteen.

Someone tapped her leg. She craned around. Noble. She squirmed from the crawlspace.

'What?'

He mimed hush and beckoned her outside.

Noble took a folded photograph from his pocket. He handed it to Frost. She rubbed her eyes, let them adjust to sudden sunlight.

She studied the picture.

'What am I looking at?'

'The target site. Bunch of pictures in Hancock's dossier. This is the only photograph that shows any activity on the ground.'

Criss-cross tyre tracks. Black SUVs.

'What are those? Couple of house trailers?'

'Looks like,' said Noble.

'Hardly seems worth a bomb.'

'I suspect they are a preliminary outpost. The start of something bigger. Look at the vehicles. Four-by-fours. What do you reckon? Suburbans?'

'Hard to say.'

'What if they are still there? Could be our ticket out of this mess.'

'Shit, yeah.'

'Let's face facts. You got a bust leg, and Hancock's got a split skull. Neither of you in much shape to travel. But I could make the journey. I can move real fast on my own.'

'Got to admit, it makes sense.'

'Hancock won't like it.'

'Fuck Hancock. Get your shit together. Leave at sundown. I'll explain the situation after you've gone.'

TRANSMISSION FAIL

TRANSMISSION FAIL

TRANSMISSION FAIL
TRANSMISSION FAIL
TRANSMISSION FAIL
TRANSMISSION FAIL

Hancock hit Break and cleared the screen. He leant forward, used the black glass as a mirror.

He tried to lift the bandage wrapped round his head. Gummed by fresh blood. He peeled it loose. He glimpsed inflamed flesh. Rot stink. He pulled the bandage back in place.

Hand to his forehead. Running a fever.

He lectured his reflection:

'We're all in fucked-up shape. No use whining about it.'

He dragged the trauma kit closer, unzipped internal pockets and popped tablets from a strip of Tylenol into his palm.

He looked around. His canteen rested on the flight controls.

He got to his feet, eased himself into the pilot seat and swigged back the pills.

He had, in his previous life been stationed at Bagram and charged with providing preliminary intel assessments of captured insurgents. Despite the belligerence broadcast by the morale patches on his sleeve, 'DON'T TREAD ON ME' and 'PORK EATING INFIDEL', he had thumbed through a Qur'an while drowsing in his bunk late at night and developed a furtive admiration for the Taliban and their Spartan ideology. He was particularly struck by the injunction to avoid intoxicants. Couldn't help feeling nostalgic for the sun-blasted purity of the Hindu Kush once he found himself back in the Birmingham suburbs surrounded by purposeless folk smothering ennui with Prozac, Adderall and bourbon.

He lifted the blast screen and sat back, gazed at the sandscape with a half-closed eye.

Brief glimpse through blurred vision. Three figures

standing on a distant dune, backlit by the glare of the afternoon sun.

He sat bolt upright.

His uncapped canteen hit the floor and spilt water across the deck plate. He snatched it up and secured the cap.

He leant forwards and stared out the window, blinked and struggled to focus. He shielded his remaining eye, tried to mask sun-glare.

Three silent sentinels.

Looked like they were wearing flight suits.

Hancock ran from the plane out into harsh sunlight. He ran for the dunes in front of the plane.

He stumbled and fell face down. He got to his feet spitting sand. He waded the steep slope, struggled to chamber his pistol.

He crested the dune, came to a panting halt, Beretta raised.

Nothing. Empty terrain.

He lowered the pistol. He wiped his brow with the sleeve of his flight suit.

Frost's distant voice:

'What's going on?'

He hauled himself upright and slowly headed back to the aircraft.

'What's up, boss?' asked Frost, as he walked past.

He didn't reply. He returned to the fetid cave-dark of the flight deck.

The payload bay.

The missile bathed in blood red light.

Frost ran her hand across the million-dollar weapon's hardened steel hull, intake to radome.

She coughed.

During the past couple of days she had grown used to the vastness of the desert, the way it drew power from her words, rendering her voice thin and small. But the tight confines of the bomb bay rendered every sound, every breath and footfall, oppressively loud.

She sat cross-legged on the floor. She set the camcorder on a horizontal wall girder and pressed REC.

'It's late afternoon. Losing track of time. The days, the nights, last for ever out here. Honestly not sure if this is my second or third day marooned in the desert.

'It's grim. A killer sandstorm replaced by merciless heat. And later tonight, we'll freeze. Fucking place is utterly hostile to life.

'We're pretty strung out. Morale is low. Each of us trapped in our own misery, getting weaker by the hour.

'Remember that plane crash in the Andes years back? The one where survivors turned cannibal, had to eat the bodies of their friends? I read a book about it. Those guys froze on a mountainside a whole month before a couple of them got their shit together and walked to fetch help. I couldn't understand it. Why wait a whole month? I wanted to shout at the pages: *Move. Act. Save yourselves.* But now, here I am, marooned and dying of thirst. I understand the trauma, the debilitating shock. One of the reasons I'm talking to a camera. Trying to organise my thoughts.'

She swigged from her canteen.

'Hancock wants to drag the bomb to the aim point. Happy to let him plot and scheme. He isn't going anywhere. His head wound smells bad. Septicaemia. Hate to say it, but if he doesn't get help soon, he'll die.

'Noble is holding up well. Sure, he's feeling the pressure. Lost it for a while. Thought he could hear choppers. But he's in good physical shape. He intends to walk out of here tonight. Take some water, some food. Our lives are in his hands.

'Maybe one day someone will find this recording and play it back. A messed-up flygirl recounting her dying days.

'This is a pitiless place. We're parched, exhausted, pretty much at the end of the line. Looks like I got to make some hard decisions.

'Just remember: you got no right to judge.'

She reached forward and pressed Off.

29

Trenchman and Akingbola sprinted across the sand. They scrambled up dunes, tumbled down gradients in a cascade of dust. Exhausted. Dehydrated. Cooked by merciless sun.

They looked around as they ran, regarded the featureless sandscape with terror.

Akingbola stumbled and fell to his knees. He panted with fatigue. Trenchman grabbed his arm and pulled him to his feet.

'Don't stop. For God's sake keep moving.'

'I can't.'

Trenchman cuffed him round the head.

'Move your ass.'

They stumbled onwards. The limestone peaks of the Panamint Range emerged from the heat haze up ahead, ghost-crags taking solid form.

'There,' pointed Trenchman. The nearest outcrop was half a mile away. 'Firm ground.'

They sprinted, fast as they could, burned last reserves of strength as they made for the rocks.

They reached boulders projecting from the sand. Jumped, gripped, hauled themselves up onto sun-baked rock. They climbed higher, anxious to be away from the dunes. They turned, sat and looked back at the silicone ocean.

Wordless exhaustion.

Trenchman looked around. He pointed to an overhang.

'Shade,' he croaked.

They crawled on hands and knees, dragged themselves to shadow.

Akingbola cracked a Coke, sucked froth, and shared the can.

Ochre rocks. Oxidised iron salts stained boulders the colour of rust.

'I'd say we were moderately fucked.'

'I will not allow fortune to pass sentence on myself,' said Trenchman.

'Pershing?'

'Seneca.'

'Want to rest here?' asked Akingbola. 'Sleep out the day?'

Trenchman shook his head.

'We ought to get further from the desert. A mile at least. Then we can rest. Take turns to keep watch.'

They slowly got to their feet and began to haul themselves upwards. One plateau after another. Rocks marbled with mica, manganese and iron salts. Pinks, yellows and purples. They scrabbled for hand-holds. They helped each other climb ledge to ledge.

'Watch out for Diamondbacks.'

They reached a pinnacle. Trenchman threw his head back and basked in a gentle breeze.

'Man, that's sweet.'

Akingbola checked out the view.

'Dude. Better take a look at this.'

A steep gradient leading down to dunes. They hadn't reached the mountains. They were sitting on an island of rock. Another hundred yards of desert before they reached the comparative safety of the Panamint Range.

'A short sprint,' said Akingbola.

'Yeah.'

'Cross it in a few seconds.'

'Yeah.'

'Can't imagine any those infected fucks followed us all the way out here. Crazy to think they'd be lurking in the dust like freakin' piranhas.'

Trenchman nodded.

'We ought to rest a moment, get our strength back. Then make the run.'

They sat a while and relished the parched desert breeze. Trenchman looked up at the sky.

'I've been trying to make sense of it. Infected burrowing beneath the sand. Must be hiding from the sun. I mean, lizards and snakes burrow to escape the desert heat, right? Maybe these bastards are trying to prolong their lives. Wouldn't last a day or two in the open. Their bodies would putrefy, their brains would cook in their skulls. So they head below ground.'

'Hard to credit them with that kind of intelligence.'

'Maybe the virus is thinking on their behalf. Maybe it has a game plan.'

Akingbola shook his head.

'It's a disease, no better than gonorrhoea. It doesn't follow any grand strategy.'

They stood and stretched, shook out tired limbs.

'Ready?'

'Yeah. Fuck it.'

Akingbola got fifty yards before an emaciated hand erupted from the sand, gripped his leg and began to haul him below ground.

'It's got me. It's fucking got me.'

Trenchman doubled back. He fired into the sand. He grabbed Akingbola's arms and pulled.

Akingbola's leg jerked free, minus a boot. He got to his feet. He slapped Trenchman on the back:

'Go. Just go.'

Trenchman ran. He covered the last fifty yards tensed like a sprint across a minefield: each footfall a coin-flip with death.

He headed for a vertiginous cliff face, the point where jagged limestone crags rose from the desert dust.

He covered the last few feet convinced he would, at any moment, be snatched beneath the sand.

He gripped a boulder, hauled himself up onto its grit-dusted surface. He scrambled one-eighty, intending to offer Akingbola a hand, but the guy wasn't there. He was a hundred yards away, sitting on the outcrop they just fled.

Trenchman cupped his hands.

'What the hell are you doing?'

Akingbola pointed to his torn and bloodied pant leg.

'I got bit,' he shouted.

Trenchman sat head in hands. Tired, defeated.

'Sorry I dragged you out here. Didn't have the right.'

'No sweat,' shouted Akingbola. 'It's a fucked-up world. Nobody's fault. Just the way it is.'

They sat, looking at each other, separated by a hundred yards of sand.

'You better get going,' shouted Akingbola. He gestured to the rock face. 'Sunset. You don't want to climb that thing in the dark.'

Trenchman nodded.

Akingbola pulled a miniature bottle of rum from his pack and twisted the cap with a gloved hand. He stood at the jagged peak of the atoll and raised the bottle in salute.

'Take it easy, bro.'

'And you.'

Trenchman stood, turned and started to climb.

CAUTION

ROCKFALL

KEEP OUT

30

Moonlit rocks.

Trenchman pulled himself upwards ledge by ledge. Gloved hands brushed grit aside to clear handholds. He looked down at the crags below. Icy lunar light messed with perspective.

Timeless terrain. Easy to imagine Palaeolithic man scaling the heights to chew a psychotropic root and commune with the savage gods of the wilderness. Maybe, in daylight, these rocks would reveal themselves to be stained with ochre handprints, representations of horses and hunting kills, the petroglyph dream-life of men that lived in the penumbral regions of the desert.

His ascent blocked by vertical rock spurs. Smooth, nothing to grip. He couldn't climb higher, so he worked sideways, headed right, clambering one shelf to another.

Some kind of mine entrance. A cave mouth framed by prop beams. Dug by prospectors looking to strike borax, or locate a uranium seam.

Trenchman shone his flashlight into the darkness. Jumbled rubble. Tunnel collapse a few yards inside the shaft.

Good place to rest. A chance to shelter from a cold desert wind.

He lowered himself to the ground, shuffled his ass to get comfortable and leant back against one of the prop beams.

He thought about the journey west. Maybe he would find

water in the mountains. Somewhere, in a shaded canyon, he might stumble upon a rockpool.

Half-remembered advice from survival class: if you find a basin of deliciously clear water, don't drink. Could be tainted with sulphur or arsenic. If, on the other hand, you discover a pool green with algae, then the water is probably free of toxins, so drink hearty.

He drowsed, pleased that he was thinking straight and true, had yet to succumb to the manias and night terrors that could play out during prolonged isolation.

Faint noise.

Shifting grit. Skittering stones.

Couldn't see a damned thing. Too dark. Maybe he disturbed a desert critter, something that made the mine entrance its home.

Clattering stones. Rubble mounded against the shaft wall began to shift and bulge. An emaciated, dust-caked figure slowly pulling itself free as if reluctantly emerging from deep hibernation.

The creature drew itself fully upright and stepped clear of the rubble pile.

It stood over Trenchman. It reached for him.

Trenchman snatched the pistol from his holster and fired. Three shots, centre of mass. Muzzle flash lit the rotted revenant in a series of freeze-frame contortions as bullet hits sent it stumbling backwards out the mine entrance into moonlight. A red jumpsuit. A skeletal, eyeless face. Something buckled round each wrist as if the thing had broken free from heavy restraints.

Two more bullet strikes nudged the creature to the cliff edge.

Headshot. The figure toppled over the ledge, and fell out of view. Muffled sound of impact somewhere below.

Trenchman slowly got to his feet. He edged towards the

lip of the stone shelf. He switched on his flashlight, leaned over the precipice and trained the beam downwards.

The body lay forty feet below, sprawled face down on rocks.

White stencil on the back of the jumpsuit:

NEVADA
DEPT OF
CORRECTIONS

Clatter of stones from the rock face high above him.

Trenchman quickly shut off his flashlight. He stepped back and pressed against the rock wall, willed himself to become a shadow. He stood still as he could. He held his breath.

Skitter of shifting gravel to his far left.

Might be grit displaced by a scorpion or snake. Might be frost-shattered scree shifting, settling, of its own accord. Or it might be a rotted, skeletal thing prowling the ridges above his position, searching for a route down.

Trenchman ducked beneath the cross-beam of the mine entrance and crouched in darkness. He trained his pistol on the moonlit entrance, ready for whatever might come.

BOUNDRY - NO STEP

31

Frost stood on the ridgeline and watched the sun descend towards the western horizon.

Noble climbed the dune and joined her.

'I'll head out in an hour,' he said.

'Be another cold night.'

'Then I better not stop to rest.'

'I'll explain the situation to Hancock when you're gone.'

'He won't like it.'

'Not much he can do,' said Frost. 'He's in no shape to chase you down.'

'His head wound smells pretty cankerous.'

'I'll remind him you're his best shot at survival.'

'Reckon you'll be okay?' asked Noble.

'Bring back one of those SUVs. We can drive out of this damned desert, find a pharmacy, maybe hook up with a MASH. Shit, if Hancock is still set on detonating the bomb we can toss him the keys once we reach safety and let him drive back here. Fucker can do as he likes.'

'I don't like to leave you two alone together. Watch your ass, all right? Not sure the guy is thinking too clear.'

The flight deck.

They sat cross-legged on the floor.

Hancock solemnly broke an energy bar and shared it like he was re-enacting the Last Supper.

Noble turned the hunk of granola between his fingers.

'Right now, I want a cheeseburger more than I've wanted anything my whole life.'

'Ever eaten lizard?' asked Frost. 'I hear they taste like tuna.'

Hancock glanced at the cockpit windows. Amber light.

'Sundown in an hour or two,' he said. 'Ought to pack. Figure how to remove the warhead and carry it to the sled.'

Frost didn't meet his eye. She examined a split nail.

'I'll load a backpack,' said Noble. 'Bottle as much water as we can carry.'

'Well, best get to it. We'll need food. Survival blankets. Might be worth bringing the trauma kit. And don't forget the map.'

'I'm on it, boss.'

'Navigation should be easy enough. We'll head for Capricorn. Adjust our heading five degrees an hour to compensate for natural deviation. That should keep us on the right heading.'

'Okay.'

'I'll remove the core element from the missile. The warhead itself weighs less than a hundred pounds. We'll strap it to the sled, take turns to pull.'

Frost looked like she wanted to argue but Noble threw a glance, a barely perceptible shake of the head. *Just let the guy talk.*

Hancock got to his feet, stumbled and gripped the wall.

'I'll need your help down in the bomb bay, lieutenant.'

'Be with you directly, sir.'

Frost stepped outside.

Daylight curdled red. The low sun cast long shadows. Her silhouette stretched across the sand.

She tied the sleeves of her flight suit round her waist and tucked the Beretta into the waistband.

She lifted the nuclear authorisation lanyard from around

her neck. She snapped the plastic tab, extracted the code slip, and hurled the spent lanyard as far as she could.

She unfolded laminate paper. The authorisation sequence. Ten digits that would arm the nuclear device, transform a canister of rare metals into a new sun.

She held the slip in her hand, felt the power that resided within the row of inked symbols.

She flicked open her Zippo and wafted the flame beneath the paper. The slip browned and caught alight. Text blackened and shrivelled. She let the paper burn down to her fingers, dropped the stub and kicked it beneath the sand.

Noble emerged from the plane. He bent and double-tied his boots. Then he stood and shouldered the backpack.

'Guess it's time to leave,' he said.

They embraced. They stood back and looked at each other.

'*Via con Dios*, brother,' said Frost. 'Don't forget about us, all right? Once you reach the world, come get us, you hear?'

He nodded, smiled, adjusted straps.

'Back before you know.'

He set out, big strides, crested a high dune. He glanced back, parting wave, then dropped out of sight.

Frost stood alone and contemplated his footprints in the sand.

CAUTION

LIQUID

OXYGEN

NO SMOKING

WITHIN 50 FEET

KEEP FREE FROM
OIL AND GREASE

FOR BREATHING
PURPOSES ONLY

32

Moonrise. Dunes lit ice-white.

Residual day heat quickly radiated into a cloudless sky. Skin chill. Each exhalation fogged the air. Noble zipped his flight suit to the neck.

He was awash with adrenalin, tempted to break into a run, try to cover as much ground as he could before morning.

'Calm the hell down,' he told himself. 'You're a rational man, a trained professional. You got a solid plan. Stick to it.'

Machine mode. Steady respiration. Breathe from the diaphragm. Inhale: three paces. Exhale: three paces. He zoned out and let his body eat miles.

He knew better than to sing or hum. If he summoned a tune it could easily turn into a tormenting earworm he couldn't shake no matter how hard he tried. An endurance lesson learned during Basic. Pre-dawn reveille. Hauling himself across an assault course in cold morning light. High wall, water trench, belly-crawl under wire. The unmastered mind will break and fail long before physical collapse.

He wanted to pause and tighten the straps of his backpack but knew if he stopped for any reason, sat a while to sip from his canteen or relace his boots, he might be crippled by lactic acid. His limbs would seize, leaving him unable to walk another step.

He monitored the rotation of the constellations. Figured he'd been walking four, five hours. The wrecked B-52 lay far behind.

He strode the first mile fast as he could, in case Hancock

put up a star shell and tried to chase him down. Didn't know the guy well enough to predict how Hancock would react once he discovered he'd split. He might regard him as a mutineer and, in his fury, climb a high dune and lose a few shots from his Beretta. A mile would put him out of reach.

He tried hard not to think of the vast aridity around him. An implacably hostile landscape. Three-sixty desolation.

Absolute silence.

Absolute stillness.

A barren sea of silica.

The death-dry plains of an alien world.

Mixture of terror and exhilaration. Marooned, yet absolute master of his fate.

He looked up at the sky. Wheeling constellations. Scorpio, Cassiopeia, Draco.

He was heading north-east towards Dry Bone Canyon. He looked up, used the handle of the Big Dipper to confirm the position of the North Star. It would be visible most of the night, shifting position approximately fifteen degrees each hour. He would take precise compass readings every three hours.

He tried to imagine what lay over the horizon ahead of him. A way to fill monotonous hours.

The reconnaissance photograph showed SUVs and a couple of house trailers. Perhaps it marked the establishment of a permanent military site. An advance team staking out the ground-plan of a secure compound to be built far from urban pandemonium.

He pictured crew cabins, generators, sealed food, jerry cans of water.

He might find fresh underwear. He might find toiletries on a bathroom shelf, a chance to freshen up and shave, foam the dust from his hair, wipe the fried-onion stink from his armpits.

Most of all, he wanted to find a vehicle with a full tank of gas and keys in the ignition. Big, black government SUV with tinted windows. A sweet journey back to *Liberty Bell*: blast the air con, crank the music, relish soft leather seats.

He tried to recall a Discovery Channel doc he once saw about the Paris/Dakar. Bunch of rich guys bouncing dunes in a tricked out Mitsubishi Pajero. A half-remembered tip for driving through desert: bleed air from your tyres. Wider they spread, less likely the vehicle will bed down.

Absurd wish? A fuelled automobile waiting for him to climb inside and turn the key to IGN? What the hell. About time they caught a break.

He kept walking.

Easy to picture old-time settlers crossing the dunes, trying to make is west. Near-dead horses hauling covered wagons merciless miles. Gaunt, hollow-eyed men and women, reins in their hands, praying for the landscape to change, anxious for any hint of vegetation.

They might be beneath his feet right now. Consumed by the landscape. Submerged cartwheels and planks. Horse skulls and tackle. Coffee pots and griddles. Boots, bonnets and bone.

His canteen hung from a lanyard slung from his shoulder. He uncapped and took a single swig, rolled the water round his mouth, sluiced cheek-to-cheek, finally swallowed. He licked the neck of the canteen in case a droplet of moisture hung from the screw thread, then recapped.

Eyes fixed on the starlight horizon. Part of him prayed for daybreak and rest. But it would be tough to sleep during the day. Heat would put him in a delirium. Physical exhaustion replaced by mental torment.

He began to fear the wilderness went on for ever. Boundless dunes, like he was lost within some kind of simulation. A game environment. A world built from code. Each time he crested a ridge a new section of virtual terrain, a wire-frame scaffold overlaid with plates of sand texture, would snap into being. The landscape would curl on itself like a Möbius

225

strip. Walk long enough and he'd find himself back at the plane, back where he began.

He shook his head, tried to arrest his free-spinning imagination and return to the present.

How long had he been walking? A long while. Didn't necessarily mean he'd covered much ground. Wading through soft sand. Laboriously hauling himself to the top of each dune. His calves and ankles burned.

He reconsidered his decision not to stop for rest. He wanted to cover as much ground as possible before sunrise. But if he drove himself to walk ten hours straight he might collapse.

Ought to conserve some energy for the following night. And the night after.

Better stop a moment and eat.

He came to a halt and stretched. Didn't want to sit down. If he sat down his legs might stiffen up, make it impossible to walk.

He tore open a protein bar.

The eastern sky had begun to lighten. He must have walked most of the night. Might be able to cover a couple more miles before sunrise. Then he would have to pitch camp, arrange a survival blanket as a parasol.

He finished the energy bar and pocketed the wrapper.

He blew to warm his fingers.

He allowed himself another sip of water.

He reslung the canteen over his shoulder, tried to ignore the slosh of liquid that signalled the declining water level within the canteen.

A glance back. A trail of footprints receded to the horizon.

He touched his toes, swung his arms, then resumed his journey. He strode double-pace to cover as much ground as he could before sun-up, mouthed '. . . one, two, three, one, two, three . . .' to set a rhythm.

He crested a high dune, and found a limousine.

STAND CLEAR DURING
SPOILER OPERATION

33

Frost stumbled through the tear in the cabin wall. Her flight suit snagged and tore.

She hurriedly shunted equipment trunks against the aperture, sealing it shut.

Frantic scramble up the ladder to the flight deck. She disregarded jarring pain from her injured leg.

She threw herself into the pilot seat and pulled down the blast curtains, blocking out a blood-red sunset.

Hancock climbed the ladder and switched on cabin lights.

'What's going on?' he asked.

Frost ejected her pistol mag and thumbed bullets into her palm. Four rounds. She reloaded, chambered, sat clutching the gun.

'Seriously. What's the deal?'

Frost sat, panting hard.

Hancock crouched beside her. He clicked his fingers for attention.

'Hey. Lieutenant. Look at me.'

She looked at him. She slowly got her breathing under control, regained her composure, ashamed of her panic.

'We need light,' said Frost. 'Lots of light. We should dig trenches and fill them with fuel. Circle the plane with fire.'

'Slow down. What the hell is going on? Are we under attack?'

'The bastards are out there, circling the plane.'

'You saw them?'

'Fuckers are getting bold. It's like they got a purpose, a schedule.'

'What did they look like?'

'Pinback, Guthrie, Early.'

'You saw their faces?'

'They've come for us.'

'Slow down,' said Hancock. 'I've seen thousands of infected bastards. So have you. They're dumb. They got the intelligence of an earthworm. They don't stalk their prey.'

'Maybe there are different grades, like ants. Drones. Soldiers. Queens.'

'It's a fucking virus. A protein chain. A string of RNA. It doesn't have a social structure. It can't dictate tactics, strategies.'

'It out-flanked humanity without much trouble.'

Hancock struggled to his feet.

'Show me. I need to see for myself.'

The dying light of day.

Hancock staggered across the sand. He stumbled and fell. Frost reluctantly left the plane, gripped his arm and helped him upright.

She kept her pistol drawn, fearful of the gathering gloom.

'Where were they?'

'Over there. The ridgeline. Moving east, like they were on some kind of patrol.'

'Sure it was Pinback and the guys?'

'Yeah.'

'Where's Noble? Did he see any of this?'

'He's gone.'

'The fuck?'

'He went for help.'

'Dammit. We got a job. A mission.'

'He's headed for the target site. Figured he might be able to find something of use. A truck. A radio that actually works.'

They stood by the wing, weapons drawn, surveying shadows which seemed to lengthen and reach for them.

'This is fucked up,' murmured Hancock. 'We're through the looking glass. We're into nightmares.'

'Keep your eyes peeled.'

'I'm not even going to blink.'

They circled the wing, crouched and shone their flashlights into deep darkness.

They inspected the engine, examined the intake turbine and exhausts.

'You think they were fucking with the plane?' asked Frost.

'They got to be somewhere close by. Maybe they've built themselves a nest.'

They climbed onto the wing and peered into tears in the aluminium skin, inspected internal spars, control lines and fuel tanks looking for a telltale smear of blood.

'Look,' said Frost. She crouched and trained her flashlight on the wing surface. 'See?'

Footprints.

They slid from the wing and dropped to the sand below.

They walked the length of the wrecked aircraft.

Hancock examined tears in the buckled hull.

Frost kept her flashlight trained on the roof of the plane in case they got jumped.

The broken tail section. Buckled support struts and fluttering insulation foil.

Frost shone her flashlight over surrounding dunes.

'Hey. Look.'

Prints trailed across the sand. The tracks terminated in a small depression.

'Looks like they went below ground,' said Hancock.

The lower cabin.

They shunted equipment trunks against the wall fissure once more to create a barricade.

They leant against the ladder, wiped sweat and shared sips from a canteen.

'Ought to check the bomb bay,' said Frost. 'Make sure the package is secure.'

Hancock switched on his flashlight and climbed into the crawlway. He inched along on his hands and knees until he reached the payload door.

He pulled back the hatch and peered inside. His flashlight played over the ribbed walls of the compartment, the massive rotary launcher, the missile.

'Are we cool?' called Frost.

Hancock didn't reply. He climbed from the crawlspace and stood in the stifling cave-dark.

He flicked the light switch. Red night-mission lamps.

He cautiously crept the length of the compartment, murmuring.

He checked the launch apparatus, checked wall stanchions and roof girders.

'You all right in there?' called Frost.

'Yeah,' said Hancock. 'Yeah, we're clear.'

The flight deck.

They sat facing each other.

'Let's think it through,' said Hancock. 'Guthrie was infected for sure, right?'

'Yeah. Advanced stages of infection. The rot, the spines. Must have been pretty far gone when he climbed aboard the plane. Looking back, he had his suit zipped to his neck and gloves on his hands during the briefing. Didn't think much of it at the time.'

'You shot him in the head.'

'Yeah. Took a pretty big chunk of skull and brain. But maybe not enough to take him out the game. Plenty of frontal lobe damage, but it's not like these bastards need much higher brain function. His cortex might be intact. Basic motor skills. Enough to keep him animated.'

'So he could be walking around out there.'

'There's a chance.'

'Pinback. You saw him die, right? Crash injuries.'

'His spine was shattered. Guess he died of organ failure. The internal haemorrhaging and tissue cavitation associated with a massive impact. But his body might have been fresh enough to host the virus, if he were infected soon after death. Maybe Guthrie got to him, brought him back to some kind of life.'

'And we got no idea what happened to Early. So we got at least three potential prowlers out there.'

'Reckon so.'

'Think they're toying with us? Fucking with our heads?'

'Not dealing with people any more. Dealing with a virus. Can't attribute human motivations. No telling what it's got in mind.'

Hancock lifted a blast screen and stared out into the night.

'Why don't they attack?' he murmured. 'Perfect opportunity to take us out.'

'Maybe they went after Noble. He's out there alone. Easy prey.'

FWD →

34

Noble skidded down the lee side of a dune in an avalanche of dust.

The white Humvee limo.

Under his breath:

'What the fuck?'

He circled the vehicle. It was smashed up. A couple of windows were broken. Need a tow truck to get it moving.

He ran a finger along a rubber window seal. Thick accumulation of dust. The limo had been sitting in the desert a while.

The driver's door was open. Noble peered inside. A dead guy slumped on the passenger seat.

Heart stopping thrill as he glimpsed Diet Coke in the door pocket. Anger when he lifted the can and found it drained dry. He scrunched the can and threw it aside.

He climbed inside the vehicle.

He checked the steering column. No ignition key.

He checked out the dead guy. Mismatched fatigues. Desert boots, G-Shock, pocket vest, ballistic wraparounds. One of Trenchman's rag-tag contingent.

Noble pulled on gloves and searched the body. Pat down: SOG multitool in a belt pouch, couple of cigars in a breast pocket, pistol but no ammo.

Dog tags:

OSBORNE.

O NEG.

The guy had been shot in the back where he sat. A bullet had ripped a big exit wound in his belly and hit the dash, punching a hole in the facia of the Bose five-point surround.

Noble reached across and released the passenger door. He kicked the corpse out the car into the dust.

Sunlight through the sunroof, the side windows. Daybreak. The temperature was already beginning to climb. Better use this unexpected refuge, this gift of shade, before moving on at nightfall.

He climbed over the driver partition into the rear.

Dead plasmas. Bent stripper pole. Empty mini-bar.

He swept a coach seat free of dust and empty vodka miniatures. He sat down, unlaced his boots and massaged sore feet.

He took *The Little Prince* from his backpack and tenderly turned pages.

To Malcolm, Have a very happy birthday, All my love, Dad.

He lay down and positioned his backpack for a pillow.

Motes of dust swirled and swarmed in the heavy air of the passenger compartment.

He hugged the book to his chest and closed his eyes. If he slowed his breathing, imposed stillness on a restless body, perhaps he would sleep until darkness fell.

Nightfall.

Noble trudged across the moonlit sandscape. He tried to estimate ground covered the previous night. He had kept a steady pace for hours. Ten miles? Twenty? Easy to overestimate distance. Delude himself a moderate stroll had been an epic trek.

He swung his arms, blew fingers to warm his hands.

Knees and ankles fatigued from the exertion of wading through dust.

He set up a rhythm. Inhale: three paces. Exhale: three

paces. He tried to shorten his strides to minimise muscular effort.

Getting close to the Panamint Range. Crags and mesas blotted the stars.

The horizon up ahead was sharply delineated by the scintillating starfields of the Milky Way. Jagged peaks. But behind him, the southern sky was a soft blur. He glanced back once in a while to make sure the haze was not an approaching weather front: one of the desert's rare downpours. But the fog remained constant. Maybe Vegas was burning. A vast atomic plume that would darken the sky for months.

Daylight.

Wind blew across the dustscape. Dunes fumed like banks of smouldering coals.

Noble strode across infernal, brimstone terrain.

Curling vortices of sand. He needed water, but didn't dare uncap his canteen in case it filled with dust.

The desert used to be a seabed. There were small shell fragments among the quartz particles, the shifting mineral powder. He was wading through primordial silt. The granular remains of bones and carapaces, detritus of the old ocean floor.

Vertiginous sense of geologic time.

Maybe some future tectonic upheaval would drain the Pacific and flood the mainland. Ruined cities, submerged apartments and office buildings, would become home to darting fish and colonies of crustaceans. The sunless depths of the Mariana Trench would be transformed to a sun-baked, bone-dry canyon.

The wind tore away his face mask. He chased the scrap of chute fabric, dove to retrieve it. He spat, purged a mouthful of dust, then tied the mask back in place.

He looked around. The wind had erased his footprints.

He looked up. Orange twilight. Hard to locate the sun.

No way to navigate. No way to strike out without potentially retracing his steps and undoing the effort of the last few hours.

He sat cross-legged in the sand. He took a survival blanket from the pocket of his flight suit and flapped it open. He wrestled against the wind, pulled the blanket over his head and shoulders, and cocooned himself in Mylar.

He crouched within his foil shroud. He battled claustrophobia. A silver, storm-lashed effigy perched on the side of a dune, lost in vast nothing.

CAUTION

FAST ACTING DOORS DISCONNECT ACTUATOR STRUT BOTH ENDS BEFORE WORKING IN BOMB BAY AREA.

35

Frost leaned from the fissure in the cabin wall and looked out into the desert.

She scanned the dunes for any sign of movement. She crouched and peered beneath the starboard wing.

Silence. Stillness.

She had improvised trip flares: marine pyros lashed to a couple of plastic rulers with duct tape. She staked them in the sand. Monofilament fishing line tied to the ring-pulls, unreeled, pulled taut. Any prowlers approaching the nose of the aircraft would trigger a series of concussions like canon fire.

Best seal the plane. Shut out any potential intruders.

She shunted equipment trunks against the fissure and blocked merciless light.

The payload bay.

Red night-mission lights. Trapped heat.

Hancock inspected the missile. He pulled a bandana from his pocket. He dabbed sweat from his face and towelled his hands.

Tools laid out on the ALCM hull like a row of surgical instruments.

He had released a tubular section of casing, fully exposed the physics package and surrounding control electronics.

Brief pause before he began the delicate procedure of disconnecting the core from the weapon's redundant guidance system. The GPS gear and TERCOM terrain correlator had to be cut in sequence to avoid tripping a tamper cut-out.

'How's it going?' called Frost. She was in the lower cabin, peering down twenty feet of crawlway.

'Okay.'

'Still messing with that warhead?'

'That's right.'

'Radiation?'

'Negligible.'

'There are lock-outs, aren't there? Screw up, and the bomb will disarm itself.'

'There's a kill-switch. Stops the device falling into enemy hands in the event of a crash landing on foreign soil. Pull. Turn. The firing circuits fry themselves. The weapon instantly transformed into a giant paperweight.'

'Don't suppose you'd care to show me that switch?'

'Can't say I would.'

Boredom.

Hancock sat in the pilot seat. Windows blacked out by blast screens like he was flying a night patrol.

He drowsed, slowed his breathing, kept still as he could. A tear of sweat ran from his bandaged scalp, down his temple into beard stubble. He ignored it.

Cruising at the edge of sleep. Each time his head nodded forwards he heard phantom engine alerts, stall warnings. He smelled smoke, the sulphurous stink of shorting fuse banks. He felt the judder and shake of the plane shaking itself apart.

He jerked awake and grabbed the yoke.

Frost lay on the deck of the lower cabin.

She tried to think her way cooler.

She opened her mouth wide and exhaled, visualising each breath as a rippling jet of expelled body heat. Sweltering discomfort purged from her lungs leaving her cool and rested.

She let her imagination transport her from the desert.

The Sierras.

Kayaking down a wooded valley. A double-blade paddle. Gentle oar splash, left and right. Ponderosa pines on either bank. Trout darting beneath the boat. Osprey wheeling in the sky. Each bend in the river, each serpentine twist, revealed fresh scenes of verdant wilderness to explore.

She opened her eyes and sat up.

She needed a piss.

Frost crouched, flight suit unzipped, pistol in her hand.

Urine splashed and frothed in the dust. Almost instant evaporation. Dark, wet sand dried pristine white in seconds.

A person dead-set on survival would, she supposed, store urine. Squat over a mess tin then decant liquid into a bottle. But no matter what happened she couldn't put a stale, part-fermented bottle of piss to her lips and drink. Rather eat a bullet than let herself be dehumanised by the futile struggle to survive an extra couple hours.

She stood and zipped her suit.

Cruel heat baked the plane metal, baked the sand.

She and Hancock would run out of water in a few days. They would lie in the shattered aircraft wracked by fierce kidney pain and shivering chills, visited by dead friends, relatives, lovers. A bunch of wailing, leering apparitions spitting accusations and reproach. The madness would last for a couple of hours. Then, without being aware, they would slide into a merciful coma and death.

Maybe, once she had shaken the last drops of water from her canteen, she should take a walk among the dunes to speed her demise. Kick off her boots, shrug off the warrior carapace of flight suit and equipment yoke, and walk naked into the sun.

She stepped out of shadow into merciless light, flinched as searing radiation hit her face.

She climbed a high ridge, shielded her eyes with her Beretta and surveyed the terrain for any sign of Noble. She wanted to see a 4x4 heading her way, lurching over dunes. A SUV kicking up a dust plume. Hum of a distant engine. Glint of sunlight on glass and chromium trim.

Nothing.

The distant horizon merged with rippling fata morganas that shimmered silver-wet like distant ocean.

They rebuilt the barricade and climbed to the flight deck.

They sat opposite sides of the cabin, backs to the wall.

Hancock: the improvised bandaged wrapped round his head was stained with pus and blood. Stubble turning to beard.

Frost: crazy, sand-dusted hair, peeling skin, cracked lips.

'Long fucking day,' said Hancock.

Frost nodded.

Her eye was drawn to the trauma kit. A clear bag of saline protruded from a zippered pouch. The liquid sparkled as it refracted sunlight, like the surface of a lake inviting her to dive and swim. Tempted to pierce the bag with the tip of her knife and suck on it like a tit, guzzle salted water until the bag crumpled dry. She blinked to dispel the reverie.

'Looks like we're fucked,' said Hancock. 'Noble should have reached the target site by now. If there were serviceable vehicles to be found, he would be back already.'

Frost ignored him. Hancock seemed to revel in their predicament, seemed anxious to discuss every catastrophic possibility. She just wanted to rest.

'How's your head?' she asked. The side of Hancock's face was dark and swollen. She could smell rot. He didn't seem to be infected by the virus. He was succumbing to septicaemia. They needed to make it to a pharmacy, find some antibiotics. 'Want me to take a look at that wound?'

'Can't see the use.'

They sat a while.

'So how long do you intend to wait?' asked Hancock.

'For Noble? A while yet. He's got a long way to walk. Lot of rough ground. Might take him a few days. Can't give up on the guy just yet.'

'How much water has he got?'

'Some.'

'And if he doesn't show up? What then? Given any thought?'

'Walk.'

'What the use?' asked Hancock. 'You're lame. Those fucks hiding in the dunes would attack before you got a mile from here.'

'Maybe.'

'They'll be back for sure, once the sun goes down.'

'And we'll be waiting.'

Hancock shifted position, tried to get comfortable.

'We still got a mission,' he said. 'We still got something to achieve.'

'Don't start with that shit.'

'We could make it to the target. You and me. Cover each other's back. We could hold off those fuckers long enough to deliver the bomb.'

'This whole kamikaze deal is turning into some kind of freakin' monomania. You're fucked up. You fall on your ass every couple of steps. You aren't going anywhere. Let it go.'

'I'm still AC. Remember that.'

'Come on. Chain-of-command doesn't mean a thing out here. The badge on your sleeve isn't worth a damn. You're like some shipwrecked guy on a desert island, driven mad by solitude. Crowns himself emperor of all he surveys. Sits on his bamboo throne, all regal and ragged. Lord of the Coconuts. King of the Crabs. I mean look around you, Jim. Aircraft Commander? There's no aircraft to command. Just a pile of half-buried scrap.'

'How do you want to die, Frost? That's the only latitude

we got left. We get to choose. A luxury most folks didn't have these past months. Think back. Took a lot of guts to get those wings, right? A lot of sweat. The Academy. The graduation salute. LaNitra Frost. Officer of the United States Air Force. Flew these birds for Uncle Sam, and proud of it. Used to mean something. So why not put on war paint one last time? There's a battle to be fought.'

'No there isn't. Remember those Japanese soldiers that hid in the jungle for decades because they didn't know Hirohito surrendered? That's us, right now, marooned, fighting a lost fucking cause.'

'I still believe in you,' said Hancock. 'That's the tragedy. I can see the officer you used to be. Wish I could hold up a mirror, make you understand.'

He drew his pistol, chambered and cocked. He pointed the weapon at Frost's head, aimed with his one remaining eye.

They stared each other down. Hancock's unblinking gaze lining the front and rear sights.

'What the hell are you doing?' said Frost.

'Take out your side arm. Do it slow.'

She thought about it, tried to get the measure of the man's resolve.

He let her see his finger whiten on the trigger.

She pinched the butt of her pistol between thumb and forefinger, and lifted it clear of the holster.

'Eject the clip.'

She slid the magazine across the deck towards him.

'And the gun.'

She span it across the floor.

'Good. Now give me the authorisation code.'

244

36

Noble clambered across the rockface. He worked north, shuffled ledge to ledge. His arms burned with fatigue. His fingers cramped.

A low sun threw long shadows, turned the crags and boulders rich caramel. He could already see the moon in a darkening sky. A minor boon in a string of catastrophes: at least he would have good visibility tonight.

High above the desert. Could almost see the curvature of the earth.

An hour since he woke. He had spent the day on a plateau, curled in the shadow of a boulder. A febrile semi-sleep. He had an eagle's eye view of the desert. The centre of the limestone outcrop had been burned black by camp-fires. The place had almost certainly been used as a vantage point by native Americans. Bet if he kicked around in the dust he would unearth flint arrowheads. If he climbed higher he would find rocks stained with alien, aniconic art. Handprints and swirls. Markers left by aboriginals who climbed to this remote elevation to commune with gods and vultures.

The plan: head north across the mountainside. Sooner or later he would find himself overlooking the aim point, the site targeted for destruction. He guessed he'd know it when he saw it. Must be something out here, some kind of significant installation.

Faint clatter of rocks to his left.

He looked up, studied the crags and ledges above. Trickling dust.

Couldn't shake the skin-crawling sensation of being watched, the suspicion his steps had been dogged by an unseen presence ever since he reached the Range. He hoped any infected that might be haunting the mountainside wouldn't develop the smarts to roll a boulder on his head.

A mine entrance. Truck rails. A couple of yards of shaft, then rubble.

He picked a tin DANGER sign from the ground and wiped away dust.

ANACONDA MINING CORP.

A shaft sunk by uranium prospectors looking for a seam. One of the few reasons a person would visit this blighted place.

Adventurers scoured the Panamints. They dynamited the cliffs and sifted scree, looking for a telltale sheen of gold. A fresh wave of chancers chipped samples with a rock hammer, scanned rubble with a Geiger rig, whooped like wildcatters when they struck a pocket of uranium ore. A Faustian deal. Euphoric prospectors would stake a claim with the county recorder, clothes matted with radioactive dust. A few years rolling in big money, then thyroid cancer.

Vague memories of *The Conqueror*, the god-awful Genghis Khan biopic staring John Wayne. Filmed in the desert downwind of the Upshot-Knothole nuclear tests, the night detonations that had Hughes-era tourists partying around the roof pools of their Vegas hotels, toasting the gamma flash as it lit the horizon like summer lightning. The crew spent a month filming their Mongol turkey. They erected a barbarian camp, marshalled a galloping hoard for the battle scenes, nursed embryonic carcinomas as they breathed dust tainted with lethal isotopes cooked in the radiant millisecond of fission.

The atomic desert. An implacably lethal environment.

Noble allowed himself a sip of water. His canteen was half empty. Another day, two at the most, and he would enter the terminal stages of dehydration. At which point he might as well eat a bullet, or swan-dive from a high crag.

He didn't feel scared. He'd bet his life on a roll of the dice, the gamble he would find salvation at the target site. It might be a vain hope. He might die out here in the barren wastes. But at least he would uncover the object of their mission, the reason they flew a cataclysmic payload into the desert.

Something on the ground near the mine entrance. Some kind of wrapper. He picked it up, squinted in the failing light.

An energy bar. Same brand Guthrie grabbed from the Vegas food store before the flight.

He examined the wrapper under the beam of his flashlight. Pristine. No accumulated dust.

Someone from the 2nd Bomb Wing must have spent the day in this mine entrance very recently. Someone from the limo.

He stepped outside and cupped his hands.

'Hello,' he shouted. 'Hello, anyone?'

His voice echoed back at him from surrounding crags and crevices. *Hello, anyone?*

'Anyone out there?

Anyone out there?

'Hey.'

Hey.

No reply.

He sat a while and listened to the night wind.

Noble stood on a high ledge and looked out over moonlit desert.

An installation on the desert floor beneath him. A wire-ringed compound. Hard to make out details. Vehicles, trailers, geodesic tents. The place looked pretty smashed up.

He descended the mountain wall. He dropped ledge-to-ledge, slid down steep accumulations of scree kicking up a dust cloud.

Concrete pylons staked in the sand supported a nine-foot razor wire fence hung with volt-zag danger signs.

The main gates hung off their hinges.

Noble walked into the compound, stood in tyre-rutted sand and looked around. Spectral ruination. Moonlight and deep shadow. Wrecked accommodation units. Burned-out vehicles.

No movement. Deathly silence.

A shot-up guard booth near the gate. Ballistic glass frosted by bullet strikes, splattered with blood. A phone hung off the hook. Casings scattered underfoot. Looked like someone ran to the guard booth to summon for help, got mown down before the call could connect.

He shone his flashlight into an adjacent tent. A diesel generator. A 2500 kVA CAT, big as a van. Gunfire dings, but it seemed to be intact. The fuel level hung a couple of notches above zero.

Key Turn.

Screen menu: AUTO.

Green button: START.

The generator coughed smoke and fired up.

He backed out of the tent to escape exhaust fumes.

The compound floodlights buzzed and glowed with restored current. They lit the installation harsh white.

Some kind of Agency black site. Half a mile square, with a helipad at the centre. A bunch of bunkhouse cabins. Accommodation for about a hundred guys.

The place was a battle zone.

A bulldozer, presumably brought to the location to level and compact the ground prior to construction, had been used to trash dormitory huts and offices. The dozer had crushed the row of blockhouses flat. Splintered wood, flutter insulation, torn roof felt. Scattered mattresses and blankets matted with dust.

Four SUVs had flipped and burned like someone tossed grenades.

A bunch of airstream trailers riddled with bullet holes, methodically strafed by .50 cal.

A toppled flagpole lying across the chalk H of the helipad.

Pop and crackle from a bunch of pole-mounted tannoy horns, as if restored power had trigger a PA system. Faint hiss, then 'Surfin' USA'. Beach tunes echoing over war-torn desolation.

Noble followed tannoy cable snaking in the dust, hoping to find the installation main office and shut off the music.

One of the PA poles had been toppled by a chopper. The charred remains of a JetRanger lying on its side. The fuselage had been ripped open by an internal detonation. The doors were cratered by bullet strikes. It seemed like someone made a methodical attempt to wipe out the camp. Tossed grenades, destroyed every vehicle, every building, made sure no one could leave.

He sniffed the air.

The smell of incineration hung over the site. Burned synthetics. And behind it, the sweet stink of cooked flesh. He'd yet to see a single body but somewhere, close by, there was a corpse-pyre.

A truck lying on its side. Looked like it jackknifed and rolled.

A freight container had spilled from the trailer. It sat on its roof, doors ajar.

Noble pulled one of the doors wide and peered into the darkness of the container. Foul stink. He switched on a flashlight. Blood-smeared walls.

He stepped inside. Ceiling beneath his feet, floor above his head. Manacles hung down, swung and clinked. The place reeked of shit, desperation and death.

He crouched. Discarded blister packs. Vet tranquillisers.

A message scratched on the container wall:

GOD SAVE US ALL

Fig 1.

37

Frost spoke slow and clear, super-calm, placating a madman.

'I haven't got the code.'

Hancock lowered the pistol and took aim like he was about to put a bullet in Frost's good foot.

'Seriously, I swear I haven't got the code.'

'I think we've already established, by your willingness to disregard the oaths you took when you put on that uniform, your word isn't worth a damn.'

Frost cautiously reached up, unzipped her flight suit and pulled at her shirt to demonstrate nothing hung round her neck.

'Where is it?'

'I burned it.'

'Bullshit.'

'Check outside. The signal fire. You'll find the clasp somewhere in the ashes.'

'The code. The paper slip. You watched it burn?'

'To a crisp.'

'But you read it. You read the code before you set it alight.'

'No.'

Hancock smiled and shook his head.

'You're lying. You looked at the digits.'

'No.'

'The authorisation slip was sealed in a heavy plastic tag. In order to destroy the code you must have cracked open the tag and unfolded the paper. Only way to ensure the slip got totally incinerated. Which means, as you flicked open your Zippo and sparked a flame, you looked at the digits. You saw the code sequence, an instant before it burned. And now it's in your head. Just got to wheedle it out.'

'And how do you intend to do that? Hypnosis?'

Frost deploying a standard bar brawl distraction technique. The urge to completion.

Throw your glass in the air. Your opponent will watch its trajectory, wait for it to hit the floor and smash. Use the pause as an opportunity to aim a jab at their throat.

Or ask your opponent a question. *What the fuck did you call me?* Wait till they start to speak, then crush the bridge of their nose with the heel of your palm.

'I'm sure, given a big enough incentive, you can . . .'

Frost snatched up her crutch and lashed the pistol from his hand. The Beretta hit the wall and fell to the floor.

She drove the crutch into his face. Roar of pain and anger. Hancock snatched the crutch from her hand.

She lunged for the pistol. Hancock was crippled by pain, but managed to throw himself forwards and pin the weapon beneath his body, putting it out of her reach.

Frost scrambled for the ladderwell.

She pushed the barricade aside. Tumbling equipment cases. She stumbled into the sun, momentarily overwhelmed by heat and light.

She couldn't outrun Hancock. Too lame. Her only chance of safety: ambush the guy as he tried to hunt her down.

She quickly limped towards the ridgeline, then hurriedly retraced her path, matching her footprints like she was jumping stepping stones across a stream.

She reached the wing tip. She reached up, gripped the lips of the aerofoil and hauled herself onto the wing surface. She hobbled back towards the body of the plane, boots scuffing dusted metal.

The flight deck.

Hancock curled foetal and clutched his head. His hands were smeared red. He could feel his scalp wound through the chute-fabric bandage. Sutures binding torn flesh had ripped open. Fresh blood leaked from the improvised dressing.

He rolled onto his side and retrieved the pistol. He crawled to the ladderwell and part-climbed, part-fell to the cabin below.

He leant against the ragged metal of the wall fissure, shielded his eyes against the sun.

Footprints led across sand to the crest of the ridgeline.

He adjusted his grasp of the Beretta. His palm was gummed to the polymer butt-grip by blood. He stepped from the plane, but immediately brought himself to a halt.

Frost was smart. She wouldn't run into the desert leaving a follow-me trail of prints.

Stark shadows on the ground around him. The curve of the wing. The flag pole. His own silhouette, stretching across the sand ahead of him.

His attention was drawn by an irregularity in the wing shadow. A slight prominence, as if something were resting on the upper surface.

Hancock trained his pistol on the lip of the wing. He swayed. He leant against the fuselage to restore his aim.

He kept his attention trained on the wing while his left hand groped for the radio tucked in a chest pouch. He raised the handset to his mouth and keyed Transmit:

'Where are you, Frost?'

Frost lay on the starboard wing. Baking metal. Drops of sweat ran down her face, dripped from her nose, splashed on the dust-matted aluminium in front of her.

She gripped her knife. Palm-sweat greased the leather grip. Seven-inch blade poised to stab.

Crude plan: listen out for Hancock. The guy was messed up, struggling to stand. Laboured breathing, dragging steps. He couldn't move around without making a racket. She would wait until she heard him beneath the wing, then jump his ass.

Rustle of flight-suit fabric. Muffled cough. Hancock had emerged from the plane and was standing close by.

She listened hard, tried to gauge his location.

Silence.

Had he moved away? Was he creeping around the wreck site, trying to hunt her down? Or was he standing still, stifling his breath, waiting for her to make a move?

Faint crackle. Her radio. The static squelch that preceded an incoming transmission. She quickly rolled onto her chest-pouch to smother the sound.

Muffled radio voice mixing with Hancock's voice from down below:

'Where are you, Frost?'

She lay still as she could.

'Here kitty, kitty.'

She lay flat, pressed herself against hot aluminium, willed her body to merge with the wing.

Her POV: a vista of rivet-seamed metal rippling heat.

She waited. Long minutes.

She thought she could smell Hancock, just for a moment. The sour stink of flesh-rot carried on the breeze.

Did she actually want to kill him? The guy pulled a gun. But he was sick, clearly not thinking straight. Succumbing to fever and delirium. He needed help.

Never the less, she might have to cut Hancock in order to subdue him. She resolved to aim for muscle, if she could. Avoid major organs, major blood vessels.

Insidious voice in her head: *If you tussle over a gun, you*

*may have no option but to kill him. And then you could keep all
the remaining water for yourself.*

She lifted her head.

Slow commando crawl to the lip of the wing, sliding on sand-dusted metal. She psyched, prepped to launch and stab.

She reared up, knife raised above her head, then froze. Hancock was gone. A disturbance in the sand like he stepped from the plane, walked a couple of yards, then turned and headed back inside.

Voice from above:

'Be obliged if you dropped the knife.'

She looked up.

Hancock standing on the roof of the aircraft. The sun was behind him, his body fringed by a brilliant halo.

He must have returned to the flight deck and climbed through one of the vacant escape hatches.

Frost slowly got to her feet. She shielded her eyes.

'How about we call time-out?' said Frost. 'This bullshit is escalating way too fast. Maybe we should hit Pause, talk it through.'

'Drop the knife.'

'Really want to shoot me?'

'I need you alive and conscious. Rest is up to you.'

'These wings are full of kerosene vapour. Bullet might send us both to hell.'

Gunshot. A 9mm round punched a neat hole in the aluminium panel between Frost's feet. Wisp of smoke.

He took aim a second time.

'Ever played Russian Roulette?' said Hancock. Gunshot. Frost flinched. A second smouldering hole punched in the wing metal at her feet. 'Want to see how far our luck will hold?'

She threw the knife aside. It fell and stabbed deep into sand.

Code of Conduct

Article I: I am an American, fighting in the armed forces which guard my country and our way of life. I am prepared to give my life in their defense.

Article II: I will never surrender of my own free will. If in command I will never surrender the members of my command while they still have the means to resist.

Article III: If I am captured, I will continue to resist by all means available. I will make every effort to escape and aid others to escape. I will accept neither parole nor special favors from the enemy.

Article IV: If I become a prisoner of war, I will keep faith with my fellow prisoners. I will give no information nor take part in any action which might be harmful to my comrades. If I am senior, I will take command. If not, I will obey the lawful orders of those appointed over me and will back them up in every way.

Article V: When questioned, should I become a prisoner of war, I am required to give name, rank, service, number, and date of birth. I will evade answering further questions to the utmost of my ability. I will make no oral or written statements disloyal to my country and its allies or harmful to their cause.

Article VI: I will never forget that I am an American, responsible for my actions, and dedicated to the principles which made my country free. I will trust in my God and in the United States of America.

38

Hancock lashed Frost's wrists with wire. Gun to her back. He forced her to climb the ladder to the flight deck. They sat facing each other. Sullen silence.

Time passed slow.

'What do you hope to achieve by all this shit?' she asked.

'Encourage a little cooperation.'

She curled and pretended to doze.

She waited until Hancock's eyelid drooped closed and the pistol slackened in his hand. Finger light on the trigger, barrel angled at the floor.

She leaned forwards and reached for the gun. He shifted in his sleep. Brief hesitation. She abandoned her attempt to snatch the Beretta. She slid down the ladder and fled the plane once again.

She limped across the sand, hands still bound at the wrist.

She crawled up a dune and rolled down the shadow side. Her vague plan: travel in a wide arc. Put as much distance as she could between herself and the B-52. Create the illusion she had headed into the desert. A trail of footprints stretching to the horizon. She would then circle back to the wreck site in the early hours of the morning and plunder supplies. Creep into the lower cabin while Hancock lay beneath survival blankets in the cockpit. Stealthily remove food, meds, water. Then head east.

She tried to walk. Her legs gave out so she crawled on her knees.

Panting ascent of the next dune. Uncontrolled roll down the other side.

A splinter of her consciousness watched her progress with detached interest. How much pain could she endure? How much suffering could she shoulder while willing her limbs to keep moving forwards? When would her body finally fail, pitching her face-forwards in the sand, motionless, muscles finally no longer able to respond to her will?

She kept crawling. She threw a long shadow.

A second shadow by her side. A figure keeping pace.

'I admire your determination,' said Hancock. 'Hotter than hell. Crack an egg on the ground and watch it fry. Yet here you are. Exhausted, thirsty, broken. But determined to fight. Admirable.'

She rolled and looked up.

'It's a shame,' said Hancock. 'You put me in a difficult position.'

Hancock laid the crutch across Frost's shoulders like a yoke. He lashed her arms with wiring stripped from the flight-deck walls, forcing her cruciform.

He tied a length of data cable round her neck as a leash. He dragged her stumbling across the sand to the dead signal fire. A tyre half buried in sand. He tied the leash to the hub.

Shove to the back. She fell to her knees, head bowed, arms forced wide.

Hancock slowly circled.

'Hate to do it,' he said. 'But I can't have you running off again.'

He checked knotted wire, made sure she was bound tight.

'This can end any time you want. We can start treating each other as adults. All you have to do is cooperate.'

Frost didn't reply.

'It'll be a cold night. Any time you want to come back inside, holler. I got a blanket, if you're willing to work for it. Back in a while. Think it over.'

Hancock retreated to the plane for a couple of hours. He got some sleep.

He woke and decided to check on Frost.

She was still knelt in the sand, head bowed, arms pinned wide. Her skin and hair were white with dust. Her lips were cracked and dry.

Hancock sat crossed legged beside her. He sipped water. He made it torture. He slurped and smacked his lips. He sloshed the canteen.

'How are you feeling?'

She didn't look up. She didn't reply.

'I'm sorry. Appalled it came to this. Hoped we could resolve our issues by reasoned discussion.'

Frost licked parched lips.

'You pulled a gun.'

'Had no choice.'

'Cut me free.'

'You know I can't do that.'

'You've gone crazy. Think. Just think. Step back a moment. You must be able to see. This stopped being about the mission a long time ago. This is some kind of death trip.'

'I have to believe there's still a government out there, trying to salvage what's left of America.'

'Come on. That old tune. We're on our own. Anything else is a wish, a daydream. The best we can do for the world is survive.'

Hancock shook his head and turned away. He limped back to the plane.

'What about Guthrie?' shouted Frost. 'His buddies. You'll

261

need me. When they come. You'll need all the help you can get.'

He kept walking.

Hancock switched on the bomb bay light. Blood-red glow.

He sat on the sand floor of the payload compartment and powered up the satcom unit.

Internal battery at 18%. The power level dropped to 17% as he watched.

His only contact with the wider world: a thin-as-gossamer thread of data, likely to be cut within hours.

The unit winked an alert.

Incoming EAM:

URGENT
PROVIDE STATUS UPDATE

He typed:

RADAR NAV
UNCOOPERATIVE.
REQUEST SECOND TRIGGER CODE.

An almost instantaneous reply:

TRIGGER CODE UNAVAILABLE
LIEUTENANT FROST MUST
SUPPLY ARMING SEQUENCE
USE ANY MEANS NECESSARY
TO FORCE COOPERATION

He typed:

CLARIFICATION.

WHY CAN USSTRATCOM NOT SUPPLY TRIGGER CODE?

No reply.

He typed:

REQUEST STATUS OF USSTRATCOM.

No reply.

He typed:

REQUEST STATUS OF SECOND BOMB WING, VEGAS.
REQUEST INFO
RE: POSSIBLE SAR EXTRACTION.

No reply.

WHO AM I TALKING TO?
REQUEST COMSEC IDENT AND LOCATION.

No reply.

WHO ARE YOU?

He stared at the winking cursor a long while. He powered down the satcom and closed the lid. He pushed the unit away.

He turned his attention to the laptop jacked to the warhead. He wiped dust from the screen. A request for a ten-digit sequence.

SCNDRY AUTH
_____

The final arming sequence. Simple as withdrawing money from an ATM.

He caressed the Return key. The little square of plastic that would end his life once he delivered the warhead to its designated target. There would be no countdown, no chance to get clear. The moment he hit Enter to confirm the detonation command, the hotwired nuke would fire. He would wink out of existence. Delete himself with a single key-tap.

He sat with his head in his hands. Turmoil. The will to live overwhelmed by exhaustion and despair.

Flashback to Bagram.

The canteen hall. Mortar-proof hard shell. One of the chefs brought a fresh tray of fusilli to the pasta bar. He noticed a local translator in the queue. Guy had his shirt buttoned to his neck. He was sweating, despite a torrent of cool air from an overhead duct.

Two minutes later the canteen was clear. Upturned chairs and tables. Spilt food.

The translator sat in the middle of the hall, shirt unbuttoned, C4 patties taped to his belly and a command wire running down his arm to a push-button trigger in his hand.

Hancock cautiously entered the empty canteen, set a chair upright and sat down. He sat fifty feet away and tried to talk the man down.

'The moment has passed,' argued Hancock. 'You came here to kill a bunch of Americans. So what now? Your death will amount to nothing. If you press that button, all you will do is wreck some furniture.'

The translator didn't reply. He sat, finger on the button, panting with indecision.

Hancock tried a different approach.

'What did he tell you? The man that strapped you into that vest? How did he persuade you to throw your life away? What would it achieve?'

The translator's fear and indecision was replaced by a beatific smile.

'They said it will be like stepping through a doorway into a perfumed garden.'

Hancock threw himself from the chair and hit the floor. They pulled him from the wrecked canteen fifteen minutes later suffering from tinnitus and smoke inhalation.

Frost knelt in the sand, head bowed, dripping sweat.

Flashback to Thompson Falls, Montana.

Escape and evasion. Forty-eight hours fleeing through woodland, Frost finally brought to her knees by a German Shepherd dispatched by a Delta pursuit team.

The next phase of the SERE exercise: interrogation.

Hooded and zip-tied, curled on the floor of a flatbed truck as it jolted down a forest track.

Dragged from the vehicle and nudged down concrete steps to an unheated basement, gun at her back. Stink of mildew and rot.

They called it The Red Room.

Buckets of cold water. High-decibel Slipknot.

Endless hours.

The desolate, Arctic terrain of sleep deprivation.

Periodically propped in a chair, unhooded, dazzled by strobes.

'Just give up your key word, and it will all be over.'

Stripped, beaten, compelled to remain in a stress position for hours. Sticking to name, rank and number until she finally heard herself blurt 'flintlock' and the suffering stopped.

'How long did I last?' she asked, as they draped a blanket round her shoulders and gave her water.

'Thirty-eight hours, forty-nine minutes.'

'How does that compare to the others?'

'Irrelevant. You battle yourself. Always.'

Frost talked it through with other members of the class as they rode the bus back to base.

Plenty of bravado:

'Blow my fucking brains out rather than be taken alive. No way I'm letting myself get beheaded for some sick-ass jihadi video. Wouldn't give those ragheads the satisfaction.'

Each of them secretly wondering if, when their moment came, they could tough-out adversity, or would break and beg for mommy.

Sunset.

Stars in a darkening sky.

Frost tethered to a tyre. Hancock crossed the sand and stood over her.

'Feeling a little more circumspect?'

'You have to let me go,' said Frost. She stretched as best she could. 'You won't kill me. And I sure as shit won't give you the code. So what then? You can't keep me tied up like this.'

Hancock shook his head.

'You think you know me. But you don't. Can't say I want to leave you out here all night. But I sure as hell will, if that's what it takes.'

'Whacking an unarmed colleague? How does that fit with your honour code?'

'I'd leave it to those bastards out there in the dunes.'

'Murder by inaction. It would still be on you.'

'You know how it is with an assignment of this gravity. The standing orders. *Anyone or anything that interferes with the execution of the mission can be considered hostile and can be engaged.* You became an enemy combatant the moment you turned your hand to sabotage.'

Frost stared past his shoulder.

'Well, then I guess this is the moment we test your resolve,' she said quietly. 'Look. They're here.'

266

Hancock turned.

Two figures standing on a high dune, silhouetted against starlight.

He drew his side arm.

'Cut me free,' hissed Frost. 'They want your ass, as well as mine. Cut me loose. Give me a weapon.'

Hancock got to his feet and slowly walked towards the figures, pistol raised.

Silhouettes against starlight.

The first figure had half a head. The left side of his body slouched limp and unresponsive.

The second figure stood bent to one side, body kinked by a shattered spine.

Hancock crept towards them, Beretta gripped in both hands.

'What the fuck are you?' demanded Hancock.

One of the creatures turned away and shambled back into the desert.

Hancock took aim at the remaining silhouette. He fired. Pinback lit by muzzle flash. Slack face. Black eyes.

Bullets punched tufted holes in his flight suit.

Hancock lowered the smoking pistol. He fumbled a reload as he backed away from the impassive figure. He raised the pistol like he intended to loose a second volley of shots. He changed his mind. He turned and ran.

Observation Log - Subject 034

Day 19 - May 21st

0915: Subject refused breakfast and water. Continues to demand
      lawyer.

0945: Subject declined water. Requested music be shut off.

1000: Scheduled strip search as per standing orders. Bathroom
      bucket removed. Subject received fresh fatigues. Weight
      logged at 202 pounds. Subjected refused to shave.

1025: Subject declined to view legal documentation pertaining
      to his detention. Repeated request for lawyer.

1120: Subject received haircut and beard trim. Did not resist.
      Uncommunicative. Nurse asked subject if he would like to
      pray. Subject cried for approximately nine minutes.

1230: Subject refused lunch.

1335: Subject appears to have smashed wall speaker. Hands
      treated for slight knuckle abrasions. Subject cuffed.
      Declined water.

1445: Subject continues to refuse water. Appears agitated.

1515: Subject sedated and restrained. Blood samples taken.
      Vitals normal. IV established in right arm by corpsman.
      Administered 1lt 0.9 sodium chloride.

1630: Subject prepped for X-ray.

39

More Conex containers, ringed by a double perimeter of concertina wire.

Noble shone his flashlight inside one of the containers.

Foul stench. Cuff-chains and a latrine bucket. Crude air holes burned in the walls by an oxy-acetylene flame. He couldn't imagine what it would have been like to be imprisoned inside one of the shipping units. Must have been hell during the day. A stifling steel coffin. A fucking oven.

Noble stepped inside one of the containers. Bare footprints on the sand-dusted floor. Bloody scratches on the wall like someone tried to claw through steel.

He kicked at a tattered red jumpsuit.

NEVADA
DEPT OF
CORRECTIONS

Something scratched on the back wall of the container. He used the balled jumpsuit to brush dust.

FIGHT

He stepped outside to escape shit-stink and claustrophobia.
A water trailer next to the containers. It had been punctured

by bullet strikes. He hit it with his fist. Dull reverberation. Near empty.

He crouched, put his lips to the tap and let the last few drops of water drain into his mouth.

He stood and wiped his lips with the back of his hand. He looked around.

A couple of watchtowers overlooked the detention area. A clear sector of fire. Anyone attempting to bust out of the Connex cells would get dazzled by searchlights, torn by twin streams of 5.56mm, before they had a chance to climb the wire.

He did the math. Seven units. Twenty guys in each. And what about that message scratched at the back of one of the containers?

FIGHT.

Some sorry soul left a warning for future inmates. Implied the cells had been filled and emptied a few times.

Hell of a body count.

A thin avenue of barbed wire. A tight rat-run that led from the freight containers to a couple of Airstream trailers.

A bunch of R20 batteries scattered in the dust. The guards must have used cattle prods as a compliance tool. Stood outside the wire and goosed recalcitrant prisoners with a livestock wand, propelled them towards the Airstreams.

'California Girls' segued to 'Sloop John B'.

He approached one of the trailers.

A couple of the corner jacks had buckled. The trailer listed to the left.

Noble drew his pistol and pulled open the door. He climbed inside, Beretta in one hand, flashlight in the other.

The Airstream had been stripped of all furnishings. The interior was dominated by a padded table. Restraint cuffs for ankles, chest and wrists. Extensions welded either side of the table to extend the subject's arms cruciform. Looked like the kind of prison gurney used for lethal injections.

He circled the table. The trailer rocked as he moved around.

Stained canvas pads. The carpet beneath the gurney was worn threadbare. Place had seen plenty of use.

The walls and windows were crudely lagged with foam. Soundproofing. Same purpose, Noble supposed, as the music blaring outside: an attempt to muffle screams.

'Help Me Rhonda' abruptly stammered and stopped.

Noble ducked outside. He took shelter from the arclights, hid in the shadow of the trailer. He waited a long while, scanning the desolate compound, the trashed buildings and wrecked vehicles. Maybe he wasn't alone. Maybe someone cut the music. Or maybe the CD player, wherever it was, glitched and shut off.

No movement. No signs of life.

A large, geodesic tent. He stepped through the arched doorway. He looked up. He could see stars through tears in the vinyl dome.

Three dissection tables. Zinc slabs with drain holes.

A metal chair equipped with leather arm and leg restraints. A tripod video camera and a couple of mikes positioned in front of the chair ready for some kind of interrogation.

Bloody surgical instruments scattered on the polythene floor. He bent and picked up a pair of rongeurs. He scissored the blades. Crusted blood and tufts of hair.

A voice behind him.

'Hands. Hands where I can see them.'

Noble froze. He held out his pistol and let it drop to the floor. He tossed the bone cutters aside.

He raised his hands and slowly turned around.

Trenchman. Dust-matted clothes. Couple of days of stubble. The guy looked sunburned and exhausted.

He lowered his side arm.

'Shit. Noble. Noble, right? *Liberty Bell.*'

'What the hell are you doing out here?'

'Looking for you guys,' said Trenchman. 'Anyone else make it?'

'Two survivors, back at the plane.'

Noble bent and scooped up his Beretta. They both holstered their weapons.

'We should get out of here,' said Trenchman. 'The lights, the music. Might as well ring the dinner bell.'

They scrambled up the mountain slope.

Trenchman led Noble to a high ledge. A sleeping bag, bottled water, canned food.

'This where you've been camping out?'

'Managed to elude the fuckers so far.'

Trenchman pointed to the floodlit compound beneath them.

'There. See that? Next to the truck.'

'Can't see a damned thing. No, wait. Yeah. I got him. Deep shadow.'

'They come out at night. Might be dumb, but they got enough sense to stay out of the noonday sun.'

'How many?'

'I don't know. A bunch.'

'Reckon we'll be okay up here?'

'They've left me alone the past couple of nights. They don't climb so well. A couple of them try to make it up that scree slope down there. Guess they wanted to take a bite out of my ass. They got a little ways, then brought a bunch of rocks down on themselves.'

Twisted bodies at the bottom of the gradient. Red jump-suits, snapped limbs, part-buried beneath stones. One of the revenants was pinned under a boulder. Skeletal hands feebly slapped the massive stone, tried to roll it aside.

Noble sat a while and contemplated the compound.

He gestured to the wrecked buildings.

'So what is this place? Evidently some pretty dark shit going down, some army docs getting in touch with their inner Mengele, but is it truly worth a nuclear weapon?'

'Wait till sunrise,' said Trenchman. 'I'll give you the full tour.'

REMOVE BEFORE FLIGHT

40

The lower cabin.

Hancock pulled the barricade aside as quietly as he could and leant through the fissure in the fuselage wall. The desert night. Deep darkness. He shone his flashlight left and right. Undisturbed sand.

'Frost?'

He reluctantly stepped from the plane, torch in one hand, Beretta in the other.

'Frost? You still there?'

He approached the extinct signal fire. Anxious three-sixty scan of surrounding dunes.

Frost still knelt with a leash round her neck, arms locked cruciform.

'You okay?'

She looked up. She didn't speak. Haunted, terrified eyes.

He held the flashlight under his armpit, took a knife from his pocket and flicked it open. He cut the leash.

'Let's get inside.'

Hancock rebuilt the barricade.

He cut Frost free of the crutch. She sank to the floor, still set cruciform. She slowly flexed her shoulders, winced as she tried to bend her elbows and lower her arms. Sensation gradually returned to numb limbs.

Hancock kept the gun trained on her head.

'Climb the ladder.'

Frost pulled herself upright. She gripped the ladder for support.

'Take a long, hard look at yourself,' said Hancock. 'Dead on your feet. Planning to throw some kung fu my way? Best think again.'

She gripped the ladder rungs. She tried to climb. She gnashed her teeth and snorted in pain as her injured leg refused to hold her weight.

Hancock pushed her ass, forced her up onto the flight deck.

She fell on her hands and knees.

He climbed the ladder. He stood over her, pistol trained at her head.

He took wire from his pocket and bound her hands to a wall stanchion.

'Stay there. Don't fuck around.'

He set his flashlight on top of the avionics console.

An eerie stillness. They could hear a rising night wind whistling through the broken cockpit windows, fluttering the nuclear blast curtains. They could hear the tick and creak of the plane's superstructure contracting in the evening cool.

The flashlight beam flickered and dimmed. A dying battery. They stared at it, like they were contemplating a guttering candle flame.

'We need more light,' said Hancock. He checked lockers.

'Why did you change your mind?' asked Frost. 'Why bring me inside?'

'I got lonesome.'

He found a large 3xD cell Maglite. He tested the beam.

'You were out there, in the dark, for a full hour,' he said. 'See anything? Hear anything?'

'I heard them walking around. They paced the site like they were checking it out.'

'They didn't come near you?'

'One of them stood behind me,' said Frost. 'I didn't dare move. He stood there a long while. Stank to high heaven. Then he moved off.'

'Why did he leave you alone?'

'No idea.'

He sat in the pilot seat, lifted one of the blast screens and peered into the dark.

'Anything?' asked Frost.

'No. But I reckon they're out there, circling like sharks. Wish I could make sense of it. Fucking mind games. It's as if they're trying to drive us nuts.'

'Doing a pretty good job,' muttered Frost.

'It's a virus. Nothing more than a strain of flu. Hard to credit any kind of smarts. Maybe it's studying us. Testing our resolve, trying to find a common breaking point. Sort of thing a general might do in wartime, right? Send out a raiding party. Use provocation to draw the enemy out, gauge the strength of its forces.'

Frost shook her head.

'It's already got the measure of us.'

'Well, in that case, maybe it's just having fun.'

Hancock bent and peered through a vacant cockpit window.

'I can see one of them. About fifty yards, dead ahead. Just standing there, in the moonlight.'

'Who? Pinback?'

'Can't tell.'

Hancock continued to squint into the darkness.

'What's it doing?' asked Frost.

'Nothing. Just standing there, looking at us.'

'Looks like we got a straight choice. Hide in here all night and hope they don't attack or suit up and take the fight to them. I vote we head outside and push for a stand-up fight. Fuckers aren't supernatural. They're flesh and blood, just like us. A well-placed bullet will put them down for good.'

'You shot Guthrie in the head. Didn't slow him down much.'

'Then let me finish the job. Put a round in his medulla. That'll stop his clock.'

Hancock thought it over.

'Time to decide,' said Frost. 'You wanted to be AC. You wanted to be the boss. So how do you intend to play it? Do we cower in here all night, or head outside and seize the initiative?'

Hancock sipped from his canteen.

Frost watched him drink, listened to liquid slosh in the metal flask. She was tempted to lick parched lips, but didn't want to betray any signs of weakness.

He saw her attention fixed on the canteen.

'Cheers,' he said. He toasted her and took another gratuitously long sip. He screwed the cap back on the metal bottle.

'You know the deal. All the water you want, in return for the code.'

'I told you. I don't remember a single digit.'

'You'll remember. When you are strung out, desperate enough. Your subconscious will offer it up.'

'Untie my hands, at least. What if those things outside decide to attack? I got a right to defend myself.'

Hancock shook his head.

'Ain't got the energy to keep chasing you around. I'm going to keep you on a very short leash from now on.'

'You got the gun,' she said. 'I'm in no shape to give any trouble.'

He thought it over.

'All right.'

He cut her free from the wall stanchion.

'Thanks.'

She flexed her arms and rubbed wrist welts.

'Hold out your hands.'

'For God's sake.'

'If they attack, you can run. Save yourself. But that's all you get.'

He retied her hands.

'Shift that trunk. Block the ladder.'

A Peli trunk full of life preservers. Frost shunted the box to cover the ladderway hatch.

She gestured to the windows.

'Maybe you should check outside one more time. See what those bastards are doing.'

He hesitated. He didn't want Frost to call the shots.

'Come on,' she said. 'We need to know what's going on out there.'

Hancock crossed the flight deck and pulled back a blast screen. He checked over his shoulder to make sure Frost was still sat on the floor.

'Anything?'

'Nothing. No sign.'

Hancock sat opposite Frost.

Frost exhaled and watched her breath fog the air.

'Getting pretty cold.'

He didn't reply. He stifled a yawn.

'Long night, huh?' she said. 'How long do you think you can stay awake?'

'I'll sleep sound enough, once you're lashed to the wall.'

Frost cocked her head.

'Hear that?'

'Best if you shut up a while. I'm done talking.'

'No. Seriously. Listen.'

Faint footfalls. Boots on metal.

'Something's walking the port wing.'

Brief pause.

Heavy footsteps above them.

'It's climbed the fuselage,' whispered Frost. 'It's on the roof.'

They both slowly got to their feet and looked up at support spars, cable conduits and escape hatches, trying to project their vision through the superstructure like X-ray.

Footfalls directly above their heads. Shuffle and scuff. The thing on the roof had come to a standstill.

'It's right above us.'

Hancock instinctively raised his pistol and trained it at the roof.

'What the fuck?' he murmured.

'Pinback,' whispered Frost. 'Heaviest of the bunch. Got to be Pinback.'

Hancock adjusted his grip on the pistol, like he intended to shoot.

'Don't. Wait for a clear shot.'

'What do you think it's doing?' he murmured.

'Messing with our heads. Trying to spook us out.'

Bootsteps moved towards the front of the plane.

Hancock edged towards the pilot seat, swinging the pistol back and forth, trying to keep Frost covered and trying to position himself in case Pinback dropped through a vacant ejection hatch.

The footsteps reversed direction. They slowly retraced their path, walked overhead and aft towards the rear of the aircraft. Bootfall reverberation diminished to silence.

'Think he'll be back?' he asked, attention still fixed on the roof.

Frost grabbed the pistol with bound hands and pushed it aside. Gunshot. Spark and ricocheted whine. The bullet exited the plane leaving a neat, smoking hole in the fuselage.

Vicious headbutt. Hancock staggered backwards snorting blood.

He tried to take aim. Frost knocked his weapon aside, balled her bound fists and delivered a double rabbit punch to his shattered nose. He yelled with pain. He kicked. She twisted and evaded the flailing boot.

They fell to the floor and wrestled for the Beretta. Frost drove her elbow into the bandage covering his rotted, vacant socket. Bubbling pus and blood. He screamed. He convulsed and released his grip on the pistol.

Frost jammed the smoking weapon against his temple. He recoiled from the hot gun barrel. A faint circle and a trace of the front sight, branded on his skin.

'Don't move. Do. Not. Fucking. Move.'

She got to her feet. They glared at each other, both panting, both catching their breath.

'Empty your pockets.'

He reluctantly tossed spare mags.

'And the knives.'

Her K-Bar was tucked behind the webbing of his chest rig. He pulled it free and tossed it clattering on the floor.

'And the other one.'

He pulled a lock knife from his pocket and threw it at her feet.

'Sit on your hands.'

He sat cross-legged on his hands.

She picked up her knife, reversed the blade and cut her wrist restraints.

'Over there.'

She gestured to the wall stanchion. He shifted position, as if he were about to stand.

'No, stay down.'

He crawled to the wall. He sat, resigned, as she bound his wrists to the fuselage frame.

She lowered herself to the floor. She uncapped Hancock's canteen and drank deep.

He used his sleeve to wipe blood from his nose and upper lip. He stared at Frost, beaming cold hate.

She stretched, massaged her injured leg.

Hancock opened his mouth like he was about to speak, but Frost suddenly froze and mimed hush.

Footsteps on the lower deck. Someone moving around in the cabin beneath them.

They stared at the trunk blocking the hatchway to the compartment below. They listened to the muffled clump of boots, the clatter of equipment and survival gear thrown aside.

'Shoot,' said Hancock. He spat blood onto the deck plate beside him. 'Pull the box aside. Do it quick. Put a bullet in the top of the fuck's head.'

Frost looked towards the hatchway. She listened as the lower cabin got ransacked.

'Think it knows we're here?' asked Hancock.

'Of course.'

She slid across the floor to the trunk. She gripped the sides of the box, prepped to push it aside, then changed her mind.

'Hey,' she shouted. 'Hear me down there?'

Sounds from below abruptly ceased.

'Pinback? Is that you?'

'Bitch, you're going to get us killed,' murmured Hancock.

'Pinback. Daniel Pinback. Do you remember your own name?'

Long pause.

'Think, Daniel. Think back. Reach deep. Your wife. Michelle. Remember Michelle? The plans you made. The house you were going to build.'

Crash from down below. Tools kicked by stumbling feet. Pinback resumed his search of the plane.

Frost barked a bunch of take-off commands:

'Engine four start. Spooling. Increase thrust.'

Sudden silence.

'Yeah. You remember how to pilot a plane well enough. The very last thing you would forget.'

282

No sound.

'Pinback? You still there?'

No sound.

She ejected the mag from the pistol. Couple of rounds left. She loaded a fresh clip.

She slowly pushed the trunk aside and shone a flashlight down the ladderwell.

The lower cabin was empty. A couple of lockers torn open. Tools strewn across the deck.

Frost sat on the lip of the hatchway and contemplated the detritus.

'What were you doing down there, Pinback?' she murmured. 'What was on your mind?'

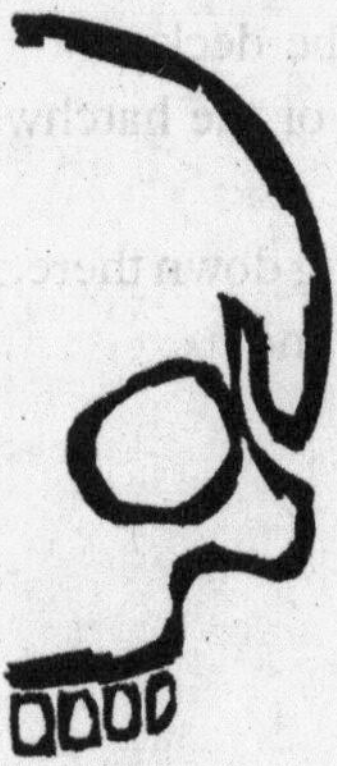

41

Sunrise.

Noble and Trenchman walked through the ruined compound.

Absolute devastation. Not a building or vehicle untouched.

A couple of smouldering SUVs. Melted plastic trim sent up black smoke.

'Site Apache,' said Trenchman. 'CIA oversight. Been here three months.'

Scattered shell casings. Fragments of rotor blade. An exploded kerosene drum, sides peeled back like the petals of a steel flower.

'Jesus.'

Trenchman shrugged.

'I wasn't here when it happened, but I heard them screaming for help over the radio. Infected broke out of their pens. Things got apocalyptic.'

Noble kicked the dirt. Enamel white shards. He crouched. Scattered teeth.

'So how many people died out here? In total?'

'A bunch.'

'Where are the bodies? Who cleaned up?'

'Handful of survivors.'

'You've checked the place out? Done a thorough search? Anything to scavenge?'

'Not a whole lot.'

'So what's the story?' asked Noble. 'What was going on out here?'

'Do you really need me to spell it out?' Trenchman gestured to the freight container cells. 'Seems pretty self-evident. They were a bunch of CDC specialists out here studying the virus. Bunch of guys from Fort Detrick. They needed test subjects. They got convicts trucked in from Lovelock and Ely. Kept them penned, fed and watered, while they waited to go under the knife.'

'Humans? Used as labs rats?'

'Murderers. Rapists. Pederasts.'

'But people.'

'Barely. In a fucked-up world, this was one of the easier decisions.'

'Kept them like cattle.'

'Look around. Agency guys didn't live much better. Human race hanging in the balance. It was tough for everyone. Nobody relished what they were doing. Death stink and merciless heat. All the docs, all the guards, sitting around guzzling Tequila. Cork high and bottle deep, all day long.'

'How many guys did they kill?'

'Couple of hundred. But they would have died anyway. The penitentiaries were abandoned. COs fled, leaving convicts in their cells to starve. It's not like anyone was going to throw open the prison gates and let a bunch of gangbangers and maniacs loose on the streets. This way, they got a few days more life.'

'What was your part in all this?'

'Logistics. Second Wing delivered some of the trailers. Sling loads beneath the Chinook. Brought a couple of CDC guys from Florida as well. Want me to feel bad about it? The killing? The guys working out here were fucking heroic. Proud to play a part.'

They kept walking.

A burned-out office unit. No roof. A single wall left standing.

The unit looked like it had been converted to a bio containment lab. Scraps of polythene suggested the unit might once have been hermetically sealed. Lengths of silver hose suggested elaborate air filtration. The skeletal frame sagging against the unit suggested a sequence of decon showers.

Toppled drums of solvent. Discarded bottles of bleach. A couple of ripped Tyvek suits.

Noble approached the charred wreckage. A zinc necropsy table at the centre of the ruined lab.

He kicked at sample containers among the debris, the kind of high-impact, flip-latch boxes used to transport donor organs.

Some kind of weird half-skull symbol on the lids, like someone improvised danger signs with a Sharpie.

'I'd stay away from that shit, if I were you,' said Trenchman. 'That was the dissection room. They used to joke about it. Called it The Deli, cause people got laid on the counter and sliced real fine. They played music over the tannoy, but it didn't smother the screams. Everyone hated the place. Seriously. Keep away. Bad hoodoo.'

Trenchman led Noble across the helipad to a mobile office unit. They ducked inside.

Scattered papers. Toppled chairs.

Trenchman sat on a desk.

Noble picked a ring binder from the floor and flipped pages.

'Doesn't anyone else want this stuff?' asked Noble. 'All this research, whatever the fuck it is. Might be useful to someone. Ought to be preserved.'

'There's nobody left. There used to be a mirror team working out of Bellevue, New York. Guess they died when the bomb dropped. Another bunch down a missile silo in Florida. Lost contact a while back.'

A sheaf of black and white photographs.

A convict strapped to a chair. A big, Slavic guy with a biker beard. A swastika tattooed at the centre of his forehead, Manson style. He exhibited the first signs of infection: one eyeball haemorrhaged black and a bunch of irregularities beneath the chest fabric of his jumpsuit hinting at the tumourous knots and ropes erupting from his skin.

A couple of tripod microphones set up in front of the guy. Headphones clamped to his head.

'What's the deal with the microphones? Some kind of indoctrination? Were they trying to create super-soldiers or something?'

Trenchman shook his head.

'Most infected folk are dumber than cockroaches. Trace metabolic function. Negligible brain activity. No memories, emotions. They are effectively dead. But now and again one of these bastards starts to demonstrate a sly intelligence. And one or two of them can talk.' Trenchman gestured to the photo in Noble's hand. 'That guy. Valdemar. Russian mob. Low-level enforcer. He was a star exhibit.'

Trenchman poked through clutter on one of the desks until he found a digital recorder.

'Listen to this.'

He pressed Play.

'Let's start with the basics. Tell me your name.'

Long pause.

Louder, clearer:

'Tell me your name.'

A guttural, unearthly slur:

'Franklin Delano Fuckyourself.'

'Do you know where you are?'

'West of hell.'

'Do you understand what's going on here?'

'Better than you.'

'According to the ECG, your heart is beating about once a minute. You shouldn't be conscious. Hell, you shouldn't be alive. How do you feel, Valdemar? Tell me what it's like.'

'Guessing you'll find out soon enough.'

Long pause. A faint slurp suggesting the interrogator was taking a meditative sip of coffee, gathering his thoughts.

'Okay. I want to talk to someone else, Val. There's something inside you. Something keeping you alive.'

Long pause.

'Can you hear me? I'm talking to the thing inside Valdemar. Can you understand what I'm saying?'

Long pause.

'I know you're in there, looking through Val's eyes. Use him. Use his mind, his speech. Please. Talk to me directly.'

Another long pause, then the microphones picked up a slow exhalation like a venomous hiss.

'Val. The thing in your head. The thing that's taken over your body, invaded your mind. What can you tell me about it? Can you tell me what it wants?'

The convict's voice, tired, broken:

'Help me. Please. It won't let me die.'

Trenchman shut off the recorder.

'Is that what all this shit is about?' asked Noble, gesturing to the paperwork and trashed laptops carpeting the floor. 'They were trying to talk to the disease?'

'The virus isn't some mutated strain of Ebola or Spanish Flu. It's way more complex. Super-lethal, super-adaptive.

Some of the guys that studied its behaviour started to think it might, on some level, be sentient.'

'A self-aware disease?'

'It dropped out of the sky with a bunch of contaminated Soviet space junk. Maybe it's some kind of messed-up bioweapon. Or maybe it originated from somewhere else entirely.'

'Somewhere else.'

'That's the one question that nags at anyone who studied this disease. Where exactly did it come from?'

Trenchman thumbed through pictures.

The same convict, strapped in the chair, the crown of his head removed, exposing brain. Electrodes sunk in his parietal cortex like a row of acupuncture needles. The convict was looking up, and to the left.

'Eyes always point to the site of a stroke, ever hear that?' said Trenchman, gesturing to the picture. 'They turn towards the point of cerebral occlusion.'

'Talking to a virus,' said Noble, shaking his head. 'Unbelievable.'

'Pretty interesting project, right? What if you could interview a brain tumour? What if cancer could talk? What would it have to say?'

'So how did they go about negotiating with a virus?'

'They tried everything to establish a common language. They used mathematics as a universal baseline. Fired synaptic impulses, ran sequences of prime numbers, logic gates, all kinds of shit way beyond my pay grade.'

'Did the disease ever answer back?'

'No. The head CDC guy was the conservative type. Didn't say much. But last time I was here he was in a bad way. Big sense of failure. He and his boys came out here looking for some kind of breakthrough. But, in the end, they achieved jack shit, so he took to his trailer with a case of Scotch. I got him talking. He reckoned the virus understood their communications well enough. Reckoned all the while Disease Control were studying the disease, it was studying them back. Some kind of hive mind. A single intelligence. Every infected bastard the world over is a facet of a vast, all-seeing eye.'

'So I guess that's definitive,' said Noble. He crouched and stuffed jumbled papers into his backpack. 'No vaccine. No cure.'

'That's right.'

'And no reasoning with it.'

Trenchman sombrely nodded his head.

'It simply wants us dead.'

The compound.

The sun was high. Heat starting to build.

'There's nothing left to see,' said Trenchman. 'I could show you dissection footage, autopsy photos, but you wouldn't learn anything more than you already know. Even horror gets monotonous after a while. We should find shade.'

They walked through a break in the perimeter wire and headed for the mountain wall.

Trenchman sniffed the air. Stink of burning flesh carried on the breeze. Seemed to be coming from behind an outcrop to the north.

'They burned the bodies?' asked Noble.

'A big pyre, behind those rocks over there.'

'How many?'

'A lot. You don't want to see it, believe me.'

They climbed the crags and boulders until they reached Trenchman's camp. Blankets, cached food and water.

They sat in shade and looked out over the battle-torn compound. They opened a couple of bean tins and ate with sporks.

'So you've been waiting for us?' asked Noble.

'Seemed a better idea than chasing you guys round the

desert. Figured you folks would head this way sooner or later. Better sit tight and wait for you to show up.'

'So what's the plan?'

'Wait until sundown, then head west across the mountains. Try to find a backcountry road, see where it leads.'

'Frost. Hancock. I can't leave them.'

'I came out here hoping to scoop you all up, get you to safety. Not sure it's going to be possible. This is your only shot at survival, dude. Come with me. Tonight.'

Noble shook his head.

'I have to go back.'

They sat a while and ate.

'I'll leave a stash of food and water,' said Trenchman. 'If you make it back here with your friends, there'll be enough supplies for you guys to recuperate a while, then try to cross the mountains. Who knows? Maybe we'll meet again, somewhere down the line.'

They sat looking out over the vast aridity and relished a parched desert wind. They listened to the unearthly silence.

'Seen so many people die,' said Trenchman. 'Still have a hard time comprehending it will happen to me. One day the sun will rise, and I won't be there to see it. Leaves on the trees, birds in the sky, but I won't exist.' He took a sip from his canteen. 'They say you shouldn't be scared of death. Pure nothing, same as before you were born.'

'One last question for you,' said Noble.

'Go ahead.'

'Why drop a bomb? They nuked the cities. I get it. Exterminating a termite nest. But this place? Apache? Sure, nefarious shit went down, but there's no one left alive to give a damn.'

'No idea. But I'd be willing to speculate. The continuity government. Bunch of politicians and generals hiding in a

NORAD bunker. They signed the order for these human trials. Command responsibility. So now they are covering their tracks.'

'Like I said. Why give a damn? It's not like they'll ever face trial. There'll be no Nuremberg tribunal. And even if there were, who would blame them for trying to defeat the virus?'

'They're rewriting history. If the human race survives this mess, if there's a new America, then the decisions that were made, the battles that were fought in these dark days, will be part of a new founding myth. The guys in that bunker, the generals, the cabinet officers, know they'll be dead soon enough. Entombed deep underground, sealed behind a thirty-ton blast door. But they want to be remembered like Lincoln or Jefferson. One day, if the nation is rebuilt, the country may have a new capitol, a new Washington. The top brass expect to be commemorated. Sculpted in marble. Printed on dollars. So that's why they want to erase this place. To sanitise the historical narrative. To make them undisputed heroes.'

'All this death, to serve some fucker's ego.'

Trenchman smiled.

'Same as it ever was.'

42

The lower cabin.

Frost picked through ransacked gear. A nylon tool roll. Wrenches and sanitary wipes scattered on the deck plate. A parka, ripped down the back, spilling synthetic down.

Pinback had stumbled around the cabin, kicking over equipment boxes, punching open wall-mounted lockers.

Frost tried to make sense of his actions. Had there been any method to his search? What had he hoped to achieve? The ladder to the cockpit was visible enough. He could have climbed, pushed aside the trunk blocking the hatchway and attacked. Yet he seemed intent on exploring the interior of the plane rather than acquiring fresh victims.

She threw an empty chute pack aside. She pushed scattered meds back inside the trauma kit.

She studied handprints on the fuselage wall. Dust streaks where fingers raked metal.

A strand of flesh hung from a fractured spar at hip level. She leant close and inspected it.

Skin tissue dried like jerky.

The horror of infection. A living death. The parasite that colonised her fellow crewman was vibrantly alive, swelling and spreading through blood vessels and musculature, but his body was a fast-decaying hunk of meat. The creature that explored the plane the previous night, clawed metal and stumbled against the walls, was effectively a walking cadaver.

The stench of rot-gas still hung in the air.

Boot prints on dust-matted deck plate. She examined the overlapping trail, tried to reconstruct Pinback's movements. Scuff marks centred on the rear of the cabin: the crawlspace that led to the bomb bay.

Frost shone her flashlight into the narrow passageway half expecting to find Pinback curled foetal, hibernating until nightfall.

She climbed into the steel tunnel and crawled on her hands and knees. She inspected the hatch leading to the payload bay. Palm prints and scratch marks. A crude attempt to force his way inside.

She stroked abraded metal.

'Why did you want to get inside the bomb bay, Pinback? What was on your mind?'

Frost stepped from the plane into dazzling morning light. She shielded her eyes and let them adjust.

Blurred prints heading away into desert.

She drew her pistol, and limped in pursuit. She followed the trail across the sand, up the lee side of a dune.

Additional prints. Three people walking side by side. Pinback joined by his companions. Equidistant tracks, like they were marching in lock-step.

She stood at the crest of the ridgeline, squinting into the low morning sun.

The tracks led away across the sand, then abruptly terminated as if the three figures simultaneously dropped to their knees and burrowed beneath the ground.

She led Hancock outside. His arms were lashed to the crutch with chute harness straps. She tied cable round his neck like a leash, and tethered him to the undercarriage wheel.

He knelt and looked up at her. He was gaunt. Skin blistered and peeling. Stubble lengthened to a scraggy beard.

'Reckon you've aged twenty years these past few days,' she said. 'Can't imagine I look much better.'

She gestured to the sun.

'Ready to catch a few rays?'

Hancock didn't reply.

Frost uncapped a bottle of water and held it to his lips. He hesitated, like he wanted to refuse but was too parched to turn down the offer.

She let him take a couple of long swigs, then pulled the bottle away.

He swilled water round his mouth like he was debating whether to spit it in her face.

'Enjoying your revenge?' he asked.

'Yeah. Yeah, I am.'

She walked to the B-52 and sat in the shadow of the nose. Hancock shuffled around, turned his back on the sun.

'How long will you leave me out here?' he shouted.

'Haven't given it much thought.'

Frost pulled a bandana from her pocket, dabbed perspiration from her brow and neck.

'If you want me dead, then man-up and put a bullet in my brain.'

'I'll sit you in the shade soon enough. Just want to see you sweat a little first. Childish retribution, but fuck it. Maybe it'll encourage you to act like a reasonable human being.'

She browsed the survival manual and studied a line drawing.

She leant forwards and dug a hole. She fetched a plastic beaker from the plane and set it in the hole. She slit open a plastic bag, placed it over the hole and pegged it down with a couple of wrenches.

'Condensation still. Might be able to decant a dribble of water if we leave it overnight. And it's a good way to purify urine. Use evaporation to filter the liquid clean. So if you need a piss, you let me know, you hear?'

She unzipped the trauma kit.

She pulled off a boot, untied the splints and examined her injured leg.

'Still planning to take a walk?' asked Hancock.

'Yeah. Head for the mountains. Hoping you'll see sense and join me.'

'If I don't? Going to leave me tied to this fucking wheel?'

'I'll cut you lose when I go.'

'How about water?'

'Fifty-fifty split. I'll drain half from the tank, carry it on my back. Leave you with the rest.'

'What about Pinback and his pals? How am I supposed to defend myself?'

'That won't be a problem.'

'How do you figure?'

'Because, when they show up tonight, I aim to kill them.'

43

Sunset.

Noble stumbled through endless dunes.

'Bobbi,' he shouted. 'Bobbi, you there?'

Noble willed her voice to come to him.

'Come on, Bobbi. Talk to me.'

Hours teetering on the edge of madness. Why couldn't he will himself over the precipice? Why couldn't his broken mind allow a retreat into dreams?

Countless times he had stood outside the barracks at Andrews Air Force Base, ignored CANNOT CONNECT TO NETWORK and thumbed his wife's number.

Torrential rain. Standing on the barrack porch, phone pressed to his ear.

'Love you, babe.' Feeling connected to his Cedar Street home despite the absence of signal bars. The kitchen counter where he often ate breakfast, hair still wet from the shower. He would sip coffee, watch birds perch on the yard fence. 'I miss you. Love to Malcolm. Hope to see you both soon.' A kind of prayer. Committing his love to UHF.

Why couldn't she be here now? Why couldn't he summon her from memory?

'Hey. Bobbi? You there?'

No sound but the rasp of his own breathing, the crunch of his boots, the blood-rush in his ears.

He was irrevocably sane, fully present, condemned to endure merciless heat, merciless light.

Noble staggered across sand, determined to cover as much ground as he could before dark.

A glint on the horizon. The wrecked limo still sitting beached among the dunes.

Trenchman's parting words:

'Don't get caught in the open at night. Not if you can help it. Find shelter. Once they get your scent, they won't quit.'

Noble broke into a run.

The limo.

Noble tossed his backpack through a shattered side-window. He squirmed through the window and rolled onto a bench seat. He lay on sand-dusted leatherette, panting with exhaustion.

Fitful moonlight shafted through the windows. The limo interior glowed with phosphorescent light.

Noble pulled down his bandana mask, bit the fingers of his gloves and tugged them from his hands.

He uncapped his canteen and let water wet his lips and tongue. He quickly resealed the cap in case he lost self control and drained the canteen dry.

He unlaced his boots and kicked them off. He slapped sand from crusted socks. He massaged blistered feet.

No sound but the mournful wind-whisper of the desert night.

He sat back, pulled a sheaf of research notes from his backpack and thumbed pages by torchlight. Too tired to make sense of the text. He shut off his flashlight and set the pages aside.

He turned up his collar, curled foetal on the back seat and fell into a fitful sleep.

Noble snapped awake. Vague sense of unease.

He lay beneath a blanket of research notes. He shuffled them neat and stuffed them in his backpack.

He sat up.

Stench of rotted flesh.

A heavy thud. He flinched.

Slow, deliberate footsteps. Someone pacing the roof.

He snatched the Beretta from its holster. Footfalls directly above his head. Heart-pounding adrenalin rush.

He looked out the window. Moon shadows. The silhouette of a man crouched directly above him on the limo roof.

A guttural, dirt-clogged voice:

'How you doing, Harris?'

'Early?'

'Long journey. Bet you're exhausted.'

Noble took aim and fired a shot into the ceiling. The retort made his ears sing. Coiling barrel fumes filled the compartment like cigarette smoke.

A smouldering notch in the roof vinyl. A pencil beam of moonlight shafted through the bullet hole.

The moonbeam flicked as the figure on the roof paced back and forth.

'What if this landscape exists in your head? What if you're not actually here, in the desert? Ever think of that? Remember that mountain bike you used to ride round town? Maybe you fell off and hit your head. You could be in a hospital bed right now, comatose, surrounded by beeping machines. What do you think this fucked-up desolation would say about your subconscious? Must hate your own guts. Every dune, every grain of sand, built it to punish yourself. Your mind could have taken refuge in a tropical paradise. You could be reclining on a beach right now. Palm trees, bikini girls, mojito. Instead you chose this nightmare.'

'You're not Early. You're an echo, reflex. All this talk. It's like zapping the legs of a dissected frog to make them twitch.'

Long silence.

'Trenchman was right, wasn't he? You. The virus. You're studying us.'

Long silence.

Noble slowly pulled the flashlight from his vest pocket.

'You could snuff us out in an instant. Me. Frost. Hancock. Why play games? Are you tormenting us, like a kid frying ants with a magnifying glass?'

Noble lunged out of a side window, pistol at the ready. The light-cone of his flashlight lit the empty roof.

He shone the flashlight at surrounding dunes. No tracks.

'You're nothing,' he shouted, bellowing into darkness. 'A germ. A string of RNA. Come on. Face me, motherfucker.'

The limo shuddered and lurched. Noble fell back inside the vehicle. He dropped his flashlight and gripped the seat. Deafening torsion and metal shriek.

The limo shook like it was taking a series of heavy side-impacts.

He hit the floor.

Another sudden jolt. The front of the Humvee dropped like both front tyres had simultaneously blown out.

Sudden wrench. Explosion of dust beyond the hood of the limo. The vehicle began to tilt nose-down, front fender disappearing beneath the sand as it was dragged below ground.

Noble grabbed his flashlight as it rolled past and trained the beam on the driver's compartment. Sand pouring through the side windows, the windshield, filling the footwells, engulfing the dash.

Groan and judder. He gripped the stripper pole. Some

303

Herculean force continued to wrench the limo below ground in a series of powerful jerks.

The gradient inside the vehicle grew more precipitous as the nose sank further. Noble hugged the stripper pole. Boots pedalled carpet as he scrambled for a foothold.

The mini-bar flipped open, spilling garbage. He was pelted with snack wrappers, empty cans and plastic vodka bottles.

The Humvee at forty-five degrees. Noble clung tight to stop himself sliding into the streams of dust slowly inundating the body of the limo.

He dropped his flashlight. It tumbled along the limo floor, bounced over the driver partition, beam quickly smothered by cascading sand.

He grabbed his backpack as it slid past.

He clawed towards a side door, kicked at it, desperate to get clear of the vehicle before he got buried alive.

He rammed the door with his shoulder. Jammed.

He climbed towards the rear window, desperate to escape the fast-filling passenger compartment.

Roof glass burst inwards. A stream of sand slammed his head and shoulders like it was jetting from a fire hose. He fought the torrent, pawed dust from his eyes, coughed and spat.

The rear window was cracked and frosted. Noble punched an opening. Glass crumbled to granules as he forced his way through the aperture.

He squirmed out the rear window and tossed his backpack. He jumped and rolled clear.

Shriek of rending metal.

He lay on his side and looked back.

The limo jerked fully vertical, dust streaming from the rear wheels and transmission.

The vehicle was relentlessly hauled beneath the ground. Awful cracks and groans as body panels buckled and the roof collapsed. Windows frosted and shattered. Sand poured into the passenger compartment.

Last glimpse of the trunk, the chromed rear fender and canary yellow SINCITY plate, as it submerged.

Sudden silence.

Noble got to his feet. He stood at the lip of the crater and tried to comprehend what he had seen.

Granules of glass glittered in the sand. Empty whiskey miniatures.

He backed away.

He turned, snatched up his backpack and ran.

**EVS MONITOR
FILTER STORAGE**

44

Noonday sun.

Frost sat in shadow, back to the fuselage. She kept still as she could, tried to breathe steady and slow. Eyes half closed. Sweat dripped from the tip of her nose. She watched heat ripple from surrounding dunes.

Hancock knelt in full sunlight, head bowed, arms lashed cruciform. He cooked in the heat. Cracked lips, peeling skin.

'Sure you don't want some shade?' said Frost. 'All you got to do is say please.'

'Fuck yourself.'

She uncapped her canteen and took a swig.

'Let me know if you change your mind.'

Movement at the top of a distant ridgeline.

Frost got to her feet and shielded her eyes. A figure stumbling out of thermal haze. Olive green flight suit. Black hair. Noble.

Frost ran as best she could. She reached the foot of the dune. Noble collapsed and tumbled down the gradient towards her.

Cracked, bleeding lips. Burned and blistered skin. He looked up at Frost slack-faced and blank eyed. He had retreated within himself, no longer aware of his surroundings.

She struggled to get him to his feet.

'Come on. Couple more yards, then you're done.'

She put a supporting arm around his shoulder. He showed no reaction as she half-guided/half-carried him to shade and lowered him to the ground beside the fuselage. He didn't react until she held her canteen to dust-dry lips and let him gulp.

Noble lay in the shade, back propped against the slate hull of the B-52. Heatstroke had set his ears ringing. Hours of sand glare had messed with his sight, made him blink away sunspots like bad concussion.

Frost leant into his field of vision. She waved a hand. She clicked her fingers.

'Harris. Can you hear me? Can you hear my voice?'

'Let me rest,' said Noble, almost inaudible.

'What happened? How far did you get?'

'Give me water.'

She held the canteen to his lips and let him drink some more.

'Did you find anything? Anything at all? Did you make it to the aim point? Did you make contact with anyone?'

Noble wearily shook his head.

'Bullshit. The entire mission. Nothing but bullshit.'

'But what did you find?'

'Death.'

'Nothing we can use? Nothing at all?'

He shook his head.

Frost fetched the trauma kit. She unzipped it and took out a clear bag of saline.

She stabbed her knife through the aluminium skin of the fuselage and hung the bag. She uncoiled clear tubing, tore open a sterile wrapper and took out a wide bore cannula. She held Noble's arm and slapped for a vein.

She hesitated, needle poised over skin as she tried to find a trace of blue beneath dust-matted, sunburned skin.

Noble leant forwards. He slowly raised a trembling hand and took the needle. He pumped a fist to boost bloodflow. Needle sunk into a vein. He slumped back against the plane.

Frost lashed the cannula in place with micropore tape and attached the IV tube. She checked the tube for kinks, made sure there was a clear feed.

'How's that?' she asked. 'Feel better?'

He nodded.

She took a bottle of burn gel from the trauma bag.

'I'm going to put some of this on your skin, okay? I'll be gentle.'

She squeezed gel onto her fingers and massaged it into his shoulders and arms.

He held out his hands and let her rub gel onto red-raw fingers.

He tipped his head back and let her wipe gel across his forehead, nose and cheekbones.

She unzipped a side pocket. Saline wash. She held back each lid with a thumb and flushed dust from his eyes.

'Thanks.'

He blinked away the artificial tears and tried to focus on Hancock. Blurred glimpse of a cruciform figure kneeling, head bowed, in the sand.

'What's going on with the AC?'

'Tell you later,' said Frost. 'Rest. Get your strength back.'

He leant his head against the hard metal of the fuselage and closed his eyes.

Frost watched the sun sink low and approach the horizon.

She inspected the drip. Two-thirds depleted.

She examined Noble, leant close and checked he was still breathing. She lifted his wrist and took his pulse.

Nothing to do but let him rest.

She untethered Hancock and led him to shade. He fell and lay still.

'Guess you're done for the day, give or take.'

She stood over him and sipped from her canteen. They

stared each other down. She crouched, held the canteen an inch from his lips and let a few drops fall on his tongue. He greedily licked the water, gaze still locked, beaming pure enmity.

She recapped the canteen.

She sat on the sand and released the ligatures binding her injured leg. She pulled up the pant leg of her flight suit.

'Swollen. Not as much as before. Guess it was a facture. And it's starting to heal.'

She talked to Hancock, expecting no reply. She used him for company, same way a person might confide in a cat or dog if they found themselves alone.

She unlaced her boot and pulled it free. She slid the crusted sock from her foot. She felt her toes.

'Still got circulation.'

Noble opened his eyes.

'Feeling any better?' asked Frost. 'I'd offer you something to eat, but we're out of food.'

He pointed to the backpack he'd brought with him.

She unzipped and searched the main compartment. A wad of documents. Empty water bottles. A plastic bag full of loose medical supplies.

'Found some meds, huh?'

'Morphine,' he croaked.

'You want morphine?'

'No. For you. For your leg.'

'Thanks, fella,' said Frost, genuinely touched. She slotted a couple of hypos into her bicep pocket. 'Thanks. That means a lot.'

Noble cleared his throat, shifted position, tried to straighten his back.

'Agency compound. Human experiments. That's why they wanted to drop the bomb. Cover their tracks.'

'Sure there was nothing at the site we could use?'

'Everyone dead. Everything burned.'

'Christ.'

'Trenchman was out there. Poor bastard drove into the desert trying to save our hides. Got himself stranded.'

They sat and watched the sun sink further towards the horizon.

'Cool breeze,' said Frost. 'Feel that? Bliss.'

Noble looked around, as if fully comprehending his surroundings for the first time. Eyes began to widen in fear.

He slowly rolled and began to crawl on all fours. The IV line pulled taut and plucked the needle from his arm.

'Hey.' asked Frost. 'What's up?'

He crawled towards the ragged break in the fuselage.

'Dude. Where are you going, Harris?'

Noble pointed at the sky.

'Darkness is coming.'

'Yeah.'

'Sand. Got to stay away from the sand.'

U.S. Department of Justice

Office of Legal Council

Office of the Assistant Attorney General   *Washington, D.C. 20530*

Memorandum for Declan R. Leuch

Senior Deputy General Counsel,

Central Intelligence Agency

Re: Circumstances Pertaining to the Use of Non-Voluntary Human Trial Subjects During Steps to Secure a Vaccine/Antidote to Virus MP01.

You have asked for our Office's view regarding the non-voluntary use of human test subjects during attempts by USAMRIID, FEMA and other Federal agencies to develop a vaccine or antidote to the virus designated MP01.

In Part I, we examine the meaning and implications of the President's sanction of 'special therapeutic measures' and 'enhanced medical procedures'.

In Part II, we examine the statutory limits of Presidential emergency powers in this regard.

In part III, we examine the jurisprudence of potential measures which

[cont'd]

45

Frost helped Noble to his feet. He put an arm round her shoulder for support.

They shuffled towards the rip in the fuselage.

'That's it,' said Frost. 'One foot in front of the other.'

Noble glanced over his shoulder at Hancock. The guy was propped against the fuselage, arms lashed cruciform. Sunburned, clothes white with dust. Eyes closed, head hung limp.

'What the hell happened while I was gone?'

'Touch of cabin fever.'

'You or him?'

Frost lowered Noble to the floor.

'Need any painkillers?'

He shook his head.

She took a foil strip from the trauma kit.

'We got codeine. No need to dope up on opiates.'

'I'm all right.'

'Take them anyway. Make me feel better.'

He lifted his head and swallowed the pills with a gulp of water from her canteen.

She leant against the nav console. She looked out the rip in the fuselage at the dunes.

'They came back, while you were gone. Pinback. Guthrie.'

'For you?'

Frost shook her head.

'They could take us anytime. Not sure what they want.

They come after dark. Ever seen a cat toy with a mouse? Bat it around, throw it in the air? Sounds crazy, but I think the disease is playing with us. Could kill us in the blink of an eye, but that would end the fun.'

'I saw Early,' said Noble. 'At least I think it was him. Dogged my steps the whole way.'

'Early.'

'Yeah.'

'Did you actually see him?'

'Not directly.'

The low sun framed by the ragged tear in the airframe. A strip of twilight projected across deck plate. They contemplated the coming night.

'They're under the sand,' said Noble. 'They're beneath us, hiding in the dust.'

Frost nodded.

'I saw an entire vehicle dragged beneath the sand,' he said. 'Starting to think there's a whole bunch out there.'

'A vehicle.'

'Trenchman's limo. He drove it into the desert hoping to rescue our asses, God bless him. Saw the entire thing dragged beneath the sand. Must have weighed two, three tons. Thrown around like it was nothing at all.'

'A subterranean army.'

'Telling you what I saw.'

She took an electronic thermometer from the trauma kit.

'Open your mouth.'

He sucked the thermometer while she took his pulse.

Normal pulse. Normal temp.

'Mind if I ask some questions?'

'Like what?'

'What's your full name?'

'I'm not nuts. I know what I saw.'

'I got to check for heatstroke. You were out there a long

while, head cooking in the sun. It's a marvel you made it back.'

'Hundred per cent sane.'

'Humour me.'

'Noble. Harris. Lieutenant, United States Air Force.'

'What's my name?'

'LaNitra Frost.'

'Where are you?'

'The armpit of the world.'

'What day is this?'

'Not a fucking clue.'

'Me neither,' smiled Frost. 'Totally lost track.'

She took the pistol from Noble's shoulder rig and ejected the mag. She put it in her pocket.

'What are you doing?'

'Things got a bit tense while you were away. Me and Hancock, not exactly seeing eye-to-eye. Best keep tabs on the weaponry. Don't want any future arguments to escalate into a fire fight.'

She patted Noble's chest pockets and removed a couple of spare clips. She thumbed bullets into her palm.

'More than a dozen rounds for each prowler. Normal circumstances, that would be plenty. But something tells me those bastards will go down hard.'

'Really want to take them on?'

'We've got no choice.'

She slotted bullets back into their magazines.

The flight deck.

She leant over the pilot seat, looked through the window and surveyed the dunes. She picked up duct tape and resealed the ejection hatches and windows. Wouldn't slow an intruder down, but she'd hear them coming. Rip and tear. They couldn't make it inside the plane without taking a full clip to the head.

She could block the ladderway with a trunk, but it might be better to leave the hatchway open. A good fire position. Pick them off as they climbed the ladder. Hard to imagine any of the prowlers would be dumb enough to make a head-on assault, but maybe she would get lucky.

Ought to decant water from the fuselage reservoir and stow it on the flight deck. Meaning to do it for a day or so. Stalling because she didn't want to face how little water they had left.

She descended the ladder to the lower cabin.

Frost stood over Noble.

'Reckon you can walk?'

'You're kidding me, right?'

'If we had to leave tonight, reckon you could cover a little ground?'

'Hurts to lift my arms right now.'

'If I shot you up with painkillers, could you move?'

'I don't know. Maybe. What about you? What about your leg?'

'I'll cope.'

'And what about Hancock?'

'Comes with us. Doesn't have a choice in the matter.'

'What's the deal? Why's he tied up?'

'The guy wants to complete the mission. Load the physics package on a sled, drag it to the target site and detonate the thing. Happy to let him do it, except that he wouldn't get a quarter of a mile before his legs gave out. Then he'd probably fire the nuke there and then, take us all to hell.'

'Why was he staked in the sun?'

'Payback. He did the same to me.'

'If I told you a week ago you'd be torturing some poor bastard to the brink of death, you wouldn't have believed me.'

'I didn't instigate this shit.'

316

'But you can put an end to it. The guy's tapped out. Let him inside.'

Frost went outside.

She crouched and examined the trip flare. It should have fired the previous night when Pinback entered the plane. He must have stepped over it.

Cunning motherfucker.

She sat in the shade.

Hancock lay on his back beside her, staring into the reddening sky with half-closed eyes.

The fuselage creaked and ticked. Metal contracting in the cool evening air.

'Kill me,' he whispered. 'Cut me loose or kill me.'

'You brought us to this. Remember that. Waving your gun around.'

'You don't have the guts to pull the trigger. Sooner or later you'll set me free.'

'I don't want to shoot you. I don't want to shoot anyone. Convinced yourself this is some kind of zero-sum face-off. Fighting me because I'm human, a quantifiable enemy, unlike those infected fucks out there in the sand.'

'You're a fucking coward.'

Frost took a tube of toothpaste from her pocket. She squeezed a nub onto her finger and rubbed it round her teeth.

'I'm getting out of here, and I'm going to take you with me. Sit you on the sled and drag your ass, if that's what it takes.'

'The Great Trek. You've been talking about it for days. Haven't taken a single step.'

'We leave tonight. Pinback, Guthrie, the rest. They'll show when darkness comes. We'll force a confrontation, put them down for good.'

He gave a derisive snort.

'You need a major reality check,' said Frost. 'You're dying of septicaemia. Forget the mission. You won't be striding off across the desert to a hero's death. Your skin is necrotising, rotting from your skull. Smells bad. Real bad. You need antibiotics. If we make it to a town, we might be able to find a pharmacy that hasn't been looted bare. Grab what we can. Then we'll find some kind of army unit, some place with a surgeon, some place that can perform a graft. Either that, or you can sit here and let the flesh peel from your bones like a leper.'

Frost held her canteen to Hancock's mouth. He struggled to lift his head and drink.

'This is a chance to become someone new,' said Frost. 'Ever think of that? This anarchy. A chance to erase your past. Pick up a dead guy's wallet and take a new name.'

Hancock drank some more.

'I don't need a new name. I know exactly who I am.'

Frost unsheathed her knife.

'Am I going to regret this? If I cut you loose, going to give me any trouble?'

'Think I'm going to beg? Go fuck yourself.'

Frost cut him free. He groaned and stretched, massaged stiff, welted arms.

'We ought to get inside,' said Frost.

'Sit in the plane and wait to die? That's your big fucking plan?'

'Like I said. We get our shit together then walk out of here.'

'Never make it. Look what the journey did to Noble.'

'He reached the foot of the Panamints. Could have gone a lot further, if he hadn't turned back.'

'He would have died in those mountains. Barren as the desert. Nothing living up there but vultures. He would have been carrion.'

318

'He had a shot.'

She held out a hand. Hancock hesitated, then let her pull him to his feet.

He swung his arms, tried to restore circulation. He bent and stretched.

She waited to see if he were about to throw a punch. Too strung out. He sagged, exhausted, against the fuselage.

'You better get inside,' said Frost. 'It'll be dark soon.'

Hancock climbed through the rip in the fuselage. He stood a while, holding the wall for support, letting his eyes adjust to darkness.

He blinked to clear sunspots from his vision. He saw Noble lying on the deck, head propped by a parachute.

'You look fucking awful,' croaked Noble, looking up at him.

Hancock slid down the nav console and sat on the floor.

'Take a look in the mirror. You're no prom date.'

'Your head. Looks bad. Smells bad.'

'Not a whole lot I can do about it. And you smell pretty ripe yourself, by the way.'

Hancock spat dust. He sat, head in hands.

'They'll be coming for us, soon as night falls,' said Noble.

Hancock pointed to Noble's side arm, the vacancy in the butt.

'She took your magazines.'

'Yeah.'

'Worried I would take your gun?'

'That's right.'

Hancock smiled and shook his head.

'You need to sort your shit out, you and her,' said Noble.

'Going to help me suppress a mutiny?'

'I'm not picking sides in this fight.'

'I'm still AC, no matter what. And we got orders.'

'Do I have to spell it out? That satellite link you've been fooling with? There's no one at the other end. Those flash EAMs? Figment of your imagination. Just you, at the keyboard, typing little messages to yourself. There is no chain of command. We are utterly alone.'

'Tell yourself whatever you like. The orders were real. They stand. We got a mission to execute, so are you going to do your job, or pussy out like her?'

'I went out there, Captain. I saw the target site. Apache. Some kind of multi-agency installation. A FEMA/CDC slaughterhouse. You know full well this mission has no purpose. An attempt to whitewash the reputations of guys that probably died weeks ago. Pure bullshit. But you're in a headlong rush to die for it anyway.'

'Some folks choose to live by a code. No point trying to explain.'

'Never understood guys like you. Itching to jump on a grenade.'

They each retreated into silence.

Noble supported himself on an elbow and sipped from a canteen. He offered it to Hancock as a conciliatory gesture.

Hancock hesitated, then took the steel flask.

'I saw the damndest thing while I was at Apache,' said Noble.

'What?'

'There was an office. Paper scattered everywhere. Some of it Japanese. Dense pages of kanji.'

'Yeah?'

'And there were pictures. Look.'

He dug in his backpack. He handed Hancock monochrome sheets. Poor quality. Copies of old woodblock prints, kind of thing held in a Tokyo museum. Stylised, grotesque.

Hancock examined the pages. One showed a city on a hill. Townsfolk leaning from their windows, watching some

320

kind of shooting star fall to earth. Another showed a samurai warrior, sword drawn, confronting an army of deformed skeletal things.

He studied the samurai. Black armour. A white, half-face skull painted on the snarling helmet mask.

'Japan.'

'Maybe this isn't the first time humans have faced off against the virus. Maybe it's been here before.'

Frost paced the dunes. She took a last look around before sunset.

She sat on the half-buried undercarriage. She disassembled her Beretta and held the components in her lap. She blew them free of sand.

She sharpened her knife on the ragged stump of a hydraulic actuator. Steel-on-steel. Each rasping stroke honing the blade razor-sharp.

Section II. FIELD-EXPEDIENT WEAPONS

To survive, the soldier in combat must be able to deal with any situation that develops. His ability to adapt any nearby object for use as a weapon in a win-or-die situation is limited only by his ingenuity and resourcefulness. Possible weapons, although not discussed herein, include ink pens or pencils; canteens tied to string to be swung; snap links at the end of sections of rope; kevlar helmets; sand, rocks, or liquids thrown into the enemy's eyes; or radio antennas. The following techniques demonstrate a few expedient weapons that are readily available to most soldiers for defense and counterattack against the bayonet and rifle with fixed bayonet.

46

Frost uncapped a hypodermic auto-injector.

'You're pretty liberal with that shit,' said Noble.

'We got a fight on our hands. Need you fully functional.'

'Don't think a head full of opiates counts as functional.'

'It'll get you on your feet.'

She took his arm and sunk a needle into his vein.

Frost stood beneath the starboard wing. She reached up into the cavity behind the spoilers and worked at a fuel line.

'Hold that flashlight steady.'

She loosened a nut joint with a wrench.

'Ready with that jerry can.'

She unscrewed the joint. Noble held the can to catch a steady dribble of JP8. Dregs from a wing tank.

'Better not breathe the fumes,' said Noble. 'Be tripping your ass off.'

The dribble slowed to a stop.

They capped the can and carried it back to the plane.

The lower cabin.

Noble held out empty mineral water bottles. Frost decanted fuel.

Hancock watched them work.

'Don't spill any of that shit.'

Frost tore strips of chute fabric and stuffed them in the neck of each bottle for wick.

'These bottles are plastic,' said Noble. 'Throw them quick, once you light the fuse. Likely to burn through and blow up in your face.'

'Touched you guys are so concerned for my welfare.'

'Might as well just shoot the fuckers,' said Hancock. 'Only way to be sure.'

'Fire will finish them well enough,' said Frost. 'Minute or two in the flames will turn eyeballs to steam. Couple more minutes will cook muscles rigid. Burn long enough, and their brains will poach in their skulls.'

She lined Molotovs on the nav console.

'You guys better wait upstairs.'

'Not sure I can move,' said Hancock.

'Give him a hand.'

Noble helped Hancock to his feet.

Hancock gripped the ladder.

'Honestly can't pull myself up.'

Noble held Hancock's hips and helped him upwards rung by rung to the flight deck.

He put an arm round Hancock's shoulder and steered him to the pilot seat.

Frost joined them.

'You should be safe up here.'

She slid down the cockpit ladder, letting her good leg take the impact.

She fetched her crutch from outside and crouched on the floor of the lower deck. She opened a parachute pack, slit fabric and wound it round the crutch. Wadded nylon lashed in place by paracord.

Noble climbed down the ladder.

He stumbled, grabbed the nav console for support.

'I want to help,' he said.

Frost handed him the crutch. She picked up the jerry can.

'Let's get a fire going.'

The setting sun turned the desert rich caramel. Dunes cast lengthening shadows.

The extinct signal fire. A part-buried tyre.

They knelt and shovelled sand aside.

Noble stood back as Frost slopped aviation fuel. She flicked her Zippo and jumped back as vapour ignited with a thump and a fireball. The wheel burned blue and belched acrid black smoke.

'Should tip the scales when our friends come calling. Rob them of darkness. If they want to bite a chunk out of our derrières they'll have to step into the light.'

She held an improvised torch in the flames. Chute fabric caught alight. Nylon melted to bubbling tar.

'Sure this is a good idea? None of us in much shape for a fight.'

'We'll have to face these bastards sooner or later. Might as well dictate terms. The plane is a good killing ground. Plenty of bottlenecks and fallback positions. It'll give us an edge. They can't try for us on the flight deck without leaving themselves fully exposed. I'd rather face them here than out there in the sand.'

'Must admit, I'm a trifle apprehensive.'

'Between you and me, never been so scared,' said Frost. 'But it's good to be taking action.'

Frost looked up. A dusting of stars across a darkening sky.

'We better get inside.'

They walked back towards the B-52.

'So you want to head for the Panamints tonight?' asked Noble. 'Is that the plan? Wipe out these bastards then hit the road?'

'Maybe I should give you guys longer to recuperate, but

you know what? There will always be a reason to postpone, to sit around, making excuses, until the water runs out. Been here less than a week, but this plane has become my world. Everything else is a fading dream.'

'We can't leave Hancock behind.'

'Guess we help him all we can. But in the end, it's down to him. He'll need to forget his plans to deliver the warhead to the target site, and decide to live.'

Frost staked the torch in the ground near the aircraft entrance.

Noble looked up at the emerging constellations.

'It's going to be a beautiful night.'

The flight deck.

Frost took Hancock's lock-knife from her pocket. A Benchmark Griptillian. She flipped it open, put it in his hand. Burned fingers closed round the silicon grip. He contemplated the blade.

'You could put it in my back easy enough,' said Frost. 'But I'm the only thing standing between you and our friends outside. Think it over.'

She unsheathed her K-bar and gave it to Noble.

'So what's the plan?' he asked.

'I need you guys to watch my back. That's all. If I can lure them into a stand-up fight, I can take them down. Don't care how sly these bastards are, how resilient. A full clip to the face, and the dance is over.'

Noble examined the heavy survival knife. Seven-inch blade. Curved Bowie tip. Blood channels.

He saw the pink blur of his face reflected in steel. A gaunt stranger. Stubble. Blistered skin. Bloodshot eyes.

'Want me to guard the windows?'

'Yeah. You and Hancock. And watch the hatches. If you hear a sound, the slightest hint they are trying to worm their way inside, holler.'

He tested the tip of the blade, adjusted his grip.

'Forget it,' said Frost. 'You're in no shape to tussle. If any of those fuckers gets in here, just stand aside. I'll deal with them.'

'I can still handle myself. Soft entry point. Eye socket, base of the skull. Put them down for good.'

Frost sat with her back to the wall, gun in her lap. She massaged her leg.

Noble sat against the opposite wall. He used the knife to dig dirt from his fingernails.

They listened to the tick of cooling metal, the symphonic contraction of the fuselage.

A muffled thud from down below.

They froze: Noble picking his teeth with the knife tip, Frost biting cuticle.

Clumsy, shuffling footsteps. Boots on metal.

Frost rechecked her pistol. Safety to Off. Brass in the chamber.

She towelled the butt free of sweat on her sleeve. She wiped the palm of her shooting hand on her pant leg.

She crawled across the floor to the equipment trunk blocking the ladderway to the cabin below.

Rumble of a heavy object dragged across deck plate.

'Sounds like they're moving something around,' whispered Hancock.

'How many of them do you reckon?'

Frost listened to stumbling footsteps.

'One, I think.'

'You're sure?' asked Noble.

'The others must be holding back.'

'I don't like it.'

'What's to like?'

They listened a while longer.

Heavy bootfalls.

'Pinback?' asked Hancock.

'Dragging foot. Hear that? Definite limp. Probably Guthrie.'

327

Fingernails raked metal. Frost listened hard, tried to picture the geography of the cabin below.

Clatter and thud.

'Sounds like he's trying to climb into the crawlspace. Fuckers are fixated on that payload hatch. They instinctually make for the warhead. Drawn back to it, time and again.'

She gripped the Molotov. She pulled the Zippo from her pocket.

'You ready?' she asked.

Noble crawled across the cabin floor. He put his shoulder to the trunk and got ready to push.

'Count of three.'

He nodded.

She brought the lighter flame to the Molotov and lit the wick.

'. . . One . . . two . . . three . . .'

Grit-grinding rasp as Noble pushed the trunk aside.

Frost held the bottle over the ladderway, using the fluttering wick-flame to illuminate the cabin below.

Stumbling footsteps. Something monstrous lurched out of shadow, gripped the foot of the ladder and looked up at her.

Guthrie. Half a head. Half a brain.

Frost hurled the Molotov. The plastic bottle hit Guthrie's face and split open.

Fuel splash.

Fireball.

The creature ablaze. It thrashed and shrieked. The lower cabin was filled with fire and smoke.

Frost threw herself aside to avoid the wave of roiling fire rushing up the ladderway to envelope her. She kicked away from the hatch, covered her mouth and nose to mask the stink of kerosene and cooking flesh.

She waited while Guthrie burned.

FIRE EXTINGUISHER

RECHARGE & INSPECTION

RECORD

INSTRUCTIONS

Attach this tag to the fire extinguisher. Recharging and inspection records are to be entered by inspectors:

CO_2

Weigh and inspect monthly.

DRY CHEMICAL (CARTRIDGE TYPE)

Weigh cartridge monthly.

Check chemical every 6 months.

DRY CHEMICAL (STORED PRESSURE TYPE)

Check gauge for proper pressure.

PRESSURIZED WATER

Check gauge for proper pressure.

Operating personnel should inspect extinguishers daily and report broken seals or defects immediately to the Safety Officer.

DATE	BY	DATE	BY

47

Frost lay on the flight-deck floor. She gripped the lip of the hatchway and looked down into the lower cabin. Flame and smoke. Splashed fuel burned blue.

Pop and crack of bubbling cable insulation.

The lung-searing stink of melting seat foam.

She covered her mouth and nose with her hand.

She jumped back as Guthrie slammed against the ladder below her. He burned and flailed. His Nomex flight suit was fire retardant, but his desiccated body was alight. Slow-cooking body fat. Hands and face sweated boiling grease.

He gripped the ladder like he intended to climb but instead hung from the rungs, limbs locked and trembling, like the metal was delivering high-voltage current. Exposed brain tissue boiled and fizzed. The creature wracked by a long epileptic convulsion. Lolling tongue. Weird cackling scream.

'Shoot,' shouted Noble. 'Shoot the damned thing.'

She took aim. She tried to centre the pistol sights on the remaining quadrant of Guthrie's forehead. He was dancing around too much to get a clear shot.

The creature wrenched itself clear of the ladder, leaving a couple of crisped fingers glued to a rung.

Frost was overwhelmed by thick smoke. She retched. She shook her head and attempted to clear her vision.

She rolled clear of the hatch and kicked the trunk back in position.

She sat back, hands pressed over burning, watering eyes.

'Let him fry,' she said. 'Maybe the poor bastard's brain will cook. Save us a bullet.'

She blinked away tears. The dark cockpit interior slowly came into focus. Detail reasserted itself.

The flight deck was slowly filling with black smoke, fumes curling from cable conduits and vents recessed behind wall insulation.

'You ought to get down there and put out the fire,' said Noble. 'It's starting to spread.'

Frost shook her head.

'No need to panic. Let him roast a little longer.'

She checked her leg, adjusted the bindings holding the calf splint.

Hancock watched from the pilot seat. He gestured to his missing eye.

'Wears you down, doesn't it? Constant pain.'

Frost didn't reply.

Wisps of smoke from the trunk blocking the ladderway. The sides of the vinyl case starting to bubble and warp in the heat.

Frost lay her hand on deck plate beside her. Metal warm from the fire below.

Muffled thud. An inhuman, mewling shriek from the lower cabin.

'Unbelievable,' said Noble. 'Son of a bitch just won't quit. This guy's so hard to kill, it's almost funny.'

Squeals of rage gave way to pitiful moans.

'No point waiting any longer,' said Noble. 'Better head down there and finish him off.'

Frost pulled on gloves. She opened a locker, threw clutter aside and retrieved an M40 respirator with a charcoal hood. Anti-radiation gear left from the days *Liberty Bell* carried gravity nukes during stand-off patrols near the Arctic Circle.

She put on the mask and adjusted straps.

She pushed the trunk aside.

Hancock held back a cockpit blast screen to vent thick fumes which immediately filled the flight deck. He fanned his hands, tried to encourage the noxious fog out the window.

Frost pulled the ring-tab from a wall extinguisher and trained a jet of carbon smoke into the lower cabin. She swept the nose cone back and forth, blasted every surface.

She dropped the depleted extinguisher through the hatchway. Metal clang.

She fumbled her flashlight and hit On. The beam shafted downwards into the smoke-filled lower compartment. Seething, swirling fumes. Black combustion smoke replaced by white, dry-ice mist from the extinguisher.

She turned and slowly climbed down the ladder, craning to make sure Guthrie didn't lie in wait.

She stepped to the floor.

Harsh filter rasp. Each panting exhalation amplified to a guttural breath-roar.

She looked around through the fogged portholes of her mask. Broiling suppressant smoke. A sweep of her flashlight lit deck walls and control surfaces cover in glittering carbon rime.

Double take: her ejector seat was back in position. The metal chair frame had been shunted in front of the nav console. She reached out and tentatively touched the headrest. The seat had fallen miles from the plane. Fell out the sky at three-hundred miles an hour and buried itself among the dunes. Yet here it was, back in situ, warped by impact and gritted with sand.

She continued her search.

She crouched and checked the bomb bay crawlspace. Metal conduit leading to the payload hatch.

No sign of Guthrie.

★

Frost left the plane. She leant against the fuselage to take weight from her injured leg. She pulled off her mask.

She looked around. Dunes lit infernal red by the signal fire.

'Where are you, Guss?'

She took a gyrojet flare pen from her pocket. She twisted a shell the size of a shotgun cartridge onto the head, pulled back the spring bolt, and fired the cartridge. The shell soared skyward. Crack. Starbust. The landscape lit harsh white.

Guthrie lay face down in sand. Blackened, smoking flesh. A grotesque stick creature hauling itself towards the dunes. Fingers raked dust. Crisped skin split and wept pus. It left a drag-trench flecked with flaked flesh and scraps of suit fabric.

Frost unholstered her pistol and walked towards the prone man.

'How you doing, Guss? Think it's about time you got some sleep.'

Hancock pulled back a blast screen and peered through the shattered cockpit window. He watched Frost cross the sand towards Guthrie, pistol drawn.

'One down,' he murmured.

A hand lunged down from the exterior roof, reached through the cockpit window and snatched at Hancock's head. It gripped the dressing wrapped round his scalp and seized a fistful of hair. He felt sutures tear. He felt skin rip further open and a warm wash of blood behind his left ear and down his neck.

'Jesus fucking Christ,' he shouted. He grabbed the emaciated hand, tried to prise fingers, but they dug into scalp-flesh like talons.

He struggled and thrashed as he was wrenched from his seat. He looked up, glimpsed a cracked Luminox and a rot-streaked sleeve. He punched at the arm, tried to break bone.

'Frost,' he bellowed, 'Frost, fucker's got me.'

He grasped at avionics, gripped thrust levers as he felt himself drawn inexorably up and out through the cockpit window.

334

48

Frost limped across the sand. Cold magnesium radiance turned the dunescape to ice. Each foot-crunch left a boot-print like she was walking through powdered snow.

Guthrie squirmed through the sand in a series of spastic convulsions. Flailing limbs churned a shallow trench.

She watched him crawl. Only the left side of his body retained function. He kicked with his left leg, clawed with his left hand.

She held her pistol in a double grip.

'How you doing, Guthrie?'

The broken creature turned towards Frost. Face burned away. Stump nose. Skeletal grin. Its remaining eye socket was a charred pit.

'Where are your friends? Are they coming out to play?'

She circled the prone creature.

'Why don't you folks attack en masse? Drawing us out? Is that the idea?'

Guthrie slowly turned his head, drawn by the rustle of her flight suit, the faint crunch of boots pressing sand.

He slowly pulled himself upright, balancing his weight on his leg. He faced Frost. She continued to circle. He followed every move.

'Tracking by sound. Smart motherfucker.'

They continued their slow dance. Frost gripped her pistol, ready to put Guthrie down the moment he lunged.

'What are you? Some kind of super-species? Some kind of evolutionary leap?'

'Reesus,' hissed Guthrie.

Frost cocked her head.

'What did you just say?'

'Reesus.'

Hancock crouched on the riveted metal of the cockpit roof. Dust-caked boots in front of him. He wiped blood from his eyes and looked up. A ragged flight suit matted with sand. Name strip: PINBACK. Hancock craned to see the man's face. Black eyes. Peeling flesh. Hancock struggled to his feet. He pulled the lock-knife from his pocket and flipped open the stubby blade. He gripped the knife with a trembling hand.

'All right, bitch.' He swayed and stumbled, almost fell from the plane, then regained his balance. 'Let's boogie.'

Hancock slashed the knife back and forth, waited for Pinback to make a move.

'Show me what you got. Come on. Let's go.'

Sound of ripping fabric near his feet. Noble forcing his way through one of the patched ejection hatches. He squirmed through the aperture onto the roof.

He stood between Pinback and Hancock. Classic knife-fighter crouch, knife hugged to his belly.

He gestured to Hancock.

'Get down below.'

'To hell with that shit.'

'Seriously. You're in no shape. Get below. I got this.'

'So what are you waiting for? Kill the fucker.'

Noble addressed Pinback.

'Hey. It's me. Harris. Remember? Think back. You got to remember.'

The blank face stared back at him.

'We all said it, right? Every guy in uniform, some time or other, sitting in a bar. *Shoot me. If I get fragged by an IED, if some jihadi motherfucker takes my legs, my dick, shoot me in the*

337

damned head. Don't let me suffer. Don't leave me paralysed. That night at The Barracuda. You and me. We shook. We had a deal. Take care of each other, no matter what. Do what's got to be done.'

No response.

Noble shuffled closer to the cadaverous figure.

'I'm talking to Pinback, Captain Daniel Pinback. You in there, Dan? Let me help you. Let me set you free.'

Pinback turned away and walked aft down the spine of the fuselage.

'So what do you want from us?' shouted Noble. 'Rip out our throats? Go ahead. Turn around and take a shot.'

Pinback kept walking.

'Fucking with our heads, is that it? To see how bad we want to survive?'

Noble spread his arms wide.

'Come on, you bastard. Get your ass back here. Try and take a bite.'

Frost and Guthrie continued their dance.

She tried to work out if he were struggling to talk, or if the vocal sounds were an involuntary convulsion of the throat. One of the blackly comic aspects of infection: belches and long, rippling farts. A consequence of internal decay, bodies starting to bloat with rot gas.

'Raysus.'

'What are you trying to say?'

'Raysus.'

He tried to run at her. A loping, convulsive limp. She shot him in the thigh, shattering his femur. He fell to the ground.

Frost dug the flare pen from her pocket and sent up another star shell.

The flare hung in the sky projecting harsh light and sliding shadows.

Guthrie lifted his head.

'Joysus.'

'Jesus. Is that what you're saying? Jesus?'

'Joysus.'

'Can you remember your old life? Is some of you left?' She stepped closer to the prone figure. 'Guss. Are you still in there? Concentrate. Think. Can you remember who you used to be? Hail Mary, full of grace. Can you say it? Hail Mary, full of grace. Say the words.'

Guthrie lunged, snapping, biting. She backed off. She lowered herself to her knees, well out of reach.

'What's it like? Death. You died, remember? Your parachute failed. Hit the ground full speed. Guess the virus jump-started your heart. What was it like on the other side? Can you tell me? Did you go someplace? What did you see?'

'Joy. Suss.'

'Is there anything at all?'

'Joy.'

'Tell me it's all true. There's light on the other side. Light and love.'

He snarled and reached for her, tried to crawl. She got to her feet. She stamped on his ankles until they broke.

'Joy.'

She stood over him.

'Infection. Is it better than death? Can't help wondering. If I injected the virus to avoid dying of thirst, would it be worth the extra days? Surely some kind of sensation, some kind of half-life, would be better than nothing at all.'

'Joy.'

Frost kicked Guthrie's shoulder, rolled him onto his back. She planted a foot on his chest.

He broke teeth trying to chew the splint binding her leg.

She stamped on his neck, boot jammed beneath his chin.

'Joy,' he hissed, head pinned to the sand.

339

She took aim.

'Join us.'

She fired a full clip into his face. Muzzle roar and gun smoke. Sand splashed with brain, teeth and splintered skull.

LINE – NO HAND HOLD

49

Frost climbed up the ladder into the cockpit.

'Hancock? Noble?'

She checked the cabin interior. The beam of her flashlight shafted through residual smoke haze.

She checked the pilot's chair, made sure Hancock wasn't sitting with his back to her.

The seats were empty.

One of the blast curtains was pulled back. Blood and tufts of flight-suit fabric on broken polycarbon.

She looked through the window. She shone her flashlight down at the sand fifteen feet below. No sign of Hancock or Noble. No disturbance in the dust.

Cold air on the back of her neck. She looked up. Starlight. A vacant ejection hatch above the co-pilot station.

She jumped, gripped the lip of the hatch, hauled herself up and out.

The fuselage lit by moonlight. The huge body of the plane. The vulpine wings.

Hancock and Noble fifteen yards distant, facing aft.

She got to her feet and limped towards them.

'You guys okay?'

They turned. Faces full of exhaustion and fear.

'Fucker is messing with our heads,' said Noble.

'Who?'

'Pinback.'

'He was here?'

'Didn't you see?' asked Hancock. 'Didn't you hear us shout?'

Frost gestured to her left. Guthrie's body lying in the sand seventy yards distant, lit by weak flame light.

'Otherwise engaged.'

Hancock's exposed head wound glistened with fresh blood.

'Jeez. You okay?'

Hancock ignored the question, stared towards the aft of the plane as if he expected Pinback to return.

Frost trained her flashlight on riveted roof plates. Boot-prints in the dust. She followed footprints aft to their abrupt termination.

'Looks like he jumped,' she said.

Noble squinted at the body lying near the signal fire.

'Who was it?'

'Guthrie.'

'Dead?'

'Yeah.'

'You're sure?'

'Yeah, I'm sure. He's down for good.'

'Then I guess we've got two to go.'

'It's cold. Let's get back inside.'

They turned to retrace their route back to the cockpit roof hatch.

Muffled thump from down below.

'Dammit,' muttered Frost. 'Hear that? They're still trying for the bomb bay.'

Hancock shook his head and said:

'Persistent sons of . . .'

His foot slipped on the sand-dusted curve of the fuselage. He fell on his back and began to slide legs first from the plane. He rolled onto his belly. His hands slapped the hull as he tried to find purchase. His boots thumped against smooth aluminium fuselage panels. No foothold. He tried to grip flush rivets and broke fingernails.

'Take my hand,' said Frost.

She reached down and gripped his right hand. Noble grasped his left.

Hancock continued to slide, threatening to pull them both from the roof.

They lost grip. He fell from the plane.

'Christ.'

Frost leant forwards and shone the flashlight downwards. Hancock sprawled on the sand.

'Are you all right?' shouted Frost.

'Think so,' said Hancock. He raised his head. He flexed his arms. 'Think I'm okay. Don't think I broke anything.'

The sand behind his head began to shift and bulge.

'Get up,' shouted Frost. 'Get off the sand.'

Hancock looked around. He saw dust ripple and seethe.

'Shit.'

He tried to galvanise sluggish limbs and get to his feet.

'Just get off the damn sand,' yelled Frost.

She ran down the spine of the plane, sat on her ass and pushed herself from the roof. She slid, fell, and hit the starboard wing. Clumsy parachute roll on sand-dusted metal. She crawled to the leading edge of the wing. She hung, arm outstretched.

'Get over here. Grab my hand.'

Hancock staggered towards her and reached up. Their fingers brushed. Too high.

Frost pointed to the tip of the wing where the drape of the metal brought it close to the ground.

'Run.'

Hancock ran for the tip of the wing. He stumbled like a drunk.

Frost ran a parallel course, limping along the wing surface.

She reached the tip of the wing and threw herself to her knees. Noble joined her. They stretched out their hands.

'Come on,' shouted Noble. 'Keep running.'

Hancock lurched across the sand, desperately trying to keep his balance. He toppled and fell. The ground behind him began to bulge and undulate.

'Get up,' shouted Frost. 'Get up, you fuck.'

Hancock climbed to his feet. He grabbed at their arms. He missed. One eye: no depth perception. Second try. They seized his wrists and pulled.

Explosion of sand. Glimpse of a dirt-clogged, skeletal thing, reaching from the dust.

Early.

Helmet. Matted flight suit. Skin like leather. It grasped at Hancock's ankles.

Hancock kicked and jerked his legs free. They hauled him onto the wing. They lay panting on the sheet-metal surface.

Frost rolled, pulled the pistol from her waistband and fired a volley into the sand.

Stuttering muzzle flash lit the cadaverous creature as it squirmed below ground. Meat-smack. Bullets hit flesh. Spark and whine: a round grazed the visor hinge of a flight helmet and deflected into the night.

She swept the dunes with her flashlight. Churned sand. The figure was gone.

She and Noble helped Hancock to his feet. They walked the length of the wing, leaning against each other for support.

Hancock climbed onto the roof of the aircraft using split panels as foot holds. He leaned down, proffering a hand, helped Frost and Noble reach the roof.

'Sly bastards. Do anything to avoid a straight fight.'

Frost wasn't listening.

'My God,' she murmured, looking past Hancock and Noble to the darkness at the rear of the plane.

345

She pulled the flare pen from her pocket, loaded a cap and fired.

Crack. The star shell streaked skyward. Magnesium burn. The crash site lit harsh white.

'Jesus,' murmured Noble.

The tail section of the plane sat fifty yards away.

'Tell me I'm not going nuts,' said Noble. 'That wasn't there before, right?'

Frost shook her head.

'It was a quarter of a mile back in the debris trench.'

'Fuckers are trying to reassemble the aircraft,' said Hancock. 'Putting it back together, piece by piece.'

'That thing has to weigh fifty tons,' said Frost, pointing at the tail. 'Couple of guys couldn't drag it on their own. There must be more of them out there, working in concert. A lot more.'

DITCHING
HAMMOCK
0016

50

They lowered themselves into the flight deck.

Frost retaped the insulation blanket, sealed the ejection hatch.

Hancock lowered himself to the floor. He tried to steady his breathing. He placed a hand on his chest.

'Heart like a jackhammer. Might keel over right here. How about that? All of this shit going down, and I drop from a cardiac arrest.'

Frost peered down the ladderway into the lower cabin, pistol drawn.

Empty.

Noble picked a sand-dusted flight helmet from the pilot seat.

'Hey. This wasn't here when we left, right?'

He threw the helmet to Hancock.

Hancock examined the name stencil-sprayed above the visor.

GUTHRIE.

'They left it on your seat,' said Noble. 'Must be intended for you. Maybe it's some kind of message.'

'What do they want from me?'

'Damned if I know.'

Frost sat on the deck beside him. She ejected the pistol mag and counted bullets.

'Whole lot of running around and not much achieved,' said Hancock.

'Achieved plenty. Lured Guthrie inside and took him down. Proves they can be killed.'

'Took a lot of effort, a lot of bullets, to finish the guy. And there are a bunch more out there. Guess we stirred a nest of the creeps at Apache, brought them our way. Out there right now, hiding beneath the sand. We'd need a Gatling gun and grenades to make a fair fight.'

Noble sat in the pilot seat, lifted a blast blind and peered out into the moonlit night.

'He's gone. Guthrie. His body is gone.'

'You're sure?'

Frost joined him at the window.

Blood on the sand. Bone and brain. But no Guthrie.

'They took him. He didn't get up and walk. He's dead for sure. Guarantee it.'

They listened to the low wind-moan.

'What time is it?' asked Frost.

'No idea. Midnight, at a guess.'

'How long since you two got any sleep?'

'Can't sleep in a situation like this.'

'How's your leg?' asked Noble.

Frost flexed her foot.

'All right.'

Noble turned to Hancock.

'How's your head?'

Hancock gestured to torn flesh and crusted blood.

'How do you think?'

'Smells pretty rank.'

'So everyone keeps telling me. You two aren't exactly shower-fresh, so pardon me if I invite you both to go fuck yourselves.'

Frost uncapped her canteen. They passed it back and forth. Shallow sips.

Hancock shook the canteen and listened to water slop in the half-empty bottle.

'Who are we kidding?' he said. 'We're not going anywhere. All of us in fucked-up shape. Guess we could have walked days ago, but the moment has passed.' He looked around the flight deck. 'Face it. This place is our tomb.'

Frost looked like she wanted to argue, but didn't have the energy. She contemplated the gun in her hand. She stroked the grip with her thumb.

'Don't let me end up like them,' she said. 'Take care of it, all right? Make me that promise. I don't want a living death.'

'Maybe you were right all along,' said Noble, addressing Hancock. 'Maybe we should fire up the nuke. Take the fuckers with us.'

They sat in silence a while.

Hancock's eyelids began to droop. His head nodded towards his chest. Deep breaths evolved into a congested snore.

Frost struggled to stand.

The sound of her boots scuffing deck plate jerked Hancock awake.

'Where are you going?' asked Hancock.

'I'm going to take a look at the tail section. Try and figure out what these bastards have planned.'

'Outside? On your own?'

She shook her head.

'I'll cut through the bomb bay.'

'Then give me a gun. Anything happens to you, Noble and I will be left defenceless.'

Frost thought it over. She took a spare mag from her pocket and tossed it to Noble.

She reached up and fumbled on the ledge above the Electronic Warfare Officer console. She retrieved Hancock's Beretta. She handed it to him butt first. He loaded a clip and chambered a round.

'Watch where you're pointing that thing.'

Noble unclipped a pocket of his survival vest and tossed Frost a radio.

'If you run into trouble, holler.'

Frost climbed down the ladder to the lower cabin.

She climbed into the crawlspace. She examined the bomb-bay door. The steel hatch was heavily dented. One of the creatures had been unable to figure out the D-ring latches and tried to punch its way inside.

She twisted the latches and pulled back the door.

The interior of the bomb bay glowed infernal red, like she was crawling into a furnace mouth.

She slid from the walkway and stood straight. Trapped day heat. She wiped sweat.

She side-stepped the disassembled Tomahawk hanging from its launch bracket. First glimpse of Hancock's work. The payload cowling unscrewed and set aside. The physics package disconnected and part removed. Tools scattered on the floor.

She walked the length of the bomb bay, balanced along a narrow grate walkway. She hugged wall conduits and held wall spars for support.

Sudden jolt. Shudder and metal shriek. The airframe shook. Frost fell to her knees. The missile suspended above her creaked and trembled in its cradle.

Static crackle:

'Frost? You feel that?'

She pulled a radio from her pocket.

'Yeah. Whole place shook.'

'Okay down there?'

'Something going on at the rear of the plane. Fuckers are up to something. Let me check it out.'

'Watch yourself.'

She got to her feet.

She reached the rear hatch.

She crouched and released the door latches.

She opened the door slowly, pistol in one hand, flashlight in the other.

She shone her flashlight into the narrow crawl channel. She climbed inside and headed for the tail.

Fifteen yards of conduit that took her past the aft gear well and fuel bladders towards the ECM equipment.

She reached a seam of ragged metal and scraps of foil insulation. The tail had been restored, crudely shunted back in position. She probed the crude join with her fingers. Glimpse of stars through fissured metal. Whistling night wind.

The flight deck.

Frost sat on the floor and wiped sweat from her face.

'They've shunted the tail back in position. God knows how. Didn't see anyone. Just reached the rear, and there it was. Think they're planning to fly out of here? Jam this bird back together, take her for a ride?'

Hancock sat staring at her. A look of apprehension on his face. He nodded towards the pilot seat.

'What's up?'

He mimed hush.

Frost got to her feet. She pulled the pistol from her waistband. She crept towards the pilot seat.

Noble reclined in the chair. His flight suit was unzipped. His belly was a blackened mess. He stroked the metallic spines that furred his skin like chest hairs and stared, unfocused, at the flight controls in front of him.

'Oh Christ.'

'Best stay away,' he said, without looking round.

'Dude, I'm sorry.'

He shrugged.

'When did it happen?' asked Frost.

'I honestly don't know.'

'Said you were attacked on your way back from Apache. The limo. Reckon you got bitten?'

'Before then, I think. Maybe back in Vegas.'

'You can't remember?'

'Maybe the virus breached the wire. Obvious scenario: one of Trenchman's guys got bit when he left the compound on a supply run. A raiding party sent out to loot a supermarket. They got jumped while they loaded a train of trolleys with canned goods. Kind of situation they could deal with easy enough. Minor skirmish in the grocery aisles. Bunch of head-shots. But one of the guys got bitten on the wrist or ankle, and hid the wound from his buddies. He brought the disease back to camp and, in the days that followed, started to infect his comrades. Picked his moment. In the showers, in the barracks. Waited till he was alone with a guy, then took them out. The virus quietly, methodically, taking over the camp.'

'A hunch, right?'

'Yeah. Supposition. We arrived on base. Someone infected Guthrie. Guthrie infected me. Then we all climbed aboard the plane.'

'He bit you?'

'Maybe he spat in my food. Or maybe he sneezed. Ever think of that? The virus could, under the right circumstances, be inhaled. The nasal membrane is pretty thin. It would be an effective entry point.'

'You've been sick the whole time we were out here?'

'I think so.'

'How can you not know? We're talking like it's guesswork. Why can't you remember any of this shit?'

'I'm not real any more. I'm a simulation. I have Noble's memories. I have the architecture of his personality. But Noble's long gone.'

'You're here, now, talking to me.'

353

'But no longer conscious.'

'You're aware that you're unaware?'

'I'm not aware of anything. You ask a question. The ruin of Noble's mind vocalises a response. It's not a conversation. More of a seance.'

'What does it want? This disease. This sentient cancer. What does it want with us?'

'An unanswerable question. It's a viral organism. You can't judge it on human terms. You can't hope to understand its designs and desires.'

Noble casually reached up and tore a flap of skin from his forehead. The ribbon of dried flesh tore away revealing glistening muscle and, beneath it, white bone.

A dribble of blood rolled down his temple. He wiped it with the back of his hand like he was mopping sweat.

He reached up and tore his hair away like he was peeling off a wig. He threw the scalp aside. It hit the deck with a wet slap.

Frost adjusted her grip on the Beretta. Safety to Off.

'One last question. The crash. Mechanical failure? Or did you guys sabotage the plane?'

Noble turned and smiled. He leapt onto the pilot seat, punched his way through the patched ejection hatch and began to haul himself out onto the roof.

Gunfire. Frost aimed for a headshot, but Noble was already half through the aperture. Bullets blew chunks out of his chest. Spark and metal-slam as a round ricocheted from the hatch frame, deflected off a couple of control surfaces. Frost ducked. Hancock covered his head. The bullet punched a neat exit hole in the fuselage. A pencil beam of moonlight shone into the flight deck, projecting a radiant disc on the floor like a shiny nickel.

Frost stood on the pilot seat, intending to follow Noble out the plane. She glanced at her weapon. The gun was jammed slide-back with a spent cartridge case wedged in the breech.

Frost worked the slide, struggled to clear the mechanism. Rasp of sand-clogged metal.

'Motherfuck.'

She stepped down from the pilot chair and backed away from the ejector hatch.

Hancock struggled to his feet.

'This is so fucked. We can't stay here. We need to get somewhere more secure.'

DANGER

MISSILE FUELED

51

The bomb bay.

Hancock removed fresh bandages from his head and examined the near-gangrenous wound using a pocket signal mirror.

Frost disassembled her Beretta and blew grit from the mechanism.

'Noble was infected,' said Hancock, 'but he didn't know.'

'It wasn't him any more. Nothing but a shell.'

She reassembled and reloaded the weapon.

'Makes you wonder,' said Hancock. 'If I were infected, how would I know? I think I'm real. I think I'm me. But I can't be sure.'

Frost didn't reply. She retreated to the corner of the bay, balanced the video camera on a thick wall cable and hit REC.

She looked at her image in the playback window. Cheeks sunken with dehydration. Eyes dark with exhaustion. Hair matted with dust. She looked like she had aged twenty years.

She tried to compose her thoughts. 'It's Thursday. Thursday? Yeah, Thursday. Must be one, maybe two in the morning. It's cold. Got to admit, I'm tired. Bone tired.'

She coughed.

'I can hear them outside. They're moving stuff around, moving with a purpose. Get the crazy impression they are trying to rebuild the plane. No point trying to understand, I guess.

'We're the last survivors. Myself and Captain Hancock. We're sealed in the bomb bay. Seems the safest place. Easy to defend. Easier than the flight deck, at any rate. Nothing to do but wait until dawn. We'll have more options once the sun comes up.'

She sipped water.

'There was a mist in the sky yesterday, way to the east. A dark haze. I didn't pay it any mind. But only one thing it could be. Vegas. Unchecked fires setting whole streets ablaze. Plenty of timber structures in the older suburbs, whole neighbourhoods baking in the sun, waiting for a spark. Must be a hell of a firestorm.'

She rubbed her eyes.

'New York. Chicago. Los Angeles. All those cities. Hard to picture the death, the desolation. The horror is too damned big for my head.

'I mean, Washington is gone. Who gives a shit, right? Piss on them. But Jesus. The White House. The Capitol. America, the idea of America, swept away. Nice while it lasted.'

She glanced up as red compartment lights flickered.

'Not sure how much longer we'll have power.

'Know what? I haven't smoked since college but, Jesus, I could use a cigarette right now.'

She reached for the camera and signed off.

'Lieutenant LaNitra Frost, United States Air Force.'

She pressed Stop. She stuffed the camcorder in her pocket.

Frost and Hancock sat side by side, backs to the curve of the fuselage wall, each lost in thought.

'So hungry I could weep,' said Hancock.

'Yeah?'

'Been craving apples. Lovely crisp apples. Hard to think of anything else. Tried singing to myself. Doesn't help. Can't get them off my mind.'

Frost glanced at the Tomahawk suspended above them.

'So how about it?' she asked. 'Want to disable this thing, or detonate?'

'Tempted to fire her up. Painless way to go. And we'd have the satisfaction of taking those fuckers outside with us. How about you? Want to call it quits?'

Frost thought it over. She shook her head.

'Think I'd rather go down fighting.'

Hancock stood up. His laptop balanced on the hull of the missile. He refreshed the screen. A winking cursor. An eight-digit input screen.

'There's a disable code?'

'Yeah,' said Hancock. 'Shuts it down, nice and simple.'

Fingers poised over the keyboard.

A hand erupted from the sand floor of the bomb bay. It seized Frost's ankle.

'Fuck,' she yelled. 'Got my leg.'

Her injured leg hauled knee-deep below the sand. She snatched her pistol from her shoulder rig and fired a volley, kicking up dust.

Hancock grabbed the collar of her flight suit and tried to drag her clear.

'Hands. Claws. Pulling me down.'

She kicked with her good foot, tried to push herself clear. She felt herself dragged deeper. She thrashed. She strained.

'Help me for God's sake.'

Hancock pulled the Beretta from his waistband and fired into the dust near Frost's feet.

Frost jerked her leg free. The fabric of her suit was torn. Her makeshift splint had been ripped away.

'Help me up.'

Hancock helped Frost to her feet.

The ground bulged and seethed.

'Got to get out of here.'

They lunged for the crawlspace hatch. Frost scrambled inside. Hancock followed.

Frost shuffled on hands and knees towards the crew cabin.

'Shit. They got me.' Hancock's voice resonated loud and metallic in the confined space.

Frost squirmed around and trained her flashlight.

Hancock scrabbling for purchase on the smooth sides of the conduit.

'They got my leg.'

Frost grabbed his wrists, but he was wrenched from her grasp.

'Jesus, help.'

His hands slapped and squeaked as he tried to grip smooth metal. He was relentlessly dragged backwards towards the bomb bay.

'Shoot me,' shouted Hancock. 'Fucking shoot me.'

Frost drew her pistol, but he was wrenched out of sight.

She crawled forwards, approached the infernal compartment light of the payload bay.

More screams.

She reached the hatchway.

Hancock chest deep and sinking fast.

She took aim.

'Do it.'

She fired. His head jerked back. Neat bullet hole between the eyes.

His limp body was pulled beneath the dust. Sand closed over his head. Arms and hands dragged below ground.

Sudden stillness.

DE OPPRESSO LIBER

52

The flight deck.

Frost slowly climbed the ladder. She crouched, weapon raised. Sweep of the compartment, flashlight in one hand, Beretta in the other. A vague plan. Twelve rounds in the clip. Eleven for any prowler she might confront. Last bullet for herself.

The two missing ejector seats, co-pilot and electronic warfare, were back at their stations. She shone her flashlight at the roof. The jettisoned ejection hatches were jammed back in position.

She stood and approached the flight controls. Glittering chunks of polycarbon piled on the sill above the EVS controls. She picked up a transparent chunk and turned it in her hand. Fragments of cockpit window. Collected from the half-mile debris trench. Picked from the sand, and mounded next to the empty window frame. A crude restoration.

The blast screens flapped and billowed. A rising night wind. She tore a couple of strips of duct tape to lash them down, but the screens tore open immediately. She tossed the tape aside.

Hard to estimate time. Must be heading towards dawn.

She looked down at Noble's backpack. Maybe she should strike out at dawn. Pack water and meds and head into the desert at sunrise. But she was overcome by an enervating wave of what's-the-point. The infected crewmen hiding amongst the dunes wouldn't let her leave. She was a part of their unfathomable plan.

Thud. A tremor ran through the plane. Frost pulled back a blast blind and stared out into the darkness.

Swirling sand. Brief moonlight.

The engines were back in position. The connecting pylons were a fractured mess of fuel line and cable, but the turbojet pods were stationed neatly beneath each wing.

She glanced around the flight deck looking for anything that might provide additional firepower.

A thin steel wall pipe running the length of the cockpit at eye level. The hydraulic line. She traced the pipe and found a screw joint. Leatherman pliers. She pinched the joint, loosened the screw for a moment. Hydraulic fluid dripped onto the deck plate at her feet.

She crouched, flicked open her butane lighter and sparked a flame. The fluid fizzed and burned blue.

She stamped out the flame.

An empty water bottle. She uncapped the bottle and shook it into her mouth in case the slightest droplet of moisture remained.

She pulled an Arctic parka from a locker, slit the quilted liner and pulled out tufts of synthetic down. She stuffed the wadding into the bottle.

She unscrewed the hydraulic line and let clear fluid dribble into the bottle, soaking into the foam, then rescrewed the cap.

Down the ladder to the lower cabin. She put her ear to the stacked trunks blocking the tear in the fuselage wall, tried to hear if anyone were moving around outside.

Duct tape. She strapped the bottle to a strut above the door. She lashed a gyrojet flare pen to the bottle. She pushed the barricade aside, ran a monofilament trip line across the aperture and tied it to the deck grate.

She stood back and inspected the trap.

Nod of satisfaction.

★

Frost sat in front of the Camcorder and pressed Rec:

She wiped away tears of exhaustion.

She composed herself.

'*You never know what you got until it's gone.* Who said that? Johnny Cash? Kind of thing he would say. Never a truer word spoken. Can't help but think back to stuff I took for granted. Queuing in the post office, pushing a trolley round the supermarket. Feels like a long-lost paradise. Guess everyone with a cancer diagnosis feels the same way. Leaving the clinic full of heart-pounding death-terror. Suddenly that hour you spent mowing the lawn the previous day feels like a lost Eden. Give anything to turn back the clock to that bored, complacent humdrum.

'Right now I'd give anything to be back at home, cleaning my oven or something, living an average day.'

She re-angled the camera.

'They'll come for me, sooner or later. Wait until I'm least alert. Sneak inside, or rush en masse. Depends if they want me alive, I guess. Depends if they have a use for my ass.

'I've got no illusions. Fight long as I can, but they'll win for sure. Dead by sunrise. Am I scared? Tired. Just tired. Fuck it. If those bastards outside want my hide, they'll have to work for it. Make them pay a heavy price.

'I'll hide this tape in the cockpit. My last testament. Maybe someone will find it, years to come. Long shot, but what the hey. And remember: if you are standing here in this cockpit, listening to my message, then take my warning. Get away from here. Get away from the sand. Nothing out here but death.'

She leant forwards and reached for the power button.

'This is Lieutenant LaNitra Frost, signing off.'

Rising wind. Whisper to a moan. The fuselage creaked and ticked. Sand gusted through torn blast screens, coated control surfaces with dust.

She unzipped her flight suit and sponged herself with wet wipes. A grey layer of grime and grey dermis stripped away. Her bicep tattoo revealed clean and clear.

She combed her hair and freshened her face.

She squeezed toothpaste into her mouth and rubbed it round her teeth. She squeezed worms of paste onto her fingers and wiped stripes across her cheekbones and the bridge of her nose like warpaint.

Codeine for her leg.

She strapped a gas mask pouch over her shoulder. The respirator would protect her airway if she found herself outside in a dust storm.

She rezipped her flight suit and buckled her survival vest. Pocket check. One spare clip. One in the gun.

She double-tied her laces, lashed duct tape round each ankle and wrist to proof her suit against sand.

She stood in the centre of the flight deck. She stretched and flexed her limbs, shook out cramp and cold.

She pulled on Nomex gloves and unsheathed her father's survival knife. A Nam-era jungle blade. Rangers stamp on the weather-worn sheath. He used it to probe undergrowth for trip-wires. He used the tip to punch open beer cans. Visible strapped to his chest in the platoon group shot hung on his office wall. 151st. Eight grinning guys sitting on the roof of an M113 APC. Boonie hats, camo faces, jungle backdrop. Peace signs and a couple of fuck-you middle fingers.

She swept the blade back and forth, sliced the air.

Ready for war.

If she had to die, let it be here, let it be now.

Out onto the roof.

Strengthening wind. She wore the M40 respirator to protect her face from driving sand.

She looked up. Vaporous clouds scudding past the moon, east to west.

The signal fire had been extinguished. At first she thought the flames had been smothered by wind and sand, but she focused her flashlight and saw the tyre that provided fuel for the pyre had been removed. No doubt remnants of undercarriage, the buckled actuators, hydraulic cable, burned and shredded radials, had been returned to their respective wheel wells.

Conscious determination to get her shit together.

She stamped her aching, injured leg and savoured the invigorating jolt of pain.

The desert swept by intermittent moonlight. Deep shadows, pools of blackness coagulating around the plane and between each dune.

A dark shape near the extinct signal fire. The discarded jerry can. She held the pistol in both hands, took aim, and waited for moonlight to gift her with a clear shot.

Guncrack.

A neat hole drilled in the side of the can. The container pissed a thin stream of aviation fuel. The fuel spattered on sand, a spreading stain of wet.

Guncrack.

The bullet sparked metal. Vapour ignition. Double fireball: the spilt fuel caught alight then, a moment later, the fuel can blew with a concussive thud.

A slow-blossoming mushroom of fire rose over the crash site. Dunes and wreckage lit by flickering flame light.

A figure, standing at the ridgeline. Ragged flight suit. A patient sentinel, oblivious to the storm.

She pulled back her respirator to get a better view. Sand stung her face.

She threw her arms wide.

'Come get some, motherfucker.'

*

She sat in the dark a while, perched on the lip of the ladderway.

She looked down into the lower cabin. Her eyes projected phantom shapes into nothingness. After a while, her sight adjusted, and she could see intermittent washes of moonlight filtering through the rip in the fuselage.

She shifted and stretched each time she felt herself sliding into sleep.

Flicker.

She sat still, breathless and unblinking, as she tried to discern movement below.

She followed her survival training: used peripheral vision to monitor deep shadow.

Flicker.

Someone, or something, outside the plane, hesitating at the threshold.

She slid a hand over the pistol butt and rested her forefinger on the trigger.

She waited. It seemed like an age.

The arachnid movement of fingers curling round torn aluminium. A grotesque silhouette. A guy in prison red, framed by ragged metal, about to pull himself through the rent in the fuselage.

Frost willed the creature to advance into the plane. It was inches away from the monofilament trip wire. All it had to do was step forwards.

The creature stood motionless.

Frost tried to regulate her breathing.

Minutes passed.

No movement.

She released her grip on the pistol, carefully unsheathed her knife and pricked her thumb. She squeezed a bead of blood and smeared it on the lip of the ladderway.

The creature stepped over the threshold into the

lower cabin. Flicker of hesitation as its arm brushed monofilament.

The thread pull taut.

Frost shielded her eyes. Crack of ignition. The cabin instantly filled with magnesium fire.

The flare burned through the plastic bottle in an instant. Hydraulic fluid ignited in a flame-burst. The creature's head and shoulders were engulfed by liquefied plastic, and melting insulation foam.

The revenant thrashed and bounced off the walls. It pawed at the flames, tried to wipe them from its face. Burning plastic adhered to its hands in glutinous strands. Bubbling, blackened flesh. Fingers quickly fused to charred clubs.

Frost got to her feet. She slid down the ladder.

She side-stepped the blinded figure as it slammed into the nav console, careened into the walls as it tried to find its way back outside to roll in sand and smother the flames.

She snatched up her crutch, held it at waist level like a pike staff, and rammed the jagged tip in the creature's belly.

It thrashed. It fought. Frost threw all her weight, propelled the figure backwards until it slammed against the fuselage. The crutch bored deep into the creature's stomach, grated against vertebrae. Foul rot-stink. She twisted the pole back and forth. It broke through the creature's back. Metal screech as the jagged tip of the crutch punctured the skin of the plane like the blade of a can opener. She continued to twist and push. The pole speared through aluminium plate and pinned the burning revenant to the wall.

She stood back and caught her breath. She shook out cramped fingers.

The creature snapped and snarled as it was consumed by fire. Lips crisped and curled. Eyes burst and boiled away.

Frost checked out the prison fatigues.

'What the fuck are you?' she murmured.

368

She unsheathed her knife and drove it into his empty eye socket. She twisted the blade and churned brain.

She gripped burning hair and began to saw through the creature's neck. Bone. She dug the knife tip between the joint and shucked vertebrae apart.

The head lifted free and clear.

She tossed it through the rend in the fuselage wall, out into the dust storm. The burning head hit the ground, bounced, rolled and came to a standstill face up. Flames guttered and died. Sand began to accumulate in empty eye sockets and an open mouth.

'Fuck you,' she yelled into the night. 'Fuck the lot of you.'

She turned her attention back to the decapitated body.

An extinguisher lifted from a wall holster. She pulled the ring tab and trained the nozzle cone. Fire smothered by a jet of gas. The corpse pinned to the fuselage, white with carbon crystals like it was sculpted from ice.

Frost threw down the extinguisher, then cleaned her knife.

**THIS AIRCRAFT CONTAINS A
PYROTECHNIC ACTUATED EMERGENCY
ESCAPE SYSTEM EQUIPPED WITH
EXPLOSIVE CHARGES**

**SEE NAVAIR B-52AAD-2-4-3- FOR
COMPLETE INSTRUCTIONS**

53

The blast blinds masking the cockpit windows billowed and cracked. The screens were fringed with a halo of phosphorescent blue. Oncoming day. The sun ready to breach the horizon. Soon, a tide of gold light would pour across the dunescape, burn away the sandstorm and dissipate turbulent air currents.

Frost blew her hands for warmth. Jet of steam breath.

'Daybreak, fuckers,' she murmured, anxious to hear her own voice, anxious to break the oppressive solitude of the cabin.

'You bastards got an hour left before the heat begins to build. Storm will clear soon enough, then you'll have to take cover. Dig in and hibernate. Won't last a day above ground. Few hours in the sun and you'll dry out like jerky. Cook rigid as a plank of wood.'

She allowed herself a sip of water.

'Endurance, right? The desert will finish you soon enough. I've just got to sit here and outlast you.'

She casually picked through the trauma kit.

She found a small plastic bottle of eyewash. She squinted at the label. She unscrewed the spout and sniffed the contents. Sooner or later water would run out. She would close her eyes, knock back 75ml of saline and try to hold it down.

She tossed the bottle into the backpack.

'I'll outlast you fucks,' she said, facing the fuselage wall, addressing the desert that lay beyond. 'A parasite. Can't live without a host. If you wipe out the human race, you'll die with us. All I got to do is find an island someplace and wait. Couple of years you'll be gone like a bad dream. All I got to do is endure.'

A cursory, time-killing search through a storage locker. Arctic gloves, foil blankets, hexamine blocks.

Something silver at the back of the locker. She tugged it free. A Thermos flask matted in dust. Must have belonged to the previous crew of *Liberty Bell*. A relic of night missions, stand-off patrols over Arctic waters. Thirty-six hours in the sky. Mid-air refuelling by a KC-10A extender. Caffeine to stay sharp.

She unscrewed the cup and cap, shone her flashlight into the flask interior.

Empty.

She sat back in the gunner's chair. Her eyes wandered to the EWO seat beside her, the ejection rail that anchored the seat to the plane. An object in the base of the seat sprayed black and yellow. She stared blankly at the wasp-warning stripes, then she finally made the connection.

She leapt from her seat and knelt on all fours.

DANGER
EXPLOSIVE CHARGE

A cylindrical steel firing tube, thick as a length of drain pipe, beneath the seat. It contained a powerful pyro charge primed to propel the EWO's chair up and out the plane once the egress systems were activated. A quarter ton of flesh and metal accelerated to 12g in less than a second.

She reached beneath the seat, tried to squeeze her hand past the catapult pylon and grip the firing tube. Couldn't reach. The seat would have to be disarmed, unbolted and lifted clear before the divergence rockets could be removed.

She checked the headrest. Ought to be a small explosive cartridge rigged to fire a stabilisation drogue.

She sawed through nylon packing and cut through the chute harness.

She flipped open the cross-head screwdriver attachment of the Leatherman and unbolted the pyro tube. She lifted it clear and turned it in her hand. A silver cylinder with a red cap. Size of a cigar.

Early leant through a rip in the fuselage and surveyed the lower cabin. Transformed vision cut through shadows bright as day.

Burn-streaked walls and instrumentation. A decapitated corpse pinned to the wall.

He stepped out of the rising sandstorm, the wind moan and swirling particulates, into the stillness and shadow of the plane's interior.

Careful footsteps. The grit-crunch of heavy soled boots on sand-dusted decking.

He could smell Frost in the upper cabin, hear her heartbeat, her breathing.

Fresh meat.

He gripped the ladder rungs and began to climb. Clumsy, jerking movements. Desiccated muscle and tendons hardened like leather.

Head above the hatchway. Frost asleep in the EWO seat, face to the wall, body blanketed by an NB3 parka. He slowly climbed the ladder and stepped onto the upper deck.

Frost slumped head to one side, still as she could. She breathed slowly, tried to calm her heart rate.

Faint creak of decking.

She opened one eye. A flight helmet on the console beside her. The dark visor reflected the flight deck in fish-eye distortion.

She watched Early climb from the ladderway and creep towards her.

Early stood over Frost and listened to deep respirations.

He bent and reached for her. Diseased, dirt-caked hands. Broken fingernails.

Her eyes snapped open. She threw the anorak aside. The Thermos trailing wires: a 9v battery lashed to the cylinder with duct tape. She trained the blunderbuss barrel at his head.

'Thanks for stopping by.'

Frost touched wire to a battery terminal.

Spark.

Flame-roar.

Thick smoke haze.

Frost lay with her face pressed to the decking. She searched out clean air. Her ears rang. Her belly bruised from the recoil of the rocket charge.

Her hands hurt. She bit the fingers of her torn Nomex gloves and slowly pulled them off with her teeth.

The trauma kit. She teased burn dressing from the Ziploc bag and tore wrappers with her teeth. She squirted anaesthetic burn gel onto her hands and lashed the dressings in place with bandage.

The flask lay beside her, smouldering, sides peeled open like petals.

She rolled. She crawled to the ladderway.

Early lay on the floor of the lower cabin. His face and torso were a pulped mess. Splintered bone and shredded muscle protruding through the fabric of the flight suit. His body glittered with embedded cockpit glass.

His leg danced. Fingers twitched. Last nerve signals from a shattered brain.

US Rangers, Standing Orders

1. Don't forget nothing.
2. Have your musket clean as a whistle, hatchet scoured, sixty rounds powder and ball, and be ready to march at a minute's warning.
3. When you're on the march, act the way you would if you was sneaking up on a deer. See the enemy first.
4. Tell the truth about what you see and what you do. There is an army depending on us for correct information. You can lie all you please when you tell other folks about the Rangers, but don't never lie to a Ranger or officer.
5. Don't never take a chance you don't have to.
6. When we're on the march we march single file, far enough apart so one shot can't go through two men.
7. If we strike swamps, or soft ground, we spread out abreast, so it's hard to track us.
8. When we march, we keep moving till dark, so as to give the enemy the least possible chance at us.
9. When we camp, half the party stays awake while the other half sleeps.
10. If we take prisoners, we keep em separate till we have had time to examine them, so they can't cook up a story between em.
11. Don't ever march home the same way. Take a different route so you won't be ambushed.
12. No matter whether we travel in big parties or little ones, each party has to keep a scout 20 yards ahead, 20 yards on each flank, and 20 yards in the rear so the main body can't be surprised and wiped out.
13. Every night you'll be told where to meet if surrounded by a superior force.
14. Don't sit down to eat without posting sentries.
15. Don't sleep beyond dawn. Dawn's when the French and Indians attack.
16. Don't cross a river by a regular ford.
17. If somebody's trailing you, make a circle, come back onto your own tracks, and ambush the folks that aim to ambush you.
18. Don't stand up when the enemy's coming against you. Kneel down, lie down, hide behind a tree.
19. Let the enemy come till he's almost close enough to touch, then let him have it and jump out and finish him up with your hatchet.

54

A steady wind blew over the dunes, skimming granules from the crest of each ridgeline, gradually reordering the landscape.

The sky filled with serpentine dust eddies. A blizzard of sand particles. The weak sun glowed through the vaporous storm like Martian twilight.

Mournful wind-howl. Absolute desolation.

The thing that had once been Captain Pinback looked out over the storm-lashed wreck site, surveyed the reassembled plane.

The tail shunted back in position.

Battered engine pods resituated beneath each wing.

The fuselage scoured by sand, an unrelenting hurricane blast which would, in time, abrade shark-grey paint exposing silvered panels beneath.

Pinback descended the dust gradient. He gripped the tip of the starboard wing where it hung low to the ground and lifted himself effortlessly onto the wing surface.

A slow, purposeful walk towards the main fuselage. Wind snatched and whipped the flight suit hanging from his emaciated frame.

He climbed onto the roof.

He looked aft down the spine of the plane to the crooked tail.

He looked forwards towards the nose.

One of the retrieved ejection hatches had been pushed aside. Darkness within.

He approached the hatch. He could hear the low murmur of a woman's voice above the unrelenting wind-roar. He crouched and listened. Frost talking to herself, mordant, resigned.

'*. . . Can't help but think back to stuff I took for granted. Queuing in the post office, pushing a trolley round the supermarket. Feels like a long-lost paradise . . .*'

Nothing left of Daniel Pinback, no pang of empathy for the exhaustion, the terror, in Frost's voice.

The creature stepped into the vacant hatchway and dropped into the flight deck below.

He hit the gunner's seat, fell hard and snapped his right arm near the shoulder.

He stood up, right arm limp and useless.

He approached the pilot chairs.

'*. . . that hour you spent mowing the lawn the previous day feels like a lost Eden. Give anything to turn back the clock to that bored, complacent humdrum . . .*'

He craned round the high-back frames.

No sign of Frost.

Something on the pilot's seat. A video camera. Frost's gaunt, weathered face in the playback window.

'*. . . Fuck it. If those bastards outside want my hide, they'll have to work for it. Make them pay a heavy price . . .*'

Pinback slammed across the head by an empty extinguisher. He reeled. He turned. Frost wielding the canister.

She threw the cylinder at his head. He ducked. It bounced off avionics.

He lunged, left arm outstretched.

She snatched the pistol from her shoulder holster and fired. Three bullets smacked into his chest, knocked him sprawling across the refuel controls.

She tried to get a clear shot at his head. He rolled aside. A couple of mis-aimed rounds smashed fuel gauges.

He stood up.

He shielded his face with his hand. Bullet punched through his hand. Bloodless entry, neat stigmata. The round shattered his cheekbone. Pinback ducked a couple more headshots. One of them caught his clavicle, span him one-eighty and threw him against the wall.

Frost took aim: split-second opportunity to put a round in the base of his neck.

Gun jam.

She struggled to clear the breech. No good. The slide gummed with sand.

Pinback turned to face her.

She tossed the weapon, pivoted on her good leg and delivered a belly kick that sent him to the floor. Jarring pain from her injured shin.

Knife snatched from its sheath.

He reached for her leg.

She swept the blade, slashed his arm, sliced flesh to the bone.

She lunged at his left eye socket. He deflected the blow. The knife slit open his forehead.

She danced round his prone body. He tried to get up. She kicked him in the face. She stabbed downwards, once again aiming for his eye. He jerked his head clean. The tip of the blade shrieked across deck plate.

He gripped her ankle, threw her balance and sent her stumbling backwards. She fell between the pilots' seats, thrust levers jammed in the small of her back. She dropped the knife.

Fingers gripped her hair. Hancock crouched on the nose outside, reaching through a broken cockpit window. She punched his arm, tried to tear her head free. She reached for her knife wedged between the arm rest and seat cushion of the pilot chair. Out of reach.

Rotted hands gripped her head and shoulders. She was slowly pulled through the window, out into the storm. She kicked and squirmed, tried to hook her legs round the window frame as she was pulled onto the nose of the plane. She lost grip, fell fifteen feet, and hit the sand below.

Face down in the sand. She spat dust from her mouth.

Boots. She looked up. Noble and Hancock looking down at her.

Noble: a fleshless, grinning skull face.

Hancock: empty eye socket, grey skin, face slack and dead.

She scrambled to her feet. She put her back to the wind, to shield her eyes from driving sand.

The two creatures stood motionless.

She balled her fists.

So here it was. The moment of her death.

The dojo above Suds Laundromat. Monday night. Rain-lashed windows.

Frost and her Sensei circling on the mats.

Kumite: block, punch, kick. Orange belt versus black belt, fourth dan.

Frost was exhausted. Panting for air, gi hanging dark and heavy with sweat.

Sensei jabbed at her face. She blocked the blow.

'Breathe. Breathe like I showed you.'

Feint to the head. She raised her arm to block and got punched in the side. She staggered backwards, cursing with frustration.

'You done?' asked the instructor. 'Been a long session. You looked wiped out.'

She nodded and dropped her guard.

'Want to quit for the night?'

She nodded.

Sensei smiled.

'Nice work. You busted your ass tonight.'

He held out his hand for a shake. She took it. He twisted her fingers back, sent her to the floor. She lay, snorting with pain, arm twisted at near-breaking point.

'Today's lesson. The fight doesn't end just because you want a rest. When you are at your lowest, when you are beaten down, exhausted, ready to quit and crawl away, that's when you are truly tested. Seen it countless times. In here, out on the street. When the battle seems to be over, that's when it truly begins.'

He released her arm and stepped back.

'Now get up and fight.'

'So what are you waiting for?'

Noble and Hancock immediately diverged and began to circle. Frost backed away, careful not to be caught between them.

Hancock stepped close and grabbed her arm. She twisted free, pivoted on her good foot to deliver a knee-break kick to his leg. Mistimed. He backed off.

Sixth sense: Noble behind her. She turned, ducked beneath grasping arms and shouldered him to the ground. She tried to stamp on his face. He rolled out of reach and got to his feet.

They moved in, trying to crowd her. She skipped clear.

She lunged at Noble. A sharp shuto strike should have crushed his larynx, but he took the blow like it was nothing and straightened up.

Kick to the chest. She heard ribs break.

She backed off and flexed her shoulders. Faint smile on her face. Fear turning to weird exultation. This was her last dance. She would go down fighting, go down throwing a punch.

An emaciated hand erupted from the sand and gripped her ankle.

'Fuck.'

She tried to wrench free. She kicked at the fingers. Her boot tore skin from knuckles, but the hand didn't slacken its grip.

Hancock and Noble moving in to finish the fight.

'Yeah, come on, you pricks.'

A shotei strike to Hancock's chest sent him staggering backwards. A right-hook to Noble's head sent him reeling sideways.

A hand grabbed Frost's other foot. She was dragged knee-deep into the sand. She fell on her back. She tried to deliver a knee-break punch to Noble's leg. Couldn't reach.

Hauled waist-deep

'Utter fucks. Utter pieces of shit.'

Chest deep.

She tried to kick free. She pawed and clawed at the sand as she was dragged further below ground.

Neck deep.

Pinback. He hugged her tight, pulled her down.

A last glimpse of storm-lashed desert. Noble and Hancock standing over her.

'You can all go to hell,' she spat, then sand closed over her head and she was gone.

MORPHINE

AUTO INJECTOR

DO NOT USE
IN CASE OF INTOXICATION
WITH ORGANIC PHOSPHORUS COMPOUNDS

1 ◀ REMOVE STERILE SLEEVE
PRESS THE RED END
TO THE PLACE OF
INJECTION

PULL THE WHITE SAFETY-
TIP AND KEEP IN PLACE
FOR TEN SECONDS ▶ **2**

-MEDTEC-

Contains:

Morphine sulphate – 15mg

LOT:

55

Frost rolled on deck plate and vomited sand. She clawed it from her eyes, snorted it from her nose. She choked, gagged, gasped for breath.

She looked around, tried to blink away blurred vision.

Bright light. She was lying on the floor of the lower cabin. She looked up. Hancock, Pinback and Noble stared down at her.

She closed her eyes and shook her head. Sickening memory of suffocation and buried-alive immobility.

She threw up a fresh bout of bile and sand.

She rubbed her eyes. Someone sat in the Navigator seat. Early. His pulped body held in place by harness straps.

Guthrie. A scorched cadaver propped at the radar nav station.

The cabin lit harsh white. Lamps on full. Residual power from the batteries.

Frost looked down at her arms and legs. She ran gloved hands over her body.

'Am I bitten?' she coughed. 'Did you bastards infect me?'

She ran hands over her face, checked her fingers for blood, any sign of broken skin. Nothing.

'Kill me. Have done with it.'

Hancock crouched beside her. Close-up view of the man's face. Death pallor. His remaining eyeball cataract white.

He opened a pocket of his survival vest and took out a morphine auto injector. He fumbled the cap, jabbed Frost in the thigh and hit the plunger.

'Fuck are you doing?'

He threw the spent needle aside. He took another hypo from his pocket, cracked the cap and jabbed her thigh.

She tried to crawl away, head spinning from the sudden opiate rush.

Another needle jab to the back of her calf. And another.

'Bastards.'

Hancock uncapped another couple of hypos.

Frost looked up at Noble's skinless face.

'This is all about you, isn't it? Everything that has happened since we crashed. All part of your fucking death wish.'

Two more shots to the small of her back.

She rolled foetal, lay in a slack-jawed stupor.

'Cunts.'

Hancock crouched by her side.

'The code,' he grunted, his one dead eye staring unfocused beyond her shoulder.

'Is it you talking?' asked Frost, 'or is Noble pulling your strings?'

'Don't tell us the code. Whatever happens, you mustn't tell us the code.'

Frost shook her head. Tried to clear the opiate fog. She lay back and closed her eyes.

'You have to keep the code to yourself. You know the digit sequence. You have it clear in your mind. But you must keep your secret.'

Frost lost in memories, halfway between waking and sleep.

Interrogation training, Montana. Succession of Air Force personnel hooded and hog-tied, given the full POW treatment.

Deep forest. Cellar of an abandoned house.

The Red Room.

Lying stripped, bound and cold. Loud music and strobe lights. Sleep dep and stress positions.

'*Give up your key word. Just say it. Say the word, then you can rest.*'

She lasted thirty-nine hours. Beat most of her class. One hard-ass held out the full three days. Sent back to his unit marked for potential transfer and BUDS.

Hancock's guttural slur:

'Don't tell us the code. Keep it in your head. Keep it to yourself.'

Frost's mind drawn back to the moment she stood at the signal fire, broke open the plastic code tab and removed the digit strip. A febrile, opiate-fuelled vision. Vivid, like she was reliving the moment all over again.

She could feel the heat of the flames.

She could feel sand beneath her boots.

She could see the digit strip in her hand.

A distant voice, sounded like her own:

'X-ray. Five.'

Montana. Blindfold, zip-tied to a chair. The interrogator screaming in her ear.

'*Give up the word. Give up the fucking word.*'

Frost trying to blank it all out, concentrate on the music blasting from the speaker on a table behind her. Sounded like Daft Punk 'Derezzed' played backwards.

'Seven. November.'

'You mustn't speak the words aloud, Frost. They must remain sealed in your head.'

That vivid memory. Thin strip of laminated paper between her fingers.

'Tango. Delta. Four. Four.'

Flicking open her Zippo. Wafting the paper above the flame, watching it brown and curl.

'Foxtrot.'

'You got to hold out as long as you can. Name and rank. Nothing else. This is the moment you prove your strength, your endurance. You've got to tough it out. Lives depend. You mustn't break.'

'Three.'

'You're doing great. Doing yourself proud.'

'X-ray. Five. Seven. November. Tango. Delta. Four. Four. Foxtrot. Three.'

'Thank you, airman.'

The payload compartment.

Blood-red light.

Noble squirmed from the crawlway and got to his feet.

The Tomahawk hung from its cradle at shoulder height. Cable hanging from the exposed physics package. The laptop sitting on the hull of the missile, beside the intake.

Noble booted the laptop from sleep mode and typed the final authorisation sequence.

He hit Enter. The screen cleared and flashed:

ENABLED

Frost felt herself lifted from the floor and pushed towards the ladder. Rotted, skeletal hands raised her up, hauled her onto the flight deck and dragged her towards the pilot seat. Her head hung limp. Her boots dragged across the deck plate. She tried to struggle, tried to galvanise numb limbs, but couldn't find the strength.

They sat her in the pilot seat, buckled her harness and lashed her arms to the rests with paracord. Too weak to resist. She lolled, doped, barely conscious.

She fought to raise her eyelids, raise her head. Dimly aware of movement around her. Shuffling feet. Click of harness buckles. Men wordlessly taking position on the cramped and crowded flight deck.

Someone climbing into the co-pilot seat beside her. She

tried to focus. Hancock. He smelled faintly of shit. Bowels must have evacuated during the interval he spent dead. Smothered by sand then, minutes later his heart and lower cortex booted back to life as the virus colonised his inert body.

He leant forwards, tore duct tape and raised each blast screen. He folded the nylon blinds and pegged them above each window.

The swirling dust storm. Orange, Venusian light. Wind gusted through broken windows. Low, whistling moan. Dust immediately began to accumulate on the floor, control surfaces, Frost's forearms and legs.

Hancock sat forwards, looked out the windows left and right with his blank dead eye. Took a moment before Frost recognised the familiar movement. A standard pre-flight check. The guy was establishing the power cart had been unhitched, the fuel truck had finished decanting JP8 and withdrawn, chocks had been pulled from the undercarriage bogies, engine intake/duct plugs had been removed.

He gave a thumbs-up to a non-existent crew chief, confirmed the plane was on internal power.

He sat back in his seat and fumbled the five-point harness, locked the straps one by one.

Interior inspection. He examined the thigh window-pocket of his flight suit like he was running through a tick-list. He checked avionic pre-sets. Adjusted dials and switch panels.

Rasp of dead, dirt-clogged vocal chords:

'Battery start.'

The plane was already on internal power, draining dregs from the tail cell, but he reached for the switch anyway and made a perfunctory performance of turning to On.

He tripped the wing lamps. The nose and surrounding dunes suddenly illuminated harsh white. Sand swirled in the twin light-cones.

Trim check. Another thumbs-up for the phantom chief.

Frost turned in her seat and craned to see the crew positions behind her.

Pinback, head hooded by a nuclear blast helmet, slumped in front of dead banks of Electronic Warfare instrumentation.

Noble sat in the gunner's seat, checked missile launch controls.

Hancock pulled on a helmet. He fixed the mask. The torn oxygen hose and frayed interphone cable hung loose.

'Engine start.'

Thud. Jolt. Flash of flame outside.

Frost craned as best she could.

The plane's remaining starboard engine pod attempting a cartridge start.

'Hey,' grunted Frost, fighting through the opiate fog. 'Hey. Going to blow us to hell.'

Second thud. More flame from the engine exhaust. Black smoke. Turbofans trying to turn over.

'What the hell are you doing?'

Gruff motor roar. The turbofan caught and settled to a spluttering idle, sucking residual kerosene from starboard wing tanks. The engine out-take blasted a sand plume. The airframe shuddered like the fuselage was shaking itself apart.

Hancock:

'Starting one, starting two . . .'

He adjusted throttles, checked dead rpm dials.

'Clear to taxi.'

Flaps lowered. Brakes released.

Hancock eased the throttles forwards.

Another flame-crack from outside. The starboard engine sucked sand, jerked and torqued the wing.

'That thing could blow any minute.'

She pictured catastrophic engine failure, whirling fragments, shards of turbine blade puncturing the hull of the plane, slicing through the flight deck like the lethal flechettes of an anti-personnel mine, transforming crew to meat-pulp in an instant.

'Gonna get us all killed,' she slurred. Empty warning. The men around her were already pretty much dead.

Pop and spark. She flinched as the mid-air refuel panel to her right shorted out. First wisps of smoke from overhead vents. Reignition of the electrical fire that brought the plane down.

Hancock stared forwards, rode the thrust levers, adjusted the stick.

Frost wondered what was going on in the dead man's head. Was he drawing dim memories of previous flights? Did the cockpit appear intact? Were dead control panels responsive, blinking green? Did he see inert output needles twitch and rise?

He stared ahead at wind-lashed dunes like he was rolling the B-52 out the hangar onto a floodlit slip, heading for the runway, jinking to align the plane with the strip.

Did he see runway strobes receding to the distance?

Did he hear the ghost-voice of tower control talk him through final checks?

Frost turned in her seat.

'Noble. Hey, Noble. Look at me.'

Noble turned in his seat. Grinning, bloody, skull mask.

'This is your deal, right? You're pulling the strings. Come on. What are you trying to achieve?'

No reply.

'The missile is primed. You realise that, right? Moment you hit Weapon Release the barometric fuse will detonate the warhead.'

He turned back to the missile panel.

'You'll die. You'll all die. Is that what you want?'

As if in response Hancock gripped the throttle levers and eased them further forwards. The airspeed indicator rested at zero but he fixed his attention like the plane was heading down the runway, approaching take-off speed.

He leant back in his seat, as if subject to acceleration only he could feel.

He shouted like he was fighting to be heard over escalating engine roar:

'. . . Twenty knots. Thirty . . .'

'Hancock. Hey. Jim. Look at me. Look at me, you fuck. You in there? Any of you left? Think. Think about what you're doing. This is madness.'

Hancock looked straight ahead, as if gauging how much runway he had left.

'. . . sixty, sixty five . . .'

Attention fixed on the dead airspeed clock like he was urging it to hit seventy.

'Nose up.'

In the ruins of his mind, they took to the sky.

He leant back in his seat as if, somewhere with the collapsing architecture of his mind, he pictured *Liberty Bell* leaving the runway, engines at full thrust. They climbed and banked, eight black fume-trails tracing the massive bomber's ascent.

'Gear retract.'

Brief pause like he was receiving confirmation from base ATC.

'Roger that. Ascend twenty thousand, maintain bearing two-two-zero.'

He gripped the flight controls and stared, unseeing, into the storm as he ascended to cruising altitude, mind's eye showed him empty skies.

Thickening smoke from overhead vents. Electrical fires spreading through wall conduits.

The cockpit shook. The plane's one remaining engine

sending jolting tremors through the airframe. Frost craned and looked out the window. The jetwash from the bedded engine was kicking up a hurricane of sand. The twin turbofans shook on their pylon and spat flame.

Hancock checked cabin pressure and released his oxygen mask.

Frost turned in her seat. She fought the dope, fought to be present and alert.

'Hey. Jim,' she shouted. 'Why are you doing this? You're dying. But why does everyone have to die with you? Why destroy everyone and everything.'

Noble turned to look at her. He answered through Hancock.

'The bomb is a doorway. A route out of this world. At the moment of detonation a quantum singularity will exist for a millionth of a second. A tear in the fabric of the real. And we will pass through to the other side.'

'You want to fly this plane to an alternate universe? You're out of your fucking mind.'

She used the moment of conversation to check for weapons. Pinback's holster was empty. Hancock and Noble were packing 9mm Berettas. Both weapons were caked with dirt. Doubtful they would fire.

Something dug into her thigh.

The hilt of her father's knife. She'd dropped it on the pilot seat earlier. But her wrists were firmly bound to the arm rests by paracord. No matter how hard she stretched her fingers, the knife remained four inches out of reach.

'Roger that. Ascend thirty thousand. Maintain course two-two-zero.'

She could see the brightly lit cabin behind her reflected in cockpit polycarbon.

She studied Pinback slumped in the EWO seat. The screen in front him, the cracked sheet of black glass, should have been delivering a constant radar sweep, RWR sensors ready to beep an alert tocsin if the plane were targeted by enemy acquisition radar.

She checked out Noble. He sat patiently staring at the emerald Go lights of the weapons panel. Pre-arms active. If he were recreating their bomb run to the target site, he would expect to reach the missile drop point fifteen minutes from the target site. According to the original mission plan, the bomb-bay doors would whine open and the ALCM would be released from its retainer clamps. A moment of freefall as the Tomahawk left the plane, then wings would unfold and the solid fuel booster would fire. It would head for the target using terrain recognition and inertial navigation for guidance. It would enter a terminal dive a quarter of a mile from the aim point, then blink out of existence.

But on this flight, this earthbound non-journey, the missile would never leave the payload compartment. Every PAL failsafe had been circumvented. The instant the Tomahawk received the launch command, the moment the B-52 weapon control system ceded full independent control, the barometric trigger would detonate the warhead. No pause. No count-down. Soon as Noble lifted the switch cover, and flicked WPN REL, *Liberty Bell* and the surrounding quarter mile of desert would transmute to vapour.

'Why me? Why do I have a front row seat?'

'Because you are part of the crew. You belong with us.'

Hancock performed a routine instrumentation check.

'Adjust heading two-two-five. Visibility good.' Pause. 'Yeah,' he said, answering a query only he could hear. 'No traffic. We got a straight run.'

The wind picked up. It screamed through breaks in the cockpit glass. Frost caught a face full of sand. She spat grit and blinked her eyes clear.

The fuselage around her shook and groaned. Thrust from the misfiring engine threatening to tear the airframe apart.

Movement outside. Figures at the periphery of light thrown by wing strobes. She glimpsed red prison fatigues.

Frost took deep breaths and got her shit together.

As far as Noble and Hancock were concerned, they had just taken off from Runway One, McCarran International, Vegas. They had passed over the southern suburbs and were now banking west.

A couple of hours to target.

She had three options:

One. Escape her restraints, then take out Noble. Do it quick and clean before he had the opportunity to trigger the bomb. Hancock wouldn't be a problem. He was an extension of Noble's will. The instant Noble were dead, Hancock would probably flop to the floor like a puppet with cut strings.

Two. Escape her restraints, then somehow flee the plane. The Tomahawk was tipped with a tactical nuke, not a high-yield city-killer. If she could put five or six miles between herself and the bomb, she might be able to survive the blast.

Three. Stay put and die.

She shifted her foot. Clink of broken glass.

She craned to look down, discretely as she could.

A couple of nuggets of thick polycarbon on the footwell floor.

She pinched the glass between her feet, shuffled a shard until it rested on the sole-seam of her boot. She slowly crossed her leg, bringing her boot up to her hand.

Looking around out the corner of her eye. Noble couldn't see what she was doing. She was shielded by the ejector seat. Hancock engrossed by dead avionics.

She stretched fingers towards her boot and snagged the shard. She held it between her knees and sawed the wrist-cord back and forth across the jagged edge. Nylon weave began to fray.

The cord broke and immediately slackened.

She psyched herself.

'One . . . two . . . three . . .'

She snatched the knife from beneath her thigh.

She sliced the cord binding her left arm to the chair.

Hancock reached for her.

She gripped the knife ready to stab, swung her arm and buried the blade in Hancock's throat, nailing him to the backrest of the chair. He croaked and spluttered, fumbled the knife hilt and tried to pull it free.

She snatched the gun from his chest holster, jammed the barrel against his good eye and put a bullet in his brain. He slumped limp.

She twisted round, tried to take aim at Noble while simultaneously scrabbling at the release catch of her seat harness. He had already drawn his Beretta. Simultaneous exchange of fire. Rounds blowing bloodless holes in Noble's chest. Bullets sparking off Frost's seat back, puncturing control surfaces, blowing out a window.

She tossed the gun, faced front, primed the arm rests and wrenched the ejection trigger between her legs.

Deafening roar.

Horrific g-force.

Hurled up and out into the storm.

The flight deck filled with smoke and typhoon backwash.

Noble released his seat harness and got to his feet. He walked to the vacant pilot position and looked up through the open ejection hatchway. He raised his pistol like he intended to fire into the storm raging above the plane then slowly, wearily, lowered his arm.

The seat rockets propelled Frost two hundred feet into the air. The chair detached and she was in freefall, chute unfurling

394

behind her. Not enough height for the canopy to fully deploy, but enough to slow her descent.

She slammed into the side of a dune and rolled.

She released her harness and untangled chute cord.

Last glimpse of *Liberty Bell*. The plane lit by the unearthly light from wing spots and strobes. The misfiring engine vented fire, turbojet scream merging with the howling wind.

The sagging flag pole. Tattered stars and stripes fluttering over the wreck site.

Spectral figures ringed the plane. Grotesque silhouettes part-veiled by driving sand.

She turned and ran.

Noble wrenched the knife from Hancock's throat and threw it aside. He hauled the corpse from the chair and dumped it on the deck.

He took the co-pilot seat and checked inert instrumentation. He adjusted the throttle, adjusted the yoke, settled back in his chair and continued to pilot a plane full of dead men on their journey to nowhere.

PYLON UNLOCK   **WPN REL**

56

Frost turned her back on the wreck sight and ran. A journey out of nightmares. Minutes to put as much distance as she could between herself and the plane, yet each footfall bedded deep in sand. Each gradient was a laborious scramble. Each down-slope turned to a tumbling avalanche

She sprinted headlong into the storm. Driving sand. She nose-breathed, kept her eyes screwed shut much as she could. Dust in her hair, her ears, working into her flight suit.

Heading west. Not that it mattered. If she could cover six, seven miles in an hour, she might survive the bomb.

Noble sat at the flight controls. He adjusted altitude and heading.

The fuselage shook. Overhead cable runs smouldered and sparked.

Dual perception:

Dead avionics. Smashed gauges, all needles resting at zero. Indicator lights extinguished. All screens dead.

But at the same time he saw switch panels winking green, altitude gimbal holding steady, EVS screen relaying desert terrain twenty thousand fleet below.

Part of him understood he was sitting in the broken hulk of a crashed plane, going nowhere, but another part of his mind was plotting course and flight time to the target sight. Gnawing confusion. He would reach his destination in a little over an hour, then all ambiguities would be resolved.

★

How far had she run? One mile? Two?

Might have been better to stay aboard the plane. Ground zero. Would have been instant, painless. But if she were caught three or four miles from the blast she would die in agony. The firestorm would wash over her. Slow incineration.

Panting for air.

She settled her mind, steadied her respiration, and doubled her pace.

Noble checked his watch. Twenty minutes to the drop point.

'Captain Pinback,' he called over his shoulder.

Pinback clumsily unbuckled his harness and left the EWO station. He stood at Noble's shoulder.

'Take over. Fly the plane.'

Noble stood up. Pinback sat in the remaining pilot seat, secured straps and checked instrumentation. Hand on the thrust lever, hand on the stick. The twin portholes of his blast helmet reflected the storm beyond the cockpit windows.

Noble patted him on the shoulder.

'Thank you, Captain.'

Noble headed to the back of the flight deck. He ducked beneath viscous drip-strands of melted insulation hanging from overhead cable runs as if they were cobwebs.

He settled in the gunner seat in front of the launch controls, and buckled his harness.

He checked his watch.

Seventeen minutes to target.

Frost's leg gave out.

Pain grew until she could feel the jarring impact of each footfall in her fingers, her teeth.

She covered a full mile so consumed by agony it filled her senses, rendered her near deaf and blind.

Then her leg simply ceased to function and she fell face down in the sand.

She massaged the limb, punched it, cursed it. She tried to get to her feet, but immediately fell on her ass.

How far was she from the plane?

Had she reached safe distance?

She dragged herself up a high dune and rolled down the other side. She took shelter in a deep depression, hoping to avoid the worst of the gamma flash.

She unhooked her belt canteen and shook it. Dregs. She emptied the bottle, shook last drops into her mouth, and tossed it.

She looked at the sky. The storm was clearing.

Weird serenity. She had done what she could to survive. Live or die. It was out of her hands.

She touched the empty sheath strapped to her chest rig, stroked the Ranger insignia stamped on the leather. She put up a good fight. Her father would have been proud. He would have nodded approval, said, 'Good job.'

The gas mask pouch, still slung round her chest and shoulder. She pulled the hood over her head and secured the mask.

She pictured the warhead, sitting in the blood-red light of the payload bay. A simple steel canister bedded into the flight-frame of the missile. The exposed physics package, trailing cable, ready to fire the moment the Tomahawk received the Go signal from the B-52's weapon management system and became a self-governing entity.

She sat and waited for the blast.

Noble checked his watch.

'Sixty seconds. Hold her steady.'

He flipped open the twin WPN REL switch covers.

Missile status panel: all green.

His battered copy of *The Little Prince* sat on the console beside him. He picked it up and hugged it to his chest.

He stared at his G-Shock and counted down the final seconds.

He reached forwards, put his fingers on the twin release switches.

'Ten . . . nine . . . eight . . . seven . . .'

Mix of exhaustion and relief in his voice, like a guy making it home after a long, long journey.

'. . . three . . . two . . . one.'

One moment *Liberty Bell* lay broke-backed and beached in sand. Next moment she was consumed by unholy light.

57

Frost sat looking down at her gloved hands. She thought about being alive, the fact of existence.

Gamma flash.

For an instant she could see finger bones, look right through her hand like an X-ray.

She blinked her vision clear.

She ought to duck-and-cover, but the instinct to take shelter was overcome by a compulsion to see the blast.

She scrambled to the top of the dune.

Ten megaton ground burst. Stellar heat. The fission core rose over the desert like a second sun, a dust vortex drawn skywards, blossoming into a vertiginous mushroom cloud.

The monstrous thunderclap of detonation.

The firestorm rushed towards her across the desert. An oncoming juggernaut of flame.

She threw herself against the side of the dune, scrambled and squirmed to get beneath the sand before she was engulfed by a wave of superheated air.

58

Miles of desert fused to iridescent glass.

Scalloped dunes, shaped by blast-wind, formed the petrified troughs and waves of a frozen ocean. Sand, momentarily liquefied by supernova heat, frothed at the crest of each ridgeline like delicate, glassy foam.

An infernal, smouldering landscape. Gunshot cracks as the crystalline crust began to cool.

A gloved fist punched through vitrified dust. A succession of blows broke an aperture wide enough for Frost to twist and squirm free.

She climbed to her feet. Dust streamed from her flight suit and respirator. Boots slid on silica glazed slick as ice. She struggled to retain her balance.

Heart-hammering asphyxia. She tore off her mask and threw it aside, part suffocated by sand-clogged filters. She bent double, whooped for air.

She caught her breath and straightened up.

She climbed to the crest of the dune, each footstep crunching through a brittle layer of trinitite, and stood looking east towards the crash site.

The mushroom cloud risen thirty thousand feet, a mighty column of dust and smoke blocking the sun, turning day to red twilight.

She stared in awe.

Somewhere, within the cloud, were the remains of *Liberty Bell* and her crew. They had been reduced to their constituent atoms, transmuted to rare isotopes, and were now diffused among the mesosphere.

She tied a bandana over her mouth and nose. A rudimentary fallout mask. One last glance at the thunderous cloud, then she turned and headed for the mountains.

Lacquered dunes glittered red sunlight. Her boots crunched glass as she travelled west across a transformed world.

LaNitra Frost. A solitary figure limping across a crystal sea.

Acknowledgements

I would like to thank Charles Walker and Katy Jones at United Agents, and Oliver Johnson and Anne Perry at Hodder.

All illustrations by Noel Baker.